LICENSE TO DIE

A JAMES FLYNN ESCAPADE

HARIS ORKIN

Black Rose Writing | Texas

ISBN: 978-1-68513-224-8
PUBLISHED BY BLACK ROSE WRITING
www.blackrosewriting.com

Printed in the United States of America
Suggested Retail Price (SRP) $24.95

License to Die is printed in Book Antiqua

*As a planet-friendly publisher, Black Rose Writing does its best to eliminate unnecessary waste to reduce paper usage and energy costs, while never compromising the reading experience. As a result, the final word count vs. page count may not meet common expectations.

Other Titles by
HARIS ORKIN

YOU ONLY LIVE ONCE

ONCE IS NEVER ENOUGH

GOLDHAMMER

Praise for
LICENSE TO DIE

"Orkin's brilliance, and his gift to the reader, is the innate ability to create dark characters worthy of a *Thomas Harris* thriller and mingle them with James Flynn, the Everyman of our time; damaged, heroic, humorous and heartbreaking."

–James L. Cox, author of *Silver or Lead*

"Haris Orkin returns with *License To Die* and turns up the storytelling to eleven. Full of suspense, humorous twists, edge of your seat thrills, and, most importantly, heart. This is easily the best *James Flynn* novel yet. Orkin's realism had me reminiscing about my time on the job and his witty writing kept me smiling the entire time."

–Ken Harris, Retired FBI and author of the *From the Case Files of Steve Rockfish* crime fiction series

"Haris Orkin has renewed not-so-secret agent John Flynn's license to thrill in this delightful mash-up of James Bond and Maxwell Smart in another charming, thrilling and amusing page-turner that makes me sad for the rest."

–Mark A. Altman, author of *Nobody Does It Better: The Complete Oral History of James Bond*

I dedicate this book to my mother, Blanche Natalie Orkin. (AKA Bunny). She was wild and outrageous. A free spirit who never let the truth get in the way of a good story. She loved to read and laugh and loved physical comedy, whether it was Lucille Ball or one of her kids taking a header. She was always my biggest fan, and her unflagging belief in me actually made me believe in myself.

ACKNOWLEDGEMENTS

I couldn't do what I do without the help of so many people.

Like my intrepid agent, Darlene Chan, and my inspired and indefatigable editor M.J. Moores, who pushes me to be a better writer with every book.

Like my friends and fellow writers who take the time to read my early drafts and offer their thoughts and ideas and endless encouragement. In particular, I want to thank Dwight Holing, Richard Procter, Jeff Fisher, Ken Harris, James Cox, Tom McAffrey, Matt Coyle, Mark Altman, and Antony Johnson.

Next I want to thank Reagan Rothe and his whole fantastic team at Black Rose Writing.

My siblings, Mike, Lisa, and Lynne, and my Uncle Sandy are constant supporters and cheerleaders and make my life so much better just by being there.

My wife, Kim, and my son, Jakob and his wife Charlotte, patiently listen to me prattling on about characters and plot and then read much of what I write, including this book in all its many iterations. They are my sounding boards and my proofreaders, and I greatly appreciate their love and encouragement.

Finally, a shout to our little rescue mutt Penny. She's a little old lady now who has lost much of her sight and hearing, but is still a force to be reckoned with and keeps me on my toes. She is my constant companion and always much more interested in what I'm eating than what I'm writing.

LICENSE TO DIE

Forget your troubles, c'mon get happy
You better chase all your cares away
Shout "hallelujah", c'mon get happy
Get ready for the judgement day.
–From *Get Happy*, by Harold Arlen and Ted Koehler

CHAPTER ONE

James Flynn crouched behind the low wall and listened for the footfalls of his prey. Even as he hunted them, they hunted *him*. Flynn never felt more alive than when faced with the possibility of his own demise. Close proximity to danger sharpened all his senses.

The air was moist with an early morning drizzle. The earthy aroma of damp dirt, wet cement, and fallen autumn leaves filled his nostrils. He expected that the birdsong and buzz of insects would pause on the approach of his adversaries. The cool, crisp, late October air energized him, along with the adrenaline coursing through his veins.

Kosovo had witnessed many battles over the years. Much of it lay devastated and in ruins. Wrecked and rusted cars blocked the streets. The windows in the one- and two-story wood and metal structures had no glass. The doors were gone along with all the innocent civilians. Only armed combatants fighting for supremacy remained.

Flynn stood stock still and kept his breath even and calm. The trick when facing danger was to stay relaxed. Never tense up. Never react out of fear or panic. Practice and preparation separated the amateur from the professional. He had trained for this. Drilled relentlessly and rehearsed every possibility. The object? Reduce surprise to a minimum. As a seasoned secret agent, he anticipated every enemy action.

The rest of his squad did not have his discipline. They fidgeted. Whispered. Scratched. Coughed. He shushed them

1

and they quieted for a moment, but they didn't have Flynn's patience or self-control. Not everyone possessed his natural talent as a predator. He'd honed those skills over many years and, after proving himself time and again, his superiors had promoted him to double 0 status.

Double 0's have a license to kill.

Everyone has a license to die.

Flynn caught a slight movement in the brush forty meters in front of him. *An animal? An enemy?*

"Steady," Flynn whispered to his squad.

He double-checked his semi-automatic. The Stormer Tactical had a red dot sight and a six-position collapsible stock. The high-impact composite body, vertical grip, and high-performance barrel made it one of the most accurate and powerful weapons on the market. He kept the stock against his shoulder and scanned the shrubbery.

He tracked his quarry and set the red dot on a beefy, bearded face wearing a camo helmet with a Plexiglas face shield. Flynn rested his finger on the trigger and released his breath in preparation for a kill shot. A sudden rustle in the bushes caught him off-guard.

His teammate Ty exploded from the shrubbery like a rampaging bear.

The twenty-three-year-old's three hundred pounds strained the seams on his surplus Army camouflage pants and jacket. He bellowed and roared, firing wildly as he charged the enemy, crossing directly into Flynn's line of fire.

Three enemy soldiers popped up across the way and peppered Ty with direct hits. Ty grunted and screamed. The shots only infuriated him. He charged forward as the enemy combatants fired again. He took hit after hit and kept on running, kept on attacking.

Ty wouldn't stop.

Ty refused to fall.

Ty wouldn't die.

Flynn couldn't see the faces of his helmeted enemies due to their black balaclavas and goggles, but their body language communicated terror. Ty moved fast for a man his size and was so intent on attacking he didn't see a protruding root.

Ty tripped, slamming face-first into the dirt. He didn't spring back up or even make a sound. He just lay there, legs and arms akimbo, motionless and silent.

Flynn and his other squad mate rose from behind the wall to fire on their enemies. His mate took a direct hit in the chest, staggered back, tripped and fell. Flynn ducked for cover. Since he couldn't help his fallen comrade, he focused on the enemy.

He peeked over the edge. The leader of the opposing squad peeped over a hedgerow a distance away. Ty lay between enemy lines like a large motionless lump. The enemy squad leader disregarded him and focused his attention on Flynn.

That was a mistake.

Ty flipped over and unloaded on him, shooting right over the top of the hedgerow. From six feet away, the high-powered shot hit the enemy squad leader directly in the neck.

"Ow! Shit!" the man shouted and dropped his weapon as another enemy, angered by Ty's *never say die* attitude, popped up and shot Ty point-blank in the face. Ty screamed and fired wildly along with his adversary until both their weapons clicked empty.

Every single member of both squads bore bright splotches of red, blue, and green.

Everyone but Flynn.

The last man standing.

. . .

Sancho Perez couldn't catch his breath. Ty's shot to the throat nearly took him to his knees. He lost his gun and saw his last remaining soldier unload on Ty until they both were out of ammo.

Still clutching his injured neck, Sancho tried to keep his cool as he castigated a grinning Ty. "You were dead," Sancho said. "We shot you twelve times."

"Do I look dead to you?" Ty held out his hand. "Hey, help me up here, brah!"

Sancho grabbed Ty's arm and tugged, strained, and struggled to get the three hundred-pound mental patient back up on his feet.

As a newly minted registered nurse at City of Roses Psychiatric Institute in Pasadena, Sancho Perez had proposed this paintball outing to help foster self-confidence and create a sense of camaraderie among his patients.

City of Roses was privately owned, but had a contract with the city of Pasadena. They catered to patients with addiction issues, depression, anxiety, OCD, mild cases of schizophrenia, and delusional disorders. Those convicted of violent crime or deemed criminally insane were sent to more secure facilities. Sancho spent the last six years working there as an orderly while attending college and nursing school. Having spent so much time there, his patients were like family.

Big-boned, freckled-faced, fifty-something Mary Alice had anger issues and wasn't too happy that Ty refused to die even after being hit by multiple paintballs. She took off her helmet to reveal faded red hair with gray roots. Her three pack a day habit turned her southern accent into a feral growl. "We shot you dead as a dang doornail, Ty! Don't you know the freakin' rules?"

Mary Alice's teammate, eighty-one-year-old Quentin Smith, also removed his helmet to express his dismay. The wiry octogenarian believed himself to be one of the greatest scientific minds of his generation. "This is exactly how he plays Uno," Quentin shouted. "Like an idiot!"

"Who the hell you calling an idiot, old man?" Ty tried to get in Quentin's face.

James Flynn inserted himself between them. "Now, now, Ty, you know Q doesn't suffer fools gladly. Being a genius, he doesn't understand us lessor mortals."

"Who you calling a fool?"

"Not you. You're a man of action, and I applaud your bold stratagem. You did exactly what they weren't expecting, and that is a good lesson for us all. Fortune favors the bold."

Sancho had grown especially close to James Flynn, the patient he picked to lead the other team. Flynn had arrived at City of Roses over twenty years ago. He believed the hospital was the headquarters of His Majesty's Secret Service and that he served his country as a super spy with a license to kill.

Not that Flynn had ever killed anyone. Although, he'd come close while literally saving the world more than once. Sancho had accompanied him on each of those hair-raising misadventures. He understood the best way to keep Flynn from going off the reservation was to make sure he didn't become bored or restless. That was partly why Sancho proposed this paintball outing. He knew the patients would appreciate getting outside and getting physical. It was a constructive way to safely express aggression, build self-esteem, and work on their coping mechanisms. Flynn, however, believed this paintball outing was a training exercise. Sancho didn't dissuade him from that notion. Bitter experience taught him it was better not to challenge Flynn on his delusions.

Besides Ty, Sancho chose Rodney Shoop as Flynn's other squad mate. The recovering alcoholic's prodigious beer gut and bushy white beard gave him a vaguely Santa-like look. As Rodney stepped closer, Sancho noticed a splotch of green paint decorating his plaid flannel shirt.

"I could stand to take a load off and sit my ass down." Rodney scanned the tired faces of his fellow patients. "Who could use a cold drink?"

Ty raised his hand. "Me. I'm thirsty as hell. D'you think they got snacks here?"

"I sure hope so," Rodney said.

"Yeah, like you two fat asses need another damn snack," Mary Alice snarked.

Rodney raised an angry eyebrow. "Give it a rest, Mary Alice."

"Bite me," she replied.

"Jesus, woman, what's your problem?"

"You, for one. For another, I could use a goddamn smoke. It's bad enough I can't smoke at the hospital, but I thought maybe, out here in the fresh air, I could have myself a dang cigarette. But no, that's not legal here in California. Not even outside. All these stupid laws impinging on my God-given rights are pissing me off."

Flynn stepped closer to Mary Alice and offered her a smile. "I don't disagree, Mary Alice. Life is not what it used to be. The world was once freer and less politically correct. Back then, governments weren't trying to legislate behavior. Living came with a certain level of danger, and vices were accepted as a way to let off steam. You could smoke in bars. Drive a car without a seatbelt. Flirt with a woman without worrying about offending her. But this is the world now and all we can do is make the best of it."

Sancho watched as Mary Alice's entire angry demeanor changed. She had a long-standing crush on Flynn, as did many other female patients at City of Roses. And many of the nurses. Tall and powerfully built, Flynn was movie star handsome and charming as hell. That, combined with his endless confidence and British accent, made him a chick magnet of the highest order.

Mary Alice sidled up next to Flynn and offered him a gap-toothed grin. "It's like you can see right inside my soul."

"We all have our needs, don't we, Mary Alice?"

"We do."

"Rodney would like a cold drink. Ty would enjoy a snack. And you would enjoy a fag."

"A fag? What? No, I like real men. Manly men."

"By fag I was referring to a cigarette. English slang. My apologies."

"You got *nothing* to apologize for. Not to me, James." She took his hand and pressed it against her not inconsiderable chest. "I am ready and willing to give you whatever you need, honey."

Sancho looked at Flynn's hand pressed against Mary Alice's chest and remembered the time Flynn's hand pressed down on his own chest. To staunch the bleeding from a gunshot wound. That trauma took Sancho six months to recover from. But he *did* recover. He even proposed to Alyssa, his long-time girlfriend. He would never have even asked her out if not for Flynn.

■ ■ ■

Tired, pretend soldiers crowded the outdoor snack area at Small World Paintball Park. Sancho found a table and went to the counter to buy everyone cold drinks, hot dogs, and chips. Sancho purposely bought Ty a caffeine-free diet soda to go with his hot dog since too much caffeine and sugar tended to amp Ty up. He handed Mary Alice an orange soda, and brought Flynn a hot, black coffee in a Styrofoam cup. When Sancho arrived with Ty's food and diet soda, the big guy was already eating. He had a tray packed with two huge slices of pizza, three hot dogs, a Snickers bar, three bags of Fritos, and two Monster energy drinks.

Sancho pointed to Ty's tray. "Where'd that come from?"

Ty gave him an answer, but Sancho couldn't understand him around his mouthful of pizza.

Sancho tried again. "I didn't buy you that. Where'd you get it?"

"He took it," Mary Alice said as she crunched down on a potato chip.

"From where?"

Rodney pointed to the snack bar counter where a tall, beefy guy with a Mike Ditka mustache argued with the skinny, pimple-faced kid who worked the counter. As if on cue, the kid aimed an accusatory finger at Ty and the beefy guy and his burly squad headed in their direction.

"Oh, shit." Sancho steeled himself.

Streaks of gray decorated the Ditka mustache of the leader, matching his salt-and-pepper flattop. The four guys with him ranged in age from late twenties to late thirties. All dressed in cammies, each had the weight, height, and build of a defensive lineman. The mustache leading the charge pointed at Ty's giant pile of food. "I believe you picked up the wrong tray."

Ty looked at him like he was crazy. "What?"

"That's our tray. Our food."

"Then why do I have it?" Ty jammed more pizza in his maw.

"Because you stole it!" The largest of the group growled. A broad-shouldered thirty-something who looked like a beardless Viking.

Ty was not the least bit cowed or intimidated as he turned to face his accuser. "What did you say to me?"

Sancho, a head shorter and hundred-seventy-five pounds lighter than Ty, leaped into the fray to diffuse the situation. He sidled up next to the guy with the Ditka mustache. "I think there's been a misunderstanding."

"Yeah, that fat asshole took our food!"

"Who you calling fat!" Ty shouted, spraying the immediate area with half-chewed pizza.

Sancho raised both his hands. "An honest mistake. I'd be glad to cover the cost of whatever he took and buy you guys lunch to make up for it." That seemed to mollify Ditka, who slowly unclenched his massive fists.

It didn't mollify the Viking, who locked angry eyes with Ty. "What the fuck you looking at, boy?"

"Your stupid, ugly face."

The Viking's eyes hardened with fury and he tried to push Ditka out of the way to get to Ty, but Ditka held him back. Sancho whispered in Ditka's ear. "My friend here is developmentally disabled and doesn't know what he's saying."

Ditka pointed at Ty. "Are you saying he's a retard?"

"Who are you calling a retard?" Ty shouted.

"He didn't mean that, Ty!" Sancho turned back to Ditka. "We're here from City of Roses on a field trip."

"City of Roses?" The Viking smirked. "Isn't that a nuthouse?"

"It's a psychiatric institute." Sancho pulled two twenties from his wallet. "Will this cover what Ty took from you?"

Ditka didn't take the money. Instead, he looked outraged. "You brought a bunch of mental patients out here to play paintball? Are you fucking kidding me?"

"Sir, please. Go enjoy your day and we'll be on our way."

"Retards are playing paintball now?" The Viking looked incensed.

"Guess so if *you're* playing!" Mary Alice retorted.

Ditka tried to restrain the Viking, but he was fit to be tied. "Who the hell do you think you're talking to, bitch?"

Flynn put down his coffee. "Sir, that's enough."

"Excuse me?"

"Tempers are frayed. Emotions are heated. But the level of disrespect you're showing Mary Alice is ugly and unwarranted. I believe you owe the lady an apology."

Mary Alice grinned at Flynn's defense of her.

The Viking poked Flynn in the chest. "Who the hell are you?"

"You a doctor?" Ditka asked.

"No, sir, but I am a civil servant. My compatriots and I risk our lives daily for queen and country, and I would hope you could show us at least a modicum of respect."

Ditka laughed at that, snatched the twenties out of Sancho's hand and turned to go. "Let's get out of here."

"Or…" Flynn said with a smile. "You could take what Sancho just gave you and try to double it."

"Say what?"

"I'm proposing a competition. Your squad against ours. Winner takes all."

"No, no, no," Sancho said.

"They believe we don't belong here, Sancho, and I'd like to prove them wrong."

"We can't play against civilians, man," Sancho said.

Ditka laughed and shook his head. "Your people against mine? Are you kidding me?"

"Unless you're afraid we might best you?" Flynn replied.

"Afraid? We're all military veterans, son. Each and every one of us works for the L.A. County Sheriff's department."

"So you accept the challenge?"

"Don't be stupid."

"Don't be a coward." Flynn smiled.

That lit a fire in Ditka's eyes. "Fine. One round. Team deathmatch. Winner takes all."

CHAPTER TWO

Charles Nelson of the Nelson Paint Company designed the very first paintball gun in the mid-1960s. He created it so loggers and cattlemen could easily mark trees and cattle. The original balls were gelatin horse pill shells injected with oil-based paint. To this day, paintball guns are still called markers. Sporting goods retailer Bob Gurney came up with the idea of using paintballs in mock survival games. He wondered whether a city person could hold their own against a country person. The first such game took place in 1981 in a wooded area of New Hampshire. The game exploded in popularity after an article in Sports Illustrated. Gurney opened the first commercial paintball field in '82. By 2020, the U.S. had over 1750 paintball fields.

Flynn held a huddle with Ty, Q, Rodney, Mary Alice, and Sancho. He laid out some simple strategies and tactics. Everyone except Sancho played close attention. "I propose we form three two-man squads. My partner and I will move up the middle to draw enemy fire, while the other two squads work their way around the flanks to hit them from the sides. If the enemy is too deeply dug in, I will call a retreat, but it will be a false retreat. My partner and I will take flight down the middle. As our enemies come out of cover to shoot us down, our other two squads will lie in wait to ambush them."

"From the flanks?" Rodney asked.

"Exactly."

"Dude, we can't do this," Sancho said.

"Of course we can. It's a time-tested stratagem and our opponents don't appear to be the sharpest tools in the shed," Flynn replied.

"When Dr. Michaels agreed to this, he said we could only play amongst ourselves."

"But to really test ourselves we must face unknown opponents. Expect the unexpected." Flynn looked at Rodney. "Rod, weren't you a marine?"

"Semper-fi! Do or die!"

"What's the motto they taught you in basic training?"

"Improvise, adapt, and overcome."

"Indeed, once the battle begins and chaos ensues, all we have to rely on is our training and our instincts."

Ty nodded his head. "It's like what Mike Tyson said. Everybody has a plan until they get punched in the mouth."

"Exactly, Ty." Flynn pointed at Mary Alice. "Mary Alice, you're with Q. Rodney, I'm pairing you with Ty. Sancho, you come with me."

"Look, I'm sorry." Sancho held his hands up. "But I can't allow this. We had our fun, but now it's time to go home. You all need to come with me to the rental office and turn in your markers." Sancho motioned for them to follow and started across the field. He looked over his shoulder. No one stood behind him. "Come on, guys!" Sancho whined. "Don't be like this."

The field ref screamed through a bullhorn. "Team Deathmatch! One shot, one kill! Ready! One! Two! Three!"

"*No!*" Sancho shouted.

"*Go!*" boomed the ref.

A shrill whistle cut the air.

Mary Alice charged off into the brush with Q trailing behind. Ty and Rodney headed in the opposite direction into the trees. They didn't do it quietly. Flynn moved forward up the middle.

He covered fifteen yards before he realized Sancho wasn't beside him. He glanced back. Sancho hadn't moved an inch.

"Get to cover, Sancho!" Flynn whisper shouted. "You're a bloody sitting duck!"

"What did I tell you? We can't—" A paintball smacked Sancho square in the nose, splattering his face with fluorescent orange, and staggering him back.

The ref thrust a finger towards Sancho. "OUT!"

Sancho sighed and dropped his shoulders, shaking his head.

Meanwhile, with Sancho eliminated, Flynn had no choice but to attack on his own.

The Small World Paintball Park had seventeen separate fields, all named after famous battle zones in formerly war-torn countries. Vietnam, Stalingrad, Bosnia, Beirut, Kuwait, Fallujah, and Kosovo.

This battle was being fought in South Vietnam.

Dense vegetation and a variety of wooden structures surrounded shipping containers decorated to look like huts in a Vietnamese village. Flynn moved through the thick brush and tried to catch a glimpse of his enemies. The rapid fwap-fwap-fwapping of paintball fire erupted all around him. Multicolored balls zipped overhead and slammed into trees as he kept low and kept moving. He was drawing fire, but then that was the plan.

He ducked and zigzagged, leaped and rolled, danced and stutter-stepped as the enemy unloaded on him. When he reached the edge of the trees, he dove behind a low wooden barrier. A dozen paintballs slammed into the plywood. Peeking between a gap in the planks, he saw all six members of the enemy squad taking cover inside and behind several thatched huts. They shot from windows and doorways, focusing all their fire on Flynn. The wide open ground between him and his enemies offered no cover.

He wanted his opponents to advance and attack, but apparently they weren't as stupid as they first appeared. He glimpsed the Viking and a squad mate darting from their hut to another in an obvious attempt to flank him.

Ty and Rodney burst out of the trees to outflank the flankers. It was more of a lurch than a burst and they weren't exactly sneaky about it, but the Viking and his squaddie were so intent on taking out Flynn they didn't hear the two rampaging elephants crashing through the brush. The Viking turned as Ty nailed him with multiple shots in the back and side. The Viking's partner hit Ty with a myriad of splotches. Rodney sprayed and prayed. He tagged the partner and the partner tagged him. The ref pointed them all to the neutral zone, shouting, *"Out! Out! Out! Out!"*

The Viking looked furious. Ty seemed reluctant to go, but Rodney grabbed him by the sleeve and urged him off the field.

With the rest of Ditka's team distracted by the Viking's elimination, Flynn retreated to draw the last of them out. He shot a few markers to get their attention and even hit one of Ditka's squad.

"Out!" shouted the ref.

Flynn popped up from behind cover and spotted Ditka, his gray mustache twisted in a furious snarl. Flynn took off and Ditka abandoned his cover to chase after. His other teammates followed, but stayed low and used trees and shrubbery as cover while hunting the fleeing Flynn.

Clumsy footfalls tramped behind him. Whizzing paintballs zipped past. Where were Q and Mary Alice? Where were they hiding? Why hadn't they attacked? Ditka was big and slow, but his other three squad mates, all young men in their twenties or early thirties, closed in.

Flushed with adrenaline, Flynn knew that the time had come to stand and fight. He took cover behind a large tree and turned to take on his attackers.

Q and Mary Alice exploded out of the brush, catching Ditka and his squaddies totally by surprise. They fired at point-blank range.

And missed.

Completely.

Inexplicably.

Ditka and his squaddies fired back, peppering Q and Mary Alice with paintballs in a variety of Day-Glo colors.

They stood there stunned as the ref shouted, "*Out! Out!*"

Elated to have narrowly escaped certain defeat, Ditka and his men laughed. Flynn made his move. He leaped from cover, diving sideways through the air as he took out two of Ditka's men mid-flight. Flynn hit the ground and rolled into cover before any of them got off a shot.

"*Out! Out!*" shouted the ref as Ditka ducked behind a tree.

Ditka's last standing squad mate had six inches on Flynn and his stride matched his height. Within seconds, he stood toe to toe with Flynn. Before he could pull the trigger, Flynn side-stepped and the paintballs whizzed right past. The angry young Sheriff's deputy slammed his shoulder into Flynn, knocking him flat on his back.

Flynn fired straight up, nailing the young deputy in the knackers. He folded forward, grabbing his gonads. Ditka tried to fire on Flynn and shot his teammate in the bum.

Flynn rolled to the side and then back onto his shoulders, performing a no-handed kip-up before hitting Ditka center-chest with three neon-green splotches.

"*Out!*" shouted the ref.

Ty pumped his fist from the sidelines. "That's what I'm talking about!"

Mary Alice cackled wildly and Q and Rodney hugged each other.

Sancho, his face splattered with bright orange paint, couldn't help but smile. An angry Ditka stalked over and handed him his cash back, plus two more twenties. Sancho returned the last two double sawbucks and said, "Let's just call it even, dude."

Ditka hesitated, but then took the twenties and motioned for his men to follow. The Viking did not look happy. Mary Alice grinned at him with her gap-toothed smile, stuck out her tongue, and flipped him a double bird. The Viking started to come after her, but Ditka grabbed him by the elbow and directed him the other way.

Sancho's nose trickled a bit of blood from the direct paint ball hit to the beezer. Flynn handed him a hanky. "May I offer a suggestion for next time?"

"I guess."

"Try ducking."

CHAPTER THREE

The Southern California Asylum for the Criminally Insane opened in San Bernardino in 1893. A wide variety of mentally ill were held captive in the facility after being judged insane by politically appointed "lunacy" commissioners. Among those incarcerated were drug addicts, alcoholics, epileptics, and schizophrenics, as well as those suffering from Down syndrome, autism, and dementia. Many were convicted of crimes ranging from public drunkenness and indecency to theft to assault, rape, and murder. Treatments in those early years included forced hydrotherapy, sterilization, rectal loosening, electroshock treatment, and full-frontal lobotomies. Modern mental institutions that house the criminally insane are now called forensic psychiatric hospitals. California has six of them spread from San Bernardino to Sacramento. A few are medium security, but the institutions that house serial killers, child molesters, and mass murderers are maximum security.

Mendoza stood six foot one and weighed two hundred and ninety-two pounds. Most of those pounds were muscle, gristle, and bone. He spent the last two years in prison, which gave him ample opportunity to pump iron. His massive chest and arms filled out the top of his orange jumpsuit, but they weren't nearly as intimidating as his dark brown eyes. Or eye. As one eye was missing and covered by a piratical black patch. That single eye exuded a cold, merciless fury. He had used that fury to inspire fear since the age of ten when he went to work as a lookout for

Mexico's Juarez Cartel. At age twelve, the cartel sent him to a camp in the mountains where they taught him how to kill.

On their first day of training, the instructor asked the fifteen recruits if they had ever taken anyone's life.

No one raised their hand.

Two cartel *soldados* dumped a naked corpse in front of the assembled trainees. The instructor handed a machete to the boy next to Mendoza. "Dismember that body," he'd ordered. The lanky pre-teen froze and the instructor walked up behind him, rested his hand on his shoulder, and put a bullet through his head.

He next handed the machete to Mendoza.

Mendoza didn't hesitate. He would do what was necessary because he knew what he wanted. He wanted to live. He also wanted money. Power. Respect.

By age eighteen, the name Mendoza was synonymous with terror. He once hoped to play professional soccer, but being a *sicario* was even better.

Everyone feared the *sicarios*.

As the war between the cartels heated up, bodies piled up all over Mexico. They hung corpses from bridges. Others they dismembered and arranged the pieces in public plazas. Each cartel tried to top the other with their garish displays of murder.

And no one outdid Mendoza.

He not only killed rivals, but local criminals who drew too much police scrutiny. Thieves. Rapists. Snitches. By the time he was twenty, Mendoza had the blood of over two hundred dead on his hands. He didn't murder for sport. It was business.

When a rival gang slaughtered the leaders of the Juarez Cartel, Mendoza suddenly had no one to watch his back. He was an outcast. A killer without a crew. His enemies retaliated and had their revenge. Shot and stabbed and left for dead, Mendoza had awoken in a hospital bed in Ensenada. The man who saved him, Francisco Goolardo, was just as much of an outcast as Mendoza.

Goolardo grew up in Brazil. A common street thug who rose through the ranks until he ran Brazil's most notorious drug cartel. He made alliances with Mexican and Columbian drug traffickers and extended his reach. When his Mexican counterpart tried to take over his network in Brazil, he turned the tables and took control of their operation in Baja. He murdered those who wouldn't bow to his will in the most gruesome and public ways possible. He created an army of the most fearsome killers he could find. Knowing Mendoza was now a Ronin, a warrior without a master, he rescued him from his enemies and set him on a course of revenge that was breathtaking in its savagery. Goolardo had promoted Mendoza to be his *teniete,* his personal bodyguard, and second-in-command.

The Goolardo Cartel grew in power and reputation, running guns and drugs all over the world. But that wasn't enough for Goolardo. He wanted to inspire not just fear, but respect. And not just from the criminal underworld, but from the economic elites. The cream of society. He saw himself as a billionaire business mogul no different from those on the Forbes 400 list, and he wanted the world to recognize him for his accomplishments. To that end, he'd hatched a daring plan. If he'd succeeded, he would have become one of the world's wealthiest men. But he didn't succeed. All because of James Flynn.

Mendoza knew something was off about Flynn from the first moment they met, but Goolardo couldn't see it. He saw Flynn as an equal and regarded Mendoza as nothing but a blunt instrument. A weapon to send against his enemies. Mendoza wanted more from his *jefe*. He wanted Goolardo's respect, but instead he gave it to that madman. That mental patient. That *idiota*. From the moment Flynn arrived, he turned Mendoza's life into a nightmare. He tried to kill Flynn many times and every time he had failed.

The last attempt cost him more than just an eye. It cost him his pride. It cost him his freedom.

Even though Goolardo didn't approve of Mendoza's attempt on Flynn's life, he still paid for Mendoza's defense. The expensive attorney he'd hired couldn't prevent Mendoza from being convicted, but saved him from a supermax prison. Instead, the fancy lawyer convinced the jury to find him not guilty by reason of insanity. The irony of all ironies.

Perhaps Flynn had indeed driven him crazy. His obsession to end Flynn's life burned inside like a white-hot fire. Mendoza couldn't let it go. Wouldn't let it go. Nothing else animated him. The promise of revenge gave him purpose. A *razón de ser*.

The court sentenced him to Hornitos State Hospital, a forensic psychiatric facility in Hornitos, California. They assigned him to the co-ed locked unit for those considered not guilty by reason of insanity. Unit G. It held only those convicted of the most violent offenses. Like Mendoza, many had committed murder. Some multiple times. Unlike Mendoza, the majority weren't professionals. They were serial killers or mass murderers or spree killers. Killers who killed for their own insane reasons or no reason at all. There were rapists too. Of women. Men. Even children.

Mendoza knew how to navigate prison life. Knew how to establish himself as an alpha. He would identify and then take down the prisoner who commanded the most fear. He did this quickly and brutally. But a forensic psychiatric hospital didn't have the same pecking order as a prison. A handful were career criminals, but most were just straight out loco. One crazy asshole killed his mother with her own assault rifle and cut her up into mailable chunks. The police caught him trying to jam the bloody packages into a mailbox. A skinny little *pendejo* named Robbie blew up his school. A psycho bitch named Judy chopped her boyfriend up with an electric chainsaw, boiled the body parts in a large pot, and turned him into soap.

It was hard to intimidate someone that insane.

Which was why Mendoza could never intimidate Flynn. The *estúpido* had no fear because he had no clue. No relationship with reality. It's not easy to scare batshit crazy.

Though one *cabrón* in the Unit G still managed to rule the roost. He intimidated patients, nurses, and doctors alike. And he didn't even seem all that insane. His name was O'Haney, and before they locked him up, he rode with a motorcycle gang. Satan's Slaves. Mendoza knew this because O'Haney had the word Satan tattooed across his forehead. One of many colorful and creative tattoos that covered his giant, hairy body.

O'Haney had four inches and fifty pounds on Mendoza, making him the biggest maniac in the place. Unlike prison, Hornitos had no guards walking the halls. A nurse explained to Mendoza this was because Hornitos was a hospital. Not a prison. Armed guards would create an atmosphere of intimidation and fear.

The Office of Protective Services and its hospital police stood by in case of an emergency and transported patients for court appearances, medical appointments, and to other hospitals. A police unit just outside Unit G had Tasers, wooden batons, handcuffs, and shotguns loaded with beanbags. Nothing lethal. When shit went down, a terrified doctor or nurse would push their personal panic button and the cops would come rushing in. But if no one saw the intimidation happening, then no one would come to the rescue.

That gave O'Haney free rein.

The biker sold cigarettes and drugs. Oxy and other prescription medication. Most of which he got from the nurses for protecting them from the other patients. He also ran dice and poker games and even pimped out some of the better-looking female and trans patients as prostitutes.

Mendoza had to hand it to him. O'Haney knew how to work the system.

Right from the start, Mendoza didn't defer to him. Didn't scrape and bow to him. Instead, he looked at him with contempt. O'Haney saw that as a challenge to his authority.

Two weeks after Mendoza joined the unit, O'Haney brought the hammer down. He grabbed Mendoza by the throat, slammed him up against a wall, and told him he could either comply or die. He did this in front of everyone in the cafeteria to show the others what happens when you challenge a slave of Satan.

Mendoza had a problem with depth perception ever since he lost his eye. The doctor explained he would always have trouble accurately tracking moving objects, judging distances, and perceiving depth. Back in prison, he had some occupational therapy to help with that. By adding non-visual signals like touch, he could overcome this. He learned to use his hands to help him judge distance and location more accurately.

That was why he grabbed O'Haney's head with both hands and squeezed it with every ounce of strength he had. O'Haney tried to pull away, but Mendoza had a strength born of an unrelenting rage and continued to squeeze. The biker screamed as Mendoza jammed his thumbs deep into each socket. After gouging out both his eyes, Mendoza slammed O'Haney's face into the cinderblock wall. He considered snapping the slave of Satan's neck, but let him live as an example of what happens to those who stand against him. He broke O'Haney's arm and shattered his left kneecap before the hospital cops rushed in.

The screaming, clanging, deafening alarm made speech impossible. So he couldn't hear what the cops shouted as they put their handcuffs on him. He didn't resist. He had no reason to. Sure, they could arrest him, but what would be the point? If they charged him with assault or attempted murder, he'd only be judged not guilty by reason of insanity again.

The brutal attack terrified and cowed nearly every patient on Unit G. Most wouldn't meet Mendoza's gaze. They'd all look away, afraid to set him off. Like any pack of predators, they considered direct eye contact a challenge for dominance.

Only one other patient in the unit didn't shy away from Mendoza or show him any fear. Though she also didn't confront him or directly challenge his authority. She kept to herself and everyone kept away from her. Caitlyn. Her intense and intimidating green eyes were as menacing as they were dazzling. More handsome than beautiful, she had thick black hair cut short and spiky, and possessed an unnerving stillness. Mendoza recognized her for what she was. Another predator. Tall and athletic, with wide shoulders and muscular arms, she looked to be in her early thirties. She moved and carried herself with confidence and never cracked a smile. Caitlyn apparently established her place in the pecking order soon after her arrival by snapping the neck of a notorious serial killer who wanted to make her his Unit G girlfriend.

Mendoza left her alone. As long as she left him alone, they wouldn't have a problem.

With O'Haney out of the picture, Mendoza took over his operation. He ran gambling and drugs and supercharged the protection racket. He became Unit G's de facto guardian and kept order in a way O'Haney never did. Once one of the most violent and dangerous wings of the hospital, Unit G now was the safest. This inspired the doctors and nurses to give Mendoza special privileges. Like a private room. Like extra portions at dinner. He even convinced one nurse to buy him a burner phone.

That was when he put his plan against Flynn in motion.

Mendoza called a private detective in Los Angeles he had a long-standing relationship with. Soto was an ex-LAPD detective who lost his job after the Rampart scandal. He worked for criminal defense attorneys to protect the same drug dealers he used to put away. As a father of eight, he had a lot of mouths to feed and couldn't afford to let his scruples get in the way. Not that he had many to begin with.

Soto was the one who originally helped Mendoza prove to Goolardo that Flynn was out of his mind.

He picked up on the third ring. "Soto."

Mendoza heard kids laughing and playing and yelling in the background, along with a barking dog and an aggravated woman shouting at the mutt to shut up. "What did you find out?"

Soto moved away from the pandemonium of his household and into some other room. A door shut. "Fucking kids, man."

"Enough with the small talk. I'm burning minutes."

"All right, all right, I got some good news."

"You find out who pays Flynn's way?"

"After his parents died, the only family he had was a cousin in Van Nuys. The court made this cousin the boy's legal guardian and the trustee of the trust his parents left him. But this guy was almost seventy and didn't want to take the kid in. That's why Flynn went into the system. There wasn't much of an estate. Not enough to pay for any kind of fancy boarding school. So the kid went into foster care. At least until the state decided he was crazy. Between that pathetic trust and what he could get from Medi-Cal, the cousin was able to send him to City of Roses. That was twenty years ago. Since then, that trust account has grown. It's worth over a million now."

"So who's this cousin?"

"His name was Warren Stettmeier."

"Was?"

"Because he's dead. Died six months ago at age ninety-six."

"Who's in charge of it now?" Mendoza asked.

"His son, Dennis."

"Can we get to him?"

"I did a credit check, and he's over his head. Unemployed. Seventy-two thousand in credit card debt. A home loan that's upside down."

"That's perfect."

"Perfect how?"

"I want to talk to him. Tell him if he sent Flynn to a state hospital like Hornitos, he could save a lot of money. And if something unfortunate were to happen to Flynn while at Hornitos, he would stand to inherit everything. He could have it all."

Soto chuckled. "He might like that idea."

"Bad things happen in places like Hornitos."

"No shit. It's a fucking psych ward for serial killers."

CHAPTER FOUR

The first gold in California wasn't discovered at Sutter's Mill in 1848. It was discovered under a tree in Placerita Canyon in 1842. Francisco Lopez was napping under that particular oak when he dreamed he was floating on a pool of gold. Upon awakening, he plucked a few wild onions from the ground for a mid-day snack and found flakes of gold glittering in the roots. Lopez studied mineralogy at the University of Mexico and knew gold when he saw it. His discovery sparked a tiny gold rush, much smaller than the one seven years later. Over two thousand people traveled from Sonora to what was then known as Rancho San Francisco to prospect for gold. Back then, that territory was still part of Mexico. California didn't become California until 1848, when Mexico ceded a vast portion of the southwest to the United States in the treaty that ended the Mexican-American War. The tree where Lopez took his nap is now known as the "Oak of the Golden Dream" and still stands to this day in Santa Clarita, a suburban town thirty miles northwest of downtown Los Angeles.

Sancho studied his face in the bathroom mirror. The paintball didn't break his nose, but gave him two black eyes. Alyssa's mom hid the shiners under some concealer so he wouldn't look like a racoon in the wedding photos. He sweated in the rented tux and had trouble keeping his zipper up. The pants were tight, and the zipper refused to stay shut. Not a great look while walking down the aisle.

Alyssa's parents lived in a new gated community in Santa Clarita. Bouquet Canyon Estates had a clubhouse and community recreation center with a pool, a spa, a patio area, an outdoor kitchen, and a community room perfect for parties and events like weddings and bar mitzvahs.

Alyssa's extended family decorated the entire area with white tables and chairs, flowers, banners, colorful ribbons, and strings of white Italian lights for the reception after the ceremony. Sancho set up the dance floor and the sound system for the DJ. His cousins handled the catering.

The ceremony itself would take place under a ribbon and flower bedecked gazebo. Alyssa's uncle, a priest, would be officiating. A family affair from top to bottom. Sancho wasn't just marrying Alyssa. He was marrying her entire family. Her father and one brother were both fireman for the city of Glendale. Her other two brothers were plumbers. Alyssa was the youngest and the only girl.

The first time Alyssa took Sancho to meet her family, her father asked him probing questions and tried to suss out his intentions. Sancho liked that. How protective he was. The brothers took pride in Sancho's fame from his many adventures with Flynn. Only Alyssa's father still seemed skeptical. He worried those adventures could put his daughter in danger. But Sancho assured him that his days as Flynn's sidekick were at an end. Sancho had graduated from nursing school and now worked full-time as a psychiatric nurse at City of Roses. He promised her dad he was more than ready to settle down.

So why am I so nervous? His hands trembled. He stared at himself in the mirror and struggled to fasten his tie. He caught Flynn's eye in the reflection.

"Need some help with that?"

Sancho mumbled as he struggled to make it work. "I got it."

But he didn't have it and Flynn stepped in and attached the tie in seconds. Flynn then flicked some lint off one of Sancho's lapels, smoothed down his shoulders, and stood back to take in the full effect. "You should dress like this more often. A tux adds a certain air of elegance."

"It's a little tight and I can't keep the zipper up."

Flynn reached for Sancho's crotch and Sancho batted his hand away. "Whoa, whoa, I got it." Flynn smiled as Sancho tried to attach his boutonniere, fumbling to get the pin through. Finally, he just handed it to Flynn. "I don't know why we gotta wear these stupid things."

"Boutonnieres date back to the age of chivalry. A knight would wear a lady's colors into a battle. To demonstrate his devotion to her." Flynn carefully pinned the boutonniere to Sancho's lapel.

Sancho looked Flynn hard in the eye. "This is all your fault, you know."

"I didn't get the girl pregnant."

"If not for you, I never would have asked her out."

"I just helped you find your confidence."

Sancho nodded. "I may have misplaced it again."

"Once you have it, you never lose it." He put his hand over Sancho's heart. "It's right here. Along with your courage and your compassion. Never doubt that."

"Thanks."

"For what?"

"Being here. Being my best man."

"I wouldn't miss this for the world." Flynn swept a flower petal off Sancho's shoulder.

"I just hope I don't disappoint her."

"That's not possible. You're a good man, Sancho. A better man than me."

"I don't know about that."

"I do. And to be honest, I envy you."

"*You* envy *me*?"

"For what you have with Alyssa. That's something I'll never see."

"Never say never."

"A man who lives like I do, I can't afford to love too deeply. A wife would be a vulnerability. My enemies would use her against me. It happened once before and I can't let it happen again."

"Maybe it's time to settle down. Let someone else save the world for a while."

"I'm not ready to be put out to pasture. Not yet. Besides, I'm no good behind a desk. Some of us were born to be hunters and I'm at my best when I'm on a mission. It's what I was trained for. Bred for. Born for. I never feel more alive than when I'm risking life and limb."

"That's not me though, bro. Never was."

"That's why we made such a good team. You were the yin to my yang, but you're a man with responsibilities now. You can't afford to take the same chances I do. Not anymore."

"I'm glad you understand that, man."

"Of course I do." Flynn looked in the mirror, straightened his tie and buttoned the top button of his jacket. He wore his clothes well and dressed better than anyone Sancho had ever met. For a guy who'd spent the last twenty years living in a mental hospital, he had a hell of a wardrobe. He bought most of his vintage suits from second-hand stores and on eBay. He didn't even need to rent a tux for the wedding. He already owned one. A Brioni.

Muffled strains of the wedding march wafted through the bathroom door. Sancho stood tall. "Guess it's time to face the music."

The ceremony went by in a blur, and Sancho was surprised he remembered his vows. He looked into Alyssa's honey brown eyes and promised to care for her and share with her, to have her and to hold her, to love and to cherish her, from this day forward, in this world and the next.

Alyssa never looked more beautiful. Even with her baby bump, she fit perfectly into her wedding dress. It was a cliché to say that pregnant women glowed, but dammit if she didn't. Sancho felt like the luckiest man who had ever lived.

So what if his zipper kept falling down? So what if his ears burned with embarrassment when he took her hand and danced the first dance? After a few glasses of champagne, his self-consciousness faded and he shook his booty with abandon, his zipper as wide open as his heart.

．　．　．

N was Flynn's plus one. He picked Flynn up in Pasadena and together they drove across the west foothills through the Newhall Pass to Santa Clarita. Once they arrived, N introduced himself to the assembled guests with his cover name. Dr. James Nickelson. He claimed to be Flynn's former psychiatrist at City of Roses Psychiatric Institute.

A few of Flynn's other colleagues were also in attendance. Nurse Durkin brought young Ty and old Q, claiming she was there to keep watch over them. The fiction being they were both residents of the same mental hospital as Flynn. He had never seen Durkin out of her nurse's uniform. She took her cover identity as the tyrannical head nurse at City of Roses quite seriously. She stood over six feet tall in her heels and wore some sort of black cocktail dress that could barely contain her bulky voluptuousness. Her carrot-colored hair, usually tied tightly back in a bun, hung freely, framing and softening her pale, forbidding face. She almost looked friendly as she stood apart from everyone and sipped on a frozen margarita.

Ty wore an immense pair of black slacks and an equally large t-shirt. Eighty-one-year-old Q, or Quentin Smith, as he called himself when out in public like this, wore his usual khakis and tweed.

As the music played and the wedding guests danced, Flynn stood by the bar and instructed Sancho's cousin Jorge on how to properly mix a vodka martini. "Four parts vodka, one-part Lillet extra dry vermouth. A twist of lemon peel. Shaken. Not stirred."

He took a sip and nodded his approval to Jorge before turning and nearly colliding with a tall, dark beauty with large brown eyes and a dazzling smile. Sancho's petite forty-something mother stood beside her and beamed. "James, my cousin Justina really wanted to meet you."

Flynn reached out and took her hand. "Justina. What a beautiful name."

Statuesque and curvaceous in her low-cut black dress, Justina nearly swooned. Her wide mouth, full lips and long, jet-black hair reminded Flynn of a beautiful enemy he once seduced many years ago. Like that alluring enemy, her eyes and smile indicated she enjoyed walking on the edge. "Do you dance, Mr. Flynn?"

"Call me James."

"Do you?"

"Not often."

"Would you?"

The D.J. played some sort of electronica that Flynn didn't find especially inspiring. "I'd prefer to dance to something slower." She smiled at that and, as if on cue, the electronica ended and the D.J. played "At Last" as covered by Etta James.

Flynn took her hand in his and led her onto the dance floor. He held her, twirled her, guided her, and dipped her as they moved to Etta's smoky-velvet voice. Out of the corner of his eye, Flynn caught the other dancers watching and then staring. Finally, they all stopped dancing as Flynn glided Justina around the floor. He sensed the electricity between them as they locked eyes and moved in perfect unison. The song ended, but Justina wanted to keep moving and they did until the next song broke the spell and the other dancers returned.

They continued to hold hands as they moved off the dance floor. "You move well, Mr. Flynn," Justina said.

"I do with the right partner."

Sancho's mom appeared again. This time with Sancho's grandparents. His *abuela* and *tata*. They spoke little English, so Flynn communicated with them in Spanish. He complimented them on how well they raised their grandson and congratulated them on their coming great grandchild. Flynn towered over Sancho's *tata*, but the man had a grip like a steel vise. Broad across the shoulders with a barrel chest and powerful arms, Flynn saw where Sancho's resilience, persistence, and determination came from. His *abuela* stood a few inches shorter, but her kind, intelligent eyes also showed a fierce tenacity. She ordered Flynn to eat and led him to the buffet, where she prepared a plate for him, filling it with Mexican delicacies created by Sancho's cousins. Chicken Mole enchiladas, Yucatan pork, fresh grilled shrimp, and green corn tamales.

As Flynn moved through the party, looking for a table, he passed Nurse Durkin doing the hokey pokey on the dance floor. She held a melting margarita as she put one foot in and one foot out, sloshing it all around as she turned about. Flynn found the expression on her face unsettling. Odd. Chilling. And then Flynn figured it out. She was grinning. Laughing. Back at headquarters, Durkin never smiled. She was always so austere. Severe. Imposing. Intimidating. For the first time ever, Flynn saw who she used to be beneath the grim exterior.

It was disturbing.

N waved Flynn over to his table. Flynn greeted Ty and Q as he sat next to N. Ty chowed down on a plate piled impossibly high with food. Q sat snoring with his head tilted back and his mouth open. N aimed a finger at the dance floor. "Did you see Durkin out there? She's drunk off her ass."

"She's enjoying herself," Flynn observed.

"I worked with the woman for over twenty years. I had no idea she could hokey-pokey."

"People can surprise us sometimes."

"Indeed. Sometimes we can even surprise ourselves."

"How's life in Beverly Hills?"

"Good. My new private practice is thriving. My previous association with you has given me a bit of notoriety. Free publicity as it were. I started working with Weird Al to help him overcome his PTSD."

"Did he develop that after what happened to us all in Saratoga?"

"Yes. It was quite traumatic for everyone involved."

"You came through it okay."

"I did indeed, but it was life changing for me. Working with Weird Al has led to further referrals with other celebrity clients."

Ty looked up from his massive plate of food. "Like who?"

"I shouldn't really say."

"You can tell us. We won't tell nobody."

N hesitated and then smiled and indicated for everyone to lean in. He lowered his voice. "Kim Kardashian. Danny DeVito. Jay-Z. Jessica Alba. Chuck Norris. Liza Minnelli."

Ty raised an eyebrow at the last name. "Liza Who?"

"Minnelli."

"Who?"

"She's Judy Garland's daughter," N said.

"Who's that?"

"She was in *The Wizard of Oz*."

Ty nodded with recognition. "Was she the witch?"

"Dorothy."

"No shit?"

"No shit."

■ ■ ■

By midnight, Flynn had danced with Justina, Sancho's bride, his mom, and his *abuela*. He took a break from the crowd to step away and have a cigarette. He stood by the aquamarine swimming pool, and lit up with his gun-metal gray vintage Ronson. Flynn had quit smoking as it wasn't allowed at headquarters, but bored without a mission, he recently started up again. He used to smoke a favorite Balkan and Turkish blend custom made by Morland in London, but now he smoked whatever he could get his hands on and only in the outdoor courtyard. Though he tried to limit himself to three a day.

An enormous shadow fell across Flynn. Nurse Durkin loomed over him, off-balance in her high heels. She put her hand on Flynn's shoulder to steady herself. "Could I bum one of those?"

Flynn offered her a cigarette, which she grabbed with her lips. Flynn flicked the spark wheel of his Ronson and lit her up. She took a drag and let out the smoke with a satisfied sigh. Flynn caught the tequila on her breath. Chanel No. 5 mingled with her perspiration from doing the hokey-pokey. Flynn snapped his Ronson shut. "I didn't know you smoked."

"There are a lot of things you don't know about me, Mr. Flynn."

"Like your given name. After all this time, you think I would know that."

"Arabella."

"What a beautiful name."

"It was my grandmother's."

"Well, it's a pleasure to meet you Arabella. You can call me James."

"I know I've been hard on you, James. But it's nothing personal. I'm hard on everyone."

"You are indeed."

"It's because I care. Too much sometimes. And if I let myself feel the pain my patients feel…it's…it's too much." Tears filled Durkin's eyes.

Flynn patted the hand she had on his shoulder. "It's all right."

"It's very upsetting to me whenever I find you in bed with one of my nurses."

"I know. It's unprofessional of me."

"It is." She nodded and wiped away a tear.

"But sometimes the heart wants what the heart wants, Arabella."

Looking into her eyes, Flynn saw the young, vulnerable, open-hearted girl she once was before all the heartbreak and disappointment created the cold, callous, imperious, impenetrable shell that now protected her from the outside world. She leaned close to Flynn and whispered in his ear. "It does. And I'm going to miss you."

"Miss me?"

"I didn't think I would, but I have to admit, I'm sorry to see you go."

Flynn grinned. "But I'm not going anywhere."

Her massive shoulders shook as large tears rolled down her cheeks. Flynn tried to put his arm around her, but he couldn't reach around that far. With her heels, she stood two inches taller than Flynn and had at least fifty pounds on him. His warm gesture must have unleashed something inside of her because she threw her arms around him and slammed her open mouth onto his, thrusting her tongue down his throat. Flynn stumbled back from the shock of it, tripping over a chaise lounge, and together they fell into the pool.

The enormous splash caught the attention of everyone at the reception. Sancho raced over and tried to fish them out. Ty, however, wanted to join the fun and jumped into the pool after them, creating a tsunami-sized splash that soaked everyone standing around the edge of the pool. Others jumped in after Ty, laughing and splashing and reveling in the pure joy of celebration.

CHAPTER FIVE

The Monday after his wedding, Sancho showed up at work to find Nurse Durkin in a foul mood. She wanted Flynn found immediately and ordered everyone in her charge to track him down. "Dr. Michaels needs to see him! Find him! Now! This instant!"

Sancho decided he better find Flynn before the orderlies did. When someone at City of Roses lost their shit, it was up to the orderlies to restore order using whatever means necessary. The hospital had a handful of security guards, but they'd only jump in if things went sideways. As far as Sancho was concerned, a few of the orderlies took too much pleasure in that part of the job. Two burly assholes in particular, O'Malley and Barker, were the biggest offenders when it came to unnecessary force.

Patients at City of Roses suffered from all sorts of psychological conditions. From bipolar disorder and clinical depression to suicidal ideation and impulse control. Many patients were addicts, hooked on everything from meth, opioids, and alcohol to benzos, crack, and even ketamine.

Fifty-three-year-old Josh Birnbaum suffered from schizophrenia and experienced auditory hallucinations. He told Sancho that his mother's ghost haunted him. He claimed she followed him everywhere and never shut up, constantly nagging, kvetching, castigating him. Some were delusional, like Doris Frawley, a ninety-three-year-old former beauty queen, who claimed to have slept with everyone from Gary Cooper to L. Ron Hubbard. She was certain that in 1952 she gave birth to the anti-Christ. Quentin Smith claimed to be the greatest inventor since Thomas Edison and told Sancho he had over five hundred patents for everything from Liquid Paper to potato chips in a can. James Flynn referred to Quentin as Q and believed he supplied His Majesty's Secret Service with all their high-tech spy devices.

Is Flynn even here? He often disappeared for days at a time and would reappear with no explanation of where he went, why he left, or what he did while he was gone. Though he lived in a locked ward, it wasn't a prison and Flynn was there voluntarily. When Sancho pressed him, Flynn would usually claim he had left on a secret mission. The details were classified and on a need-to-know basis and Sancho didn't need to know.

Working from the premise that Flynn hadn't fled the hospital, Sancho searched all of his usual haunts. First, he checked the room he shared with Quentin Smith. Q claimed he hadn't seen Flynn since breakfast. Next, he poked his head in the activity room. A couple of patients played cards. Flynn wasn't among them. Ty sat on the couch next to Doris Frawley and watched a Brady Bunch rerun. Neither one had seen Flynn. Sancho checked the gymnasium and the outdoor courtyard. No Flynn. He asked the two nurses eating lunch at a cement table if they had seen him.

Nope.

Sancho checked the pharmacy and found Nurse Reyes arranging the mid-day prescription drug distribution. She and Flynn had a fling a year ago and she survived to tell the tale. The attractive forty-something Filipina divorcée managed to have her fun *and* keep her job. Not normally the case with nurses who have flings with Flynn. She kept it discreet and ended the affair after a few weeks.

Flynn's animal magnetism was responsible for the firing of more than a few young nurses. Because of that, Nurse Durkin really had it in for him. She thought that the former head psychiatrist, Dr. Nickelson, coddled Flynn. This new one sure didn't. And Sancho worried what Dr. Michaels might do if Flynn continued to flaunt the rules.

Flynn's flirtations were always innocent. He was never the aggressor. He never had to be. The ladies came to him. Sancho found it uncanny. He knew just what to say. How to be. When he and Flynn first met, girls terrified Sancho. He *never* knew what to say. *Never* knew what to do. Flynn became his tutor. Taught him the importance of self-confidence. Flynn was nothing if not confident.

Seeing Nurse Reyes brought to mind the laundry room where he'd found them bumping uglies. He hurried down the corridor to the hospital's maintenance and storage wing and approached the area, only to find the room locked tight. Sancho put his ear to the door. Washers washed, dryers tumbled, and a young woman moaned.

Sancho rapped on the door. "Flynn!" He knocked harder. "*Flynn!*" The moaning stopped, though the rumble of the washers and dryers continued unabated. "Open up, man!"

Nothing. Sancho pounded on the door and kept pounding until it finally opened.

Just a crack.

A beautiful if embarrassed face peered at him through the door, Nurse Maisie MacMillan, a recent hire. She wasn't much older than Sancho and had the pale freckled face and curly red hair of her Scottish forebears. The door hid most of the rest of her. "Mr. Flynn isn't here," Maisie insisted.

"Maisie, it's okay. I'm not here for you. I'm here for Flynn."

"I just told you he's not here."

Sancho shouted past her. "Flynn! Dr. Michaels has the whole hospital looking for you!"

Maisie's eyes went wide. "The whole hospital?"

A shirtless Flynn suddenly appeared behind her. "I was just helping Nurse MacMillan sort her... unmentionables."

Maisie blushed a bright shade of crimson and hurried away from the door.

"While Miss Macmillan finds her aforementioned unmentionables, perhaps you can tell me why M needs to see me."

"Dude, I don't have a clue."

"Well, I *was* intending to have a word with him. I suppose now is as good a time as any."

■　■　■

Flynn, dressed in a slim fit Armani suit, traipsed into the anteroom outside M's office. M's loyal secretary and girl Friday, Miss Honeywell, typed away on her computer. She'd been with the service for many years, having previously worked with M's predecessor. Flynn always enjoyed their flirtatious repartee.

"Honeywell, you look quite fetching today."

Honeywell didn't bother glancing up from the screen. "Go right in, Mr. Flynn." Honeywell, a lovely and voluptuous ebony goddess, had to be in her fifties by now. She liked to play hard to get and pretended to regard Flynn with irritation and contempt.

"Is that a new hair-do?"

She stared at her computer screen. "Nope."

"Is that a new dress?"

"I think you better go in, Mr. Flynn."

Flynn detected at hint of unexpected emotion in Honeywell's tone. "Sounds serious."

She met Flynn's eyes with her own. "It is."

"Honeywell, what is it? I've never seen you like this. Are you all right?"

She nodded and steeled herself and pointed towards the door.

Flynn walked into M's office. It once belonged to N, but M clearly made it his own, turning N's cluttered, friendly, and avuncular space into something more forbidding. The new décor matched M's icy demeanor. He had a clean-shaven head, wore steel-rimmed spectacles, and sported a black goatee streaked with gray.

"Have a seat, Mr. Flynn." M pointed to the sleek, black leather chair on the other side of his desk. Flynn stood stock still. Immovable.

"Sir, first I have something I need to get off my chest. I've been idle here at headquarters for far too long now. I have fully recovered from my last adventure and I'm as fit as I've ever been. I know the world hasn't become any less dangerous and there are still those who would do us harm. I am the sharp tip of the spear, sir, and I'd rather not lose my edge."

"Mr. Flynn, please." He pointed to the chair.

"I am a Double-0 and there aren't many of us left. I know some see us as brutal relics of a bygone age, but sometimes, sir, you must meet force with force. Unsheathe me. Unleash me. Loose me on our enemies."

"You want me to send you somewhere else?"

"Yes!"

"Well, it's your lucky day then, Mr. Flynn. Because that's exactly why I called you in."

"Where are you sending me, sir? Jamaica? The French Riviera? North Korea?"

"Hornitos."

"Mexico?"

M shook his head. "Northern California."

"When am I leaving?"

"Within the hour."

"Then I should go pack."

"You already have everything you need."

"What about Q?"

"Who?"

"Aren't you outfitting me with any special equipment?"

"Not this time."

"Do you have a file for me? A briefing? What am I up against?"

"You'll see soon enough. Go back and wait in your room. Your ride will arrive shortly."

"When can I expect to return?"

"Not anytime soon." M pushed a button on his phone. "Miss Honeywell?"

Miss Honeywell's voice came across the intercom. "Yes, sir."

"Mr. Flynn is leaving. Can you send in my next appointment?"

The door to M's office opened. Honeywell stood right outside with Nurse Durkin. Flynn detected a certain melancholy in Miss Honeywell. "This way, Mr. Flynn."

As Flynn walked out of M's office, Durkin entered and shut the door without a word. Flynn offered Honeywell a rakish grin. To his surprise, she didn't offer him her usual irritated frown. In fact, her big brown eyes brimmed with tears.

"Honeywell, what is it?"

"When you get where you are going, you be careful."

"Of course." He offered her a reassuring smile. "When am I not?"

She threw her large arms around Flynn and hugged him close, which surprised him as she'd never shown him any physical affection before. He felt her tears on his face as she kissed him on the cheek. "What is *this* all about, then?"

She held him at arm's length. "I'm going to miss you, Mr. Flynn."

"Don't you worry now, Miss Honeywell. I'll be back."

She stifled her tears and pushed him out the door.

CHAPTER SIX

A delusion is a false belief based on an incorrect interpretation of reality. Many delusional patients firmly stay stuck in this alternate reality despite clear evidence or proof to the contrary. Such patients rarely suffer hallucinations and often can function in a day-to-day setting. Delusional disorder is difficult to treat. It's highly resistant to treatment with medication alone. Individual psychotherapy is the primary treatment, but since most delusional patients don't believe they have a mental disorder, it's difficult to engage with them. Cognitive-behavioral therapy can often help patients change fanciful or dangerous thought patterns, but that can only happen if the patients recognize that they have a problem.

Following his last adventure with Flynn, Sancho could no longer work with him. Dr. Michaels, the head psychiatrist, believed that there needed to be more of a professional distance between them. He assigned Sancho to other patients. Besides, once he passed his nurse's certification, Sancho had many more duties and rarely visited with his old friend.

From the few times he had seen him recently, Sancho detected a disturbing restlessness. Flynn wanted "M" to send him on a mission, but Dr. Michaels wasn't as understanding as Dr. Nickelson and didn't indulge Flynn's delusions. He often confronted Flynn with the ugly truth and tried to get him to see reality. At a recent staff meeting, Dr. Michaels brought up the possibility of putting Flynn on anti-psychotic medication. Sancho worried what that course of treatment might do to him.

They tried medicating Flynn before and it turned him into a shuffling zombie.

After lunch, Sancho poked his head into Flynn's room and found Quentin taking a nap. A shaky, twenty-something man sat on the edge of Flynn's bed. Meth sores pocked the man's emaciated face. He gritted his gray teeth, eyes tearful with trepidation. "Do you hear that? What is that?"

Sancho didn't hear a damn thing. "What do you hear?"

The man flinched as if rocked by something and held his hands over both ears and shouted, "*That!*" The shout awakened Quentin, who slowly sat up, looked at Sancho and rolled his eyes. The young man rocked in place, hugging himself. "*You don't hear that?*"

"Can you describe it?"

He flinched again as if rocked again by some sort of explosion. "Make them stop! *Make them stop!*"

Quentin sighed and sat up on the edge of his bed. He pointed at the young man with his thumb. "Do you believe this idiot?"

Sancho put his hand on Quentin's shoulder. "Where's Flynn?"

"Gone."

"Gone where?"

"On a mission."

"What kind of mission?" Sancho prodded.

"He didn't say, but he never does. When they took him away, they took all his stuff. His clothes. Everything."

"Who took him away?"

"Barker and O'Malley. Then that kid showed up. According to Nurse Durkin, he's my new roommate." Quentin whispered. "I think he's some kind of meth head."

Sancho patted him on the knee. "Thanks Quentin." Quentin nodded. His new roommate sat with his hands over his ears, tears running down his face. Quentin looked at Sancho and shook his head.

Sancho caught up with Nurse Reyes outside of the cafeteria. "Blanca, have you seen Flynn?"

She stopped and put her right hand over her heart as if to calm herself. By the set of her jaw, he could tell she was angry. "They sent him away."

"Sent him where?"

"Another hospital."

The news hit Sancho like a kick in the stomach. For a second, he couldn't breathe. "Why?"

She fought tears as she shook her head. "I don't know."

Sancho hurried into the anteroom outside Dr. Michael's office. Miss Honeywell worked away at her computer. "I need to see Dr. Michaels."

"He's out doing his rounds."

"Do you know what happened to Flynn?"

Honeywell rarely showed any emotion other than annoyance, but Sancho's question made her eyes glisten. "He's gone."

"Gone where?"

"Hornitos."

"Are you shitting me?"

"Just telling you what I know."

"Why would Michaels do that?"

"It wasn't his call. Flynn's family requested it."

"I didn't even know he had any family. All these years and he never mentioned them once."

"Guess they were tired of paying for a private hospital."

"But Flynn got all that money from Belenki. A million-dollar trust fund. It's not like he's hurting for cash."

"I don't know what to tell you."

"Can you tell me who handles his trust?"

Honeywell shook her head. "You know I can't."

"Flynn's been here for over twenty years. Why would they send him somewhere new now? Somewhere like that? After all this time? Doesn't make sense."

Honeywell grabbed her mouse, pulled something up on her computer and wrote something down on a Post-it note. She went to hand it to Sancho, but snatched it back before he could grab it. "You didn't get this from me."

She handed it over. Three names were scrawled across the paper: *Davis, Hopkins, & Cromartie.* "Is this a law firm?"

"You need to go."

"Honeywell—"

"They didn't even let him take his clothes. Just what he had on his back."

"Why would they do that?"

"Patients at state mental hospitals can't wear their own clothes."

"So, what did they do with them?"

"Boxed 'em up for Goodwill."

"They're giving away all his clothes?"

"They're sitting out there on the loading dock right now. But you didn't hear it from me. Now go before you get me in trouble."

Sancho left Honeywell and made his way directly to the parking lot. He climbed into his Aston Martin and pulled it up around back, close to the loading dock. Workers watched with surprise as Sancho climbed from the DB9 Volante. They had to be wondering how a nurse could afford such an incredible car. The truth was, he couldn't. Flynn gave it to him after their first adventure together, and it often attracted more attention than he liked. He considered selling it more than once to help pay for grad school. Even with fifty-three thousand miles, the grand touring coupe could fetch him close to ninety-thousand dollars. A married guy with a kid on the way had to be practical and there was nothing practical about the cost of gas, maintenance and car insurance for an Aston Martin DB9.

Sancho spied the security cameras and tugged on a baseball cap. He pulled down the brim to hide his face and strolled inside. He searched various boxes, peeking inside each one. All he found were medical supplies.

Sancho looked up to see a loading dock worker staring at him. He was a short black guy in his fifties. "You know you're not supposed to be back here, right?"

"It's okay. I work here." Sancho held up his hospital ID badge. "Someone accidentally packed up clothes belonging to one of my patients. They should be in the pile going to Goodwill."

"See those boxes over there? That's Goodwill. What's your patient's name?"

"Flynn."

"Ain't that the guy who thinks he's a spy?"

"That's him."

"Usually when a patient croaks, the family donates their clothes to Goodwill. Most of the time, it's like one or two boxes, tops. But this Flynn guy had like six."

"Has. He's still alive."

"And we're talking primo designer wear. I thought about taking some of that shit for myself, but none of those clothes would fit me."

"He's not dead," Sancho said.

"I'm just saying. If he *was* dead."

"He's not."

"Right. I got it. So where do they go? Back to his room?"

"He got transferred to another hospital."

"So you're taking them to him?"

"Yep."

"You sure you're not taking them for yourself?"

Sancho ignored the question. "You got a dolly I can borrow?"

The guy pointed to a dolly leaning against the wall in the far corner and eyed Sancho suspiciously as he loaded up the tiny trunk of the Aston Martin with as many boxes as would fit. The rest he piled in the backseat. Then he hopped in behind the wheel, started the 6.0 liter V12, and roared out of there.

Once home, Sancho carried the boxes into his garage.

Alyssa watched from the door that led into the house. "What's all this?"

"Flynn's clothes."

Sancho and Alyssa pooled their money to buy a tiny house in Pico Rivera. The two-bedroom, one bath townhouse had an attached garage with barely enough room for one car let alone all six boxes of Flynn's clothes.

"Why the hell do you have those?"

"Because whoever administers his trust decided to save some money and send his ass to a state hospital."

"Which one?"

"Hornitos. It's in Northern California."

"By the look on your face, I'm guessing it's not a very nice place."

"It's what they call a forensic hospital. It's where they send the worst of the worst. Those convicted of violent criminal behavior and judged not guilty by reason of insanity."

"Seriously?"

"Rapists. Murderers. Serial killers."

"Why would they send him somewhere like that?"

"I don't know, but I looked the place up and it's a hellhole. I found a database of violent incidents at state hospitals and Hornitos tops the list. Assault. Rape. Murder. Suicide."

"You gotta get him out of there."

"First, I have to figure out who sent him there. And why."

CHAPTER SEVEN

French Egyptologist Gustuve Jéquier discovered The Code of Hammurabi in modern day Iran in 1901. The ancient laws were engraved on a seven-foot-tall pillar of black diorite that now stands in the Louvre. Considered the world's first written system of laws, the King of Babylon enacted them nearly two thousand years ago. It posits the idea of presumption of innocence and suggests that both the accused and the accuser must have the opportunity to provide evidence. It also forbids the punishment of insane people for crimes they may have committed. From that time forward, most legal systems followed that same credo. The M'Naughton Rule, established by the English House of Lords in the mid-19th century, states that a defendant must understand the nature of their actions and know the difference between right and wrong. If those two requirements are not met, then those accused shall be found not guilty by reason of insanity.

Flynn sat on a hard metal bench in the back of an armored transport van, handcuffed and shackled at the waist and ankles. The burly two-man team transporting him north wore blue uniforms. Their badges identified them as police from the law enforcement arm of the California Department of State Hospitals. Flynn soon assessed that these police were actual police and had no idea that Flynn worked for His Majesty's Secret Service. Clearly, the service wanted to keep Flynn's cover story as a mental patient intact, so he played along and didn't resist when they shackled him to the bench. They told him the ride to Hornitos State Mental Hospital would take seven hours, with one or two stops along the way for bathroom breaks and food.

M's briefing was slim on details and Flynn didn't know what waited for him at Hornitos. He assumed his mission would be explained upon arrival. Perhaps by another undercover agent posing as a nurse or doctor.

Two other prisoners rode with him in the back of the van. From their general demeanor, he determined they didn't work for the service and were, in fact, actual mental patients. One man filled the rear of the van with his muscular bulk. Even seated, he towered over Flynn. His massive shoulders, arms, and chest stretched the material on his blue scrubs taut. Black stubble covered his shaved head and face and a crudely tattooed upside-down cross adorned his forehead. With his chin tilted down, he stared at Flynn through lidded eyes. A cold, confident smirk curled his lips. A tattoo of a clock with no hands decorated his wrist and the letters E, W, M, and N covered the scraped knuckles of his right hand.

The younger man shackled next to him was much smaller. Pale with a baby face and frightened eyes, he looked to be in his early twenties. A nasty white scar puckered the top of his forehead and bisected his hairline. While the big man wouldn't stop eyeballing Flynn, the younger one wouldn't meet Flynn's gaze at all.

After twenty minutes of tense silence, Flynn broke the ice. He looked at the big man's ham-sized hands. "E, W, M, N?"

"Evil, wicked, mean, and nasty," the big man said in a southern drawl.

"And the upside-down cross. What does that signify?"

"It signifies that I am not someone you want to mess with."

"Sir, from your size and general disposition, I already made that assumption."

"What's with the suit?"

"It's what I was wearing when they picked me up," Flynn explained.

"What kind of pansy-ass accent is that?"

"British by way of Scotland. Do I detect a bit of Texas in your drawl?"

"Yes, you do. I'm originally from Houston. Name's Mason."

"Flynn. James Flynn." He glanced at the moon-faced man, who looked away as soon as Flynn caught his eye. "What about you, young man?"

"Don't get him going. Once he starts, he won't shut up," Mason said.

"Shut up about what?"

"You don't want to know."

The moon-faced young man rattled his chains. "Jocks in socks."

Flynn offered him a smile. "Excuse me?"

"Jocks in socks with cocks in box." Flynn looked at Mason and Mason shook his head as the young man continued. "Chicks with bricks. Chicks with blocks. Chicks with dicks and pricks and cocks." The young man looked directly at Flynn. Suddenly, animated and interested in communicating, he continued to rattle off sentences that made perfect sense to him, even if they made no sense to Flynn. "Chicks with frocks and chicks that rock. Hands on clocks and hands on jocks!"

"All right, Boyd, I think we're good," Mason warned.

"Dicks in socks and cocks in jocks, five big micks with big fat sticks."

"*Boyd!*"

Boyd flinched and cowered and lowered his eyes.

Flynn felt for the boy and glared at Mason. "Was that really necessary?"

"It sure the hell was. Unless you want that little asshole rhyming shit like that for the next six damn hours."

"What's wrong with him?"

"He's out of his damn mind. You wouldn't know it to look at him, but that little twitch shot up his private high school and took out a dozen of those entitled pricks. Then he put one in his own damn head and didn't die. That's why they're sending him to Hornitos on a 1026."

"1026?"

"Not guilty by reason of insanity. Same reason they put me in there."

"You shoot up your high school?"

"No, I'm not *that* crazy. I just like to pretend I am. Though I freely admit I have anger issues. That, combined with my fondness for meth and my propensity not to take any shit, has led to some rash actions on my part. What about you?"

"Me?"

"Why are they sending your fancy ass to Hornitos?"

"To be honest, I'm not really sure."

"Sure you're sure. They don't send just anybody to Hornitos. You must have quite the body count if they're sending your ass there. What did you do, Jim? How many lives have you taken?"

"I can't really say."

"Can't say. Can't remember? Or can't count that high?"

"Let's just say I've never hurt anyone who didn't deserve it."

"I feel the same way, brother. Everyone I offed had it coming. The powers that be don't agree with me, but I don't go by their rules. I make my own."

Boyd began rhyming again, but kept his eyes focused on the floor. "Boyd I is. Boyd I is. I don't like your dumb pop quiz. I don't like your rules and regs. I don't like your skinny legs. I don't like your teasing lies! I don't like your vicious eyes."

Mason glowered at the boy. "Okay, Boyd. That'll do."

"I don't like your nasty cracks. I don't like your cliques and clacks. You push and push and make me sad. You push until I get real mad."

"I said *that'll do!*"

Boyd, now bright red, his eyes squeezed tight, his mouth pursed in a firm white line, rocked in place, rattling his chains.

Flynn caught Boyd's eye. "Breathe, Boyd. Breathe. A big deep breath."

Boyd held Flynn's gaze as he took a big breath and held it. "Now let it go. Out your nose." He did as instructed. "Again. Deep breath. Hold it. Okay, let it out. In and out. That's it."

Boyd slowed his breathing and gradually his red face faded to pink and then back to pale white. "I have to wee. I have to pee. Oh, the places I'll go. Oh, the places I'll see."

Flynn banged on the wall between the cab and the rear of the van. "Hey! We have to make a pit stop! The kid needs to have a piddle."

"Not yet," came the muffled reply.

"When?" Flynn shouted.

"*When I say so!*"

Boyd rocked and held his knees together, both hands over his crotch. "Piddle and piss. Tinkle and wee. Wizz like a wizard. Oh, the places I'll pee!" Finally, he grimaced, unclenched, and let go with a long sigh as the front of his scrubs turned dark with urine.

Mason sighed. He caught Flynn's eye. "They'll stop once or twice along the way. But that's just for them. Not for us. No way in hell they're unlocking our asses out here in the middle of nowhere. You think they care if we piss ourselves? These doors aren't opening until we get to Hornitos."

After about three hours on the road, the driver pulled the van to a stop. No one opened the doors. No one let them out. The drive up I-5 cut through the heart of California's San Joaquin Valley. Flynn knew the average temperature in July and August hovered near a hundred degrees. The temperature in the rear of the transport had to be even higher. If not for the California Aqueduct, the San Joaquin Valley would basically be a desert.

Ten minutes later, they were back on the road. Two hours after that, Flynn's bladder screamed for release. Mason already wet himself, and the acrid smell of urine assaulted Flynn's senses. Finally, Flynn could hold it no longer. He let his muscles relax and his bladder release. Some distant memory arose from the depths of his unconscious. Back when he was a different person. A little boy. Fat and afraid and all alone in some foster home. An angry woman wrenching him out of bed. Stripping his sheets as he lay on the floor. Embarrassing him in front of the other children. Bedwetter, they called him. *Baby wet the bed! Baby wet the bed!*

The transport van finally stopped for the last time. The armored doors were unbolted and opened wide. Bright light flooded inside, blinding Flynn. He used his arms to shield his eyes from the unyielding sun.

A phalanx of blue uniforms stood waiting outside. They watched the driver unlock Flynn and the others from the metal bench in the back of the transport. Flynn's restraints rattled as he stepped down from the van. With his ankles chained together, he had to take tiny steps or risk tripping and falling. A guard grabbed him hard by the arm and led him away. Other guards held Boyd and Mason.

As Flynn's eyes adjusted to the brightness, he registered a guard booth behind a metal gate attached to a towering twenty-foot-tall perimeter fence. Topped with coils of razor wire, the fence extended for hundreds of yards around the grounds. It looked more like a World War II prisoner-of-war camp than a state psychiatric hospital.

A sprawling, gothic structure constructed of red brick rose from the center of the compound like a dark castle, complete with wall buttresses and copper-topped spires on multiple towers. Ornate stone archways decorated with bas-relief sculptures framed the front entrance. Other newer, blocky buildings built in the fifties surrounded the older main hospital. Chain-link fences kept each area and each building secure.

The hospital police led Flynn, Boyd, and Mason into the intake building to process their paperwork. Next, they took all three to a large shower area with tile walls and a drain in the floor. Orderlies unchained Flynn from his ankle, wrist, and waist restraints as police with sidearms, batons, and stun guns looked on. Flynn figured he could disarm them and escape with little problem, but M sent him here for a reason. He needed to play out the charade.

The officer in charge, a tough-looking bantamweight bruiser with a flat nose and cauliflower ears, barked, "Strip!"

"Excuse me?"

He clapped his hands. "Get that suit off, asshole. Let's go!" As Boyd and Mason disrobed, Flynn stripped down to his boxers. "Those too, asshole! Everything! Gotta get you clean."

Flynn complied. The tallest guard unfurled a hose from a reel. A fat guard turned a valve and a powerful stream of ice-cold water slammed Flynn back into the tile wall. The intense pressure tore at Flynn's skin, buffeting him before they turned it on the others. Flynn often finished a hot shower with cold, but not this cold. The icy torrent stung like needles. When they finally finished hosing all three down, the officers tossed them rough towels and allowed them to dry off.

The bantamweight commander clapped his hands again. "Okay! Bend over! Spread your butt cheeks!"

Flynn knew that this entire process was designed to humiliate and diminish him. Instead, Flynn kept his cool as he bent over and spread his cheeks. The squeak of latex gloves preceded the squirt of a squeeze bottle full of lube. A moment later, a fat finger violated his insides as it probed for any possible illegal contraband.

With that indignity done, the taller guard tossed Flynn an orange set of hospital scrubs and a pair of plastic slip-on shoes. Flynn put them on and pointed towards his leather loafers and

Armani suit sitting in a wet, crumpled heap on the tile floor. "What about my suit?"

"Patients held in maximum security units are required to wear hospital-issued clothing."

"What will you do with it?"

"Don't worry about it."

"That's an Armani, and those loafers are Ferragamos."

"Sure they are." The commander smirked at the taller guard, who grabbed Flynn by the arm.

The guards escorted Flynn and the others from the intake building down a long, paved pathway past shrubbery and shrieking peacocks. Eventually, they reached the towering wooden doors of the main building. A guard station with a metal detector separated the front entryway from an ornate reception desk on the far side of the room. After trading more paperwork, the guards prodded Flynn, Mason, and Boyd down a long corridor that led to a reinforced steel door with a tiny double-paned window. A sign on the door identified it as the entrance to Unit G. The taller guard unlocked the door and the smaller one ushered them inside.

They handed Flynn and the others to psychiatric aides wearing blue scrubs. Nurses sat at an intake station completely enclosed by a transparent barrier. One by one, they handed out the room assignments.

Boyd looked at Flynn as they led him away. "I like it here. I like it a lot. Said the mouse in the house to the frog in the pot."

One aide tried to take Mason by his massive arm. Mason shrugged him off. The aide didn't touch him again, he just pointed in the direction they needed to go. Mason smirked at Flynn and winked before slowly heading down the corridor.

The other aide took Flynn by his upper arm and pulled him along after Mason. Flynn tried to make conversation. "I'm James, by the way."

"I'm Mr. Bautista," the aide said. At five foot nine, he stood a few inches shorter than Flynn, but outweighed him by a good thirty pounds.

"I understand this is a maximum-security unit."

"Correct."

"What does that mean, exactly?"

"It means we take no shit and give no fucks."

Flynn pointed to a device with a red button clipped to Bautista's belt. "What's that?"

"That's my alarm. If things go south, I call in the cavalry."

Flynn passed two older men in wheelchairs sitting side by side. One glared at Flynn. The other laughed.

A heavy-set brunette covered with freckles smiled at Flynn with a mouthful of yellow teeth. Flynn smiled back and she grabbed her pendulous right breast through her scrubs and squeezed it, flicking her tongue at him.

A tall skinny man with stringy hair hummed to himself with his eyes closed, white sweat socks stuffed into both his ears.

Flynn spotted a lanky, athletic-looking woman with extremely short black hair watching him from a doorway. She looked fierce. Feral. Ruggedly beautiful. Like a fashion model left to fend for herself in a post-apocalyptic hellscape. Flynn, ever the player, offered her a charming smile. She didn't react or return it. She just stared back. Watchful. Cautious. Dangerous.

The aide escorted Flynn around a corner and opened a door, but before Flynn could walk inside, a piercing siren shook the air and multiple strobe lights flashed. The aide with Flynn took off as doctors, nurses, and techs filled the halls and patients ran every which way. A wheelchair ran over Flynn's foot and the man with the socks in his ears crashed into him, eyes wide with terror as he ducked into a room.

Flynn followed the stampeding staff to see what all the hullabaloo was about. Rounding a corner and racing through a door, he found himself in the dayroom, where a giant Samoan held an elderly black man up against a wall and throttled him. The old man's feet dangled off the floor.

Nurses, doctors, and aides all grabbed various body parts belonging to the Samoan and pulled as hard as they could. The monster of a man was immovable. His scrubs could barely contain him.

Flynn decided to lend a hand and waded into the fray. He put his arm around the Samoan's neck and attempted a chokehold, but the man's neck was the size of a tree trunk and Flynn couldn't get the proper leverage. Try as he might, he couldn't restrict the monster's airflow or put any pressure on his carotid artery. As he attempted to readjust and get a better grip, the Samoan slammed his head back into Flynn's nose.

Flynn found himself on his back, his head ringing, his eyes watering, blood pouring from his smashed nose. He tasted a coppery tang as blood leaked into mouth and looked up to see someone stepping over him before smashing a chair over the Samoan's head. That staggered the man-mountain, but still he refused to let go of his victim. The chair bashed the back of his massive head again and this time broke into its constituent parts. The man who walloped the Samoan hit him repeatedly with a broken chair leg. After a good ten whacks, the Samoan released the old man from his death grip, stumbled back, and stepped directly on Flynn's crotch.

All three hundred and fifty pounds of the Pacific Islander pressed down on his nuts. The pain was so intense Flynn couldn't even scream. The pressure eased as the Samoan toppled. He took the black man with him and crashed to the floor.

Flynn cradled his smashed gonads as he rolled to get out of harm's way. Someone grabbed the Samoan's massive arm and wrenched it behind his back. A bone cracked, the Samoan bellowed, and the hospital police rushed in to slap restraints on the man-mountain.

Doctors performed CPR on the old black man as other hospital personnel slammed an injection into the Samoan's neck. The man-mountain slowly stopped struggling as the drug cocktail worked its way into his brain.

A hand reached down, grabbed Flynn by the wrist, and pulled him to his feet. The pain radiating from his testicles nearly buckled him at the knees. Flynn took a few painful steps and plopped into a chair, wincing with agony.

He looked up into a large face looming over him. It belonged to the man who helped Flynn to his feet. The same man who subdued the Samoan. A familiar face. A furious face. The face of a man who wanted Flynn dead and had tried to murder him more than once.

Mendoza.

CHAPTER EIGHT

The next day, Sancho arrived at City of Roses an hour before his shift. Lately, he worked days. Nine-hour shifts starting at 8:00 a.m. At that early hour, a few of the patients were already up and roaming the halls.

Renata, the nurse at the reception desk, looked surprised to see him. "What are you doing here?"

"I'm way behind on my charts," Sancho said. "I need to get caught up before I start my shift."

Renata had a round face and a round body, a friendly smile, and big brown eyes. Just two years out of nursing school, Renata was a "Dreamer" brought to the U.S. by her parents when she was four. Before Sancho met Flynn, most women showed no interest in him. He was painfully shy and awkward. But then Flynn encouraged him to ask Alyssa out, and she became the love of his life. Now that he was more self-assured and no longer shy or tongue-tied, women seemed a lot more interested in him. Or maybe they were just more comfortable around him because he was more comfortable in his own skin. Renata pointed at a computer behind her. "You want to use one of the workstations back here?"

"That would be great, Renata. Thank you. Can I get you a coffee? I was going to get one for me."

She grinned. "Two sugars. No cream. Thank you."

"Got it."

Sancho returned with Renata's coffee and logged onto a computer on the far side of the reception area so she couldn't see what he was doing. He did have paperwork to catch up on, but he also wanted to look at Flynn's file. He found the transfer order and noted the law firm that sent the paperwork. The same name Honeywell scrawled on the Post-it Note. He also found out who administered Flynn's trust. Someone named Dennis Stettmeier.

Sancho glanced at Renata. She busily texted someone. He logged into his Facebook account and plugged the name Dennis Stettmeier into the search box. Sixteen Stettmeiers came up, including three in Nebraska, eight in Germany, one in Ohio, two in Wisconsin, and one in Los Angeles. Sancho clicked on the profile and looked into the face of a plump, balding, forty-something guy with an uneasy smile and squinty eyes behind rectangular horn-rimmed glasses. Sancho plugged the name Stettmeier into Stettmeier's Facebook friends list and found only one Stettmeier. Warren. The profile image showed an elderly unsmiling man wearing thick plastic glasses.

Sancho clicked on Warren to see a wall full of condolence messages. According to his profile, Warren kicked the bucket five months ago. He lived in Glendale, and Dennis was apparently his son. Sancho didn't see that Dennis had any other siblings or a mother still living. The guy had nothing posted under work or education, or any other category. Sancho checked Dennis's photos and found a few awkward pics of him posing with an irritated redhead wearing glasses. On a beach. At a restaurant. At Disneyland.

More recent shots showed Dennis with a zaftig blonde who looked to be in her twenties. Many of those photos were selfies. The blonde seemed to be a bit of a ham. She grinned or stuck her tongue out or puckered her lips in nearly every picture. Dennis's expression never changed. Every shot showed him squinty eyed with an embarrassed smile. The blonde looked much younger than the irritated redhead and wore much more revealing clothing. Each shot showed off massive cleavage. According to the tag on one picture, her name was Misty Love. Sancho clicked on her profile. Her profession was listed as exotic dancer. There were links to an Instagram page filled with pictures of Misty in very skimpy outfits. She had quite a few tattoos and a giant pair of fake boobs. Apparently, Misty worked as a stripper at the Strawberry Hippo in Burbank.

"A friend of yours?" Renata stood right behind him.

"A friend of the family."

"Misty Love?"

"Uh huh."

Renata stared at Misty Love in a string bikini, posing with a puppy. Something beeped on her computer and she hurried back to her workstation.

Sancho searched for Dennis Stettmeier on LinkedIn and found him pretty quickly. A different, less flattering photo, but the same guy. He worked as an IT manager for an insurance company. Or did, at least. According to his LinkedIn profile, he left the company almost a year ago and now worked as an "independent contractor."

Sancho logged out of Facebook and then went into the browser settings and cleared the history. He mouthed "thank you" to Renata as he left the nurses' station and started his day.

■　■　■

Over lunch, Sancho retreated to his car and placed a call to the law firm administering Flynn's trust. A middle-aged woman with a smoker's rasp answered the phone. "Davis, Hopkins, & Cromartie."

"Hi, I'm calling from City of Roses Psychiatric Institute. My name is Mr. Perez. I'm a registered nurse, and I have a question concerning one of your clients who used to be a patient here."

"You're calling from where?"

"City of Roses Psychiatric Institute. The client in question is James Flynn. Your firm administers a trust for him."

"Hold on." Sancho heard click-clacking on a keyboard. Silence. And then more click-clacking. "What's your question?"

"Mr. Flynn was recently transferred from City of Roses to Hornitos State Hospital and a few of his belongings were left behind here. Some are kind of valuable and I thought I might send them to Flynn's guardian and trustee. Mr. Dennis Stettmeier."

"I'm sure that would be fine, sir."

"Great. I just need his mailing address." Sancho flipped over an envelope to write the address on.

A pause. "Hold on." Click-clacking, followed by silence, and then someone slurping—probably coffee. "222 Maple Drive, Glendale, California, and the zip is… hold on… that's the previous trustee's address."

"Previous trustee?"

"Warren Stettmeier. Apparently, he passed away recently and this hasn't been updated. Hold on."

"When did he pass away?"

"Hold on." Clicking. Clacking. Coffee sipping. More clicking. More clacking. "The successor trustee's address is 4520 Scandia Way, Los Angeles, California, 90042."

Sancho wrote it down and repeated back. "4520?"

"Scandia Way."

"And what was the zip again?"

"90042."

"90042. Thank you."

"Is there anything else I can help you with?"

"Um…I think that'll do it. I appreciate the help."

The woman hung up.

After a thankfully uneventful shift, at 5:00 p.m., Sancho finished his day and decided to make a stop on the way home. He plugged 4520 Scandia Way into Google maps and followed the directions to Stettmeier's address. He didn't call ahead. He wanted to surprise him. See his face. Look into his eyes. People reveal more when you catch them off guard.

The ride to Stettmeier's house led him into the hills. He found the address and parked just down the block. The place was impressive. A huge contemporary house that looked out over the valley. It had to be worth at least a million and a half. A new Range Rover sat in the driveway. Apparently, Stettmeier did okay working in IT as an independent contractor.

Either that or he was paying himself a hefty salary as Flynn's new trustee.

Sancho rang the Ring Doorbell. He looked at the camera and wondered if someone was watching him. He still wore his nurse's scrubs and faced the camera in a way that displayed his hospital name tag. After waiting a respectable length of time for an answer, he went to push the bell again. A male voice startled him.

"Yes?" said an annoyed, high-pitched voice.

"Is this Dennis Stettmeier?"

"Who wants to know?"

"My name is Sancho Perez and I'm a registered nurse at City of Roses Psychiatric Institute."

A pause. "Do you see the sign on the door? No solicitations."

"I'm not selling anything, sir. I'm here about James Flynn. According to the law firm of Davis, Hopkins, and Cromartie, you're his new legal guardian and trustee."

"Any question concerning Mr. Flynn can be handled by the law firm. You should call them directly."

"I have, sir, and they gave me your address. He was recently transferred to a new hospital and I have some of his belongings. Clothing. That kind of thing."

"Just leave them on the porch."

"I'm sorry, sir, but I really need to speak to you first."

"You *are* speaking to me."

"I mean face to face. In person. There's a delicate matter we need to discuss."

"What?"

"I was hoping we could do this in person."

"Look, I don't have time for this right now."

"When would you have time?"

"What's this about?"

"Sir—"

"Either tell me what this is about or get off my property."

"It's about Mr. Flynn."

"Please get to the point."

"He recently was transferred from City of Roses to Hornitos State Hospital."

"I know. I'm the one who authorized the transfer."

"Why?"

"How is that any of your business?"

"Mr. Flynn lived at City of Roses for nearly twenty years. I worked with him there for five of those years. It's his home. He's comfortable and safe there. Hornitos is not safe for him. It's where the state sends those guilty by reason of insanity. Murderers. Rapists. Serial killers. It's a very dangerous place and—"

"Did the hospital send you to talk to me?"

Sancho sighed. "No, sir, I'm here on my own because—"

"What's your name?"

"Perez. Sancho Perez."

"My lawyers will be contacting the hospital. Mr. Flynn's welfare is my responsibility. Not yours."

"I just thought if you knew—"

"Goodbye, Mr. Perez."

"Mr. Stettmeier?"

No answer.

"Mr. Stettmeier!"

Nothing.

Sancho pushed the doorbell.

A pause and then Stettmeier's angry, adenoidal voice blasted from the tiny speaker. "Do you want me to call the police?"

"Sir, please…"

"I'm calling the police."

"No need, sir! I'm leaving. Sorry for the intrusion." Sancho backed away from the door and stumbled off the stoop before turning around and heading down the walkway. *Was Stettmeier really going to get his lawyers to call the hospital? What the hell? Why wouldn't he just open the door?*

A red Porsche 911 came racing down the narrow street and squealed into the driveway. Sancho jumped back to avoid it as it skidded to a stop next to the Range Rover. The door opened and two long legs emerged. They wore spiked heels and were attached to a pneumatic torso in a tight, red dress. Misty Love offered Sancho a friendly grin before brushing past him and heading for the house. Stettmeier's new squeeze seemed way out of his league. There was something screwed up about this whole setup. What the hell was that *cabrón* up to?

CHAPTER NINE

Bethlem Royal Hospital in London began housing the mentally ill in the 1300s. Soon after its opening, it became known as "Bedlam." Built over a sewer, the hospital often reeked of human waste. Those in charge chained up the inmates and locked them away, to starve and die in their own filth, hidden from sight so the sane would not have to think about them. Though some of the "sane" seemed to enjoy watching the insane suffer. In the 1800s, the upper crust of English society often enjoyed social outings there, where, for a fee, the most disturbed patients were put on display to be openly mocked. Early American mental institutions often made money the same way. The treatment for those afflicted included whipping, beating, teeth pulling, bleeding, electrical shocks to the genitals, and being submerged in ice cold tubs of water for long periods of time.

After Mendoza blinded O'Haney and made him his bitch, incidents of violence in Unit G dropped to nearly zero. Even the craziest of the crazy knew not to fuck with Mendoza. Especially after he sent three fellow patients to the hospital and two to the morgue. Cautionary tales to anyone who would cross him. Every nurse and doctor in Unit G appreciated how Mendoza kept them safe.

Soon after Flynn's arrival at Hornitos, Mendoza used his burner to call Soto. "Here's here."

"So Flynn made it?"

"Didn't I just say that?"

"So it's done?"

"What?"

"You *know* what."

"Not yet."

"Waiting for the right opportunity?"

"I'm in no hurry. I want him to live with it. Sit with it. Weigh on him. I want him to know that I'm coming for him."

Soto sighed. "Wouldn't want to be him."

"Can we trust this Stettmeier *pendejo* to keep his mouth shut?"

"He wants what we want. So yeah, I think so. We do have one issue, though."

"What's that?"

"Stettmeier said someone from the hospital came to his house. Wanted to know why Flynn was transferred to Hornitos."

"What did Stettmeier tell him?"

"He didn't tell him shit," Soto said.

"Did he say who this person from the hospital was?"

"Sancho Perez."

"*Mierda*. That little *puto* needs to be taken care of too."

"I'll see what I can do. Meanwhile, what should I tell Stettmeier?"

"Tell him to keep his mouth shut. And once this is done, you'll need to convince him to transfer Flynn's trust to that offshore account I told you to set up."

"It's in the works."

Mendoza nodded. "Good."

"You've put a lot of thought into this."

"I've had a lot of time to think about it."

"Goolardo will be impressed."

"That arrogant *bastardo* only ever saw me as muscle. It's time he sees me for who I really am."

"Stettmeier won't be happy once he realizes where this is going."

"Which is why, eventually, we'll have to deal with that *pinché pendejo* too."

CHAPTER TEN

Three Supreme Court decisions in the early 1970s emptied the mental institutions in America. The court ruled that a person could not be involuntarily hospitalized. Not if they could "survive" in the community. Those fighting for those decisions believed it was an issue of civil rights. Many saw it as a civilized step forward. The result was that thousands of mentally ill individuals were now left to fend for themselves on the streets. State hospitals emptied. A large percentage of the homeless mentally ill eventually ended up in jail or prison. Meanwhile, state hospitals became "forensic facilities." They now housed violent criminals deemed not guilty by reason of insanity. The end result? The nonviolent mentally ill receive no treatment whatsoever and state mental hospitals house the most violent criminals in society.

Even though his nose was as swollen and painful as his injured testicles, the nurse practitioner told Flynn it wasn't broken. Standing, his stomach lurched with nausea. His head pounded. She gave Flynn two Tylenol and released him.

A psychiatric aide escorted him to his quarters. Each room in Unit G had two twin beds, two shelving units, and two simple cabinets. A barred window overlooked the grounds.

His roommate sat on the edge of his bed and eyeballed Flynn.

Flynn nodded to him. "I'm James."

His roommate nodded back. The man looked to be in his thirties. Tall and lanky, he had powerful arms with long ropy muscles. He was missing a front tooth and his nose looked crooked and flat. Like someone had broken it more than once. "I am Gabriel."

"Good to meet you, Gabriel."

Gabriel stared at him with unwavering ferocity. Flynn checked out the artwork taped to the wall above Gabriel's bed. Drawn with colored pencil and crayon, they depicted giant bloody massacres. Crudely drawn stick figures with swords and battle-axes slaughtered each other. Scribbles of red crayon erupted everywhere. Gabriel smiled as Flynn perused his drawings. "You like those?"

"Very colorful."

"Illustrations of what's to be. Visions sent to me by our Lord and Savior."

"I see."

"Unlike most of the people in this place. I'm no criminal and I'm not crazy."

"No?"

"No, I'm an archangel in human form, sent to Earth to help lead the forces of the Lord against the armies of darkness."

Flynn nodded politely. "Of course you are."

"Humans without faith judged me not guilty by reason of insanity."

"For doing what?"

"The Lord's work! I'm here to raise an army of righteous men to meet at Armageddon. Satan sent demons to stop me, but I dispatched them all. Sent them back to burn in fire and brimstone."

"Demons?"

"Disguised as law enforcement officers. But those of little faith can't perceive what I can. Can't see the evil hidden in the souls of those they believe are righteous. So many innocent have already lost their souls. Tricked by the trickster into selling them for earthly pleasures. That's why he sent me here."

"Who?"

"The Lord of Hosts! He sent me to help those who can't see the truth. Can't see that soon everything will change. It's all in the Book of Revelations. Have you read it, James? Have you read Revelations? Have you accepted the love and salvation of our Lord and Savior?"

"Can we continue this conversation later? I'm feeling a bit knackered." Flynn sat on the empty bed and marveled at the lumpiness.

"You don't believe I am who I say I am?"

"I didn't say that."

"You don't have to. You have doubts. Primal doubts. Most do. But look at me, James. It's not too late for you."

Flynn's face throbbed with pain. He eased himself back, horizontal on the bed. "That's good to know."

"You're not like the others here. There is goodness in you. Righteousness. I could see it the first time I laid eyes on you."

"Can we pick this up later, Gabriel? I really need to rest my eyes."

"Join us, James. Join us in the fight against the forces of the Beast."

"If I say yes, will you let me take a nap?"

"If you say yes, your soul will be saved and you will sleep the sleep of angels."

Flynn wondered if there was more than Tylenol in the pills the nurse practitioner handed him. A great weariness weighed him down and he let himself sink into a sweet, deep slumber.

■   ■   ■

When Flynn awoke, Gabriel's ear was inches from his nose. Flynn firmly, but gently, pushed Gabriel away. He tried to keep the anger out of his voice, but wasn't entirely successful. "What the hell are you doing?"

"Making sure you're still alive. You slept the sleep of the dead and I wanted to make sure you were still breathing."

"I appreciate the concern," Flynn said sarcastically.

"I can't afford to lose any new recruits."

Flynn sat up on the edge of the bed. "What time is it?"

"There are no clocks in here."

"Then how do you know what time it is?"

"You don't, and that's by design. Just another way to take away your self-determination. Though the lunch bell did just ring if you need sustenance."

"I'm starving."

"Good! Come. I will show you the way and guide you on your path, introduce you to the righteous and warn you away from those who would do you harm."

Flynn followed Gabriel as he joined a steady stream of patients making their way to the Unit G cafeteria. The southwestern style décor was festive, if somewhat incongruous. Brightly colored chairs and a dozen or more tables filled the large, well-lit, surprisingly pleasant room. Flynn stood behind Gabriel in the cafeteria line.

The hulking Samoan who nearly broke Flynn's nose stood a few patients ahead of them. He held a tray that looked tiny in his massive hands. He'd tried to strangle a fellow patient just yesterday, but now he waited patiently in line for his lunch. Flynn didn't see the elderly black man the Samoan tried to murder, but he did see the men he rode with in the transport.

Mason stood just behind the Samoan. Big as he seemed in the van, the Pacific Islander dwarfed him. He nodded to Flynn. Gabriel glared at the upside-down cross tattooed on Mason's forehead.

"The mark of the beast," Gabriel mumbled. "Do you see that sacrilege? A new arrival. One of the devil's own."

"His name's Mason. He rode in with me on the transport. The pale, round-faced lad behind him, that's Boyd."

Boyd offered Flynn a shy wave. "One bird. Two birds. Red birds. Blue birds. Black birds. New birds. Old birds. Jail birds."

The woman standing directly in front of Gabriel turned and smiled at him. "Hi Gabriel."

"Grace, I'd like you to meet James Flynn. He arrived just this morning."

"Hello, Grace. It's good to meet you."

Grace offered Flynn a warm smile. "It's good to meet you, too." She looked like a plump, friendly, forty-something suburban housewife.

"Grace is one of the good ones," Gabriel explained.

Flynn reached out to shake, but instead of taking his hand, Grace reached down and grabbed him by the balls with a grip like a steel vise.

Flynn's gonads were already swollen and badly injured and the intense pain caused his knees to buckle. As Flynn fell, he took Grace to the ground with him.

"I'm so sorry," she said, squeezing tighter. "But my hand is under the control of a mysterious evil entity."

Flynn made a strangled high-pitched sound as he tried to peel her fingers back, but her digits were immovable.

Mason looked on and laughed as Grace slapped and struggled to pull her hand away. "Let go! Let him go, you bastard!"

Flynn finally got a grip on Grace's offending hand and, using a Brazilian Jujitsu move, twisted until Grace screamed and let go.

Tears filled her eyes. "I am so, so sorry."

Gabriel helped Flynn back to his feet. "You okay?"

"I will be." Flynn glanced at Grace, cradling her injured wrist. "I hope I didn't hurt you."

"I hope I didn't hurt *you*," Grace said.

"Guess that's one way to say hello," Mason joked. A few of the other patients laughed.

Grace blushed and closed her eyes in shame. "The doctors call it Alien Hand Syndrome, but I know what it really is."

"A dark spirit. An evil entity," Gabriel explained.

"I used to be a nurse before that demon possessed me. All I wanted to do was help people." She held up her right hand and glared at it hatefully. "But instead, this fiend murdered my patients right in front of me. Grabbed them by the throat and…." Grace's eyes glistened with tears.

Gabriel rubbed her back. "If we confess our failings, he is faithful and just to forgive us our sins."

Flynn sat at a bright blue table with Gabriel, Grace, and Boyd. He poked at a chicken pot pie and glanced across the dining room. Mendoza watched him. The big man sat at a purple table with an even larger man with two empty eye sockets. The sightless man fondled his food with his fingers before putting it in his mouth.

"The big guy next to the blind guy? That's Mendoza." Gabriel took a bite of cheese enchilada. "That's someone you do not want to cross. He runs Unit G. The blind one, O'Haney, used to be the big cheese before Mendoza gouged out his eyes."

One table over sat the lean, athletic-looking, dark-haired beauty with the dangerous demeanor. Flynn smiled and nodded to her, but she didn't smile back. She just held his gaze for a second or two before returning to her dinner. She had no tablemates.

"That's Caitlyn Valentine. You want to stay away from her too," Gabriel said. "Not even Mendoza messes with her."

"Why's that?"

"The week she arrived here, a man by the name of Franklin Bittaker tried to have his way with her."

"The Red River Killer?"

"You've heard of him?"

"He was all over the news a few years back."

"Murdered forty-seven prostitutes over a twenty-year period. A stone-cold psycho killer. Twice her size."

"She fought back?"

"She snapped his neck."

Flynn kept his eyes on her. "Impressive."

"That's one way to put it."

"So what's her story?"

"No one knows. It's possible she's in league with an evil entity, but it's hard to say. It could be she's just crazy. She keeps her own council and no one goes near her."

Flynn noticed Mason smiling at him from the other side of the cafeteria. Mason looked at Caitlyn before grinning back at Flynn, winking at him.

"I think that's about to change," Flynn said.

Mason scraped back his chair and stood. As he crossed the room, he passed Flynn. whispering "I'm going in." He approached Caitlyn's table, pulled out a chair, and took a seat directly across from her.

Flynn couldn't hear what Mason said, but by his body language and the grin on his face, he figured he was hitting on her. Caitlyn ignored him and continued to eat, but Mason wouldn't back off. His smile wasn't friendly. It was testy. Mocking. Aggressive. He grinned at Flynn and gave him a thumbs up. Caitlyn tried to get up and Mason took her by the wrist and pulled her back down. He said something to her and smiled as he slid his chair closer.

Flynn rose.

Gabriel said, "Best thing to do is mind your own business."

"I believe this *is* my business." With a dull pain still radiating from his testicles, Flynn limped across the cafeteria and pulled back a chair at Caitlyn's table. "Mind if I join you two?"

"Yeah, I do mind." Mason gave Flynn a wild-eyed grin. "Two is company. Three's a crowd."

Much to Mason's consternation, he sat down anyway. "The name's Flynn. James Flynn." Flynn tried to catch Caitlyn's eye, but she wouldn't look at him. She just stared at her unfinished taco pie and didn't resist as Mason held her wrist.

"This little bitch is mine. So back the fuck off!" Mason growled.

Caitlyn looked up from her pie and studied Flynn's face. "I know who you are."

"Then you have me at a disadvantage."

"I'm Caitlyn."

"What a beautiful name. In Irish, it means pure."

"As the driven snow," Caitlyn replied dryly. "But it's Caitlyn with a y and that's the Welsh spelling."

"Like Dylan Thomas's wife."

"Exactly."

Mason's smile curdled. "What the hell are you two talking about?"

"Dylan Thomas. The great Welsh poet," Flynn said.

"All right, enough. You said hello to the lady. Time to go."

"Maybe it's time for *you* to go." Caitlyn said.

Mason jerked Caitlyn to her feet. "Bitch, you have no idea who you're fucking with."

She used a Krav Maga technique to turn Mason's wrist until something cracked. He released her, his face purple with fury. He tried to backhand her, but she caught the blow and used an Aikido move to turn his momentum against him. Caitlyn twisted and flipped him over her hip. Mason crashed down on the table.

Flynn scooted his chair back and enjoyed the show as an enraged Mason rolled off the table and landed on his feet, his eyes wild, his teeth bared. An alarm siren screamed, shaking the air as he picked up a chair. He tried to break it over Caitlyn's head, but she easily sidestepped the blow, swept his feet out from under him, and slammed him face-first into the floor.

When Mason tried to get up, she stomped his head, smashing his nose into the linoleum. Keeping her foot on the back of his neck, she held him there until the hospital police arrived. She then fell to her knees and allowed them to subdue her. As they carried her off, she glanced back at Flynn and offered him the tiniest of smirks.

CHAPTER ELEVEN

Flynn lay in bed after light's out and wondered if he had a concussion. He still didn't know why M had sent him here. No contact had yet to connect with him or give him his mission. *Does it have something to do with Mendoza?*

Gabriel mumbled quietly, not to Flynn, but to the God he believed watched over them. "Beloved Shepherd of our souls. Spread your holy protection over us and keep us secure from the wickedness of the evil one. Clothe us in your holy armor, that we may stand against his diabolical machinations, resist his enticements and temptations, and overcome his darkness with the light of your righteousness. Amen." After a beat. "Flynn?"

"Yes?"

"Isn't there something you want to say?"

M didn't give Flynn a sign/countersign identifier. It was the usual way to identify an unknown contact as an agent. His roommate, Gabriel, seemed truly delusional, but perhaps that was just an elaborate ruse. Maybe he didn't believe he was actually an archangel sent to Earth to lead the forces of the lord against the armies of Satan. Perhaps he had knowledge of Flynn's mission and was waiting patiently for Flynn to offer him the proper countersign. The service used a few standard sign/countersign phrases over the years. Flynn tried one to see if Gabriel was indeed his contact. "The migrating birds fly over the sea."

"Excuse me?" Gabriel said.

"The migrating birds fly over the sea."

A long pause. "I suppose they do," Gabriel said.

That wasn't the proper response. So Flynn tried another. "The waxing moon rises at noon."

Another long pause. "What are you talking about?"

"You asked me if there was something I wanted to say."

"Because I proffered our Lord a prayer, and you didn't offer an amen."

Was *amen* the countersign? "Amen," Flynn said. Flynn waited to see if Gabriel would now reveal himself as his contact.

But Gabriel didn't say another word. And after a few minutes, he began to snore.

When Flynn was sure Gabriel was asleep, he crept from his bed and tried the door. Locked. Because Unit G contained spree and serial killers, mass murderers, rapists, terrorists, pedophiles, and mad bombers, it made sense that they would lock the doors at night.

Flynn noticed a panel on the wall next to his bed with a call button and another button marked *emergency*. Unless Mendoza had a universal key, Flynn figured he'd be relatively safe for the night. Just in case, he created a makeshift alarm using a stack of plastic cups and an aluminum bedpan that he propped in front of the door.

Flynn wondered if nefarious forces somehow compromised his Majesty's Secret Service and sent him here to die. It happened once before. A trap was set with a beautiful Russian spy in Istanbul. He barely survived that attempt, but lived to tell the tale. Was the intention here the same? *Was I sent to Hornitos to die at Mendoza's hand?*

■　■　■

The morning buzzer jarred Flynn awake. Gabriel kneeled on the floor, praying once again.

"When the wicked advance to devour me, it is my enemies and my foes who will stumble and fall. Though an army of darkness besieges me, my heart will show no fear." Gabriel used the bed to push himself to his feet and squeaked out a fart. He smiled at Flynn. "Who's ready for breakfast?"

Over the course of the morning, Flynn sidled up next to various patients and staff members and tried several sign/countersign phrases to see if he could suss out a contact.

"The red fox trots quietly at dusk."

"If a dog chews shoes, whose shoes does he choose?"

"Fuzzy Wuzzy was a bear. Fuzzy Wuzzy had no hair."

Everyone looked at him as if he were crazy.

Especially the crazy ones.

At eleven, Flynn met with a senior psychiatrist in one of Unit G's consultation rooms. From the last three letters of his name, Flynn concluded that Dr. Sahakian was of Armenian extraction. Stocky and short, with salt-and-pepper hair and a perfectly trimmed goatee, Dr. Sahakian offered Flynn a perfunctory smile before directing him to a well-worn couch. The doctor took a chair across from him and opened his file, giving it a cursory glance.

Flynn watched him carefully and said, "The migrating birds fly over the sea."

"Do they?" Sahakian said without bothering to look up.

Flynn waited for the proper countersign. It wasn't forthcoming. "The toothless tiger rules a restless jungle."

Sahakian looked up from the file. "What does that mean to you, Mr. Flynn?"

"What does that mean to you?" Flynn gave him a knowing smile.

Sahakian returned the smile, but once again failed to reply with the countersign. "I understand you've gotten into a few scuffles since you arrived yesterday."

"I witnessed a few and tried to help those being assaulted."

"I appreciate the intention, but going forward... let's let the staff manage those sorts of things. Do you think you can do that?"

"The staff sometimes seems hesitant to engage."

Sahakian repeated himself. Slowly, this time. As if talking to a mentally challenged child. "Do you think you can do that, Mr. Flynn? Not involve yourself in physical altercations?"

"If that's what you prefer."

"It is." Sahakian closed Flynn's file folder. "Do you know why you're here, Mr. Flynn?"

"I don't, Doctor, which is why I need to make a confession." Flynn leaned in closer and whispered, "I'm not actually a mental patient."

"Why are you whispering, Mr. Flynn?"

"Because they might be listening."

"Who?"

"My enemies."

Sahakian open the file folder and wrote something down. "So you don't believe you're mentally ill?"

"No, sir, that's just my cover. I actually work for His Majesty's Secret Service and I was sent here on a mission."

"What mission is that?"

"I don't know."

"Your superiors sent you on a mission, but they didn't tell you what it was?"

"I have yet to meet my contact here and fear that something might have happened to him. Or her."

"It says here in your file you were transferred from City of Roses Psychiatric Hospital."

"Also a front."

"So City of Roses isn't a mental hospital?"

"It's a foreign field office for HMSS."

"Is this a foreign field office as well?"

"Of course not. This is a state mental hospital."

Dr. Sahakian narrowed his eyes and made a notation in Flynn's file. "I'd like to prescribe some medication for you. An antipsychotic combined with something to help with your anxiety."

"I don't feel especially anxious."

"This particular combination will help you think a lot more clearly."

"I believe I'm thinking *very* clearly."

"Which is why I'll be seeing you three times a week for individual psychotherapy. You'll also be in group therapy and I'd like to try CBT as well."

"CBT?"

"Cognitive behavioral therapy to help you recognize and hopefully change unhelpful and distorted thought patterns."

"Sir, I'm not sure you're listening to me. I am *not* mentally ill."

Dr. Sahakian smiled at that. "We have several group activities here at Hornitos that many of our patients find very therapeutic. Art therapy can be extremely effective."

"Have you heard a single word I've said to you?"

"I hear you loud and clear, Mr. Flynn."

"*You are not listening to me!*"

"Let's sign you up for our anger management group as well."

Flynn bolted to his feet. "Sir, my life is in danger here. One of your patients, Mr. Mendoza, is a murderer."

"Many of our patients here are murders."

"Yes, but he has personally tried to terminate me on multiple occasions."

"Mr. Flynn, your personal safety is of paramount importance to us. We have many security protocols in place and will do everything we can to protect you. But for us to help you, you must be willing to help yourself. What do you say, Mr. Flynn? Can you make that promise?"

Flynn tamped his anger down. "I suppose."

"Start by doing what's necessary. Then do what's possible. Before you know it, you'll be doing what's impossible. Do you know who said that?"

"*You* just said that."

"St. Francis of Assisi. He also said that all the darkness in the world cannot extinguish the light of a single candle."

After their session, Dr. Sahakian escorted Flynn to the nurse's station, where they gave him his first dose of antipsychotic medication. Nurse Winston, a stocky no-nonsense nurse in her early forties, handed him a plastic medication cup with two little pills. One yellow and oblong and one white and rectangular. She waited for Flynn to take them and, rather than make a scene, Flynn humored her. He held them out on his tongue for her to see, but instead of swallowing them, he tucked them between his teeth and his cheek as he swallowed the cup of water. He removed them later on the way back to his room, secreting them in his pocket, knowing they might come in handy if he needed to drug someone.

As he passed the dayroom, he saw Gabriel watching TV with Grace and Boyd. *Good.* Flynn needed some alone time. Needed time to come up with a way to get in contact with M. He opened the door to his room and stepped inside. Mendoza sat on Gabriel's bed.

Flynn could have fled, but why delay the inevitable? Instead, he shut the door behind himself. "Mr. Mendoza."

Mendoza glared at Flynn with his one good eye. "Do you know why you're here?"

"You're the second person to ask me that today."

"Because of me."

"You?"

"Francisco Goolardo was like a father to me. He believed in me. Trusted me. And you turned him against me."

"I think that was all you."

"No, that was *you*." Mendoza balled his immense hands into fists. "Even once he knew you were crazy, he still believed you were better than me. Smarter than me. More cultured. More educated. He saw me as nothing but a stupid *pendejo* barely worth talking to."

"That's not true." Flynn crossed to his own bed and sat across from Mendoza. "He respected you. Relied on you."

"But he *doesn't* respect me. He never respected me. And that's because of you!"

"Is that why you tried to kill me?"

"Look what you did! Look where I am! They found me not guilty by reason of insanity. You made me crazy! As crazy as you!"

"But *are* you crazy? Or did you just pretend to be so you could get to me?"

Mendoza looked at the floor. He shook his head. "To tell you the truth, I don't even know anymore." Then he raised his gaze to meet Flynn's. "All I know is I want you dead."

"Killing me won't earn you Goolardo's respect."

"That's where you're wrong. When he learns what I've done here. When he understands the lengths I went to to make it happen. Then, finally, he'll see me for who I really am."

"So you still intend to kill me." A statement. Not a question.

Mendoza pulled out a sharpened screwdriver. "I do."

Flynn knew his injuries would hamper his ability to defend himself against an opponent who had at least a hundred and fifty pounds on him. A hundred and fifty pounds of prison-hardened muscle that threatened to burst from his orange hospital scrubs. Flynn eyed the alarm button on the wall between the beds and calculated how he might reach it. He scanned the room for anything that might work as a weapon.

He needed to keep Mendoza talking until he could figure a way out of this. "Even if you do manage to kill me, you'll never get away with it. They'll know it was you."

"So what if they do? What does it matter? This is the perfect place to commit murder. What can they do to me? Where can they send me? I've already been found guilty by reason of insanity." Mendoza laughed.

"I'm glad you find that amusing." Flynn edged his bum across the bed, closer to the emergency button.

"I think Goolardo will be so impressed by my ingenuity, he'll hire lawyers to push for my release. Pay doctors to testify that I am sane. Bribe judges to agree to release me. Soon I will be out of this hellhole and back at his right hand. And do you know where you will be?"

"Why don't you tell me?" Flynn kept his eyes locked on Mendoza as he inched his buttocks ever closer.

Mendoza slowly rose to his full height. "Rotting in the ground."

Flynn dove for the alarm, but Mendoza anticipated his move and kicked him in the ribs. Flynn missed the alarm button by less than an inch. His head hit the edge of the bed.

Mendoza grabbed Flynn by the throat, lifted him off the ground, and slammed him into the wall. Flynn stretched to reach the alarm button, extending his fingers as far as they would go.

Not far enough.

Mendoza raised the screwdriver high over his head and brought it down with all his might, aiming for the center of Flynn's chest. Flynn deflected the blow, but just barely. The sharpened point pierced the flesh just above his collarbone, sinking deep.

Grunting like a beast, Mendoza pulled the screwdriver out. Blood splattered Flynn's face. Before Mendoza could bring it down again, Gabriel opened the door.

The momentary distraction allowed Flynn to get a grip on the hand Mendoza had on his throat. He turned the maniac's wrist with a jujitsu move, freeing himself and falling to the floor.

Mendoza stomped Flynn in the face before turning on Gabriel. Flynn's roommate pointed a finger at Mendoza and screamed, "And I will strike down upon thee with great vengeance and furious anger!" Gabriel pulled his own shiv and came at Mendoza hard. Mendoza backhanded Gabriel before he could reach him, sending the "Angel of the Lord" right back out the door.

Flynn hit the alarm with a hand covered in blood.

The siren screamed. Lights flashed in the corridor.

Mendoza turned his attention back to his original prey. Flynn crawled between his legs and across the floor, making a beeline for the door.

Mendoza stomped on Flynn's lower back, smashing him into the dirty linoleum. He fell upon Flynn and straddled him. Flynn tried to get out from under his attacker's massive body and managed only to rotate onto his back. Mendoza glared down with his cyclops eye, holding the screwdriver high. One hand cupped over the other, he prepared to drive the sharpened point all the way through Flynn's heart and into his spine.

Pinned down by Mendoza's thighs, there was nothing for Flynn to do but die.

An orange flash blurred by overhead, striking Mendoza in the throat.

The big man gasped. Caitlyn landed lightly and executed a perfect spinning hook kick, knocking the screwdriver from Mendoza's hand. It hit the wall and clattered to the floor.

Mendoza pushed off Flynn to confront his new attacker. Before he could take a step, Caitlyn brought the edge of her foot down on the side of Mendoza's knee. Flynn recognized the karate move: Kansetsu Geri, a devastating attack.

Mendoza bellowed like a beast and fell on top of Flynn, knocking the air out of him.

Determined to finish what he started, Mendoza put both his massive hands around Flynn's throat and throttled him.

Caitlyn grabbed Mendoza by the hair and held the sharpened tip of his screwdriver an inch from his eye. "You want to lose this one too? If so, keep squeezing."

"*Pinche puta*," Mendoza mumbled. He drove his thumbs into Flynn's throat. Flynn struggled to free himself, but between the broken ribs and the puncture wound in the shoulder, he just didn't have the strength.

Caitlyn brought the screwdriver closer to the sicario's last remaining eyeball. "Let him go, *pendejo*! I am not playing!"

Mendoza let go of Flynn's throat with his left hand and grabbed Caitlyn's wrist. She tried to push the screwdriver through Mendoza's eye, but he held her back even as he continued to choke Flynn.

The hospital police arrived with their stun guns and tasers, batons and injections. First, they tased Caitlyn and then Mendoza, subduing them both before securing them with zip ties. When Flynn tried to sit up, they tased him as well, injecting him with a B-52 cocktail before flipping him over and zip-tying him too.

CHAPTER TWELVE

The B-52 is a drug cocktail often administered to agitated or violent mental patients to chemically restrain them. It's named after its constituent ingredients and induces an immediate tranquilizing effect. The ingredients include Benadryl, Haldol, and Lorazepam. Not to be mistaken for the sickly sweet B-52 shot you can order in any cocktail lounge. That one consists of Baileys Irish Cream, Grand Marnier, and Kahlúa. That particular cocktail is named not for the B-52 bomber, but for the iconic band.

The nurse practitioner told Flynn she was tired of seeing him in the medical unit as she taped up his bruised ribs and stitched up the cut on his head. The puncture wound from Mendoza's sharpened screwdriver hit no arteries, organs, or ligaments, but did injure some muscle. The largest worry was infection, so she cleaned it out, used a topical antibiotic, and gave Flynn a tetanus shot before bandaging him up.

She also patched up Caitlyn and Gabriel and returned all three back to Unit G. Hospital Police took their statements and arrested Mendoza for assault, battery, and attempted murder. They handed him over to the sheriff's deputies, who took him to Hornitos County Jail. Flynn wasn't sure how long he'd remain there. The last person taken to county jail was the Samoan, who stepped on his balls the first day he arrived. Flynn later learned his name was Manu. One day after his arrest, they returned the hulking Pacific Islander back to Unit G. A judge ruled he wasn't competent to stand trial.

Flynn still had bruises on his neck and a headache that wouldn't quit as he listened to Mr. Rabbish, the art therapist, explain their group activity. He was a smiling forty-something man with a shaved head and a close-cropped beard.

"Today we will explore the concept of joy." He motioned to a long table covered with art supplies; poster boards, crayons, colored pencils, construction paper, glitter, glue, piles of old magazines, and blunt plastic scissors. The same child-safe scissors given to preschoolers. "You will look through magazines and find images and words that make you happy. Whatever makes you smile and fills you with delight. Cut them out, paste them on the posterboard and decorate the collage anyway you like."

Flynn glanced at the faces of the other patients in the art therapy room. Grace grinned. Mason smirked. Manu glowered. Boyd seemed confused. Caitlyn looked put out.

Mr. Rabbish pointed to the piles of magazines. "Grab whatever you want, but make sure you share. There's no wrong way to do this. It's all about having fun and finding your bliss."

The patients crowded around the table and perused a wide variety of magazines: Car and Driver, Cosmopolitan, Sports Illustrated, Good Housekeeping, Popular Mechanics, National Geographic, Newsweek, Esquire, Vogue, Rolling Stone, Food and Wine.

Flynn grabbed a handful of random magazines, found a chair at a long table, and cut out pictures of whatever caught his fancy. Until he had a better understanding of why he was here, he needed to go with the flow and keep a low profile. Thanks to Mendoza, he'd already attracted far too much attention. And what was Caitlyn Valentine's story? *Where did she learn how to fight like that?* She obviously had training. He glanced across the table and caught her eye. She dismissed him with a glower and went back to reading an old issue of Rolling Stone.

From where Flynn sat, he analyzed what images the others were cutting out and pasting on their poster boards. Flynn deduced that Rabbish assigned this project to tap into each patient's unconscious mind and uncover unexpressed or unexplored feelings.

The images in Gabriel's collage mirrored the drawings and paintings he taped above his bed in their shared room. Burning buildings. Smoking rubble. Crying children. Screaming mothers. Floods. Wild fires. Tornadoes. Hurricanes. Images of death, destruction, tragedy, and terror.

Mason carefully cut out female rear ends in all shapes and sizes. Big booties. Little butts. Muscular backsides and wide flabby bottoms. No full bodies or other individual body parts. No legs. No breasts. No faces. Just every size, shape, and color of female derriere imaginable.

He caught Flynn eying his art and grinned. "What can I say? I'm an ass man."

Boyd mumbled a rhyme in a quiet monotone as he methodically went through magazine after magazine, cutting out eyes and eyeballs by the dozens and pasting them to the posterboard. "And two little puppies, and a pair of guppies, and a mouse named Haskell, and a little toy castle, and a goat and two hippies and a bowl of Rice Krispies."

Manu's giant sausage-sized fingers barely fit in the scissor handle holes as he carefully cut out pictures of cakes, pies, pork chops, pasta, roast beef, fried chicken, and fish tacos. He grinned like a little kid with his tongue between his teeth as he glued them into a giant, two-dimensional smorgasbord.

Grace used her left hand to wield the scissors as she cut out pictures of puppies and kittens, rainbows and butterflies, beautiful flowers and snowcapped mountains. Her right hand, however, had a mind of its own and would grab the pictures as soon as she finished cutting them out and crumple them into balls. "No, no. Stop, stop, *stop!*"

Flynn finished his collage and sat down right next to Caitlyn. "I want to thank you."

She didn't bother looking up. "For what?"

"For saving my life."

She shrugged and continued to read the Rolling Stone article. "Forget it."

"Why'd you do it?"

She raised her gaze. "What?"

"Save my life?"

She stared at him for a beat. "I don't have a fucking clue." And went back to reading.

"You're trained in Krav Maga and Shotokan Karate. I recognized the moves. I've trained in those disciplines as well. Where'd you learn to fight like that?"

She sighed with frustration. "Do you mind? I'm trying to read here."

"I don't mean to bother you..."

"Then stop bothering me."

Flynn noticed her blank posterboard. "I see you haven't started your assignment." Flynn watched the muscles in her jaw tense as she clenched down. He continued to push her. "You don't want to take us to your happy place?"

"My happy place is any place other than this place." Caitlyn looked at Flynn's collage and smirked. "Cars, guns, babes, and beaches." She shook her head, stood up and crossed to the far side of the room, sitting at a table as far from Flynn as possible.

Flynn felt the sting of embarrassment. He was used to women playing hard to get or giving him the cold shoulder, but this wasn't that. This was utter contempt.

Mr. Rabbish addressed the group. "Okay, class, I'll see you next week. You're welcome to take your collage with you. For those of you who didn't take part, perhaps next time you'll have a change of heart. Tonight, think about all those things that make you happy. Part of what this class is about is cultivating an attitude of gratitude. Even in here at Hornitos, you have things to be grateful for. As a wise man once said, 'Enjoy the little things, for one day you may look back and realize they were the big things.'"

Caitlyn shot out the door first. Flynn quickly followed. The crowded corridor filled with patients and staff heading for the dining room. Flynn scanned the hallway, always alert to danger as he joined the flow of traffic.

Up ahead, an unfamiliar maintenance man with a toolbox worked on a lighting fixture. Flynn caught the man surreptitiously glancing back at Caitlyn. She was indeed attractive, so that might account for his interest, but something about the look gave Flynn the impression he wasn't checking her out, but sizing her up.

The maintenance man pulled something out of his pocket. People passed back and forth in front of him, obscuring Flynn's view, but finally he caught a glimpse. A syringe. *Why would a maintenance man need a syringe?*

Flynn quickened his pace as Caitlyn passed the man. The guy took a step in her direction and raised the syringe. Flynn caught up to him and turned the syringe back on him. The man grunted. They struggled briefly. Caitlyn glanced back in time to see Flynn force the needle into the man's neck. It happened so fast no one else noticed.

Flynn kept walking as the syringe fell to the floor. The man staggered. Caitlyn stopped to stare as the man collapsed. Flynn grabbed her by the arm and pulled her along.

"That man just tried to murder you," Flynn whispered.

"Wouldn't be the first time." Caitlyn pulled away from Flynn and headed into the cafeteria.

Flynn followed and stood behind her in line. "What do you mean, it wouldn't be the first time?"

She didn't answer his question and shuffled forward, pointing to the turkey meatloaf, the mashed potatoes, and green beans. The lunch lady handed her the plate, which she put on a tray. Flynn selected the least objectionable entrée he could find: fish and chips. He followed Caitlyn to her table and took the seat across from her, asking her the same question. "What do you *mean* it wouldn't be the first time?"

"A week after I arrived here, someone tried to take me out."

"Are you talking about the Red River Killer?"

"I believe someone got to him. Sent him after me."

"Who?"

"The same people responsible for putting me here."

"And who would they be?"

"What do you care? We're even now." She took a bite of turkey meatloaf.

As patients and staff filed into the cafeteria, the major topic of conversation revolved around the maintenance man who'd just collapsed in the corridor. EMTs had already taken him away. Some speculated he had a heart attack.

Gabriel approached Flynn's table. Before he could sit, Caitlyn shot him an icy glare that gave him pause. "Mind if I join you?" Gabriel asked.

"Yes," Caitlyn said.

"Yes, I can join you?"

"Yes, I mind." She stared him down. Gabriel nodded and moved on.

"You're not really a people person, are you?" Flynn said.

Caitlyn couldn't help but smile at that.

"A smile. Well, wonder of wonders. I haven't seen one of those on your face before."

"You really are persistent."

"Why would someone want you dead?"

"What do you care?"

"Maybe I'm curious."

"Maybe it's none of your business."

"Did I or did I not just recently save your life?"

"Like I said…we're even now. Let it go."

"Who wants you dead?"

Caitlyn scraped back her chair and stood. "Do *not* follow me."

She crossed the cafeteria. Flynn honored her request. Mason eyed her as she made her way out.

CHAPTER THIRTEEN

Sancho had never been to a state hospital before and didn't expect such a pastoral setting. Golden rolling hills dotted with oak trees all set against a vivid blue sky. The original hospital, built in the 1920s, was the centerpiece of the bucolic one-hundred-and-fifty-acre campus. From a distance, the towering brick and stone structure resembled an old English estate like the one featured in Downton Abbey.

Sancho stopped at a guard gate with a security kiosk and showed his driver's license. The guard, a bored forty-something black lady, looked at him, looked at his Aston Martin, and then went off to print up his visitor's pass. She returned and handed Sancho a plastic security badge. "Make sure you keep this on you at all times."

"Got it. Where should I park?"

"Just follow the road. You'll see the signs."

"Thank you."

Sancho pulled forward, past the intimidating perimeter fence topped with coils of razor wire, and followed the road to visitor parking. He found a spot on the end and made his way up a brick path past 1950s era buildings.

Flynn's unit was in the sprawling main building. The one that looked like Downton Abbey. Sancho put his wallet and keys in a plastic tray and passed through a metal detector before moving to a screened area off to the side. A hospital police officer frisked him from head to toe to make sure he had no weapons or contraband.

Sancho continued on and showed his pass to an unsmiling middle-aged Asian lady behind some plexiglass. She buzzed him through a security door. He followed the signs to Unit G, where another security officer buzzed him through yet another locked door. City of Roses had nowhere near this level of security. Just one locked ward with one locked door.

Sancho crossed into a large lobby filled with a variety of humanity all waiting to visit with family, friends and clients. At 3:00 p.m. on the dot, a light glowed above the door and hospital police led the visitors to a long line of numbered cubicles with Plexiglas windows. A handset in each one allowed the patient to speak to their visitor at a distance. An elderly Hispanic lady waited in the cubicle to his left. On his right sat a heavyset white woman who smelled of cigarettes.

When Flynn first appeared in front of him, Sancho didn't recognize him. He walked with a painful limp, grimacing and wincing as he sat down. His puffy, unshaven face had welts and bruises and scabbed-over scratches. A bandage covered his nose and both his eyes were ringed with green and purple bruises. Seeing Sancho brought a smile to his face, but also a flinch as he cracked the scab on his fat lip.

"What the hell happened to you?"

Flynn shrugged. "It looks worse than it is."

"Dude, I don't think that's possible. We gotta get you out of here."

"Not until I complete my mission."

"What mission would that be?"

"I was hoping you could tell me. I have yet to meet my contact and I'm beginning to suspect I was sent here under false pretenses. In fact, I fear that His Majesty's Secret Service has been compromised. Do you know who gave M the order to send me here?"

"I do."

"Who?"

"The one who pays the bills. Pays your way. Paid for you to stay at City of Roses."

"What are you talking about?"

"The trust fund put in place after your parents passed away." Sancho could see the distress on Flynn's face. He'd seen that look before. Whenever someone made Flynn confront his delusion directly, his carefully constructed fantasy would collapse. He'd remember who he used to be. *What* he used to be. The pain. The loneliness. The sadness of that fat little boy who lost his family. The crushing insecurity. Sancho hated to make Flynn feel that pain, but he needed his friend to understand.

"The trust fund was administered by your mother's cousin, Warren Stettmeier. He didn't want to take you in, so you ended up in the foster system, going from family to family until they decided you needed to be institutionalized. Warren managed the trust and made sure they put you in a private hospital. City of Roses. He's been paying the bills ever since."

Flynn wouldn't look Sancho in the eye. "I don't know what you're talking about."

"And I didn't know you had any family."

"I don't."

"Warren died. His son, Dennis, took over the trust and decided City of Roses was too expensive. That's why you're here. That's why he sent you to a state hospital."

"*I don't know what you're talking about.*"

"I think you do."

"You're talking about my cover story. Who I pretend to be. A carefully constructed false identity put in place to protect who I really am. A top-secret agent with double-0 designation."

Sancho sighed. "Bottom line, mano, we got to get your ass out of here. It's not safe."

"I agree. Not with Mendoza here."

"Mendoza?"

"He tried to take me out, but a very brave young woman saved my life."

"*Mendoza's here?*"

Flynn nodded. "Masquerading as a patient."

"Are you *shitting* me?"

"He's currently in the county jail, but if a judge decides he's not competent to stand trial…he'll likely return him here."

"Man, that can't be a coincidence. Mendoza's here and this is where Stettmeier sends you? There's no way that's just bad luck."

"I need you to do me a favor. I need to look into the woman who risked her life to protect me. Her name is Caitlyn Valentine. I need to know who she is and where she comes from. I believe her life is in danger."

"From who?"

"That's what we need to determine. Maybe Bettina can help with that."

"Bettina O'Toole-Applebaum?"

"She's helped us before. As an investigative journalist, perhaps she can shed some light on the situation here."

Sancho nodded. "That's not a bad idea. If she can expose what Stettmeier's up to, maybe we can shame him into sending you back to City of Roses."

"So you'll call her?"

"Why not?"

"Good." Flynn smiled and winced, gingerly touching the scab on his fat lip.

Sancho put his hand up against the Plexiglas. "Be careful in here, brother. Can you do that for me? Can you lie low until we get you out?"

"When you talk to Bettina, don't forget to ask her about Miss Valentine."

Sancho sighed. "Will do."

"How's Alyssa?"

"Very pregnant and very pissed off."

"Hormones."

"Uh huh."

"You're a brave man, my friend."

"No shit."

"When's she due?"

"In, like, two months. Though I don't know how she can get any bigger than she already is."

"Say hello to her for me." Flynn scraped back his stool and winced as he stood. "You watch your back too, Sancho. You're going to be a father. You have responsibilities now." Flynn hung up the receiver, offered Sancho a last wave, and slowly limped away.

CHAPTER FOURTEEN

The Freemasons were founded as an upper-class fraternal organization in the early 18th century. Membership grew quickly and many of America's founding fathers took the vows. Its secretive nature, mysterious rituals, and the wealth and power of its members elicited suspicion and conspiracy theories from those who didn't belong. Because it sometimes challenged the power of the church, many framed the group as anti-Christian, even Satanic. British Author John Robison believed a cabal of Freemasons known as "the Illuminati" were secretly plotting to put an end to religion and state authority. Anti-Masonic fervor reached a fever pitch in upper New York State in the 1820s and led to a new political party. The Anti-Masonic Party. Evangelical Christians were drawn to its critique of corruption and immorality while members of the working class liked the anti-elitist rhetoric. The citizens of New York State elected dozens of Anti-Masonic party members to congress. They merged with former Republicans to found the Whig Party in 1833.

It took weeks for Bettina O'Toole-Applebaum to convince *Young Americans for Morality* that she was a true believer. Not an easy task for a gay, biracial vegetarian. Her father was the great-grandson of a slave and her mother came from a long line of Ashkenazi Jews. With her hazel eyes, auburn hair, and freckled complexion, Bettina easily passed for white. She normally dressed like a Brooklyn-based, post-punk, intellectual hipster, but for this undercover assignment she went more conservative. She never saw herself as a bombshell, but she knew some men found her attractive. So she played up the frilly and feminine. Bettina's mother swore like a sailor and so did Bettina, especially when driving, so she did her best to keep her mouth in check.

Young Americans for Morality, a fringe right-wing political action committee, pushed the fringiest of right-wing conspiracies. They recruited would-be conservatives in their teens and twenties by reaching out to them on social media and playing to their fears and feelings of powerlessness. At age thirty-seven, Bettina looked younger than she was. She could still pass for twenty-eight and that was what she put on the application when she applied for a job on their action committee as Betty O'Toole.

She investigated the existence of troll farms in America the previous year. She befriended several obvious trolls on various news sites and finally convinced one of them to contact her directly. That led to coffee and her recruitment into *Young Americans for Morality*.

The young man who recruited her obviously had more than politics in mind. His name was Matt Tombers and she didn't exactly lead him on, but she didn't dissuade him either. She let him rhapsodize about the movement, his political philosophy, his religiosity, and his worries about the collapse of the American dream. "Betty" hung on his every word and before long, Matt invited her to Y.A.M. social gatherings, official meetings, and even a religious service.

Bettina created a fake identity for Betty, complete with a Facebook page, an Instagram account, and Twitter profile. She also created accounts on alt-right social media platforms like Parler, NewsMax, WeMe, and Rumble. Matt did very little to vet her, other than check out her online profile. Once Matt accepted her, the rest of the organization brought her into the fold with open arms.

Many of "Betty's" posts pushed the same insane conspiracy theories that Matt and the other *Young Americans for Morality* believed in. Mainly, that a cabal of Satan-worshipping pedophiles secretly controlled the country. That members of this conspiracy included elitist left-wing politicians, mainstream journalists, and popular movie, TV, and rock stars. Their goal? To corrupt humankind and pull naïve and godless young people to the dark side. Satan needed their bodies and souls for his evil army. Cannon fodder for the day of reckoning. A cataclysmic battle between good and evil loomed on the horizon. The vast majority had no clue that this apocalypse was coming. Y.A.M.'s task was to warn unsuspecting innocents about the coming storm. They would do this by initiating what they called, "The Great Awakening."

Bettina or "Betty" as her new friends knew her, moved to Missouri to work with Y.A.M. She stayed in a group dormitory in a residence owned by Y.A.M., and each day rode in a van with her fellow true believers to their headquarters in an anonymous building in an industrial park. There, in a large open office, they set up dozens of cubicles. They put "Betty" in one such cubicle with a computer wired to a high-speed network. Her superiors instructed her to join multiple online news sites, establish several identities, and then comment on various news stories of the day. She and all the other apostles of Y.A.M. replied to "libtard" posts and pushed back on the brainwashing perpetrated by the "lamestream" media.

Many of those she communicated with accused her of being crazy or a Russian troll working for Putin. The scope of this disinformation operation was enormous, though as far as Y.A.M. was concerned, they weren't disseminating disinformation. They were communicating their truth. A truer truth based on actual facts covered up by those in power. They hoped to convert some of these skeptics to their side, but the main point was to question authority and even reality. Create doubt. Create fear. When people were afraid, they craved certainty. They cried out for direction. For a purpose. For a path.

Bettina secretly taped many of the meetings at the troll farm and kept notes on everything. Each night she'd return to her room and expand on her notes. Y.A.M.'s ambition was breathtaking. They literally wanted to overturn American democracy and replace it with an alt-right plutocracy. The likelihood of this was slim, but stranger things had happened. Look at the Salem Witch Trials, the Khmer Rouge, Nazi Germany. It happened before. It could happen again. A story like this could win Bettina another Pulitzer.

She started off by spreading right-wing conspiracies on center-right sites, but when they saw how well she could write, they encouraged "Betty" to find stories on news sites and platforms with a center-left point of view and create comments that would work to divide Democrats. To do so, she first needed to establish herself as a trusted voice. Someone with something interesting to say. The idea was to amass followers and accumulate likes, upvotes and retweets.

One online identity she created, @honestbetsy, won "Tweet of the Week" on HuffPost. She wanted to create an impression of fairness and impartiality as she drove subtle wedges between Democrats on issues as diverse as vaccines, immigration, Black Lives Matter, gay marriage, climate change, income inequality, and AOC. Much of what they wanted "Betty" to do was stoke distrust among millennials and African Americans in democratic institutions. The ultimate goal? Depress voter turnout.

Her story in Rolling Stone would be about the insidious plot to fill voters' heads with disinformation and sow confusion. If people understood the techniques being used against them, perhaps they'd learn to spot, verify, and resist that kind of disinformation on social media and become more sophisticated consumers of news.

She had a cellphone for "Betty" and one for Bettina. She kept Bettina's hidden in a sock in her suitcase with the ringer set to vibrate. Late at night, after everyone else went to bed, she'd check the messages. One was from Sancho Perez. They hadn't spoken in over a year. Not since he and Flynn handed her a story that won her the Selden Ring Award for investigative journalism. Bettina figured he wasn't just calling to say hello and called him back immediately.

"Sancho, it's Bettina."

"Thank you for getting back to me so quickly."

"Of course. What's up?"

"It's Flynn. He's in trouble." Sancho dispensed with any preamble and explained Flynn's current situation. The transfer to Hornitos. Dennis Stettmeier, the new trustee who sent him there. Mendoza's attempt on his life.

"Shit," Bettina said.

"No shit," Sancho repeated.

"You think there's some connection between Stettmeier and Mendoza?"

"It's kind of a big coincidence, don't you think?"

"I do."

"I'm thinking maybe if you publish a story about what happened to Flynn, it might put some pressure on Stettmeier to send Flynn back to City of Roses."

"I'll need everything you have on Stettmeier."

"I'll send you an email with everything I know."

"Good. I'll see what I can find out."

"There's one more thing. One of the other patients there saved his life. She actually took down Mendoza."

"She?"

"Her name's Caitlyn Valentine and Flynn thinks someone is trying to kill her."

"Seriously?" Bettina mused.

"He wants you to look into her and find out why she's there, what she did, and why someone would want her dead."

"I've heard of Hornitos. That's where they warehouse the worst of the worst. Everyone sent there's a psycho killer."

"Pretty much."

"Shit," Bettina said.

"No shit."

"I'll get back to you."

"Thank you."

Bettina hung up and hid her spare cell phone back in her sock. Even though she was in the middle of another investigation, this had to take priority. She liked Flynn. She cared about him. She owed him.

Her work at the troll farm gave her a perfect opportunity to surf the net. She spent the morning dividing progressives. In the afternoon, she began investigating Dennis Stettmeier.

Sancho sent her what he had gleaned from his amateur investigation, including info on the man who ran the trust before Dennis Stettmeier inherited it. She found Warren Stettmeier's obituary on Legacy.com. Working backwards, she then found the obits for Flynn's mother and father and established that Stettmeier was Flynn's mother's cousin. She confirmed Dennis was indeed Warren's son and looked up the law firm that first established the trust. Davis, Hopkins, and Cromartie seemed legit. Warren's widow was still alive and, according to public records, she inherited her husband's entire estate. Nothing went to Dennis. The only thing his father left him was control of Flynn's trust.

Other public records revealed Dennis was up to his eyeballs in debt and that he'd been sued by creditors numerous times. That all gave him incentive and a motive to go after Flynn's money. What she didn't find was any connection with Mendoza. That would require a bit more digging.

She switched gears and searched for Caitlyn Valentine and found an obituary for a black grandmother in Alabama, a high school student in New Mexico, and a mother of two in Florida.

She also found several news stories about a Caitlyn Valentine charged with murder and domestic terrorism.

That Caitlyn Valentine was accused of sending a sitting member of congress a letter covered with ricin powder. The amount you can fit on the head of a pin can kill an adult human. The Congressman, Alton Jeffers, collapsed in his office and EMTs rushed him to the hospital. Three days later, he was dead. An autopsy confirmed the poisoning. Alton Jeffers was an ultraconservative firebrand who made his bones spreading many of the same right-wing conspiracies that Y.A.M. disseminated. The case drew a lot of attention at the time and Valentine told the media that she was being framed by enemies of the state. She said she worked for the CIA and that she uncovered a vast conspiracy to bring on the apocalypse, but the CIA claimed they had no knowledge of her, and the prosecution posited she was mentally ill.

After being examined by a psychiatrist, the judge in the case decided she wasn't competent to stand trial. Eventually, she was found not guilty by reason of insanity. Once they sent her to Hornitos, media attention waned.

Delving deeper, Bettina found social media accounts on LinkedIn, Instagram, and Facebook for her, but no record of military service. According to her LinkedIn profile, she grew up in California and attended Stanford, majoring in computer science and international economics. She later graduated with an MBA from The London School of Economics. She worked for HSBC in London and eventually joined Accenture as a senior analyst and consultant, specializing in compliance software for financial institutions. She rarely posted on Instagram or Facebook. Her "about" category had nothing listed under family or relationships. She wasn't married and from her Facebook feed, it appeared she traveled extensively with her job all over the world, moving from position to position every few months. Her home base was San Francisco, but she never seemed to be there. Par for the course for a high-tech consultant working for an international company like Accenture.

It would actually be the perfect "nonofficial cover" for a CIA agent. She had very little online presence or history. The only thing suspicious was how abruptly she went from being a prosperous tech worker to a delusional and homicidal mental patient.

That night Bettina called Sancho to tell him everything she'd learned.

Sancho was astounded. "She thinks she's a C.I.A. agent?"

"She claims she was framed by a vast international conspiracy plotting to bring on the apocalypse."

"Jesus. No wonder she gets along so well with Flynn. Guess that's why they found her *not* guilty by reason of insanity."

"So Flynn thinks someone's trying to kill her?"

"That's what he claims," Sancho said.

"Not surprising, considering the whole place is packed with homicidal maniacs."

"Like our friend, Mendoza. You find any connection between him and Stettmeier?"

"Not yet. But I'll keep looking," Bettina said.

"I appreciate it, but we need to get Flynn out of there as soon as possible."

"Okay, I'll talk to Rolling Stone about running a *'where are they now'* sidebar. People love Flynn. They're not going to like what Stettmeier is doing to him. A little online shaming might get him to change his mind."

"I sure hope so."

"So are you going to tell Flynn what I found out about his new girlfriend?"

"What? That she thinks she's a CIA agent?" Sancho said.

"Maybe it'll help open his eyes to his own delusional thinking."

"Or send him deeper down the rabbit hole."

"He wanted me to find out who she is. Well, that's what I did. She has been diagnosed as delusional and that's why she's there. Same as him. Tell him the truth enough times and maybe, eventually, it'll sink in."

CHAPTER FIFTEEN

Roman aristocrat, statesman, and Stoic philosopher Seneca believed that there was no place in the civilized world for anger. He thought it was less an emotion and more of a temporary madness. He wrote, "No plague has cost the human race more. We see all around us people being killed, poisoned, sued: we see cities and nations ruined". Centuries before Seneca, Aristotle theorized that anger was an important component of courage. A useful emotion in war, not for generals, but for soldiers. Seneca believed the opposite. He thought the Germanic tribes lost to Rome because they couldn't control their rage. Even though the Romans were physically weaker, they overcame those wild, uncontrolled bands of savage warriors. He believed that force guided by reason is more effective than the furious power of unbridled anger.

Flynn sat with six other patients in a half-circle. The windowless group therapy room had a yellowing linoleum floor, a drop tile ceiling with rectangles of fluorescent lighting, and institutional white walls decorated with a few fading posters. Each one had an inspirational affirmation or saying that had to do with anger management and conflict resolution.

Take a deep breath.

Talk it out.

Take a time out.

Let go of the pain.

A balding, bearded, burly, fifty-something African American man in a short-sleeved shirt and tie sat on one end of the semicircle and smiled at everyone present. "Good morning, everyone. We have a new member starting today. Mr. Flynn, I'm Doctor Ross. Welcome to Anger Management."

"Thank you," Flynn said. He looked around the semi-circle. Only Grace offered him a smile. Gabriel looked grim. Boyd appeared distracted. Manu chewed on a cuticle. Mason glared. Caitlyn Valentine just stared at the floor.

"We'll start today, like we do each session, with a few positive affirmations. Repeat after me, all together now. I am a calm and loving person."

Only Flynn and Grace repeated the phrase. "I am a calm and loving person."

"Good, but I want to hear from everyone. Manu. Mason. Gabriel. Boyd. Caitlyn. I am a calm and loving person."

Everyone but Boyd repeated in ragged unison. "I am a calm and loving person."

"I am in control of my life and emotions."

Again, in concert, except for Boyd, they repeated the phrase.

"I am at peace and harmony with everyone and everything."

The group replied with an unconvincing singsong monotone, "I am at peace and harmony with everyone and everything."

Dr. Ross smiled at Boyd. "Boyd, we'd like to hear from you too. Is there a reason you're not participating?"

"I do not like to get all sad. I do not like to get all mad. I do not like that you're my boss. I do not like it, Dr. Ross."

"I'm not here to tell you what to do, Boyd. I'm here to help you figure out what you're feeling and find a way to process it. If you want to leave, you can leave, but I'd love for you to stay and listen if that's okay. Is that okay?"

Boyd nodded and looked away. "All ball. We all play ball."

"Thank you, Boyd." Dr. Ross smiled at the others, even as they sat there with folded arms and stubborn frowns. "Now the rules here are simple." He held up a little wooden sculpture of a man sitting with his hand on his chin. "In my hand here, I have our talking piece. This is called a thinking man. It comes from Africa and symbolizes the idea that you should always think before you react. If you want to share, you need to hold the talking piece. Beyond that, please do not raise your voice. Do not put your hands on anyone else. Everyone here deserves respect. Whatever happens in this room stays in this room. This is a safe space.

"To start, we will pass the thinking man from person to person and I want each of you to tell me something that triggers your anger. It's important for each of us to understand what our triggers are. If we know what sets us off, we can better predict our response, control our emotions, and make a choice not to respond in an angry manner. When I hand you the thinking man, please tell us your name and what triggers you." Dr. Ross handed the thinking man to Mason.

"I'm Mason and what triggers me is sitting here in this stupid room staring at your stupid face and answering your stupid questions."

"So am I your trigger? Or are you triggered by authority in general?"

"Anger is fucking necessary, you stupid asswipe. It's how we fucking evolved. The angry assholes are the ones who survived. The kumbaya motherfuckers all got their skulls bashed in. *Anger is a fucking survival mechanism!*"

"I understood how you feel, Mason, but it isn't necessary to raise your voice. We're all on the same side. We're all here to help each other."

"Fuck that. Fuck you. And fuck this stupid ass group!"

"Thank you for your point of view, Mason. Can you hand the 'thinking man' to Manu?" Mason handed the thinking man to Manu and Manu stared at it for a stupidly long time. Everyone sat there simmering in the long awkward silence until finally Dr. Ross prodded Manu. "Can you tell us your name?"

"Manu."

After another stupidly long pause, Dr. Ross prompted him again. "And can you tell us something that triggers you?"

"Double dipping."

"Excuse me?"

"When you're at a party and some *pukio* dips a chip, takes a bite out of it, and then sticks the same damn chip in the same damn dip. It's fucking disgusting!"

Grace grabbed the thinking man out of Manu's hand. "I'm Grace and you know what I hate? Lying. When someone lies to me, that feels so hurtful. So dishonest. So disrespectful. That really, really upsets me."

Grace then handed the thinking man to Gabriel, who held the tiny black sculpture high over his head. "I am Gabriel. An archangel in human form sent here to lead the forces of the Lord against the armies of darkness." Mason smirked at that, and Gabriel thrust his finger into his face. "That! That's a trigger! That condescending smile. That ugly smirk. It's pure depravity! Foul corruption. Absolute evil. This miscreant has sold his soul to Satan and the anger I feel towards him is just. Necessary. Righteous! Our God is a vengeful one! *He is the whirlwind and the storm and the mountains quake before him!*"

Mason slapped Gabriel's finger out of his face. Gabriel leaped to his feet. Mason jumped up as well.

Dr. Ross stepped between them. "Come on now, let's calm down. Remember that first affirmation. I am a calm and loving person. Say it, Mason." As the two men continued to glare at each other, Dr. Ross gently tried to push them apart. "Say it."

Mason's voice was hoarse with rage. "I am a calm and loving person!"

"Gabriel?"

Gabriel, his voice tight with fury, growled. "I am a calm and loving person!"

"Now please. Both of you. Sit. *Please*." Both men vibrated with anger as they took their seats. Ross smiled at Caitlyn. "Miss Valentine, would you like to hold the 'thinking man'?"

"No."

"Mr. Flynn?"

Flynn reached out and Gabriel handed him the little statue. Flynn tried to catch Caitlyn's eye, but she wouldn't meet his gaze. "My biggest trigger is probably dishonesty. Like Grace, I dislike being lied to and that includes lies by omission. For instance, Caitlyn here never has been truthful with me about why she's here or who she is. Recently, a good friend of mine contacted me and told me her truth."

"Mr. Flynn, we're not here to judge one another. We're here to support each other. Help each other."

"How can I help Miss Valentine if she won't let me?"

Caitlyn slowly raised her intimidating gaze. "Who asked for your help?"

"You told the authorities that you were framed for the murder of a sitting senator."

"Who told you that?"

"Framed because you uncovered a vast conspiracy to bring on Armageddon."

Gabriel perked up at the mention of Armageddon. "She did what?"

"*Who told you that*?" Caitlyn growled.

"Why didn't you tell me you were ex-CIA?"

Caitlyn stood up. "I'm done with this!"

Dr. Ross raised both his hands. "Deep breaths everyone. Just relax. Caitlyn, if you want to speak, you need to hold the 'thinking man.'"

She pointed at Dr. Ross. "Fuck you!" She put her finger in Flynn's face. "Fuck you too!" Then looked at everyone else in the room before shouting, "*Fuck you all!*"

Dr. Ross offered Caitlyn a warm, caring smile. "Clearly, Mr. Flynn has triggered you. Take the 'thinking man' and take a breath. On a scale from one to ten, how angry do you feel?"

"*Are you fucking kidding me?*"

"I'd say a nine at least. Perhaps a ten," Flynn said.

Caitlyn ripped the 'thinking man' out of Flynn's hand and snapped it in half right in front of Dr. Ross's face. The mild-mannered psychiatrist leaped to his feet, his face suddenly red with outrage. "*What the hell!?*"

Caitlyn threw both pieces on the floor and stomped on them.

"No, no, stop! Stop it! *What the hell is wrong with you?*" Ross sputtered as he picked up the broken pieces. "Goddamn lunatics! Get the hell out!" He pointed at the door and screamed, "*Out! Out! Get the hell out!*"

Caitlyn left first, followed by Flynn, and the rest of the group, all a bit taken aback by Dr. Ross's outburst.

Flynn called to Caitlyn. "Caitlyn! Come on! Talk to me!"

She ignored Flynn and stormed into her room, slamming the door.

Flynn knocked politely. "Caitlyn? Please? I just want to talk." He knew the door wasn't locked. None of the rooms had interior locks. They could only be locked from the outside. He cracked the door and poked his head in. "Can I come in?"

She sat on her bed, staring at him with a crooked smile. "What a joke."

"What is?"

"You. Me. This whole fucked up situation."

"What situation would that be?"

"Everyone out there thinks we're in here for the same reason. That we're both suffering from the same stupid delusion. But I'm not crazy, they just want to erase me. Discredit me."

"Who?"

"The powers that be."

"The ones who want to bring on the apocalypse?"

Caitlyn shook her head. "Even you don't believe me."

"I do believe you, but I'd love a few more details. How do they hope to bring on this apocalypse?"

"By provoking war between Iran and Israel. By bringing on the end of days. The second coming. The final battle between heaven and hell."

"That does seem a bit far-fetched," Flynn admitted.

"It's fucking delusional. But that's what they believe."

"And how do they plan to provoke this war?"

"I don't know. That's what I was investigating when they killed my contact and framed me for his murder."

"The Senator?"

"Alton Jeffers. He had second thoughts when it finally dawned on him what his fellow lunatics intended to do."

"Who *are* these lunatics?"

"They number in the thousands. At the highest levels of government. From Capitol Hill all the way to the Pentagon. They call themselves The Army of God."

"And you took this to your superiors?"

"Of course."

"But they didn't believe you?"

Caitlyn laughed at that. "They suspended me and sent me in for a psych eval. The very next day, Senator Jeffers received that Ricin in the mail."

Flynn sat on the bed next to her. "According to my investigator friend, there's no record of you working for the C.I.A. or any other government agency."

"Because I had a 'non-official cover' as a tech-consultant. No one in my family knew. Not my mother. Not my brother..."

"You're not married?"

"I was married to the job."

"As am I. People who do what we do can't afford one-on-one relationships. Our lives are too dangerous. Too risky. I do have one question, though."

"Just one?"

"If you've already been discredited, why would your enemies still want you dead?"

She shook her head. "Maybe they figure I'm a loose end."

Flynn studied her fierce face and came to an inescapable conclusion. "That must be why M sent me."

"Who?"

"My immediate superior. The head of His Majesty's Secret Service."

"Okay, here's the difference between you and me. I'm an actual intelligence officer who was betrayed by the powers that be. You, on the other hand, are really fucking crazy."

"Posing as a patient at City of Roses has been a remarkably effective cover, which is why M could so easily insert me inside here surreptitiously. Obviously, he discovered that the C.I.A. has been compromised. Clearly, he sent me here to assess the situation and, if necessary, rescue you."

"I appreciate the thought, but I really don't need your help."

"I've escaped from more dangerous places than this."

"What did I just say?"

"The killer I eliminated won't be the last."

"You don't think I know that?"

"So let me help facilitate your freedom and take down those who would bring down the world."

She pointed at the door. "Okay, time to go."

"I'll work up a plan."

"You do that."

Flynn knew he'd have to prove himself if he ever hoped to help her. He left and headed back to his room. On the way, the door to the unit swung open and guards escorted in a huge, hulking figure. They unlocked the monster's ankle, wrist, and waist restraints.

Flynn stepped closer to get a better look at the face of Unit G's newest arrival.

Mendoza.

CHAPTER SIXTEEN

Nurse Erickson woke up with a gun in her mouth. The man menacing her hid behind a black balaclava. All she could see were his eyes. Cold. Pitiless. She tried to scream, but he shoved his gun in deeper, muffling the shriek.

He leaned close and spoke quietly and calmly, "Your husband is at work and your adorable daughter is asleep in the other room. If you don't want her to die, you will do exactly as I say. Nod if you understand."

Nurse Erickson nodded.

"Good. I am going to remove my gun. Scream and I will hurt her."

He pulled his gun from her mouth, and she didn't scream. Tears filled her eyes. "What do you want?" she whispered.

"You work as a nurse at Hornitos. You're assigned to Unit G. You dispense the morning medication, correct?"

She nodded.

"I'm going to give you an additional pill for one of your patients. Caitlyn Valentine. You will include this pill with her daily dose of medication. If you don't, your adorable seven-year-old daughter will die a prolonged and very painful death. So will your husband. And in the end, so will you. Do as I say, tell no one what happened here today, and you'll have the opportunity to watch your daughter grow up. Your life will continue as it was and no one will ever be the wiser. You will never see me again, and it will be as if this never happened. Nod if you understand."

Dirty tears smeared Nurse Erickson's face as she nodded her head.

"Good."

．　■　■

Mendoza's fury towards Flynn seared his insides. It roiled his guts and threatened to erupt like a volcanic bomb. He'd had his hands on that *pendejo's* throat. He saw the life leaving his eyes. He was so close to ridding himself of the *hijo de puta*.

So close.

But then that bitch got in his way. Why? What business was it of hers? Why would she care if Flynn lived or died?

The hospital police dragged Mendoza to Hornitos County Jail. He didn't go willingly. Didn't make it easy. He kicked and punched and head-butted until finally they tasered, tranquilized, and zip-tied his ass. He saw no downside to totally losing his shit. The point was to make them think he was out of his mind.

Mendoza attacked anyone who came within spitting, hitting, or biting distance, including every public defender assigned to his case. He pissed his pants and banged his head against the bars until it bled, growling and snapping like a rabid dog. It felt good to let his crazy out. Laughing like a lunatic. Eating bugs off the floor. It was liberating.

They took him to the county courthouse in chains. Before the judge could ask his first question, Mendoza took a bite out of his third public defender's ear. He knocked over chairs and tables and snarled and spit that hunk of ear high into the air. It took six bailiffs to hold him down, and that was only because he let them.

One day later, he was back at Hornitos.

Flynn had to go. He had to die.

And so did that crazy bitch.

．　．　．

Caitlyn Valentine had more enemies than she could count, and all of them wanted her dead. Though that asshole Mason likely wanted to rape her before he murdered her. She could see it in his eyes. He couldn't hide his hate and hunger to inflict pain on anyone female. Now even Mendoza had it in for her. That one-eyed *sicario* was back on Unit G, and he plotted revenge.

She had to escape if she wanted to survive. Caitlyn just hoped Flynn wouldn't get in the way. *What a joke. Jesus.* The last thing she needed was that lunatic dogging her every move.

Her prosecutor actually used Flynn's famous story to help put her away. He claimed she suffered under the same delusion. A crazy, dangerous, wannabe super spy. Meanwhile, no one at the CIA stepped up to correct the record. They threw her away. Denied her very existence. She was on her own and couldn't expect help from anyone.

Caitlyn wondered if any of the higher-ups at the agency were involved. *Could they be part of the conspiracy too?* It all went to shit when Senator Jeffers decided to play ball with her. The Army of God shut him down without a second thought. They wouldn't stop until they put her in the ground.

．　．　．

Flynn stood in a long queue with the other patients from Unit G as Nurse Erickson dispensed their morning medication. He stood just behind Mason. The hulking ex-con couldn't keep his eyes off Caitlyn's bum. She stood just a few patients ahead. Mason pursed his mouth. He clenched and unclenched his jaw and eyeballed her buttocks. Flynn wondered if Caitlyn could feel Mason's eyes probing her. Probably. She seemed hyperaware of her surroundings. Secret agents cultivate that ability along with a constant kinetic sentience. Flynn, for instance, felt Mendoza's eyes boring into him from behind.

Ever since Mendoza returned to the unit, Flynn felt the *sicario* watching and waiting for the right moment to strike. Flynn would need to take him out preemptively. He didn't like to rely on his license to kill, but in this case, he had no choice. Mendoza couldn't be reasoned with and couldn't be bargained with. If he made another attempt on Flynn, there'd likely be collateral damage, and he didn't want to be responsible for anyone else's death.

Danger lurked everywhere, and Flynn felt it keenly. The molecules in the room vibrated with tension. Something bad was about to happen. Flynn was only alive because he trusted his gut, though in this case there were so many vectors of potential danger it was difficult to know which one to counter first.

He studied all the faces in the room. Mason wasn't the only one staring at Caitlyn. Nurse Erickson couldn't keep her eyes off the ostracized CIA agent. Erickson had the light blonde hair and ice-blue eyes of her Scandinavian antecedents. She appeared to be in her late thirties and sported the zaftig build of a Viking shield maiden. Her broad shoulders balanced out her equally large bust. After the nurse handed each patient their pills, she'd quickly steal a glance at Caitlyn moving up the line. Nurse Erickson's hands trembled ever so slightly. Her eyes reminded Flynn of a small, frightened animal. Usually, Nurse Erickson looked tired and bored as she handed out everyone's daily dose.

Today she seemed terrified.

The closer Caitlyn moved up the queue, the more fearful the nurse appeared. Something wasn't right. After each glance at Caitlyn, she'd quickly look down at the little plastic cups of pills. *What is she so worried about? What's she hiding?*

Flynn smoothly cut to the front of the line, stepping past Mason, Grace, Caitlyn, Boyd, and Gabriel. He glanced at the little plastic cups, each perched on a sheet of paper with the patient's name and their prescribed medications listed below. Flynn grabbed Caitlyn's cup and made a show of attempting to swallow them, but before he could tilt back the cup, Nurse Erickson grabbed him by the wrist. "No! No! No! *What are you doing?*" The panic raised her voice an octave.

"Taking my pills."

"No, no, those aren't yours! *Those are Ms. Valentine's!*" She jerked the tiny cup out of Flynn's hand and the pills went flying.

Mason was laughing when one landed on his tongue. Nurse Erickson looked apoplectic as he stuck out his tongue to show it off, grinned, and swallowed it down.

"What kind of ride does this one give you?" Mason's grin quickly turned to a grimace. He grunted in pain. He clutched his gut. The color drained from his face as he sank to his knees. The other patients stepped back, giving him a wide berth as he pitched forward and flopped around the floor.

Caitlyn glanced from Flynn to Mason. His body bucked and he bit his tongue. Blood ran down his chin. Flynn knelt by his side and flipped him over. Only the whites of his eyes were visible.

A terrified Nurse Erickson hit her alarm button. The siren screamed as they all stood frozen, watching Mason spasm and convulse. Pink foam flecked the corners of his mouth. Finally, the rest of the staff rushed in. A doctor pushed Flynn out of the way. Soon an emergency medical team arrived, shot Mason up with something in a huge hypo, and shocked his heart with an emergency defibrillator.

Nurse Erickson completely fell apart as they carted him off. She sobbed and wailed while two other nurses tried to calm her down. Flynn caught Caitlyn staring at him. She raised a curious eyebrow. Flynn offered her a grim and cryptic smile.

■ ■ ■

Caitlyn cornered Flynn in the activity room after lunch. They retreated to a far corner, out of everyone else's earshot. "That pill was meant for me, wasn't it?"

"Apparently."

"How did you know?"

"I didn't. Not definitively. Though Nurse Erickson was oddly eyeballing you and acting uncharacteristically jumpy."

"You believe someone got to her?"

"It's a possibility."

"I need to talk to her then."

"We both do."

"I appreciate what you did for me, but we are not a team."

"Neither one of us is safe in here." Flynn pointed out.

"*No one* is safe in here."

"So we both have the same goal."

"You want to escape?"

"Yes."

"Do you really think I would still be here if that was at all a possibility?"

"It might not be a possibility on your own, but if we work together—"

Caitlyn shook her head. "No."

"You haven't even heard my plan."

"I don't need to."

"It's a pretty good plan."

"No one has ever escaped from here."

"Because no one ever came up with a plan like mine."

"I think we're done here."

Caitlyn tried to walk away, but Flynn stepped in front of her. "Are you saying you're not the least bit curious?"

"About your plan?"

"Yes."

"No."

"I think you're a little bit curious."

"Jesus, you're annoying."

"I can't do it without your help. In fact, to really pull it off, I'm going to need everyone's help. Except Mendoza's."

Caitlyn sighed, already tired of the conversation. "Pull what off?"

"I thought you didn't want to hear it?"

"I don't."

"I think you do."

"I really don't."

"Fine." Flynn stepped out of the way and directed her forward. "After you."

She took two steps past him, stopped, turned around and glared. "Okay."

"Okay what?"

"What's your fucking plan?"

CHAPTER SEVENTEEN

Nurse Erickson knelt on the cold linoleum floor of the toilet stall. She kept one hand on the toilet paper dispenser and held her hair back with the other. Nausea still rocked her, but there was nothing left inside. Sweat beaded on her forehead and burned in her eyes. They'd pumped Mason's stomach. Apparently, he was still alive. Now the hospital police wanted to question her.

The men who gave her the pill also gave her a phone number. They wanted her to call them when it was done. *Do they already have my daughter?* What could she possibly tell them? Her stomach twisted with cramps. She continued to dry heave. Nurse Erickson sobbed and trembled and watched her sweat drip into the toilet, making little concentric rings. Helplessness paralyzed her.

The bathroom door rattled. Someone tried to open it.

A sharp knock.

"It's occupied," Nurse Erickson said.

Silence.

Another sharp knock.

"*Ocupada!*" she said with a voice on the edge of hysteria.

A moment of silence followed by three hard raps against the door.

"*I said there's someone in here!*" She angrily pulled herself to her feet, fumbled to unlock the deadbolt and open the door. "*What?*"

Caitlyn Valentine shoved her inside. Flynn followed and pulled the door shut, throwing the deadbolt.

Nurse Erickson's anger flashed to terror, but having worked at Hornitos for over ten years, she knew better than to show it. She tried to stay calm and keep her voice even. "This is a staff only restroom. You shouldn't even be in this part of the—"

Caitlyn put her hand over Nurse Erickson's mouth. "Shhh." Leaning closer, she whispered, "If you call for help, I will hurt you. Do you understand?"

Eyes wide and terrified, Nurse Erickson nodded.

Caitlyn removed her hand. "You tried to kill me."

"No."

"Don't lie to me."

Nurse Erickson could no longer hide the fear as tears filled her eyes, blurring her vision, her voice muffled. "It wasn't me."

"Who got to you?" Flynn asked.

"He said they'd kill my little girl."

"Who?"

"Army of God," Caitlyn said. "Has to be."

Flynn nodded. "Can you tell us what he looked like?"

"I don't know. He wore a ski mask. But he said if I didn't... if I..." Nurse Erickson tried not to cry, but the tears came anyway and she couldn't catch her breath.

"Do they have her now?" Caitlyn asked.

"I don't know, but he wanted me to call after I... but now..." Caitlyn was a blur as the tears continued to flow. "What am I going to do?"

"You're going to tell them it all went as planned. That I didn't die, but ended up in the ER. That they pumped my stomach and sedated me."

"Like Mason."

"Exactly. Tell them you intend to slip into the medical wing in the middle of the night and finish the job. Tell them you plan to inject air into my IV."

"But what happens tomorrow? What happens when they find out that you're still alive?"

"Tomorrow they'll learn that I escaped before you could get to me. Escaped in the middle of the night."

"Escaped?"

"With me gone, they have no leverage over you. No good reason to kill you or your daughter."

"Do they need a good reason?"

"Probably not," Flynn said. "But as long as there's a chance Caitlyn will be caught and sent back to Hornitos, they have every incentive to keep you alive. Helping us escape is your best and only option if you want to keep your daughter breathing."

"You want me to help you escape?"

Flynn nodded. "Tonight."

"You can't. No one's ever escaped. There are hospital police everywhere. At every entrance. Every exit. There's no way."

"Mr. Flynn has a plan." Caitlyn said with a smile.

■　■　■

Mendoza knew something was up. Caitlyn always kept to herself and never talked to anyone. Never sat with anyone in the dining room. Never chatted with anyone in the activity room. Now she and Flynn were whispering with all the other patients. That *pinche puta* was even crazier than Flynn. Did that *idioto* brainwash her the way he brainwashed Goolardo? Did he seduce her? *What the fuck are they up to?*

He cornered Boyd and tried to get him to talk, but the small, soft, pasty-faced *bolillo* made no sense at all. "Oh, my, said the rat, you do not like their play. Should I lead you astray? Disobey? Run away?"

Mendoza grabbed him by the chin and looked him hard in the eyes. "Stop it, *cabrón*. Enough with that shit. What did Flynn talk to you about? And don't fucking lie to me."

"Let's hide up high said the boy to the fly. Time to run. Time for fun. Time to roam and go home."

Mendoza could have beaten answers out of that *hombre loco*, but for what? More fucking rhymes that made no fucking sense?

He got Grace alone, but kept his distance from that grabby hand of hers. "What did Flynn talk to you about?"

"He said he's on a secret mission for His Majesty's Secret Service." She leaned closer and whispered. "I'm not sure he's entirely in his right mind."

Gabriel told him that Flynn pledged himself to the army of heaven and urged Mendoza to renounce Satan. "Do not enter the path of the wicked and do not proceed in the way of evil men. A wise man is cautious and turns away from evil. But a fool is arrogant and careless."

"Are you calling me a fool?"

"I am saying it is not too late for you. Join the fight against Satan and you will find forgiveness. Be strong in the Lord and in the strength of his might. The final battle is nearly upon us. Choose wisely or suffer forever in eternal agony."

Finally, Mendoza sat with Manu and tried to get the massive Pacific Islander to tell him what Caitlyn and Flynn whispered in his ear. "They want to get out of here and take us all with them," Manu said.

"How?"

Manu pointed straight up and grinned like an idiot.

Mendoza gave up trying to get answers out of the lunatics. Of course Flynn wanted out. They all wanted out. But there was only one way to escape this fucking place.

The Big Adios.

Mendoza would give Flynn that gift. That *pinche puta* too. He would awaken before dawn and end both of them. He would do this early before the day-staff relieved the night. He'd creep into their rooms and take them out one at a time. Breaking their necks with his bare hands.

Mendoza lay awake in the dark all night, imagining the moment. Flynn would awaken to find Mendoza's hands wrapped around his throat. He would struggle and buck, but with his air and blood cut off, he would soon fall into unconsciousness. Mendoza would then lift Flynn partly out of bed and twist his head. Hard on the diagonal. Snapping his spine. Shattering his vertebrae. Mendoza anxiously anticipated that satisfying crack.

He waited until the ward was at its most still. Mendoza didn't know the exact time. But the quiet told him the sun had yet to rise. He slowly climbed out of bed and slid his feet into his hospital slippers.

Mendoza intimidated one orderly into leaving his cell unlocked that evening. The knob turned easily, and he stepped out into the silent corridor. The fluorescent ceiling lights were dimmed at night to help reinforce a feeling of peace and quiet. Mendoza moved cautiously, soundlessly — like a three-hundred-pound ninja.

He stole a passkey to the rooms in Unit G two months previously. He hoped Flynn hadn't rigged his door with some sort of homemade early warning system. Stacked cups or something that would fall when he opened the door. If either Flynn or Gabriel hit the alarm buzzer, he might not have time to take them out before the hospital police arrived. He'd kill Gabriel too if he had to. It would be a mercy to kill every poor *gilipollas* in Unit G.

Mendoza turned the knob on Flynn's door and inched it open. The dim light from the corridor spilled into Flynn's room, but both beds lay in shadow. He quietly closed the door, trying not to make a sound. Mendoza stood in the dark until his eyes adjusted and he could make out the edge of Flynn's bed.

Finally, this *pendejo* would be out of his life.

Finally, Mendoza would have justice.

It was time to move forward and reestablish his relationship with the man who made him. His captain. His commander. His teacher. His jefe.

Francisco Goolardo.

Mendoza slowly approached Flynn's bed. No one stirred. Flynn had no idea he was there. He was a quiet sleeper. The *pinche pendejo* didn't even snore.

The lunatic would awaken just long enough to feel Mendoza's death grip. The last thing he'd hear is Mendoza's whisper in his ear. "Adios, motherfucker."

Mendoza reached for Flynn's throat. He found only a pillow. The big man felt around, but couldn't find a body. Flynn wasn't there. His bed lay empty. Mendoza turned on the light to find Gabriel gone as well.

What the hell?

He turned out the light and crept into the hall. Was he in bed with Caitlyn Valentine? Of course. He had to be. That was Flynn's M.O. Goolardo wasn't the only one taken in by that *artista de mierda*. He was a serial seducer of beautiful women. How could they not see past that pretty face to the crazy beneath? Fine. He would go to her room and kill them both. Enough was enough.

Mendoza found Caitlyn's door and slowly turned the knob. He had to open it fairly wide to fit his bulk through. Light spilled inside, illuminating Caitlyn's bed.

Empty?

Mendoza flicked on the light.

No Caitlyn.

No Grace.

No Flynn.

What the hell?

Were they hiding in someone else's room? Mendoza abandoned all semblance of ninja stealth and strode down the corridor, opening doors and flicking on lights. Boyd was gone. Manu was gone. Every patient in Unit G... gone. Except for Mendoza and O'Haney.

"What the hell!" Mendoza shouted.

O'Haney stumbled out into the corridor. "What's going on?"

"Everyone's gone. I don't see anyone."

"Welcome to my world," O'Haney shouted.

Their loud voices attracted the attention of Nurse Erickson at the nurse's station. She stood with an orderly at the far end of the corridor. "Mr. Mendoza? What are you doing out of bed?"

"They're gone!" Mendoza shouted. "Everybody's gone!"

Nurse Erickson quickly moved toward Mendoza. The orderly hurried to keep up. "Gone where?" she asked.

"I don't know! Every room is empty! They're all gone!"

Nurse Erickson hit her panic button and sirens screamed as she raised a general alarm.

CHAPTER EIGHTEEN

"No prison can hold me; no hand or leg irons or steel locks can shackle me. No ropes or chains can keep me from my freedom. But the greatest escape I ever made was when I left Appleton, Wisconsin." Harry Houdini.

Ten minutes after Nurse Erickson hit the alarm, hospital police flooded the unit. "Every room's empty!" she shouted over the screaming alarm. "I can't find anyone!"

Lieutenant Becker turned off the alarm. "What do you mean? Where could they go?"

Tears filled her eyes. *"I don't know."*

More police arrived, and they checked all the rooms. Except for O'Haney and Mendoza, every patient had vanished. The police were shocked and perplexed.

Becker questioned Nurse Erickson. "They must have passed by the nurse's station?"

She shook her head. "I didn't see anyone."

"We have multiple locked doors and hospital police at every checkpoint. This doesn't make any sense."

"I know," she blubbered. *Did he suspect her of having something to do with it?* She wanted to run off. She wanted to throw up. But she had to play innocent and not flip out.

Nurse Erickson watched as they checked the recorded video feed. No patients crossed the checkpoints or were shown leaving their rooms.

The highest-ranking officer on site, Captain Darnell, ordered every officer working the night shift into Unit G, including the ones working the checkpoints, the cops walking the grounds, and even the ones in the video monitoring room.

The police all gathered in the corridor by the nurse's station and Darnell shouted to everyone assembled. "There's no way through these locked doors and security checkpoints. No way past the cameras without being seen! They're somewhere inside and we have to find them. This building's a hundred years old! There are dozens of closets, multiple storage rooms, and a very large basement area with lots of places to hide. Look everywhere. *Everywhere!* I want them found and I want them found *now!*" He clapped his hands three times hard. "Move! Move! *Move!*"

.　■　.

Flynn held his finger to his lips and shushed the patients from Unit G. They all sat, knelt, or crouched on the roof of the building that housed their unit. All except for Manu, who still struggled to make his way up through the ventilation shaft. His bulky body wouldn't budge. Flynn and Caitlyn pulled and strained on the knotted nylon climbing rope that Nurse Erickson smuggled in, but Manu's massive shoulders and gut were hopelessly jammed.

Flynn had instructed them all to stand on their dressers after lights out and push out a ceiling tile. The tall ones did it easily. The shorter patients had to stack books or boost each other up. They all clambered up into the crawl space above. After replacing the ceiling tile so that no one was the wiser, the patients crawled carefully across the support beams and made their way towards the light. Flynn had a flashlight supplied by Nurse Erickson and he instructed them to move quietly towards him without making a sound. Most kept their mouths shut and moved softly and silently. Even Boyd refrained from rhyming. Manu's weight weighed heavily on the support beams. The joists strained and squeaked as the massive Samoan crept forward towards the light.

Nurse Erickson supplied them with a screwdriver which Caitlyn used to take apart the ductwork leading to the HVAC system on the roof.

Flynn had boosted Caitlyn up into the five-foot diameter industrial ductwork where she pressed her feet and hands against both sides and stemmed her way up. With the nylon rope tied around her waist, she made it up above the roof and unscrewed the nuts that held the ductwork together. After climbing out, she tied the rope around the base of an HVAC unit and waited while the others clambered up after her.

First Grace, then Flynn, followed by Gabriel, Boyd, and finally Manu. Flynn figured they would need everyone working together to pull Manu up, but unfortunately, Manu proved larger than the diameter of the ductwork. As he reached the top, his torso lodged itself in tighter than a carrot in a duck's arse.

When the alarm sounded, they no longer had to worry about keeping their voices down. They pulled, grunted, and strained to pull Manu through, but finally he told them to stop and untied the rope around his waist. "Go!" he said. "Get out of here!"

"Are you sure?" Flynn asked him.

"My fat ass ain't getting through. Go before you get caught, brah!"

Flynn crept to the edge of the roof and watched every hospital police officer on the grounds race for their building. As the officers flooded inside, Flynn tied one end of the rope around a steel pipe and dropped the other end off the edge. Caitlyn climbed down first. A few of the patients hesitated, but it was now or never. No police patrolled the perimeter. Most were inside searching for the "missing" patients.

Flynn motioned for Grace to come closer, but she shook her head and said, "I can't."

"It's easy," Flynn whispered.

"I'm scared."

"I'll help you."

Boyd and Gabriel pushed past her and half rappelled/half fell down the side of the building. Flynn didn't want to leave Grace, but had no choice. She offered him a smile and a little wave goodbye.

"Flynn!" Caitlyn shout-whispered from below.

Flynn stepped backwards off the building and half fell/half rappelled as well, missing Caitlyn, but landing on Boyd.

Gabriel pulled them both to their feet as Boyd whispered, "And all the king's horses and all the king's men couldn't put Boyd back together again."

Flynn led them around the perimeter of the building, where they found rolls of duct tape hidden in the bushes by Nurse Erickson. They threaded it through the exterior door handles and wrapped them tight, tearing off the ends with their teeth, securing the front doors, the back doors, and the two side emergency doors.

Through a barred window in one of the emergency doors, Flynn glimpsed a nervous Nurse Erickson staring at him. A police officer pushed past her and locked eyes with Flynn. He raced for the double doors and struggled to wrench them open. Luckily, the duct tape held.

Flynn hurried off and found Caitlyn trying to coax Grace off the roof, but the former nurse with the homicidal hand was still too afraid to rappel down.

Flynn tugged on Caitlyn's arm. "We gotta go."

"I know," she said.

Grace waved them away, her face red and stained with tears. "Run! Go! I'm good! I'm fine!"

Flynn, Caitlyn, Boyd, and Gabriel sprinted for the tall security fence topped with coils of razor wire. They found the wool hospital blankets Nurse Erickson left for them in the surrounding shrubbery and hung them around their shoulders as they climbed. Flynn held onto the fence with one hand as he tossed the blanket over the razor wire with the other. Some barbs poked through the blanket, but mostly Flynn avoided the razor-sharp metal and clambered over. Caitlyn followed right behind him. As Gabriel struggled to make his way over the top, Boyd paced and waited below.

Hospital police either cut through the duct tape securing the doors or found another way out. Half a dozen officers charged across the grounds right for them.

A blanket ripped. Gabriel fell off the fence, landing in the dirt at Flynn's feet. Boyd was halfway up the fence when the hospital police shot him with taser darts, sending him into convulsions. He fell to the ground. Caitlyn took off, running down the hill.

Flynn followed close behind, stumbling after her past clumps of California sagebrush and buckwheat. The alarm screamed in the distance as hospital police took Boyd into custody, shouting things like, "Stay down! Hands out! Face down!!"

Caitlyn, quite the sprinter, left Flynn in the dust. Stumbling footsteps followed Flynn as a panicked Gabriel hurried to keep up, half-running, half-sliding, half-tripping down the hill.

The horizon was barely blue. The sun had yet to rise.

A state park bordered the hospital grounds. Flynn followed Caitlyn down the dusty hillside into a greener area dotted with wild oak, alder, maple, and manzanita. They raced through a native garden habitat, totally deserted at this time of the night. Coyotes howled along with the sirens of the hospital police cars.

Caitlyn finally stopped running to assess the situation. Flynn caught up and tried to catch his breath.

"We need a car," Flynn wheezed.

"No shit." Caitlyn said, not the slightest bit out of breath.

Gabriel caught up with them and sat heavily on the ground, completely winded.

"We need to find a car before the helicopters get here," Flynn said.

"The hospital has helicopters?" Gabriel's voice rose with alarm.

"The county sheriff does, and you can bet they put out the word to every law enforcement agency in the county. Maybe the state." Flynn scanned the horizon.

"Lord, protect us," Gabriel mumbled.

"We should split up," Caitlyn said.

Flynn shook his head. "I disagree."

"Yeah, well, I'm not asking your permission." Caitlyn sprinted away. Flynn raced after her. Gabriel, still on the ground, staggered to his feet and followed.

Flynn spotted an old truck with a horse trailer parked in some sort of equestrian area. An elderly Asian man spread out hay. Caitlyn pushed right past the old fellow and jumped in the front seat of his truck. The keys must have been left in the ignition because Caitlyn started it right up. The engine roared, the tires spun, and dust rose. Flynn rushed to catch up before Caitlyn tore out of there. He got a hand on the horse trailer just as the truck took off.

The man feeding the horses yelled, "Hey!"

Gabriel yelled, "Hey!" as well. Flynn glanced back to see him stumbling to a stop, bent over at the waist, out of breath and disappearing in the dust.

The horse trailer bounced and rocked as Caitlyn sped out of there. The empty trailer caught air every time they hit a bump. The dirt road led to a gravel road which led to a paved two-lane highway. Peering around the edge of the horse trailer, Flynn caught sight of an SUV coming right at them. Caitlyn hit the brakes and cut sideways to avoid crashing, only to lurch to a stop, blocking the road and cutting off the SUV.

The SUV skidded sideways and nearly went off the edge. A burly bearded man leaped out, red-faced and screaming, "What the heck?"

Caitlyn jumped from the truck and ran right at the man. He staggered back as she brushed past him, climbed into his SUV, started it up, and hit the gas. A look of astonishment crossed the man's face as she backed up and turned his vehicle in the opposite direction. Flynn threw open the passenger door and climbed inside seconds before Caitlyn put the pedal to the metal. The momentum slammed Flynn's door shut. He glanced back to see the stunned man blinded by the rising dust kicked up by his own departing tires.

■　■　■

Mendoza wanted to strangle someone. Flynn would've been his preferred choice, but Flynn was long gone along with that *pinche puta*. Mendoza couldn't believe that *idiota* got away. The man had the luck of the *zumbado*. *How is it possible?* After all Mendoza did to get him to Hornitos, after all his complicated plans and machinations, now he would have to escape. Find a way out of this *casa de locos*. Hospital police searched the rooms and corridors as if there might be a clue where Flynn fled.

You couldn't outmaneuver Flynn. You couldn't out think him. *How can you out think someone who isn't thinking? How can you ever predict what a tarado like that might do?*

The police couldn't bring firearms into the unit, just pepper spray, stun guns, and Tasers. Well, those would have to do. Mendoza grabbed two hospital cops and slammed their heads together, taking a Taser from each. He tased and shocked a third *chota* before pulling out the Taser barbs, grabbing his keycard and heading for the exit. It wasn't manned because the only mental patients left in Unit G were him and O'Haney.

A muffled rumble echoed from above. Mendoza stopped to listen. *What the hell is that?* He looked up just as Manu crashed through the ceiling.

"*Chingada*," he mumbled as three hundred and fifty pounds of sweaty Samoan hit the floor right in front of him. The big Samoan lay flat on his back with the air knocked out of him, his round face and frizzy hair covered with dust and cellulose insulation.

"Where's Flynn?" Mendoza asked him.

Manu pointed up.

Mendoza stepped over Manu's massive gut and hurried for the door with his two stolen Tasers and a keycard from one of the guards.

The hospital police searched all the rooms and corridors for the missing patients. No one could understand how they all disappeared. Manu crashing through the ceiling clued Mendoza in on the escape route. He needed to get out too, but if that route didn't work for Manu, it wouldn't work for him.

The keycard got Mendoza through Unit G's security door. His abrupt appearance surprised the two hospital police on the other side. Mendoza tased them before kicking them unconscious.

One was almost as large as him, so Mendoza stripped him down and put on his uniform. It fit snugly, but stayed buttoned. Mendoza made his escape. He hurried through security door after security door, passing panicked hospital police as he left the main building.

Outside, a bone-rattling alarm continued to scream. A hospital police car pulled up and two officers hopped out. Mendoza tased one in the face and pushed the other's head through the driver's side window. He took their weapons, took their keys, took their car, took their wallets, turned on the siren, and took off.

The guards at the front entrance didn't hesitate to open the lift gate and let the flashing hospital police car through.

CHAPTER NINETEEN

Sancho never watched TV news. Hell, he didn't even have cable. Just Netflix and Amazon and Apple. But he did check the headlines on his phone. As he lay in bed, struggling to wake up, the alarm on his cell phone beeped. He considered hitting snooze, but he didn't want to be late for work again. He checked his email and the morning headlines. One news item generated a shot of adrenaline.

Escape from Hornitos.

"Shit," he mumbled, suddenly wide awake. His sleeping bride groaned and pulled the blankets tighter. Pregnant as she was, she could only sleep on her side. Sancho extricated himself from the tangle of sheets, pulled on sweatpants, and padded into the living room. He checked CNN online, but kept the sound low so as not to disturb Alyssa. The crawl across the bottom confirmed what he saw on his phone. Four patients had escaped from Hornitos State Hospital before dawn. They didn't mention them by name, but Sancho didn't need any names. He suspected he already knew who flew the coop and couldn't help but smile.

. . .

Caitlyn needed clothes and money. She also needed to shake Flynn. He was surprisingly competent for someone so delusional and yes, his stupid plan actually worked, but now she needed to lose him. His previous adventures made him somewhat of a celebrity. Eventually, he'd draw attention by doing something completely deranged, and she needed to be long gone before that happened.

She and Flynn cruised the Broadway Plaza parking lot in Walnut Creek. The elegant outdoor shopping center had a Macy's and a Nordstrom, and Flynn wanted to steal high-end clothing and a luxury car. Turned out, Flynn was a bit of a snob.

Caitlyn didn't argue. She just kept an eye out for a female shopper approximately her size and weight. If they carried bags full of newly purchased clothes from Athleta, so much the better. Flynn did the same, though there were far more ladies than men at Broadway Plaza.

"There. Over there!" Flynn pointed out a fashionable thirty-something couple lugging bags from Nordstrom, Banana Republic, and J. Crew. The man looked angry as the woman went on and on about something that clearly irritated him. The man snapped at her and she snapped back.

"Trouble in paradise," Caitlyn mused. She slowly followed them in the stolen SUV. The couple continued to quarrel as they crossed to the end of the parking lot, opened the trunk of a BMW 550i, and loaded their bags in the back. Caitlyn pulled into an adjacent parking spot. She and Flynn climbed out.

Neither the man nor the woman noticed Flynn and Caitlyn's smudged faces or dirty and tattered Hornitos hospital scrubs as they squabbled. "There's nothing going on. I can't help it if she keeps texting me. I work with the woman. I can't just—"

Flynn grabbed the man from behind. Caitlyn did the same with the woman. They both used standard carotid chokeholds to render them unconscious. Caitlyn found the key fob for the BMW in the woman's shoulder bag. She also found a wallet and a pink Sting Ring stun gun.

She jammed it against Flynn's neck, shocking him with ten thousand volts. He went down hard, twitching and convulsing as electricity ripped through his body. She jumped into the BMW's front seat, hit the ignition button, and squealed out.

Glancing in the rear mirror, she caught sight of Flynn still on his back, still flopping on the ground. She had a momentary stab of regret, which she quickly dismissed as she looked to the road ahead.

. . .

The thousands of volts that shot through Flynn's system made him lose control of every muscle in his body, including his urethral sphincters. He jerked, twitched, and pissed his insane asylum pants. Dust and bits of gravel hit him in the face as the BMW burned rubber.

Caitlyn ditched him.

She still didn't trust him.

Flynn shuddered as the effects of the stun gun slowly dissipated. He rolled over onto his hands and knees and blinked until his eyes were no longer blurry. Flynn fished the wallet out of the pants of the man he choked out before slowly working his way to his feet. The man he assaulted coughed and came to. He caught Flynn's eye. Recognition animated his face.

Flynn hurried off across the parking lot and accosted a biker climbing off a red Honda Fireblade. He snatched the guy's key fob and jumped on his bike, started her up and roared out of there.

. . .

Caitlyn heard the helicopter before she saw it. She powered down the driver's side window and the thwop-thwop-thwopping of the chopper reverberated overhead. It stayed right on top of her. Followed her even as she sped up. The sirens were faint at first, drowned out by the roar of the chopper blades, but they grew in volume and intensity as flashing cherries in her rearview mirror caught her eye.

"Shit!" she shouted to no one in particular and cut down a side street, but the chopper and the patrol cars stayed right with her. *Someone must have called the cops. Either that or the car has a LoJack. Or both.* Goddamn Flynn and his snobby-ass attitude. She should've boosted an old Corolla or some piece of shit Chevy from a Walmart parking lot. Caitlyn flew through a light and turned right, threading in and out of traffic. Up ahead, she saw more flashing lights. Cops coming from the other direction. On the right, she caught sight of a parking structure next to an office building.

She cut a hard right, crashed through a lift gate, and headed up an exit. An Acura swerved to avoid her. She clipped a headlight as she veered around it, up the wrong way into the parking garage. She reached level two. Level three. Level four. One more level and she'd be on the roof. She squealed to a stop and hopped out. Sirens wailed below and the helicopter thundered overhead.

She looked over the edge. Two patrol cars blocked the exit. By now, they must have blocked the entrance as well.

"*Shit!*"

That's when she spotted the red racing bike. Every car had pulled over to the side, leaving the center of the road wide open. The bike sped right between the cop cars blocking the exit. Its engine reverberated throughout the parking structure, louder and louder as it climbed higher, tires squealing, engine revving until finally it arrived on the fourth floor.

Flynn grinned as he skidded to a stop next to her.

He held out his hand.

Caitlyn smiled back, took his hand, and threw her leg over the saddle, scooting up close to him. He revved the engine and cut a U-turn back down into the parking structure. Four cops stared wide-eyed as they rounded the corner. All four pulled their guns. Flynn accelerated right at them. They had no choice but to dive out of the way.

Gunfire echoed as they squealed down the structure, past level two and then level one, where they blew by two cops flanking a patrol car. They weren't expecting or looking for a motorcycle. There was just enough space for Flynn to thread the needle.

Caitlyn held tight to Flynn as he twisted the throttle and shifted into fifth. She wasn't sure exactly how fast they were going, but it had to be over a hundred as they hit the highway. The most powerful racing bikes could easily hit one hundred and fifty. *Where had Flynn learned to ride a motorcycle? This didn't feel like his first time.* He maneuvered it competently, but knew if they hit a car or a guard rail they'd go flying. And since they weren't wearing leathers or helmets, they'd end up looking like raw hamburger. She pulled herself closer to Flynn's muscular back and held on for dear life. What other choice did she have?

■ ■ ■

They arrived in San Luis Obispo after dark, dumped the bike, and hot-wired an old Buick in a used car lot before breaking into a secondhand clothing store two blocks off the main drag. Caitlyn couldn't wait to get out of her filthy, ragged hospital scrubs. She found a pair of Tommy Hilfiger jeans, a black turtleneck, black leather boots, and a distressed denim jacket. Flynn went more formal with a vintage Brioni suit. Though unshaven and a little sweaty, he looked far less like a mental patient out of his scrubs. In fact, he looked good. Handsome even.

Caitlyn knew all about Flynn. She'd followed his story from the beginning and read all about how he foiled Goolardo's maniacal plot. Since then, she read everything about him, watched both documentaries, and perused all the YouTube videos. When her enemies framed her for murder, the prosecution used Flynn's case to paint her with the same broad brush. So she learned all she could about him. Including how females of all persuasions and professions had succumbed to his charms. She saw the attraction, but it was nothing more than an illusion. A carefully constructed delusion. Yes, he had some helpful skills, but they were born of a confidence untethered to reality. Still, he'd proven useful. Without Flynn, she'd probably be in police custody.

They spent the night in the secondhand shop and snuck out just as the sun came up. Caitlyn needed breakfast. She was ravenous. She didn't want to use the credit cards they stole from that yuppie couple in Walnut Creek, but their cash would spend just fine. They found a diner on Higuera Street called Louisa's Place. It had a small town 1960s vibe with a long lunch counter, Formica table tops, and red Naugahyde booths. Flynn looked out of place in his Brioni suit, as most of the other patrons were local senior citizens, day trippers, and students from Cal Poly.

Caitlyn ordered coffee and expected Flynn to order tea, but he went for the coffee too. "You don't drink tea?"

"I never drink tea."

"Not very British of you."

"I'd rather drink a cup of mud. In fact, I believe tea is one of the primary reasons for the downfall of the British empire."

The forty-something waitress grinned at Flynn's tirade. "I love your accent."

Flynn smiled back and eyed her name tag. "Thank you, Darlene, but everyone sounds like this where I come from."

"And where would that be?"

"Southern California most recently, but before that, the United Kingdom. London, to be precise. Though my father was Scottish, so I do have a bit of a burr."

Caitlyn smirked as the woman leaned closer, clearly smitten, her pencil poised over her pad. "What can I get you, darling?"

"Two scrambled eggs, two slices of whole wheat toast, and a rasher of bacon. Breakfast is my favorite meal of the day."

"Mine too," Darlene said. She started to walk away.

"What about me?" Caitlyn said. "Don't you want my order?"

"Of course I do," Darlene replied, looking a little flustered. "What would you like, dear?"

"Can I get a breakfast burrito?"

"Absolutely." Darlene bustled off.

Caitlyn sipped her coffee. "I appreciate all the help you've given me, but I really think it's time we split up."

Flynn nodded. "I disagree." Flynn must have seen the skepticism on her face because he reached across the table and put his hand on hers to reassure her. "I know you don't know me. I know you don't trust me. I know that's why you ditched me. But I believe I was sent to Hornitos to bring you in from the cold."

"Sent by who? God?"

"His Majesty's Secret Service."

Caitlyn sighed and closed her eyes in frustration. Flynn somehow incorporated her situation into his delusion. At the moment though, crazy as he was, he was the only person she could trust. "Bring me where?"

"To see my superiors at our satellite headquarters in Pasadena. Once we help Nurse Erickson, of course."

"I'm not sure I'd be safe there."

"Not safe? Why? Do you think someone has infiltrated our organization as well? Is that why M kept my mission on the QT? So secret that he couldn't even tell me?"

Rather than puncture his delusion, she humored him. "Maybe."

"Then I won't bring you into headquarters. We'll hide out with a colleague of mine. Someone I trust implicitly."

"I appreciate the help, but I think it's time for me to disappear. On my own." Caitlyn took a sip of coffee.

"What about the plot you uncovered?"

"What about it?"

"Don't you want to stop it?"

"I told you what happened when I tried. The people behind it are too powerful."

"Nonsense."

"You want to stop them? Be my guest. I'm going to have my breakfast burrito and then I'm gone."

Flynn leaned closer across the table. "What about Nurse Erickson?"

"What about her?"

"Didn't we promise to help her?"

"She tried to kill me."

"Not successfully. Besides, you know she did it under duress. She was worried for her daughter."

"There's nothing we can do for her," Caitlyn said.

"The men who threatened her will likely return to threaten her again. If we can apprehend them, perhaps we can find out who sent them."

"We know who sent them."

"Yes, but I want a name, and I want to know where to find them."

"Not me. I'm done dealing with those lunatics."

"If you want to abandon her, that's up to you, Miss Valentine. But without her help, we never would have escaped. I made a promise to her and I intend to keep it."

"Like I said. Have at it."

Darlene arrived with their food, and Caitlyn tore into her breakfast burrito. Both she and Flynn were so famished they didn't say another word. She took her last bite, drank the last of her coffee, and watched Flynn finish the last of his breakfast. He wasn't wrong about Nurse Erickson, but at this point, there wasn't anything to be done.

Caitlyn looked past Flynn at the other customers in the room and caught a guy eying her from the counter. He whispered something to the waitress refilling his coffee. They both glanced in her direction and then quickly looked away when they saw her watching them. *Shit*. She and Flynn were probably all over the news. She reached across the table and lightly touched Flynn's hand. "I think we've been made."

"Good."

"Good?"

"Yes, I figured someone might recognize us. In fact, I was counting on it. Come on…" Flynn rose, dropped a bunch of cash on the table, and headed for the doors.

Caitlyn felt eyes on her as she followed him outside into the parking lot.

Flynn climbed behind the wheel of the Buick Regal. Caitlyn rode shotgun. They headed south on Higuera street towards the 101. "The police will assume we're heading for Southern California. They'll never expect us to double back."

"Double back where?"

"To our only possible lead. To Nurse Erickson and those men who threatened her."

Caitlyn pointed to the side of the road. "Pull over."

"Why?"

"You know why."

"You want to get out?"

"No, I want *you* to get out. Pull over. *Pull over*." Flynn pulled the Buick over and sat there staring at her, trying to make her feel guilty. She locked eyes with him, intending to stare him down. But he wouldn't look away. He was waiting. Waiting for her to change her mind. To find her courage. To find her better self. Well, screw that. Screw him.

"I said get *out*," she shouted.

"Are you sure?"

"Very sure."

"Okay. If that's what you want."

"It's not what I want. It's what I have to do."

Flynn continued to stare at her. Finally, he opened his door.

"Wait." Caitlyn punched the dashboard. "Fuck it. *Fine.* We'll check on Nurse Erickson. Make sure she's okay. But then I'm fucking gone and we are *fucking* done."

"Fine."

"Fine."

CHAPTER TWENTY

They were waiting when Nurse Erickson opened the door. Mike sat tied to a chair. His mouth dangled and dripped blood into his lap, his right eye purple and swollen shut, his left staring at her in terror. A bolt of fear shot through her. *Where's Danni?*

This time, the men didn't bother wearing masks. Did that mean they intended to murder them? They didn't look like murderers. They looked like insurance salesmen as they sat there on her couch, wearing matching suits, watching *Jeopardy*. The man with the remote control muted the TV. He had short blond hair cut in a very conservative style. The other didn't have any hair. Both men stood, but only the bald one spoke. "Close the door and lock it."

She considered running, but knew they'd catch her if she did. So she turned and locked the door.

"Look at me," the bald one said. When she did, he continued. "You didn't do what you said you would."

Tears blurred Nurse Erickson's vision. "I tried, but by the time I got to the medical wing, she was gone."

"You said you were going to finish the job."

"I can't help that she escaped."

"I told you there would be consequences."

"Once she's caught and they bring her back, I'll be there to do whatever you want."

"And if she isn't caught?"

"Where's my daughter?"

"Your husband told us she's at a friend's house," the blond said.

A voice emerged from Mike's battered face. "She's at Julie's. A playdate."

"We waited for you and now we'll wait for her," the bald man said.

"Then what?" asked the blond.

"Then we'll take her husband and her daughter to some undisclosed location and hold them hostage."

The blond raised a curious eyebrow. "Why?"

"Two reasons. Consequences for what she didn't do the first time and to make sure she doesn't screw up the next time."

Nurse Erickson sobbed. "Please..."

"Too complicated," the blond man said.

"What do you mean?" asked the bald one.

"We have a find a place to hide them. We have to find someone to guard them. It's too complicated."

"Do you have a better idea?"

The blond nodded. "Kill 'em."

"All of 'em?"

The blond nodded again. "There's a time to kill and a time to heal. A time for war and a time for peace. There are those who fight on the side of Satan and those who fight on the side of right."

The bald one sighed. "But just these two, okay? Not the little girl. She's innocent and has yet to be corrupted."

Nurse Erickson's eyes glistened. "You don't have to do that. I told you I'd do whatever you want."

"See," the bald man said. "She'll do whatever we want."

"And you believe her?"

Nurse Erickson ran for the door and unbolted the lock, but before she could get it open, the bald man had her by the back of the neck. He tossed her across the room into her tied-up husband. She held Mike and sobbed.

The blond looked irritated and drew his gun.

"Hold it," the bald guy said. "A neighbor might hear the gunshot."

The blond guy re-holstered his pistol and pulled a knife. "Better?"

"Too messy. Let's load them into the husband's car and drive them up into the hills." He looked at Nurse Erickson. "Are you parked in the driveway?"

"I'm on the street."

"So you're not blocking the garage?"

"No."

The blond guy used his knife to cut the cords binding Mike to the chair and pulled him to his feet. He wobbled off-balance as he rubbed his raw wrists.

The guy slapped Mike across the face to get his attention. "Keys?" Mike pointed to a table by the front door. The keys sat next to a pile of mail.

The bald one grabbed Nurse Erickson by the arm and pulled her to the door leading to the garage.

The blond followed with Mike.

The Ericksons kept the garage uncluttered and pristine, along with their Lexus. The bald one opened the trunk. "Get in."

Nurse Erickson didn't move. Neither did Mike. There didn't seem to be enough room for both of them. Their kidnapper sighed with irritation and pulled his gun. "Get the heck in."

Nurse Erickson helped her husband into the trunk and climbed in after him. It was a tight fit. The bald guy slammed the lid down, plunging them both into darkness. A bit of light seeped in the seams along the edge of the trunk. The smell of Mike's sweat and the coppery tang of his blood filled her nostrils.

"Are you okay?" she whispered.

"I'm sorry," he whispered.

"No, *I'm* sorry. I should have told you…"

"You were afraid."

She started to cry. "I'm so sorry."

"Shhh."

The car started and the garage door rumbled open.

The bald one shouted, "What the heck?"

The car door opened and slammed shut. The bald guy banged on the trunk, his voice muffled by the metal. "I thought you said you didn't park in the driveway?"

"I didn't."

"Well, who the H-E-double-hockey-sticks did?"

"Look out!" shouted the blond guy.

A heavy thunk. Grunts. Shouts. Punches. A pitched battle. Wood on metal. Metal on metal. Metal on flesh. A single gunshot. And then silence.

The garage door closed with a rumble. A moment later, someone popped open the trunk.

Caitlyn Valentine and James Flynn stared down at them.

"Good to see you're still alive," Flynn said.

"We expected the worst," Caitlyn added.

"But hoped for the best," Flynn replied.

Flynn helped Nurse Erickson and her very perplexed husband out of the trunk. The two men lay motionless on the ground.

"Are they dead?"

"I hope not," Flynn said. "I'd like to get some information out of them once they regain consciousness."

Mike rubbed his injured jaw and winced. "Who are you?"

"Flynn. James Flynn. And this is Caitlyn Valentine."

"She's the one they wanted me to murder," Nurse Erickson explained.

■　■　■

Caitlyn and Flynn searched the men as Nurse Erickson tended to her beat-to-crap husband. They took the kidnapper's Glocks, their combat knives, and their wallets. Caitlyn found the keys to the Lexus. She grabbed the bald one's ankles. "Want to give me a hand here?"

Flynn grabbed the man under the arms and together they heaved him into the trunk. The blond was taller and heavier and took more effort, but eventually they dumped him in on top his bald and equally unconscious compatriot.

Caitlyn caught the trepidation in Mike's eyes as he stared at his torturers bleeding in his trunk. The blond's eyes opened with a start. He reached for the edge and tried to climb out. Caitlyn slammed the trunk on the man's hand. The blond screamed. She lifted the trunk lid and slammed it down again. This time on his head. The screaming stopped.

"They won't be bothering you again," Flynn said.

"They won't be bothering anyone," Caitlyn added.

Mike gingerly touched his bloody lip. "Who the hell *are* they?"

"The less you know, the better. For now, just know that you're safe," said Flynn. "As long as you don't go to the authorities. If you go to the police, you'll find yourself in their crosshairs again."

"So what do we do?" Nurse Erickson asked.

"Nothing."

"Though we will need to borrow your car." Caitlyn opened the driver's side door. "Tomorrow, you can report it stolen."

■   ■   ■

Flynn drove the kidnapper's Buick. Caitlyn took the Lexus. Together they headed south towards Southern California. They abandoned the Buick near Banning and Flynn rode shotgun as Caitlyn drove east into the San Luis National Wildlife Refuge. They found a deserted access road and hid the car in an isolated wooded area.

Flynn held both Glocks on the boot as Caitlyn unlocked it. He assumed both men had regained consciousness and would likely try something foolish. Flynn hoped the sight of their own weapons would dissuade them from that reckless course of action. The lid creaked open and the two men inside remained motionless. Both were wide-eyed and sightless. That, combined with the pallor of their skin and the rigor mortis setting in, made it quite obvious they were dead. Flynn checked their carotid arteries anyway.

"Shit," Caitlyn whispered. "Suicide pills."

"They're Army of God. I thought Christians didn't commit suicide?"

"Catholics don't, but these fanatics are another story. They don't see taking their own lives as suicide. They see it as martyrdom." Caitlyn grabbed the man on top. "Can you give me a hand here?"

Flynn pitched in and together they lifted and pulled and dragged them both out and laid them on the ground. "We need to find the men who sent them," Flynn said.

"*We* don't *need* to do anything. I am done with this."

"Didn't you swear an oath to support and defend the Constitution of the United States against all enemies, foreign and domestic?"

"I did and then the powers that be betrayed me."

"The Constitution didn't betray you. Flawed human beings did."

"It's hot out here and I'm thirsty." She climbed back into the driver's seat. "Are you coming?"

"The world is in great danger and you can do something about it."

"The world's always in great danger. If climate change doesn't turn the world into a post-apocalyptic wasteland, a fucking asteroid will. Or the singularity will happen and an intelligent A.I. will build an army of killer robots to wipe out all of humanity. Or some asshole scientist will create a bioweapon that escapes and exterminates all life on earth. Bad shit happens. It'll continue to happen. So this is my plan. I'm going to disappear and live out my life the best way I can."

"You're running away?"

"You do you. I'll do me."

"That's a very selfish point of view." Flynn said.

"Exactly. Now get in the car. I'll drive you as far as L.A. After that, you're on your own. You go your way, I'll go mine. Is there any place in particular I can drop you?"

CHAPTER TWENTY-ONE

Sancho didn't want to piss off Alyssa. Though lately, he couldn't seem to avoid it. Everything he did irritated her. Cranky was her default condition. Along with achy, uncomfortable, sweaty, and gassy. The love of his life had transmogrified into Jabba the Hutt. Every morning she woke up in a cold sweat and farted all the way to the bathroom. She had to pee every ten minutes. She even peed when she sneezed. Her face broke out and weird hairs sprouted up. He knew Alyssa felt ugly, huge, and repulsive. If Sancho made the mistake of telling her she was beautiful, she would glare at him like he was out of his mind.

At nine months, Alyssa was impossibly huge. And impossibly stubborn. She insisted on finishing out the semester at Cal State L.A. She only had two more semesters to go before she graduated with a degree in accounting and, baby or no baby, she was going to get it done. She had a class and Sancho offered to drive her to school since he had the day off, but she insisted on taking her own car.

"At least let me make you some breakfast," he said.

"No thanks."

"You gotta eat. You're eating for two. I'll make you some scrambled eggs."

"I can't stand the smell of eggs right now."

"Oatmeal?"

She sighed. "Fine. Oatmeal. But don't put any milk in it. I'm gassy enough as it is. I'm going to go take a shower." She farted as she walked off.

Sancho put the oatmeal on to cook and straightened up their tiny two-bedroom Pico Rivera townhouse. He planned to work on the baby's room until he had to get to the hospital. Sancho had an afternoon rotation this week. 1:00 p.m. to 10:00 p.m. But knew the baby could pop out at any time. If Alyssa went into early labor, he wanted to be there. California had a new family leave law that covered mothers *and* fathers. Six weeks of care time. Though it only covered seventy percent of his income, and he didn't make all that much to start with.

Such were the thoughts swirling around his groggy head when he heard a suspicious knock at the door. It wasn't a slow loud "here I am" knock, but a quick, quiet, secretive knock. So Sancho had some trepidation as he looked through the peephole.

Flynn peeped right back at him.

Sancho whispered, "Shit." He opened the door.

Flynn hurried in, followed by a slim and strong-looking woman with short dark hair and striking green eyes. The woman scanned the street and spotted Sancho's elderly next-door neighbor, Mrs. Zavala, walking her dog. They locked eyes and then Mrs. Zavala looked at Sancho. He offered her a smile and a little wave, closed the door, and looked at Flynn. "What the hell, man?"

"Sorry to drop in unannounced, my friend, but I'm in a bit of a jam. This is Caitlyn. Caitlyn, Sancho."

"You got the whole world looking for you, dude."

Caitlyn peered through the peephole. "Who was that woman?"

"That's my neighbor. Mrs. Zavala." Sancho headed into the kitchen. Flynn and Caitlyn stayed right with him. He turned off the oatmeal just as Alyssa came walking in, her baby belly ahead of the rest of her.

"Who was that at the—" Alyssa stopped mid-sentence to stare wide-eyed at Flynn. "James?"

Flynn grinned. "Look at that beautiful mother to be. You are absolutely glowing."

"What are you doing here?"

"As I explained to your new husband, we're in a bit of a pickle."

Sancho offered Alyssa a reassuring smile, but she wasn't reassured. She grabbed him hard by the arm and kept her voice calm, though Sancho could tell she was close to losing her shit. "Would you excuse us for a second?"

She dragged Sancho off to the bedroom, closed the door and shout/whispered into his ear. "What the hell?"

"I know."

"You gotta get him out of here."

"He's in trouble."

"No shit."

"Alyssa—"

"You know I love the man, but Jesus Christ!"

"He has nowhere to go."

"You know what'll happen if the police find him here?"

"I know."

"You want me to have this baby in jail?"

"No one's going to find him."

"I'm going to class. I want him gone by the time I get back." Sancho nodded. "Fine. Okay."

"I'm not playing. He's gotta go."

"I know."

"And who's that with him?"

"Caitlyn."

"Who?"

"She escaped from the mental hospital, too."

"Give him money. Do what you have to. But get him the hell out of here," Alyssa insisted.

"I said okay."

She closed her eyes, shook her head, and opened the bedroom door. Sancho followed her as she grabbed her car keys and backpack and headed for the front door. "I gotta go, but it was really good seeing you, James."

"You too."

"Where are you going?" Caitlyn asked. Her voice had an edge.

"Class," Sancho said.

"I have a class," Alyssa clarified. She was out the door before Caitlyn could say another word. Sancho closed it behind her.

Caitlyn peered out the peephole. "Is she going to call the cops on us?"

"Of course not," Flynn said. "She's a friend."

Caitlyn didn't look convinced. She focused her intimidating gaze on Sancho. "But she doesn't want Flynn to stay here, does she?"

"No, but I don't think it's such a good idea either. People know I know Flynn and I'm not that hard to track down."

Flynn nodded. "I don't disagree. We won't stay long."

"I'm not staying at all," Caitlyn said. "I said I'd drop you off and that's exactly what I'm doing."

Flynn put his hand on her shoulder. "We haven't slept in twenty-four hours. We need rest and we need food."

Sancho pointed to the kitchen. "There's oatmeal on the stove and, if you want, I can make some eggs."

"Thank you, old friend. I'll take them lightly scrambled in butter and a rasher of bacon on the side if you have it."

Caitlyn smirked. "Pretty picky when it comes to your eggs."

"When it comes to food and drink, I never settle for less than the best. After all, you only live once."

"And not for very long with all that butter and bacon."

"People in our profession don't live all that long anyway," Flynn pointed out. He glanced back at Sancho. "After we eat, we should get some sleep."

"Okay," Sancho said. "But after your naps, you need to go."

Caitlyn moved for the door and Flynn stepped in front of it. "You're hungry and you're tired. You need to eat and you need to sleep. We both do."

Caitlyn sighed. "Fine, but then we each go our own way."

"If that's what you want."

"That's what I want."

. . .

Mrs. Zavala recognized Flynn immediately. She also recognized the woman with him. Their escape from that mental hospital dominated the news. She called 911. It was her duty as a concerned citizen.

"This is 911."

"Those two mental patients who escaped? I know where they are," Mrs. Zavala said.

. . .

Deputy Steven Cronkite was exhausted. He and his partner worked nights and by hour twelve, he always needed a nap. But first he needed food. He and his partner hit Denny's for an end-of-shift breakfast. He ordered the Grand Slam, a massive breakfast that usually plunged him into a major food coma. Not a problem, since in less than an hour he'd be in bed.

They got the call on the way back to the station. The two mental patients who escaped from a maximum-security psychiatric hospital up north were spotted not a mile away. *Shit.* He looked sideways at his partner. Dave was just as exhausted as him, but food coma or no, they had a job to do. He picked up the radio and told them they'd take the call.

.   .   .

Wood heard the call on his police scanner and immediately woke Quinn from a sound sleep. The startled ex-Navy Seal took a swing at his older colleague. Knowing Quinn might react like that, Wood kept his distance. He too suffered the effects of PTSD from his time in the shit. Both fought in Iraq and Afghanistan. Both were retired special operators recruited by the Army of God.

After Valentine and Flynn's escape, the Army of God sent Wood and Quinn to Southern California to keep an eye on Flynn's known contacts. Other teams surveilled Caitlyn Valentine's family and friends. When Wood and Quinn weren't following Perez, at least one of them was always monitoring the scanner. Finally, all their days of dull and seemingly pointless surveillance had paid off.

"Drop your cock and grab your socks! We got a positive ID on our tango," Wood shouted.

"Huh?"

"Do I need to break it down for you Barney-style? We got eyes on Valentine, but we gotta move pronto if we want to beat Five-0."

CHAPTER TWENTY-TWO

Caitlyn awoke disoriented and discombobulated. Rainbows, butterflies, flowers, and pink unicorns covered the walls. A grinning sun and puffy clouds dotted the sky-blue ceiling. Fuzzy bunnies sat on the lap of a giant stuffed panda watching her from a white rocking chair. Slowly, she remembered where she was. The nursery of Sancho and Alyssa's future baby.

She rolled off the air mattress and worked her way to her feet. She wasn't refreshed or wide awake, just exhausted and full of dread. A bone-tired weariness weighed her down. She needed more sleep, but she knew she couldn't stay. Not here. Not with Flynn. She needed to ditch him. He'd be safer without her. The Army of God wasn't looking for him. They were looking for her. Sure, the police were still after him, but they wouldn't kill him. They'd just lock him back up again.

She crept from the nursery and down the short hallway, past the bathroom, where she heard a shower running. Behind the door, Sancho sang *Wake Me Up Before You Go-Go*.

She peered into the other bedroom where Flynn, wearing nothing but his boxer shorts, slept the sleep of the dead. His secondhand Brioni suit hung from a hanger hooked on top of the closet door. She would slip away while he still slept. It was better that way. No arguments. No guilt. He'd wake up, and she'd be gone.

Flynn stirred, mumbled, and rolled over on his side. There was something so innocent and charming about him. So naïve and unsullied. She wished she could live inside that fantasy of his, but to do so she'd have to be as crazy as him.

She gathered her few meager belongings, including the Glock 17 and the combat knife stolen from Nurse Erickson's kidnappers, and tiptoed past the bathroom door. Sancho now sang *Get Lucky*. She put on her denim jacket, slid the Glock into her pocket, carefully unlocked the deadbolt on the front door, and eased it open.

Two burly men stood on the other side of the door. One was older, with dark brown hair and a slightly graying goatee. The other had closely cropped red hair and a nasty scar on his chin. One had a Taser. One had a pistol. Both pointed at her. They smiled. She didn't smile back.

■ ■ ■

Flynn swam through the warm, tropical sea. Weightless. Free. The Caribbean sun penetrated the clear blue water, illuminating the coral reef and the bright, colorful aquatic creatures that swam all around him: angel fish, blue tang, parrotfish, grouper, queen triggerfish, and giant barracuda. That silvery blue predator always filled Flynn with trepidation. Its lower jaw jutted out beyond the upper, revealing an endless supply of razor-sharp teeth. They rarely attacked humans, yet Flynn gave the predator a wide berth as he kicked his flippers, propelling himself through the crystal-clear water.

A deep thumping explosion echoed above, muffled by the sea. The sound startled Flynn, and he rose towards the surface until finally he burst through and found himself awake and dry and lying in Sancho's bed. He wondered if he dreamt the sound and then he heard distant scuffling on the other side of the house.

Something thumping.

A window shattering.

A gunshot.

Instantly up, he drew the Glock 17 from the holster hanging on the headboard and hurried into the living room. The front door stood ajar. Wearing only his boxers, Flynn raced outside. Two burly men dragged Caitlyn down the sidewalk.

"Caitlyn!" Flynn shouted.

One man turned and aimed his weapon. Flynn dove sideways as the gun boomed. He didn't return fire, afraid he might hit Caitlyn. Yet he knew if they carried her off, she'd be dead anyway.

One continued taking potshots at Flynn as they pulled her towards a Ford Taurus parked at the curb. These were professionals. Trained soldiers. They moved with precision and shot with accuracy as those bullets landed all too close to him.

They popped the boot and threw her inside, continuing to fire at Flynn as they jumped in the car. They took off like a shot. Flynn tried to shoot out the front tire. His bullets punctured the front quarter panel, but missed the rubber as the Taurus roared off.

A sheriff's vehicle rounded the corner ahead, directly into the path of the Taurus. The kidnappers tried to swerve around the patrol car, but clipped the front bumper and slammed into a street sign. Two deputies leaped from their vehicle and took positions behind it, drawing their guns and returning fire as the redhead turned his weapon on the police.

They didn't know Caitlyn was in the boot. Flynn worried a stray shot might puncture the lid. He ran barefoot down the street in his boxers, shouting, "There's a woman in the boot! There's a woman in the boot!"

The police directed their fire at him now. He realized what he must look like: a nearly naked lunatic brandishing a pistol. Flynn dove behind a tree as bullets ricocheted off the wood.

. . .

Caitlyn banged her head when the Taurus crashed. Seconds later, gunfire erupted. Bullets slammed into the car. One even punctured the sheet metal inches from her leg, letting in light and the sharp sounds of the gunfight. She knew most modern car trunks had a glow-in-the-dark emergency release lever mandated by law. But she couldn't find it and figured her kidnappers had cut the cable and removed it. *Shit!*

She turned herself over, bracing her shoulders against the trunk, and kicked the back seat as hard as she could. It didn't even budge. But as more bullets slammed into the car, her amygdala alerted her hypothalamus, which sent an urgent message to her adrenal glands. They released an instant burst of epinephrine. Tiny airways in her lungs allowed more oxygen to course into her bloodstream, sharpening her senses. Her heart raced and pumped more blood to her muscles. Fear fueled her strength as she kicked and kicked until the latches on the rear seats ripped free. Pushing the seats down, she slithered through and climbed out the Taurus's right rear door.

Her kidnappers didn't notice her escape, they were too busy trading shots with the sheriffs. But then the older kidnapper must have glimpsed her in his peripheral vision, because he turned around and locked eyes with her before she took off. Her legs, stiff from being crammed in the trunk, moved slowly. A bullet whizzed past her ear. She nearly fell as she spun around to see the kidnapper correct his aim. This time he wouldn't miss. Before he could pull the trigger, a gleaming black Aston Martin DB9 Volante squealed to a stop between Caitlyn and her would-be killer and caught the bullet meant for her.

Sancho sat behind the wheel. "Get in!" he shouted.

She did, but before she could close the door, Flynn dove in after her, wearing nothing but his underwear. A bullet shattered the passenger side window. Flynn shoved Caitlyn down. Sancho flattened the gas and the DB9 squealed out and rocketed past the Ford Taurus before clipping the door on the patrol car. It banged into the cop crouched behind it and knocked him on his ass.

Caitlyn glanced out the rear window. Both kidnappers shot at the departing Aston Martin. No one pursued them, but then few cars could catch an Aston Martin DB9 Volante.

CHAPTER TWENTY-THREE

Mendoza figured Flynn had nowhere to go but south. The only people he knew were in Southern California. The *baboso* would check in at City of Roses since he believed it was the secret service's secret headquarters.

Mendoza ditched the police car in Stockton and stole a gardener's pickup truck. Being undocumented, the *vato* wouldn't report it stolen. He then stopped at a DXL Big and Tall Store and used one of the hospital cop's credit cards to buy a change of clothes.

After two Double-Doubles and a chocolate milkshake at an *In and Out*, Mendoza drove to Pasadena. He parked outside City of Roses and kept an eye on the place. He noticed an unmarked police car up the block, the lack of whitewalls being a dead giveaway, and figured they, too, were keeping an eye out for Flynn. Mendoza had to pee and had no patience. He needed to find Perez and wasn't willing to sit there and wait forever.

Mendoza drove to a nearby Best Buy, emptied his bladder, and bought a burner phone. He called Soto to see if he had an address for Perez. He did. In Pico Rivera.

By the time Mendoza got there, the entire block was shut down. Police and news teams staked out the neighborhood. A news helicopter hovered overhead. Mendoza stood behind the police line with the crowd, watching the aftermath of whatever went down.

He asked a stooped and shriveled old lady for the scoop. "You know what happened here, *señora*?"

"Huh?"

He had to shout to be heard over the helicopter and pointed to help make his point. "You know what happened?"

"Two crazy people escaped from some mental hospital!"

"Did they catch them?"

"No, but somebody got shot."

"Did they say who?"

"What?"

"Did they say who got shot?"

"They didn't say."

The police went in and out of Perez's address. They spoke with an angry pregnant woman. *Is Perez even here?* Mendoza didn't see him anywhere. Reporters shouted questions at the pregnant woman. She ignored them and went in the house, slamming the door. An ambulance left the scene. The police left soon after, followed by the TV news vans.

Mendoza waited in his stolen pickup truck as the neighbors slowly dispersed. Soon after the sun went down, he climbed over the low wooden fence and peered into the kitchen window.

The pregnant woman shouted at someone on the phone. *Could she be talking to Perez?* She hung up on whoever she was talking to and slammed the phone on the table. Then she started to cry.

Mendoza moved to the back door, broke the glass with his fist, and pushed his hand through to unlatch the deadbolt. The pregnant woman jumped to her feet. The kitchen chair fell as she ran.

Mendoza opened the door and chased her through the house. As she fumbled with the deadbolt on the front door, Mendoza grabbed her hard by the arm. "Don't make me break it."

She tried to struggle, but only for a moment, and then she started to cry again.

Mendoza didn't need to raise his voice to terrify her. "I want to know where Perez is."

"I don't know," she said.

"Who are you to him?"

"I'm his wife."

"Where is he?"

"I told you! I don't know!"

"Has he contacted you?"

"No!"

"Have you contacted him?"

"I tried, but he won't pick up."

"Is Flynn with him?"

"I don't know."

She tried to pull away, and Mendoza squeezed her arm harder.

She shrieked in pain. "You're hurting me!"

"You need to stop lying to me."

"I'm not lying! I'm not! Please! You're hurting me!"

■　■　■

Dennis Stettmeier stayed glued to the news ever since Flynn escaped. He grew sick with fear. Literally nauseous. He tried eating saltines to settle his stomach, but the salt just made him thirsty. He cracked open a beer, hoping it would relax him, but all it did was make him bloated and uncomfortable.

Flynn had to know that Stettmeier sent him to Hornitos. Perez probably told Flynn where he lived. He all but said he would. And now Stettmeier had an escaped lunatic after him. Why had he ever listened to Mendoza? How could he have been such an idiot? Flynn was dangerous. A mental case convinced he had a license to kill.

They almost had him at Perez's place, but somehow he escaped. Again. Flynn was still on the loose and Stettmeier was sure the psychopath was coming for him next. Why wouldn't he?

Stettmeier located his father's old Smith and Wesson .38 Special and a box of cartridges. He didn't know how to load it or shoot it, but maybe just brandishing it would be enough. He kept it on the side table next to the couch.

He padded into the kitchen and cracked open another beer. Stettmeier returned to the couch and channel surfed the local news stations, hoping to find any additional information on Flynn. Maybe he was just being paranoid. After all, he didn't know for sure Flynn was after him. Maybe he fled L.A. after the close call with the cops. Maybe Stettmeier was terrified for no good reason at all.

A sharp knock at the door startled him. He peed his pants a little.

Fuck!

Would Flynn knock? Or come crashing through a window? Maybe he'd just set his house on fire and wait for him to come running out.

Another sharp knock made a little more pee leak out. Stettmeier was too afraid to run to the bathroom. Too afraid to answer the door. Too afraid to get up off the couch. Maybe whoever was at the door would go away if he just…

The doorbell rang.

Followed by more knocking.

Shit!

Stettmeier grabbed his unloaded Smith and Wesson and approached the front door. He peered out the peephole, steeling himself for what he might see. A frightened young woman. Hispanic. Pretty. Her eyes looked teary. He unlatched the deadbolt and opened the door to discover that she was very pregnant.

And not alone.

Mendoza stood just behind her. Stettmeier hadn't ever met him or even talked to him before. All communication went through Soto. But Stettmeier recognized his big, wide, ugly face.

A year or two ago his scary mug was all over the news. "Mendoza?"

Mendoza pushed the pregnant woman forward and followed her inside. He slammed the door and towered over Stettmeier. "Flynn broke out of Hornitos."

"Yeah, I know."

"He's with Perez, and Perez knows where you live."

"You think he's coming here?"

"I would if I were him."

Stettmeier pointed at the crying pregnant woman with his Smith and Wesson. "Is this your girlfriend?"

Mendoza twisted the gun out of Stettmeier's hand.

"Ow, Jesus!"

"What's this for?"

"Flynn!"

Mendoza flipped open the cylinder. "It's not loaded."

"I know."

"Why isn't it loaded?"

"I don't know how."

"Were you planning to hit him on the head with it?"

Stettmeier pointed at the woman again. This time he used his finger. "So she's not your girlfriend?"

"She's Perez's wife."

"Why is she here?"

"Leverage."

"What?"

"Perez is going to lead me to Flynn." Mendoza held up the Smith and Wesson. "Do you have any bullets for this?"

"I do. Are you going to kill him?"

"I am. But you need to make it worth my while."

"How do I do that?"

"If I kill him, you inherit that trust. I deserve half."

"Half the money in the trust?"

"I think that's fair."

"I don't. That's a lot of money."

"Are you haggling with me?"

"No, I'm just saying that it's… you know… a lot of money."

The doorknob rattled. *Shit!* Was it Flynn? Did he have a gun? Stettmeier snatched up a fireplace poker as Mendoza threw Perez's wife to the floor and stood on one side of the door. Stettmeier raised the poker as the door opened. He nearly brought it down on the pretty blonde head of Misty Love.

"What the hell?" Misty croaked.

Mendoza grabbed her by the arm, pulled her inside, slammed the door, and locked it tight. Misty tried to pull free, but Mendoza wouldn't let her go.

"That's M-M-Misty," Stettmeier stuttered. "My lady!"

Misty got right up in Mendoza's face. "Who the fuck are you?"

"That's Mendoza," Stettmeier said. "Try not to make him mad."

CHAPTER TWENTY-FOUR

The National Old Trails Road Association formed in 1912 to promote a highway that would link Los Angeles with New York. Much of that same road later became Route 66. Starting in Chicago, it headed west across Missouri, Kansas, Oklahoma, Texas, and Arizona before crossing the Colorado River into California. It was the route the Joad family took in "The Grapes of Wrath." It ran right through Pasadena as Colorado Boulevard and continued on to Eagle Rock and downtown L.A. It traversed West Hollywood and Beverly Hills before coming to an abrupt end at the Pacific Ocean. The sign on Santa Monica pier still reads SANTA MONICA: END OF THE TRAIL.

The words "aiding and abetting" kept going through Sancho's head. *Aiding and abetting escaped mental patients. Aiding and abetting escaped fugitives. Aiding and abetting an assault on police officers.* He'd seen enough cop shows to know that aiding and abetting was bad.

The speeding and reckless driving charges were his responsibility. And hitting the sheriff's deputy with the door of his own car? That wasn't good. That was a hit-and-run. No aiding and abetting there. Those crimes were his and his alone.

What was I thinking?

He wasn't thinking. He didn't take the time to think. He just knew Flynn and that crazy chica needed help. And now he had no clue where to go. Sancho didn't want to put his abuela, tata, or mom in danger. He couldn't go to their house. *So where?* The police saw the Aston Martin right before it hit their patrol car.

Not exactly the most anonymous vehicle. The *popo* probably caught the license plate and called it in.

Time to get off the road and hole up somewhere far from Pico Rivera. Some cheap-ass motel. He didn't want to use a credit card. The police would trace it right back to him. And he didn't have much cash, so he needed the cheapest motel they could find. That would be the Happy Host Motel on East Colorado. A one-star shithole between a Buick Dealer and Korean BBQ.

Caitlyn looked frazzled and on edge. Her face smudged, her short, dark hair everywhere. The result of being tased and shot at and chased. Sancho knew the feeling. People who hang with Flynn tend to get tased and shot at and chased. Flynn didn't look frazzled at all. He seemed his usual unruffled self. Cool and collected, unconcerned and somewhat amused. Flynn loved this kind of shit. This is what he lived for. Sancho caught his friend's eye in the rearview mirror.

"I assume you have a destination in mind," Flynn queried.

"I do," Sancho said.

"A safe house?"

"A shithole."

"Where they don't ask too many questions?"

Sancho nodded. "Exactly."

"You came by just in the nick of time." Flynn smiled. "As usual."

"Who the hell were those guys? Are they with Mendoza?"

"Caitlyn? Would you like to tell him?"

Caitlyn shook her head like a sullen teenager. "He doesn't need to know."

Sancho took a hard right. "What do you mean, I don't need to know?"

"They call themselves The Army of God," Flynn said.

"So, people really *are* after her?"

"She discovered a vast conspiracy…"

"Of course she did."

"...to bring on Armageddon."

Sancho smiled at that and caught Caitlyn's angry eyes in the rearview mirror.

She pointed her thumb at Flynn. "You think I'm as crazy as him, don't you?"

"I don't know what to think, but I do know you're in trouble."

"We're *all* in trouble." Caitlyn sat back and sourly looked out the window.

■   ■   ■

The front desk clerk at the Happy Host Motel wasn't happy to see Sancho. The middle-aged lady was busy watching something on her phone and didn't appreciate the interruption. "What?" she barked at him.

"Can I get a room? I'd like to pay cash."

"How many nights?"

"Just tonight. For now."

"Fifty-seven dollars."

Sancho counted out the money, handed it over, and she counted it again. She picked out a key, but didn't hand it over. "Five-dollar key deposit."

"Key deposit?"

"Five dollars."

Sancho pulled out a five and exchanged it for the key, saying a sarcastic, "Thank you."

"Room 102. Don't use the pool."

Flynn and Caitlyn waited by the Aston Martin as their faces were all over the news and Flynn only wore his boxers. Sancho had parked in the back lot between a large pickup truck and a delivery van. A maid pushing a cleaning cart caught sight of Flynn in his underwear. She narrowed her eyes. Flynn smiled and waved. Shaking her head, she continued on.

The room smelled of cigarette smoke. The two double beds, mussed and wrinkled, looked like someone had recently been laying on them. Sancho tried to turn on the TV. Nothing.

He still had a box of Flynn's clothes in the trunk of his car, part of the collection he'd brought home from the hospital after Flynn was sent to Hornitos. He hauled them in and Flynn found some well-worn Bally loafers, a Sea Island cotton shirt, and a dark blue single-breasted Zegna suit. He didn't bother with a tie.

Caitlyn stood by the window and peered through a crack in the plastic blackout curtains. Flynn approached her. "What do you see out there?"

"Some asshole getting high."

"I think we're safe here for now, but we need to decide our next steps."

Sancho sat on a rickety chair by a rickety desk. He didn't want to chance sitting on the bed. "I'm thinking we should contact Dr. Michaels," Sancho said.

Flynn shook his head. "Not until we solve Caitlyn's situation. If her enemies have infiltrated the highest levels of the U.S. government, they might also have moles in our operation as well. It's hard to know who to trust. Speaking of which…" Flynn aimed his eyes at Caitlyn. "How do you think they tracked you down?"

"No idea."

"Perhaps they implanted you with a microscopic tracking device. An RFID chip inserted under your skin."

"Yeah, I don't think so."

"How do you know? I think you should take off your clothes and let me search every square inch of you. From head to toe."

Caitlyn smirked. "Yeah, like I'm falling for that."

"I'm not trying to seduce you, Miss Valentine. I'm just trying to protect you. Of course, if *you* wanted to seduce *me*, I wouldn't say no."

"Do you ever say no?"

"Not very often." Flynn glanced at Sancho. "Have you called Alyssa yet?"

"I was going to call her right now."

"She probably shouldn't go home."

"No shit." Sancho pulled out his iPhone.

"You know the police can track that, right?" Caitlyn said.

"I won't talk long. I just need to let her know—"

Flynn grabbed the phone out of Sancho's hand and cracked it in half before dropping it on the floor and stomping it into pieces.

"What the hell, dude?"

"Better safe than sorry, my friend." He pointed to an ancient push-button phone on the table between the beds. "Better you call her on that."

"If she doesn't recognize the number, she might not pick up."'

"Leave a message then."

It took Sancho a minute to remember Alyssa's cell number, as it wasn't something he usually needed to remember. It rang twice before she picked up.

"Hello?" Alyssa sounded suspicious and agitated.

"Hey, sweetie. I'm so glad you picked up."

"What phone number is this?"

"Not important. I'm not home right now and you can't go home either. Some people came looking for Flynn and we got away and I'm okay, but I'm not sure it's safe there for you right now. Can you go to your parent's house? Just for tonight. Just 'til we figure out what's going on?"

Alyssa didn't reply. The silence stretched for ten seconds. Twenty seconds. Thirty seconds. "Alyssa, you there? Alyssa?"

"She's here." Mendoza said. "If Flynn is with you, say yes."

Terror took Sancho by the throat and squeezed tight. He struggled to stay calm. *Stay strong. Stay in the moment.* "Yes."

"Do not say my name. Do not react. Do not let Flynn know I have your wife. If you understand, say yes."

"Yes."

"Good. If you say anything to Flynn, she dies along with your unborn child. There is only one way to save them. Tell me where you and Flynn are. Do this and I won't hurt her. Once I have Flynn, she will be safe. You'll be safe. Your baby will be safe. If you understand, say okay."

Sancho kept smiling as he wiped the sweat off his forehead. He caught Flynn looking at him and nodded and smiled back at him, raising a thumb. "Okay."

"Now tell me where you are."

"Honey, I'm thinking maybe you should come here instead of going to your parent's house. If they know you're married to me, they might be watching their house as well."

"What's the address?"

"I don't know the exact address, but we're at the Happy Host Motel on East Colorado. It's between that big Buick dealer and the Korean BBQ. Across the street from the Hot Yoga place you used to go to. Room 102."

"If you tell him I'm coming, I'll kill her. He won't be able to save her and he won't be able to save you. Now tell me you love me."

Sancho swallowed a mouthful of bile. "I love you."

"I love you too." Mendoza snickered wickedly and hung up.

Sancho looked up. Flynn watched him. "Is she on her way?"

"She is."

Flynn narrowed his eyes. "Are you okay?"

"Just worried about her."

"She's a strong girl. She'll be fine."

Sancho nodded. "Gotta pee." He went into the disgusting little bathroom and stared at himself in the smeary mirror. The sink had black hairs in it. He wanted to throw up, but he didn't want to kneel on the dirty floor. He also didn't want to give Flynn any reason to worry. He rinsed the curly black hairs down the sink, splashed some water on his face, and dried himself with a stiff musty hand towel.

CHAPTER TWENTY-FIVE

Sancho exited the tiny bathroom to find Caitlyn and Flynn deep in a contentious conversation. Caitlyn paced and shook her head. "No. *No*. I said *no*."

"We can stop this," Flynn insisted.

"No. We can't. I tried, but no one believed me. They locked me up. They put me away. These people are *too powerful*."

Flynn didn't back down. "So you're okay with just walking away?"

"Of course not, but you don't understand how influential they are. They are everywhere."

"Hiding in plain sight."

"Yes. They are respected. They are revered. Irreproachable. Unimpeachable. Untouchable."

"But you found out they weren't what they seemed."

"I did."

"How? How did you do it?"

"How did I do what?"

"Uncover the plot."

"It doesn't matter."

"It does to me. Start at the beginning. When did you join the C.I.A.?"

Caitlyn sighed and stopped pacing to sit on the wrinkled bedspread. "They recruited me out of college."

"Which one?"

"Stanford. I double-majored in computer science and international economics."

"You have a knack for languages?"

"I speak fluent French and Spanish and passable German and Russian."

"No wonder the C.I.A. recruited you."

"My plan was to work in cyber security. But after my initial training, they decided I might have an aptitude for deep cover operations."

"They sent you to the Farm?"

"That's right. They trained me in surveillance, counter-surveillance, cryptography. I even had classes in the science behind WMDs, chemical weapons, nuclear weapons."

"From your skill set, I assume that included paramilitary training?"

Caitlyn nodded. "Everything from weapons to defensive driving to hand-to-hand combat."

"Is that where you learned Shotokan?"

"I studied karate as a kid. From age twelve through high school. I even competed and won a few tournaments. At The Farm, they teach less formal and more lethal martial arts."

"Krav Maga?"

"And Jeet Kune Do."

"Did they assign you to the Special Activities Center?"

Sancho could tell Caitlyn was surprised by Flynn's insider knowledge. "No. Not right away. They wanted to build a bulletproof cover for me. They arranged for me to go to the London School of Economics. I graduated with a Global Executive MBA. After that, they got me in the door at HSBC as a software expert in the compliance office."

"The Hongkong and Shanghai Bank?"

"Yes."

"That's the largest investment bank in London." Flynn raised an eyebrow. "Why'd they send you there?"

"They wanted me to investigate international money-laundering."

"Any luck?"

"Oh, yeah, I uncovered all kinds of dirt. And when things got too hot, I went to work for Accenture."

"The multinational consultancy?"

"The C.I.A. has a lot of their people working undercover in multinationals."

Flynn nodded. "Makes sense."

"My remit was to monitor international banking and root out money laundering by terrorist networks, rogue governments, and transnational crime syndicates. Then to use that information to pressure various bad actors into providing additional inside intelligence."

"Is that how you stumbled into the plot?"

"As a senior analyst for Accenture, they sent me to work on a project for The Bank of the East in Cyprus. I worked with their compliance department to create an algorithm that would flag any large money transfers. I found billions hidden in hundreds of mysterious shell corporations. Money being laundered for Russian oligarchs, Mexican drug cartels, and African dictators. But then I found something even more surprising. Millions were being moved from The Bank of the East to a U.S.-based religious organization. The Church of the Prophecy."

"So this church was helping to clean dirty money?"

"And taking a generous percentage. They'd funnel millions of dollars in donations to dozens of non-profits owned by other various mysterious shell corporations."

"All controlled by those same oligarchs, drug cartels, and dictators?"

"Exactly. But here's what's really strange. The Pastor of that Church was a retired Marine Colonel. Calvin J. Henderson. The Church's board of directors are all former military men. The chairman is a retired general. Jedidiah Anderson."

"The billionaire defense contractor?"

Caitlyn nodded. "And one of the founders of The Army of God."

"Why would a bunch of right-wing religious zealots want to help dictators, oligarchs, and drug cartels?"

"Because the Church of the Prophecy holds to a literal interpretation of the Book of Revelations. They believe it is their responsibility to hasten the end of days by bringing on the Battle of Armageddon."

"And how do they plan to instigate this battle?"

"With a false flag terrorist attack so heinous it would precipitate World War Three."

"Another 9/11?"

"But much, much worse. I passed this information to my immediate superior, hoping he might authorize a full-on investigation. Do you know what he did?"

"Nothing."

"That's right. He told me to stand down. General Jedediah Anderson runs a super PAC that funnels millions to conservative causes. He is a major defense contractor and the great, great, grandson of a famous Confederate general. Richard "Fighting Dick" Anderson."

"But you didn't stand down, did you?"

"No, in fact, him wanting me to stand down only made me more suspicious. More determined. My superiors made sure that Accenture put me on another project. They sent me to the Silicon Valley to work on corporate cybersecurity. They were hoping I would let it go. But I didn't. I kept at it. I figured if I could find hard evidence on Anderson, they couldn't ignore it. So I hacked into the Church of the Prophesy and The Army of God. I accessed their private email and voice mail. I cloned phones. I broke encryption. I recorded their phone conversations and learned they had the help of at least one U.S. Senator."

"Alton Jeffers."

"Yes, and I discovered a false flag plot to foment a war in the middle east. I didn't have the specifics, but I did find evidence that they were actively trying to acquire a nuclear device to use against a target in the United States."

Worried as Sancho was about Mendoza's imminent arrival, the idea that a mysterious cabal of retired generals was working to acquire a nuke for a false flag operation was even more worrying. How could he just sit here and not say anything about Mendoza? He could save Flynn or he could save Alyssa and his unborn baby. He couldn't save both. If anything happened to Alyssa, it would break him. It would destroy him. So he sat there in silence, frozen with indecision.

This plot Caitlyn was laying out might not even be real. Even if she was once a C.I.A. officer, she could still be crazy. Sure, people were trying to kill her, but she went after terrorists and drug cartels. Any or all of them could want her dead. Didn't that make more sense than some doomsday plot to blow up the world?

Flynn rose to his feet and paced. "Did you take all that evidence to your supervisor?"

"I did and he reprimanded me for disobeying a direct order."

"He may have been involved with them. He may have been one of them."

"Yeah, that's what I thought, and I didn't know where else to turn. So I went after the Senator. I contacted him discreetly and let him know I was with *the company* and that we knew what he was doing. He admitted to me he was having second thoughts. I wasn't sure if he was trying to set me up, or simply trying to save his own ass, but in the end he slipped me actionable information and even promised to testify. This time, I went above my immediate superior's head. I went to my boss's boss. He thanked me. He promised me he would act on my information immediately. One week later, Jeffers was dead and I was in jail, framed for his murder."

Flynn sat next to her on the wrinkly bedspread. "How would you feel if you heard that terrorists detonated a nuclear bomb in Manhattan, killing tens of thousands?"

"We can't stop them."

"I don't disagree that our enemies are far more powerful than we are, but if we give up, if we walk away, if we don't even try… we stand no chance at all. You're not doing this alone now. You're doing this with me."

"And you are certifiably crazy."

Sancho pulled the rickety desk chair closer to Caitlyn and sat right across from her. "Maybe because that's what it takes. Maybe you *gotta* be a little crazy to think you can save the world. I've seen this vato loco pull off shit you wouldn't believe. Shit no sane person would ever do. Yet, here he is and so's the world."

Flynn patted Sancho on the knee. "I didn't do it alone, my friend. You were there at my side. Each and every time."

"Pissing my pants every step of the way."

"Nelson Mandela said 'Courage is not the absence of fear, but the triumph over it.'"

"And speaking of courage, there's something I need to say." Sancho took a deep breath. "Mendoza is on his way."

"Excuse me?"

"He has Alyssa, and he threatened to kill her if I didn't tell him where you were."

Caitlyn leaped to her feet, furious. "You what!"

Flynn rose as well, holding her back. "What else could he do? He was put in an impossible position." He turned to Sancho and put his hands on his shoulders. "But in the end, you did the right thing. I appreciate you telling us the truth, old friend."

"I'm so sorry, brother, but when I called her, Mendoza picked up. I didn't know what to do."

"So you gave us up?" Caitlyn shouted.

A Molotov cocktail crashed through the window and set the drapes on fire.

Flynn grabbed Caitlyn by the arm and pulled her towards the door as the wall and then the bed went up in flames. Sancho choked on the thick, black smoke filling the room. He followed Flynn out the door and that's where they found Mendoza.

He didn't have Alyssa, but he did have a gun — some kind of revolver. He aimed it at Flynn. Caitlyn kicked Flynn sideways just as Mendoza pulled the trigger. He fired again, but Flynn dove behind Sancho's DB9. Mendoza swung his gun on Caitlyn and squeezed off three shots, missing her with each one as she sprinted across the parking lot and jumped behind a dumpster.

Sancho's Aston Martin roared to life. He watched as it screamed backwards out of its parking spot and thundered across the lot towards Mendoza. The *sicario* put a bullet through the rear window an instant before the car plowed into him. His bulk left a massive dent and his head shattered the already cracked back window.

Mendoza rolled off and hit the ground hard. He fired fruitlessly at the car, his last three bullets ricocheting off the back bumper. Sancho watched as the big man staggered to his feet, flipped open the cylinder, and shook out the spent shells.

Sancho darted for his quickly departing car. By the time Mendoza's giant sausage fingers reloaded his weapon, he and Caitlyn had jumped inside.

Sancho sat in the back seat and peered out the shattered rear window to see a furious Mendoza taking aim. He ducked. Bullets peppered the back of the car as Flynn accelerated out of there, squealing into the street and down the block. Sancho looked back. A furious Mendoza stamped his foot in anger as the Happy Host Motel receded into the distance.

Sancho felt sick inside and noticed Flynn staring at him in the rearview mirror. "Fear not, my friend, Mendoza doesn't know you gave him up. Call her number. I'm sure he still has her phone. String him along. Let him think you're still working for him. Tell him you'll hand over my location as soon as we land somewhere. In the meantime, we'll work up a plan to find and rescue your sweet Alyssa." Flynn glanced at Caitlyn. "Is there some way we can track her cellphone?"

"There might be, but I'll need a decent computer with a high-speed connection."

Flynn nodded. "I think that's doable."

CHAPTER TWENTY-SIX

Sancho called Alyssa's phone from the back seat of the speeding DB9. Mendoza answered, his voice cold and furious. "Did you tell him I was coming?"

"Of course not. He was there, wasn't he? If he knew you were coming, he would have been long gone."

"Are you with him now?"

"Yes, and I'll stay with him."

"He can't hear you right now?"

"No."

"Do you know where he's going?"

"He won't say. But I'll tell you as soon as we get there."

"If you cross me, she dies."

"Hurt her, and I have no reason to help you."

"And I have no reason to hurt her. Unless you give me one." Mendoza clicked off.

Sancho studied the back of Flynn's head. "He thinks I'm still working for him."

"Good," Flynn replied.

"So what's the plan?"

"Step one, we need to regroup and reassess."

"Mendoza won't wait forever."

"He's waited this long. He can wait a little longer. He won't hurt her. She's his only leverage."

"So, where are we going?"

"A place we can hide and get some help and, hopefully, a computer."

"Where would that be?"

"Malibu."

Caitlyn turned to look at Flynn. "Malibu?"

"Sancho and I have an old friend there. It's a bit of a drive and you look rather knackered, so I'd suggest you get a bit of a kip."

"I have no idea what you just said," Caitlyn replied.

"Take a nap. Rest your eyes. We'll be there before you know it."

■ ■ ■

Caitlyn considered jumping out of the car at the next stoplight, but she had no money, no plan, and nowhere to run. She couldn't go to her mother or her brother. The government convinced them both she was crazy. She never told either one she worked for the C.I.A. It was against company policy. So when she finally told her mom the truth, that the Central Intelligence Agency had set her up, her mom looked at her like she *was* crazy and gladly signed the papers to have her committed. Caitlyn walked away from all her old friends when she joined the agency. She made a few new friends when she went through training. Friends who did what she did. But when *the company* turned on her, so did they.

Now she had no one to help her and nowhere to go. No one except for a totally delusional psycho. For now, she needed to ride this out. Besides, Sancho needed her help. Mendoza was an even bigger psycho than Flynn. So she would do what she needed to help him, but then she was out.

Caitlyn closed her eyes as they merged onto the Ventura Freeway; the next time she opened them, the Pacific Ocean stretched before her. An orange sun hovered over the horizon and slowly sank into the sea. She loved the beach. She loved to surf. And she recognized one of her favorite spots. Topanga. Caitlyn grew up in Santa Monica, but left Southern California for college. That's how she ended up at Stanford. But whenever she visited her mom, she'd break out her wetsuit and surfboard and hit the beach at Topanga.

Lines of surfers tried to catch a wave. She envied their freedom. What she wouldn't give to be out there with them. They cruised past Malibu Lagoon and then Flynn made a left at Webb Way towards Malibu Colony. *Who the hell would Flynn know here?* The most famous movie stars in the world lived in the Colony. The average house cost upwards of ten million. She also knew it was gated and heavily guarded. They'd have to pass a security kiosk with a camera.

Sancho tapped Flynn on the shoulder. "Dude, maybe you should let me drive us in. I'm not as famous as you."

Flynn nodded. "Not a bad idea." He pulled the car over onto the shoulder. Flynn climbed into the trunk and Sancho closed the lid before getting behind the wheel.

He navigated the tiny, winding road and pulled the Aston Martin up to the security kiosk. He lowered his window. The security guard approached and Sancho smiled up at him. "We're here to see Alessandra Zimmel."

The guard scrutinized the dented front bumper and blown out rear window. "What's your name?"

"Sancho Perez."

He looked through a binder. "I don't see your name on the list."

"It's kind of a surprise."

He regarded Sancho skeptically. "So she's not expecting you?"

The guard glanced at Caitlyn, who turned her face slightly away and pretended to look for something in the glove compartment.

"No, sir. Like I said, we wanted to surprise her."

"I'm sorry, but I can't let you in if you're not on the list. I'm sure you understand."

"I do. Tell Mrs. Zimmel that Sancho Perez is here to see her. She'll know who I am."

The guard went back into the kiosk, picked up a phone receiver, and placed a call. Caitlyn couldn't hear the conversation, but she saw him nod. He hung up and walked back to the car. "Can I see some ID, Mr. Perez?"

Sancho pulled his driver's license out of his wallet and held it up for the guy to see. He nodded. "Okay, thank you, Mr. Perez. Sorry I had to ruin your surprise."

"No problem, officer. I totally understand."

The man nodded and returned to the kiosk, pushed a button and the lift gate rose. Sancho smiled at him as they pulled past and headed south on Malibu Colony Road. They drove by incredible mansions sitting right on the beach. Most were mid-century or contemporary multi-storied houses standing side by side with very little yard. They finally came to a stop by a somewhat modest-looking Cape Cod-style beach cottage with a steep slate roof, whitewashed shingle siding, and an abundance of multi-paned windows.

Caitlyn climbed out, curious as hell who might live here. The trunk lid opened and Flynn climbed out, looking elegant in his Zegna suit and not the slightest bit ruffled.

The door to the beach house opened and out stepped an attractive older woman wearing faded blue jeans, a black turtleneck, and a long blue cardigan sweater. She had a big smile on her face and a tiny Pomeranian in her arms. Something about her seemed awfully familiar to Caitlyn. And then it hit her. *Of course.* Alessandra Bianchi. Caitlyn read all about how she and Flynn exposed that pig of a film producer, Gary Goldhammer. She still looked every bit the movie star. Her shoulder-length silver hair framed high, angular cheekbones. Tall and slender, she moved with a dancer's grace and posture. She had to be in her seventies, but even without makeup, she was stunning.

Alessandra and Flynn embraced. She hugged him close and then held him at arm's length. "James Flynn. What a sight for sore eyes."

"Hello Alessandra. You look beautiful as ever."

"So do you, young man." She cupped Flynn's face the way a mother might. "I've been following your adventures on the news."

"Don't believe everything you hear."

"You just can't stay out of trouble, can you?" She smiled at Sancho. "Mr. Perez. It's good to see you too."

"Hi, Mrs. Zimmel."

"Alessandra, please." She then turned to Caitlyn. "And who is this lovely young lady?"

Flynn grinned. "Alessandra, meet Caitlyn Valentine."

"Good to meet you, Caitlyn." She glanced back at Flynn. "You just can't help yourself, can you, James? Always rescuing damsels in distress."

"She's rescued me more times than I've rescued her," Flynn admitted.

"I think we're even," Caitlyn said as she shook Alessandra's hand. "It's a pleasure to meet you, Miss Bianchi. Or do you prefer Zimmel?"

"Alessandra, please. Miss Bianchi is who I used to be. Before I married my Phil. Of course, now I'm on my own again." She waved them in. "Come! Come inside before someone recognizes you."

Caitlyn's anxiety level lowered as she followed Alessandra inside her cozy and peaceful abode. If she ever had a ten-million-dollar house on the beach, she would decorate it just like this one. The high beamed ceilings, cream white walls, and beautiful Plein air paintings created a cheery sense of calm. Floor-to-ceiling windows offered a spectacular view of the Pacific. The shabby-chic furniture adorned with throw blankets and soft decorative pillows looked inviting.

"Please. Sit. Relax. Rest. Who would like a glass of wine?"

Caitlyn raised her hand as she sat on a couch and marveled at how comfortable it was. "Nice couch."

"Do you like Chardonnay? Or would prefer a glass of Merlot?"

"Chardonnay please."

"James, would you like a vodka martini? I also have a bottle of Bowmore. I'm not much of a scotch drinker, by my Phil loved a good whiskey."

"Whiskey sounds marvelous."

"Sancho?"

"Do you have any beer?"

"I do indeed."

Alessandra poured their drinks and joined them in the living room. Caitlyn sipped her excellent chardonnay and watched the sun sink into the Pacific. The tiny Pomeranian leaped up on the couch next to Caitlyn and rolled over on its back for a belly rub.

"Peanut loves her belly rubs," Alessandra said.

Caitlyn rubbed Peanut's belly and the tiny Pomeranian closed her eyes with ecstasy.

"We're in a bit of a jam," Flynn said.

"From what I've seen on the news, I would agree," Alessandra said. "Of course, you're welcome to stay here as long as you need to."

"I don't want to get you in any trouble."

"No trouble. It's wonderful to have the company."

"Even so, it's not safe for you. The people after us are quite dangerous."

"So you're not just running from the authorities?"

"No. Caitlyn here is ex-CIA, and she uncovered a vast conspiracy that reaches to the highest levels of our government."

Alessandra looked to Sancho. He nodded his head. "Somebody is definitely trying to kill her."

"And somebody has kidnapped Alyssa," Flynn added. "An enemy of ours from the past. A man by the name of Mendoza."

Alessandra nodded. "Didn't he also escape from Hornitos? They said on the news he was an enforcer for the Goolardo Cartel."

"He has tried to kill me more than once and took Alyssa as leverage. He wants my life for hers."

"Do you know where he's holding her?"

"No, which is why we need your help. Caitlyn needs a computer with a high-speed internet connection."

"I may be seventy-nine, but I'm not a complete Luddite."

Caitlyn set down her Chardonnay. "What kind of computer do you have?"

"A MacBook Pro. And I believe my Spectrum plan is the fastest they have. Nine hundred and forty megabits per second. Will that work?"

"That's perfect."

CHAPTER TWENTY-SEVEN

Caitlyn followed Alessandra into her book-lined study. The MacBook sat on an impressive antique desk near a window that looked out on the dark ocean. When Caitlyn put her nose up to the window and shielded her eyes from the room light, she saw foam and breaking waves lit by moonlight.

"My password is Peanut."

Caitlyn smiled at that and looked around the room. Framed movie posters covered the walls. All featured a young Alessandra in bikinis or hot pants or miniskirts. *What's New Pussycat* with Peter Sellers. *Fun in Acapulco* with Elvis Presley. *The Wrecking Crew* with Dean Martin. An eclectic collection of books filled the shelves; everything from *The Feminine Mystique* to *One Hundred Years of Solitude* to *Walden*. A tarnished Golden Globe served as a bookend.

"That's my only award," Alessandra said. "1963. Most Promising Newcomer."

"Pretty impressive."

"To be honest, that award was more about P.R. than talent. The studio wanted their own European sex symbol, and they paid to put me on the cover of Vogue, Elle, and Glamour. But I was just one of many. Sophia Loren, Gina Lollobrigida, Ursula Andress were all much bigger stars than me."

"I think I've seen almost all your movies."

"Really?"

"On TMC."

"I didn't know I had any fans your age."

"You grew up in Italy?"

She nodded. "I lost most of my family in the war. So it was just me and my mamma."

"It must have been hard."

"It wasn't easy. I was always hungry, which is why I love to eat. I was just a *bambina* when the Americans liberated Rome. They were so kind. So friendly. So generous. They gave me C-Rations. They gave me Hershey bars. My mom even dated an American for a while." Alessandra smiled, remembering. "Mike. He would take my mother and I to American movies and I would dream about living here. Where everything was so new and clean and no one ever went to bed hungry. I won a beauty pageant at fifteen and Vittorio De Sica saw me and put me in a movie. As soon as I could, I came to Hollywood. But my English wasn't so good. It got better over time, but I never lost my accent."

"I love your accent."

"Would you like another glass of wine?"

"No, I'm good."

"Good. If you need anything else, let me know." She pointed at the MacBook. "I hope you can find what you're looking for."

"Can I ask you something?"

"Of course."

"You seem to trust Flynn."

Alessandra smiled. "I do."

"Why?"

"Because he has never lied to me. He always watched out for me. Always did the right thing. Even if it didn't always seem like the smart thing. Or the logical thing. Or the sane thing. Yes, he's delusional, but somehow he still sees the world very clearly."

. . .

One bite and Caitlyn was in heaven. "Oh, my God! What is this?"

Alessandra smiled. "Spaghetti Carbonara. My mother's recipe."

Caitlyn pointed with her fork. "Is there bacon in this?"

"My mother used guanciale, but slab bacon works just as well. You fry it up real crispy and stir in a little garlic. Whisk up eggs and Pecorino Romano cheese with some black pepper. Some people use cream, but my mother never did and who needs that much extra fat? Carbonara has enough calories as it is."

"You still count your calories?"

"I may be old, but I'm not ready to let myself go completely. So I walk. I exercise. But I also like to eat." She looked across at Flynn. "What do you think, James?"

"It's the best Carbonara I've ever tasted."

She looked at Sancho. His food sat untouched. "So, no luck tracking Alyssa's cellphone?"

"Not yet," Caitlyn said. "But I'm using an app called Stealthtrack. It sends a text to her phone with a picture. Clicking on it installs malware, activates the GPS antenna, and sends me a message, pinpointing the location on Google maps."

"Do they know they're being tracked?"

"No, they do not. "

"What about the Army of God?" Flynn asked. "Any luck hacking into their server?"

"After I hacked them the first time, they must have put in all kinds of security software, because I can't crack it. I tried for two hours, but I couldn't get in."

"So, how do we get the information off it?"

"We have to access it directly."

"You mean physically?"

"It's the only way. I've pinpointed the IP address, so I know where the server's located."

"At the Church of the Prophesy in Orange County?"

Caitlyn shook her head. "Ten miles outside Cody, Wyoming."

Flynn's eyes widened. "Cody, Wyoming?"

"On General Jedidiah Anderson's 3500-acre ranch."

Flynn nodded and sipped some wine. "Then I suppose that's where we need to go."

"We? I don't think so."

"If they're as powerful as you say they are, there's no running from them. They'll use every resource they have to find you wherever you go."

Caitlyn put down her fork. "I'll help find Alyssa, but after that—I'm done."

"Then I'll go on my own."

"On your own? That ranch is an Army of God training camp. Hundreds of soldiers. And these aren't weekend warriors. To join, you have to be ex-military or ex-law enforcement. But unlike the Oath Keepers, these aren't just grunts. They are elite fighters. Rangers. Delta. Navy Seals. And not just noncoms, but officers. Majors. Colonels. Brigadier Generals. There's no way you're getting in there. Not on your own."

Flynn shrugged. "Easy or not, if that's how we find out what's on their server, that's what I need to do."

Sancho chimed in. "But first we get Alyssa away from Mendoza, right?"

Flynn nodded. "Of course. Saving your bride is our first priority."

Alessandra looked up from her carbonara. "General Jedidiah Anderson? Why do I know that name?"

"He was caught up in a scandal about ten years ago," Caitlyn said. "The Washington Post did a big story on it."

"What kind of scandal?" Sancho asked.

"He ran a training program for missile launch officers at Vandenberg Air Force Base. Part of that training involved religious indoctrination. He had chaplains teaching a course on the theological justification for nuclear war. A PowerPoint presentation that referenced religious figures and quotes from the bible."

"What part of the bible justifies nuclear war?"

"The Book of Revelations, according to him. The Air Force offered him early retirement and he went to work for Raytheon before finding investors to start his own thing."

Alessandra looked at Flynn. "So he's part of that vast conspiracy you referenced earlier?"

"He is indeed," Flynn said.

She turned her gaze back to Caitlyn. "And you don't think he can be stopped?"

"No. I don't."

"So you're going to let James do this on his own?"

"There's nothing to be done."

"I wouldn't be so sure," Alessandra said.

■　■　■

Flynn stood in Alessandra's white-tiled walk-in shower and let the multiple showerheads pummel his body. His muscles loosened under the hot high-pressure spray. Flynn bent at the waist as the water pounded his back. Then he turned it all the way cold, as was his usual practice, and stood in the icy stream until he couldn't stand it any longer. He dried himself off with a thick Turkish towel and wrapped it around his waist. The large bathroom was foggy with steam as he opened the door.

Caitlyn stood there wearing one of Alessandra's terry cloth robes, open at the throat to reveal a bit of cleavage. For all her cold fury and emotional distance, Flynn found her quite attractive. She wasn't a classic beauty like Alessandra, but her body was long, lean, and athletic. Her eyes were striking and she had a beautiful smile when she deigned to flash it. Which wasn't very often. She trusted no one and he understood why. Everyone she depended on had turned against her. It's why she felt she couldn't afford to show any openness or vulnerability. Even so, she checked him out from head to toe. Not bashful at all. They had an awkward moment as they stepped around each other. Flynn turned back to check her out one more time, only to see she was checking him out as well.

Later, she joined him on the outside deck for a glass of wine. For the first time in a long time, they were alone.

Caitlyn stared out at the whitecaps gleaming in the moonlight. "I used to watch her when I was a kid."

"Watch who?"

"Alessandra. I was sick a lot when I was little and had to stay home from school. I'd turn on the TV while I did my homework. They'd play all these movies from the sixties and seventies. Action movies were my favorite, and she was in a lot of them. She played this one character that really stuck with me. A female cat burglar. Veronica Steele. She wore this black cat suit and knew karate. She was beautiful and smart and she wasn't afraid of anybody or anything. She was everything I wanted to be, but wasn't. I was skinny. I had acne. I was shy. I was bullied."

"You?"

"Junior high was hell for me."

"Hard to imagine."

"Right... so I reimagined myself. I asked my mom for karate lessons. I lost weight and worked out like a maniac. I had a black belt by the time I was fifteen. I wasn't too concerned with my feminine side, but boys seemed to notice me anyway. I started hanging out with a bunch of guys who did parkour and got pretty good at that too."

"So you've always been an athlete."

"I ran track in high school and competed as a pole vaulter. I placed first in the state and Stanford gave me a full ride."

"So you became Veronica Steele?"

"More like Lisbeth Salander."

Flynn grinned. "The Girl with The Dragon Tattoo?"

"Turns out I had a real aptitude for anything that had to do with computers and I turned myself into somebody new. But that little girl who was bullied..." Caitlyn tapped her fingers against her chest. "She's still in here too."

"I understand."

"Do you?"

"I do. None of us are just one thing. And look at you now. You told the truth to the powerful and they tried to crush you. But here you are. Undaunted. Unbowed. Brilliant. Brave. Beautiful."

"Are you flirting with me, Mr. Flynn?"

"Would it bother you if I was?"

"I don't think our relationship needs to be any more complicated than it already is."

"Perhaps you're right. It's just that imminent death is often the ultimate aphrodisiac."

"Is it now?"

"Indeed. The possibility of one's potential demise often engenders a primal desire to procreate. It's part of the biological imperative to perpetuate the species."

"That's quite a come on. Does that usually work for you?"

Before Flynn could answer, Alessandra poked her head through the French doors. "Caitlyn. Looks like you got your message."

■　■　■

Caitlyn worked the mouse pad on the MacBook as Flynn, Alessandra, and Sancho hovered behind her. She clicked on a link, which brought up a map with a highlighted circle indicating the approximate location of Alyssa's cellphone.

"They're at Stettmeier's," Sancho said.

"Dennis Stettmeier?" Flynn asked.

"I told you he and Mendoza were working together. They're at his new place in Eagle Rock."

Flynn tapped the screen. "That's quite a distance away."

"So we better get moving," Sancho said.

Caitlyn nodded. "But not in your Aston Martin. By now, the police probably have an APB out on it."

"Borrow one of my cars then," Alessandra said.

"Are you sure? I wouldn't want the authorities to charge you as an accessory after the fact."

"I'll say you stole it. Along with my laptop and a few of my late husband's weapons. Philip had quite the collection."

Between the Jaguar, Bentley, and the Maserati Levante SUV, Flynn went for the Maserati. Alessandra explained she bought it to replace her late husband's Aston Martin. The one Flynn apparently totaled in their last adventure together. She then led them to her late husband's gun safe where Flynn selected a Desert Eagle Mark XIX pistol with a walnut grip and gold-plated trigger. Caitlyn recognized it as one of the largest and most powerful handguns ever made. Flynn also grabbed a Browning Citori over-under shotgun. Caitlyn selected something smaller. A Rohrbough R9 Stealth Elite. Weighing under a pound, it would easily fit into her pocket.

Sancho moved the cardboard box of Flynn's clothes from the Aston Martin into the Maserati, and Alessandra handed Flynn a large manila envelope. "It's all the cash I have on hand. There's more where that came from, of course. I'm here if you need me and ready to help. Call anytime."

"You're a lifesaver," Flynn said.

Alessandra smiled and kissed Flynn's cheek. "You be careful."

"Always."

She gave Sancho a hug and then turned to Caitlyn. "It's been a pleasure."

"For me too."

"Do me a favor, though. Don't give up without a fight. You're stronger than you think and have more power than you know." She kissed her on the cheek. "*Coraggio!*"

The trio then climbed into the Maserati and headed for Highway One.

Sancho, sitting in the back seat, tapped Caitlyn on the shoulder. "What did she say to you?"

"*Coraggio,*" Caitlyn replied. "Courage."

CHAPTER TWENTY-EIGHT

Strippers date back to the bible and Salome's "Dance of the Seven Veils." Sally Rand later updated the veils to include dances with ostrich feather fans and balloons. She didn't actually bare anything too personal, but created the illusion and became a noted star of the burlesque stage. Gypsy Rose Lee took it further by dispensing with the ostrich feathers and the balloons and putting it all out there. A 1937 law made stripping illegal in the burlesque houses of New York, and the striptease went underground into back-alley grind houses and peepshows. The 1960s saw a revival with topless go-go dancing, which eventually led to the emergence of "Gentlemen's Clubs" and the ubiquitous pole dance. The pole dance actually dates back to the 1893 Chicago World's Fair, where Coochie-Coochie dancers would sensually gyrate around tent poles to pull in a crowd.

Mendoza hated strippers. He hated the phony come-ons and the pretend passion. Like they couldn't get enough of him. Like he was Antonio Banderas, Javier Bardem, and Benicio Del Toro, all rolled into one hot package. But Mendoza knew the fear his appearance provoked. His huge, flat, scarred, and pitted face. His cold, empty eyes. Or *eye* now that he only had one. The eye patch only made him more terrifying. Like a three-hundred-pound pirate.

So it annoyed him that Stettmeier's stripper girlfriend kept coming onto him. He knew it was mainly for self-preservation. He was a danger, and she was used to using her sexuality to tame brutal men. But it was more than that. Misty Love wanted to humiliate Stettmeier. Put him in his place. She liked Stettmeier's money, but not Stettmeier. Mendoza saw the loathing and resentment behind her practiced smile and pouty lips. The hate came off her in waves. Mendoza understood what it meant to live with that kind of hate.

At least they had that in common.

He sat on the couch and waited for Perez to call. Misty sat right next to him with her massive cleavage and her clammy hand on his knee, her stripper perfume choking the air. Stettmeier sat in a chair on the other side of the room and stared at Perez's pretty wife, sitting at the opposite end of the couch from Mendoza, her wrists and ankles bound tight with duct tape.

Mendoza knew Stettmeier wanted to say something to him, but the *maricón* was afraid. Afraid to even look him in the eye. The *ñoño* opened his mouth a few times to say something, but nothing came out.

Finally, Mendoza had enough. "What? What do you want to say to me?"

Stettmeier started, but then stopped himself. He opened his mouth again, but hesitated.

"*What?*"

"I don't think it's fair," Stettmeier mumbled.

"What's not fair?"

Stettmeier shrugged and hesitated and finally blurted, "That you want half the trust."

"You don't think that's fair?"

"What if I give you a quarter?"

"You already agreed to half."

"I didn't agree to anything."

Mendoza put his finger in Stettmeier's face. "I said I wanted half and you didn't say no. To me that means yes."

"Not to me."

"Why do you need more than half if you're dead? Because that's what you'll be if I don't kill Flynn. He knows what you did. He knows where you live."

"I just think that half's a lot."

"Fine. How about this then? After I kill him, I kill you. How's that sound?"

Misty stroked Mendoza's knee and let her hand drift down his inner thigh, her voice low and seductive. "What about me? You don't want to hurt me?"

"Yeah, you die too." He looked at Perez's wife at the far end of the couch. "All of you. Everybody."

Perez's wife trembled. Big tears rolled down her cheeks.

Stettmeier sighed. "Okay, fine. Half."

Mendoza shook his head. "I changed my mind. I don't want half."

"You don't?"

"No. I want it all."

"All?"

"Everything. The whole trust. Every dime. You sign it over and in return, you get to live."

Stettmeier's eyes went wide with fear. "*What?*"

"Where the *hell* is Perez?" Mendoza angrily pulled out Alyssa's phone. The last text he sent was over an hour ago. He promised to send him an address, but he hadn't sent *mierda*. He called Sancho's number.

It rang three times before Perez picked up. "Hey, sweetie."

"Where the hell are you?"

"Mission Hills. We just got here. The Good Knight Motel on Sepulveda. We're right about to check in."

"You just keep him there. You understand?"

"I can't wait to see you."

"This time I'm bringing her with me. Either he dies or she does."

"I love you too."

Mendoza clicked off and heard a faint sound just outside the window. He turned out the light on the table next to the couch and stood, pulled his weapon, and moved against the wall next to the curtains.

He glanced at Stettmeier. "Turn off the lights."

Stettmeier sat frozen in the chair.

"The lights. Turn 'em off!"

Stettmeier bolted up and hit a wall switch, plunging the room into darkness.

Mendoza pushed the curtains back and peered outside into the gloom. There were no streetlights, but he could see the lights on in the house across the street. He heard no other sound. Saw no movement outside. It was probably nothing. The wind. A cat. His shoulders dropped as his muscles relaxed. All this bullshit with Flynn made him paranoid.

"You see anything?" Stettmeier asked.

"It's nothing. Turn the lights back on."

The lights flicked on and Mendoza pulled Perez's wife to her feet. He pushed her towards the front door and opened it. Flynn stood on the stoop, aiming a Desert Eagle at him. Mendoza took a step back, pulled her back with him, and put his .38 Special against her head.

Flynn offered her a brave smile and then leveled his eyes at Mendoza. "Let her go."

"Why would I do that?"

Flynn took a step forward. "Because if you don't, I will shoot you."

"Me too," Sancho said. He stepped into the doorway and pointed a shotgun at him.

"Not before I put a hollow point right through her pretty head," Mendoza snarled.

"We seem to be at an impasse," Flynn said.

"Not at all," Mendoza replied. "I don't mind dying and I don't mind killing."

"No one has to die," Sancho said.

Mendoza took another step back. "Yeah, they do. Everybody has to die. Might as well be today."

"Let her go and we'll let you go," Sancho said.

Mendoza shook his head. "You might, but he won't. You want her to walk out of here alive? Put your *pinche* guns on the ground."

Sancho lowered his gun and glanced at Flynn. "I think we better listen to him."

Flynn shook his head. "If we disarm, he'll kill us all."

"I got no reason to kill the girl." Mendoza eyeballed Perez. "Just him. Just Flynn. I might even let you go, too."

Flynn shook his head. "I don't think so."

Perez's wife sobbed and trembled. Perez looked about to cry too as he slowly raised his shotgun and aimed the barrel at Flynn. "Put the gun down, James."

"Mendoza will not leave any witnesses, my friend. No one's walking out of here alive."

Mendoza laughed at that. "What do I care about witnesses? If they catch me, what can they do to me? They don't execute insane people in this country. They'll just put me back in the hospital."

Tears filled Perez's eyes as he kept the shotgun on Flynn. "I'm so sorry, man."

"No reason to be sorry, old friend. Once again, Mr. Mendoza has put you in an impossible position."

"Not at all." Mendoza grabbed Alyssa by the hair and screwed the barrel of his gun into the back of her head. "I think it's pretty simple." He aimed his dark, dead eyes at Perez. "Shoot that *hijo de puta! Put him down!*"

"*I can't!*" Sancho slowly bent over and put the shotgun on the floor. Tears streamed down his face. Alyssa shook with sobs.

Misty Love looked up at Mendoza with tears in her eyes. "Can I go?"

"No." Mendoza glared at Stettmeier. "*Sit.*"

Stettmeier slowly lowered himself to the floor and sat with his back against the wall, his face pale and covered in sweat.

Flynn kept the Desert Eagle trained on Mendoza.

Perez pleaded with him. "Please, man. James. *Please.*"

Flynn locked eyes with Perez, and then his sobbing wife, and finally, reluctantly, turned the barrel of his Desert Eagle away from Mendoza and slowly set the gun on the ground.

Mendoza immediately aimed his weapon at Flynn. "Finally. *Finally.* I can't tell you how long I've waited to do this."

The window shattered behind Mendoza. Something hard punched him in the back of the head. He pulled the trigger on Flynn, but whatever hit him in the back of the head made him miss. He tried to follow Flynn with the barrel of his gun, but the world tilted. The ground shifted beneath him and came up to meet him as his face slammed into the floor. He rolled over onto his back. Someone stood in the window. *That crazy bitch from Hornitos.* She had a gun, and it was pointed right at him. Mendoza felt the back of his head. He found a hole leaking blood. So much blood. His fingers were sticky with it. Mendoza felt around for his gun, but couldn't find it. He looked back up at Caitlyn. "You shot me in the fucking head."

"But you're not dead. I guess I must have missed your tiny little brain."

"*Vete a la mierda,*" he mumbled, his voice fuzzy and muffled. "*Puta* bitch."

She shot him again.

. . .

Sancho hurried to Alyssa and held her close. She sobbed in his arms as Misty Love sprinted out the door. No one stopped her. Stettmeier tried to follow, but Flynn took him by arm and pushed him into a chair. "Mr. Stettmeier, I presume."

"That's him," Sancho said.

Stettmeier sat with his head down and his hands up, palms out. "Please don't kill me. Please, I'm sorry."

Caitlyn came through the front door that Misty Love left open and closed it. She crossed to Mendoza. His head rested in a spreading puddle of his own blood. She knelt next to him and felt for the pulse in his carotid artery. "Shit, this asshole is still alive. I shot him in the back of the head. I shot him in the chest. And he is still breathing."

Sancho used a kitchen knife to cut the duct tape off Alyssa's wrists and ankles. A faint siren wailed in the distance. "Flynn, you and Caitlyn better go before the cops get here."

Flynn put his hand on Sancho's shoulder. "What about you?"

"We'll stay here and wait for them. And keep an eye on Stettmeier."

"I had nothing to do with kidnapping your wife," Stettmeier pleaded. "That was not my idea. That was all him!" He pointed at Mendoza, bleeding out on the floor.

Flynn cradled Alyssa's face in his hands. "Are you okay?"

She nodded. "Thank you."

"You're going to be fine."

"Come on, man." Sancho pointed at the door. "Time to go."

Flynn nodded. Caitlyn handed Sancho the Rohrbough R9 Stealth Elite and took the shotgun. As soon as they left, Stettmeier stood up.

Sancho pointed the pistol at him. "Where are you going?"

"I told you I had nothing to do with this."

"Except for sending Flynn to Hornitos so Mendoza could murder him. Other than that, this has nothing to do with you."

"You going to tell the cops?"

"Not if you sell this house and the Range Rover and all the other shit you bought with Flynn's trust fund money and return it. Not if you remove yourself as the trustee and transfer those funds to Flynn personally."

"I'm not sure I can do that."

"If you don't, I'm going to tell the police everything I know about you and Mendoza and your plot to defraud and murder Flynn."

Stettmeier mulled it over. "Do you think Flynn will leave me alone if I remove myself from the trust?"

"Absolutely."

Stettmeier closed his eyes and let go with a big sigh before opening them again. "Fine. *Fine.*"

Mendoza mumbled something. Sancho recognized only one word. *Puta.* Approaching police sirens drowned out the rest. Flashing lights appeared in the front window. A voice amplified by a bullhorn shouted, "The house is surrounded. Put down your weapons and come out with your hands up!"

CHAPTER TWENTY-NINE

Mormon settlers founded a town fifty miles south of Salt Lake City in 1860. Church Apostle Erastus Snow named it after a nearby creek. Chicken Creek. Church President Brigham Young later changed the name to Levan for reasons known only to him. However, as Levan is navel spelled backwards, some believe Young chose the name because the tiny town sits exactly in the geographical center of the state. Utah's belly button covers a total area of just under one square mile. The population in 1900 was 614. In 2020, the population hit 954.

Flynn and Caitlyn jumped into Alessandra's Maserati Levante and hit the road before the police arrived. Flynn drove. He gave Caitlyn the side-eye. "Where can I drop you?"

"Cody, Wyoming."

"You're coming with me?"

"I can't let you do this by yourself."

"I'm glad to hear that."

"Which means I'm probably as crazy as you are."

Flynn smiled and found the freeway. Caitlyn navigated them north towards Wyoming and the headquarters of General Jedidiah Anderson's Army of God.

An hour later, they crossed the Tejon Pass and, nine hours after that, picked up some supplies at a Kmart in Provo before heading to a motel on the outskirts of Levan, Utah.

The Shady Dell Motel had eight rooms, and they all were empty. The lady manning the battered front desk looked almost as old as the town itself. A cigarette hung from the corner of her lip as she watched an old portable TV perched on the counter.

Some sort of evangelist preached a sermon. "The second thing that Manasseh was guilty of was immorality. He built altars to Ashteroth and Baal. Vile and obscene orgies they had. And priests would drink and violate the holy sisters who had pledged their chastity to our Lord and savior…"

She turned down the TV when Flynn and Caitlyn walked in. Flynn gave her a charming grin and checked out the name tag pinned to her blouse. "Good evening, Verna. We'd like your best room."

A huge smile crinkled all the wrinkles on Verna's face as she set down her cigarette. "I like that accent. Are you British?"

"I am indeed."

"Like Hugh Grant?"

"I suppose."

"You think he's related to Cary Grant?"

"Who?"

"Hugh? Is he his grandson or something?"

Flynn looked at Caitlyn, who couldn't help but smile. "What do you think, dear?"

Caitlyn just shook her head.

"You kind of sound like him," Verna said. "Hugh. Not Cary. Though Cary was more handsome. More masculine. A very good-looking man. My late husband actually looked like him a little. Wasn't as charming, though. Alvin wasn't charming at all." Her lips turned down and her faced turned sour.

"So, about that room?" Caitlyn said.

"Room 3 is probably the best. It's got a newer TV and the mattress isn't too saggy."

"We'll take room 3 then, Verna." Flynn said. "Is there a restaurant nearby you might recommend?"

"There's an Arby's and a Wendy's up the highway in Nephi, though I'm not sure I'd recommend either one. If you like

Mexican, *Jalisciense* might be your best bet. Everything's homemade."

"Sounds good."

"If you're going, would you mind picking me up a carne asada taco and a quesadilla?" She pulled a five out of the register. "And a large Dr. Pepper."

Flynn waved away the cash. "Our treat, Verna. For being so friendly and helpful."

"That's very kind of you."

"Our pleasure," Flynn said.

Her wrinkly face crinkled with another smile as she put a fresh cigarette in her mouth and lit it with the one still smoldering in the ashtray.

■ ■ ■

Room 3 consisted of two twin beds with rumpled and faded comforters and a beat-up dresser with an older TV sitting on top. Flynn and Caitlyn ate their supper on a rickety table after delivering Verna her own evening meal. Christian-themed pictures dominated the walls: Jesus walking on the Sea of Galilee; baby Jesus with Mother Mary; Jesus ascending to heaven; Daniel in the lion's den.

Flynn stared at them as he ate his chili relleno and chicken tamales. "Verna wasn't kidding. This is quite good."

Caitlyn looked troubled as she tucked into her carne asada tacos. "You don't think Verna recognized us, do you?"

"I think if she did, she would have said so."

"Maybe our escape wasn't a big story here."

"I doubt Verna's much of a news junkie."

Caitlyn nodded. She looked at the picture of Jesus walking on water. "That Jesus is quite the hottie." She pronounced Jesus using the Spanish pronunciation.

"He's no Cary Grant."

Caitlyn took a swig of Dos Equis. "I think if you play your cards right, you might get lucky tonight."

"I'm not sure I'm Verna's type."

"I'm not talking about Verna."

Flynn raised an eyebrow. "I thought you didn't want to complicate our relationship?"

"Wasn't it you who said imminent death is often the ultimate aphrodisiac?"

"It sounds like something I'd say."

"Well, tomorrow the odds will not be in our favor."

"I've faced similar odds before and somehow I always seem to survive."

"Maybe you've just been lucky."

"I don't believe in luck. What some call luck is simply preparation meeting opportunity."

"Speaking of preparation... I found what some claim is a satellite photo of the compound." She turned her laptop around and Flynn checked out a black-and-white satellite image. He couldn't make hide or hair of what he was looking at, but Caitlyn pointed out a sprawling central structure. "I believe that's Anderson's mansion. Those are bunk houses a distance away, and over here are what look like a couple of large barns or hangars. A twelve-foot-tall fence topped with razor wire surrounds the entire compound. I've been reading about the Army of God on 8kun."

"On what?"

"It's an off-the-grid message board on the dark web. Home to QAnon, white supremacists, and child pornographers. There's an Army of God board for current members and wannabes. I found some posts claiming they mined the entire perimeter outside the fence. They have guard dogs. Security cameras. Alarm systems. An Apache attack helicopter. A

Bradley fighting vehicle. An M1 Abrams tank. A Stryker. Two sniper towers. And multiple machine gun emplacements."

"So what you're saying is there's a chance we might not make it out of there alive."

"That's exactly what I'm saying."

Flynn studied the satellite photo. "Do you think he keeps the military vehicles in this hangar?"

"It's a possibility. I'm guessing he has an entire armory. After all, he's a defense contractor. He can get his hands on anything and everything from assault rifles to hand grenades to RPGs."

"I don't see any nearby neighbors."

"There's nothing around for miles. Most of the compound outside the fence is farmland and pasture. Though there are some woods over here to the south. I'm thinking we can approach from there."

"After dark?"

"We can, though I'm guessing the sentries have night vision goggles."

Flynn scrutinized the map. "How many men does he have training there?"

"There's no way to know for sure, but if those bunkhouses are all occupied, at least a hundred, if not more."

"Do you think the servers are in the main mansion?"

"According to the 8kun board, the mansion has a large basement bunker. Since they need to keep those servers cool and protected, that's probably where I'll find them. Meanwhile, I'll need you to create some kind of distraction so I can slip inside without being seen."

"I can do that." Flynn stood up from the table and plopped down on one of the saggy beds. "I must say, I'm a bit knackered."

"Don't tell me you're too tired to play your cards right tonight?"

"I'm not usually one to deny a beautiful woman, but we do have a big day tomorrow."

Caitlyn smiled at that. "Mr. Flynn, are you turning me down?"

"I'm asking for a rain check."

She smirked. "I'm almost insulted."

He stood and pulled off his shirt. "Please don't be. Besides, the anticipation of pleasure is a pleasure in itself. Do you know the German word *vorfreude*?"

Caitlyn smiled. "The joyful and intense anticipation that comes from imagining future pleasures."

Flynn nodded. "Indeed." He crossed to the bathroom and closed the door. Flynn turned on the shower and stripped naked before stepping into the stream. The water pressure was disappointing. It dribbled down his back, but at least the water was hot. His muscles loosened and he let go with a long sigh.

Truth was he hadn't ever met anyone like Caitlyn. She wasn't someone he could just love and leave. Yes, she was beautiful, but she was so much more. He admired her bravery and bravado; her fierce intelligence. But ever since he joined the service, he avoided deep emotional connections and sticky and unnecessary encumbrances. To love someone too deeply was a vulnerability.

The air in the room shifted as the bathroom door opened. Cool air hit Flynn as the shower curtain parted.

A naked Caitlyn stepped into the tub. "I wanted to claim that rain check while we both were still breathing."

She put arms around him and leaned against him. Her firm breasts pressed hard against his chest as she grabbed his bum with both hands. Flynn looked down into her mischievous green eyes. She had a sprinkle of freckles on her upturned nose and her short, dark hair was spiky and wet. Slender as she was, her shoulders were broad and her arms were strong. She held on tight and wouldn't let go.

She kissed him on the chest and on the neck. "For someone who doesn't believe in luck, you sure get lucky a lot."

"Luck has nothing to do with it."

CHAPTER THIRTY

After his father's death in 1860, William F. Cody headed for the gold fields of California. However, he never made it to the Golden State. Instead, he became a rider for the Pony Express. During the Civil War, he fought for the Union Army and later served as a civilian scout during the Indian Wars. In 1872, he was awarded the Congressional Medal of Honor for leading a calvary charge against a Sioux war party. He picked up the nickname Buffalo Bill when he worked as a buffalo hunter, supplying the workers of the Kansas Pacific Railroad with meat. Soon after that, he met Ned Buntline, who wrote a series of successful dime novels romanticizing his life. Buntline produced his original Wild West Show, which toured all over the world. In 1887, Bill Cody did a command performance for Queen Victoria. At the age of fifty-four, he established the eight-thousand-acre TE Ranch on the South Fork of the Shoshone River, thirty-five miles outside of what later would become the town of Cody, Wyoming.

Flynn drove while Caitlyn slept. He glanced at her in the seat next to him and grappled with an affection that surprised him. For the longest time, he thought love was too risky. Too perilous. But Caitlyn already led a life of danger. Maybe with her he wouldn't have to stay a stranger.

She opened her eyes and smiled. "How long was I asleep?"

"Long enough to miss the Boysen Reservoir. Yellowstone is just northwest of here and I believe those rather impressive peaks are the Grand Tetons." He pointed out a billboard as they passed by it. "We're coming up on Thermopolis. Do you need to make a pit stop?"

"I'm good for now. So we're only about an hour away?"

"That's my estimation."

She checked the Maserati's navigation system. "Looks like we exit at 14 and head west and then south on 291."

"This land must have cost General Anderson a pretty penny."

"Over the last twenty years, millionaires and billionaires have been buying up all the big ranches."

"Apparently, there's money in defense contracting," Flynn said with not a little sarcasm.

"He started as an arms dealer, but eventually diversified. He now sells everything from small arms and munitions to tanks, armored vehicles, and missile systems. Anderson also runs one of the largest lobbying groups in D.C. and funds several political action committees. He has dozens of politicians in his pocket. At this point, he can write his own laws and implement his own foreign policy."

"Selling arms to both sides in conflicts all over the world."

"That's his business model."

Flynn nodded. "Propagating perpetual war. Sounds profitable."

"But it's not just about making a profit. Anderson's a true believer. A millenarian who wants to bring on the end of human history."

"By creating a war in the Middle East."

"A war to end all wars. Armageddon."

■ ■ ■

The sun was down by the time they reached Route 291. A few miles later, Flynn headed up a gravel road at Caitlyn's direction. The narrow, dusty track led up a steep hill. The switchbacks were sharp and on one side the road dropped away completely. The edges looked like they might collapse under the weight of their vehicle, so Flynn kept to the center, hoping they wouldn't meet another speeding four-wheel-drive vehicle coming from the other direction. Eventually, Caitlyn directed them off-road entirely, and they climbed a steep rocky trail, crested a hill, and came down the other side into a stand of trees. They bounced and rocked as they crept ahead, threading their way through pine, spruce, and Douglas fir.

"Better turn off the lights before they see us coming," Caitlyn said.

Flynn did and the way ahead went black. The light from the dash illuminated their faces and reflected back on the windshield. "I can't see a damn—" They slammed into something. Probably a tree. Luckily, they were barely moving. Flynn turned off the ignition. "I'm pretty sure this is the wooded area just above pastureland that surrounds the compound." Flynn turned on a flashlight he bought at the Kmart in Provo. "You ready to move?"

"Let's do it."

They put on their packs, grabbed their weapons, and carefully made their way through the dark woods. Rather than reveal themselves with their flashlights, they moved slowly, letting their eyes adjust to the darkness.

The Wyoming night was bright with stars, and a waxing moon rose high in the sky, dimly illuminating their way. As they moved through the trees, the distant lights of the compound glowed below. Anderson wasn't shy about using electricity. Security lights bathed the perimeter as well as the compound itself. If you were hastening the end of the world, climate change would likely not be of much concern.

The compound seemed closer than it was because of all the light. It took a good thirty minutes before they reached the wide pastureland that surrounded it. They cut their way through a hinged joint wire fence. Dozens of large black lumps dotted across the ground. At first, Flynn thought they were large rocks, but as he crept closer he realized they were cattle, laying down in the grass, asleep.

"I thought cows slept standing up," Flynn whispered.

"Cows and horses can doze lightly on their feet, but to sleep deeply, they need to lie down."

"I do see a few standing."

"A few always do. To keep an eye out for predators."

Flynn nearly tripped when he stepped into a gopher hole. "How is it you know so much about cattle?"

"My mother's parents had a farm in Iowa. That's where I spent my summers."

"So is cow tipping really a thing?"

Caitlyn shook her head. "Not really. No."

"I suppose all these cattle give lie to the rumor that the perimeter is mined."

"I would say so. Unless Anderson enjoys watching his cows explode."

"That would be an expensive hobby."

"Well, he *is* a billionaire."

The cattle still standing reacted to them and walked or trotted away before they could get too close. All the security lights were focused on the twelve-foot-tall fence encircling the compound, creating an even greater contrast to the darkness surrounding it.

Two tall towers likely held snipers. It occurred to Flynn they probably had night-vision scopes. He hoped they were too bored and distracted to spend much time keeping an eye on the cattle.

Caitlyn motioned for Flynn to stop. He did, crouching behind a cow sleeping so deeply it had no idea Flynn was there. It snored like a human. In fact, it sounded a lot like Q, his roommate back at headquarters.

Caitlyn whispered in his ear. "It's not as well guarded as those posters on 8kun led me to believe."

"I did see one guard walking the perimeter. And that red blinking light on the building across the way? I'm guessing that's a security cam."

"A distraction might not be necessary."

"I agree. No reason to raise the alarm unnecessarily."

Flynn and Caitlyn moved around the perimeter until they found a section of fence difficult to spot from either sniper tower. Besides the flashlights, Flynn purchased various other tools and supplies from that Kmart in Provo. Their tin snips cut through the chain-link fence easily and quickly.

At 3:37 in the morning, most everyone was sound asleep and sawing logs like those cows dotting the pasture. Flynn and Caitlyn crept through the compound and kept to the shadows as they made their way towards the main house. They spotted only two guards patrolling the grounds. One wore earphones and watched something on his phone while the other looked half-asleep as he leaned against a wall and lit a cigarette.

They tiptoed past an empty firing range and the entrance to some kind of obstacle course before moving past a building the size of a large airplane hangar. Flynn tried a side door. It opened. He slipped inside and flicked on his flashlight to find an actual M1 Abrams tank. He kept the beam aimed at the ground as they moved around and discovered a Bradley fighting vehicle parked right next to it.

"Guess those guys on 8kun weren't wrong about everything," Caitlyn whispered.

Flynn noticed a large mechanic's workshop with all the tools necessary to keep those two war machines in tiptop shape. "One of these might prove helpful if we need the extra firepower."

"You know how to operate a tank?"

"Not this one specifically, but how hard could it be?"

Caitlyn rolled her eyes as she led them back outside and closed the door. They continued on past a large storage shed and one of three bunk houses. They kept low and snuck below the dusty windows, heading down a service road that led to the rear of the main house.

The massive ranch house sprawled in all directions and stood two stories tall, like some kind of rustic log-and-stone cowboy castle. Even the rear had gigantic windows that revealed vaulted ceilings and an immense man-sized fireplace that blazed with an impressive conflagration. All the furniture inside was polished wood and larger-than-life.

Flynn spotted security cameras above the double doors in the rear. A sign in the window announced some kind of alarm system. Would Anderson bother activating the alarm system this far out in the middle of nowhere when he knew he had a full complement of troops training there? Being a religious fanatic with a doomsday phobia who built his born-again army to confront Satan and the armies of Hell… probably. But maybe he was arrogant enough to think that no one could ever penetrate his outer perimeter. Or maybe he couldn't imagine that anyone would ever have the audacity to stand against him.

The mechanized cameras continuously swept the area. Flynn didn't see any motion-activated security lights attached to them, so he assumed the cameras had night vision. He and Caitlyn waited for the nearest camera to move in the opposite direction and then they scurried close to the house. They pressed themselves flat against the brick, out of the security cam's field of view, and edged along the wall. Rounding the corner, they reached a side door.

Caitlyn carefully searched the edges of the door frame.

"What are you looking for?" Flynn whispered.

"Alarm wires," she whispered back.

Flynn moved past her and peered in a first-floor window. The blinds were drawn and no light peeked out. Much to his surprise, however, the window was slightly open. He slid it up a little wider. The sound made Caitlyn jump.

"What are you doing?" she shout-whispered.

"It's open."

"Don't—"

He slid it open even wider and no alarm went off. "It's fine."

"Flynn…"

He lifted the window wide enough to accommodate his body and climbed inside, rattling the blinds. "Come on…"

"Jesus Christ…" Caitlyn climbed in after Flynn.

They found themselves in some sort of library or study. The embers of a dead fire glowed in another impressive fireplace. Not as impressive as the one in the giant living room with the vaulted ceilings, but impressive nonetheless. Dim light spilled under a closed door on the far side of the room. Flynn quietly moved to the door and put his ear against it. He didn't hear a thing.

"I need to find the door to the basement," Caitlyn whispered.

Flynn nodded and carefully turned the knob so as not to make a sound. He eased it open and stepped into the corridor. The hardwood floor creaked. He stood still and listened, hoping the creak didn't catch anyone's attention. The house remained silent. Most everyone was apparently asleep.

They stayed to either side of the corridor where the hardwood floors would be less likely to bend, bow, and squeak. Flynn scanned the ceiling corners for security cams, but didn't see any. That didn't mean there wasn't one there. Modern miniature camera technology often made spy cams undetectable. They could be hidden in a clock, a painting, or even a child's teddy bear.

Flynn eyed an original Remington bronze sculpture of a rider on a bucking bronco as they crept by. It sat upon a rustic timber-framed console table. Original paintings by other artists of the western frontier lined the walls.

The corridor ended at the entrance to the massive living room with its vaulted ceilings, twenty-foot-tall picture windows, and immense fireplace. The conflagration continued to blaze, illuminating much of the room in a warm, flickering light. A lot of the room remained in shadow, however, and Flynn and Caitlyn kept to the darker areas as they entered. Antique tables and pedestals with more Remington and Russell bronzes decorated the space. The trophy heads of a dozen dead animals adorned the walls.

Flynn checked out a long wooden antique bar with a brass rail. The polished wood gleamed and the detail and carvings were extraordinary. Anderson probably found it in some famous old-time western saloon and had it transported here to recreate his own cowboy heaven. Flynn stared at his dim silhouette in a long mirror and then noticed several bottles of fine whiskey displayed on various shelves. He stepped around the bar to get a closer look.

"What are you doing?" Caitlyn whispered.

Flynn surveyed the labels. "Oh, my..."

She whispered a little louder and with more ire. "Flynn?"

Flynn kept his voice low even though he couldn't hide the excitement. "He has a bottle of Pappy Van Winkle 23-year-old family reserve."

"*Flynn?*"

"It would be a crime not to try a taste." Flynn popped the top, found two cut-crystal whiskey glasses and poured them each a generous dollop. Caitlyn stepped up to the bar and Flynn handed her a glass.

"Are you kidding me?"

"It's Pappy Van Winkle." Flynn took a taste and let the bourbon roll over his palate. "It's like kissing God, isn't it?"

"I wouldn't know."

"Hints of oak and sweet vanilla with touches of citrus, honey, and spice. It's really quite remarkable." Flynn finished the rest of his glass and poured himself another. "Fine scotch is all well and good, but there's nothing like a premium Kentucky bourbon." Flynn crossed back around the bar and approached a large comfortable-looking sofa.

Caitlyn quickly tossed back the bourbon, carefully set the glass down, and crossed over to Flynn. "We don't have time for this."

"That's no way to imbibe a fine bourbon. It needs to be savored. It's sipping whiskey."

Flynn took a sip, sat on the sofa and immediately bolted back to his feet. He glanced down at the sofa. A Native American blanket shifted and moved. Someone emerged from beneath it.

The forty-something guard's shock of thick black hair stood out in all directions. As he was clearly hungover and still half-asleep, he seemed disoriented and somewhat confused. "Who the hell are you?"

"Flynn. James Flynn."

"Who?" It was then that the man noticed Caitlyn. By the look in his eyes, he recognized her immediately. He reached into his pocket and hit a panic button before either Flynn or Caitlyn could react.

Security strobes flashed from all corners of the room as an earsplitting siren cut the air.

Caitlyn screamed something. Flynn couldn't hear her over the siren, but he could see her point as the man climbed off the couch and pulled a pistol from a shoulder holster. Before Flynn could move to disarm him, Caitlyn caught the guard's arm in a quick trap before twisting the weapon out of his grasp and pointing it back at him. She struck him hard in the forehead with the butt of his own gun, and he sank to one knee before she struck him again. He toppled forward, face down on the bearskin rug.

Flynn had to shout to be heard over the siren. "Find your way to the basement! I'll distract the guards!"

"What?"

"The basement! Find the basement! Find the server! I'll meet you back at the Maserati when this is all over!"

She nodded and took off, disappearing into the side corridor an instant before the front doors burst open and five armed guards rushed in. Flynn already had his weapon in hand, but he didn't turn it on the guards. He turned it on the floor-to-ceiling window. His intention was to shatter it and make his escape, but the bullets ricocheted right off the glass. Flynn heard one whistle past his ear. All his assailants hit the floor. He took advantage of the chaos to take off through a doorway. The thunder of the guards' weapons nearly overwhelmed the siren as they unloaded on Flynn. Bullets ripped through the plasterboard and into the corridor. One tore through a Russell painting and another ricocheted off a Remington bronze.

Flynn led his enemies, hot on his heels, away from Caitlyn. He raced into the small study. Bullets whizzed by his head, punching holes and splintering wood. He dove for the window, suddenly wondering too late if this too was ballistic glass. Luckily, he didn't bounce off, but crashed through. More gunfire erupted. Flynn ran. Shouts and orders and the crackle of walkie talkies filled the air as guards spread out over the grounds.

An imperious voice blasted from outdoor speakers mounted on metal poles. "The intruder has fled the main house and is loose on the grounds. Run the evil doer down! Do not let him escape! The General wants him alive!"

CHAPTER THIRTY-ONE

Angry shouts and the vicious barks of guard dogs followed Flynn as he hurried away from the main house. Apparently, they kept the animals contained and only released them when an intruder intruded. Blindingly bright security lights lit up the grounds, so staying in the shadows was not an option. Sniper rifles boomed as high caliber bullets zipped through the air.

"I said alive! I want him alive! Hold your dang fire!" The general's words thundered from the compound's PA system like the voice of God.

Flynn darted past the storage shed and the bunkhouse as soldiers stumbled outside, bleary-eyed, half-dressed, and half-asleep. They all had weapons, but no one fired per the general's instructions. They did chase after, but as groggy as they were they didn't move with much alacrity.

The dogs were another story. They sprinted ahead like the hounds of hell. Huge German Shepherds. Teeth bared. Eyes wild.

No way could Flynn make it to the fence before one of those beasts took him down. So he headed for the closest door he could find. Fortunately, it was unlocked and led into the heavy equipment hangar. Flynn slammed the door shut on the closest dog's slathering jaws. It yelped and withdrew. Flynn locked the door tight. Another dog threw itself against the metal with a loud thump, snarling and growling, its paws furiously scraping to get in.

■ ■ ■

Caitlyn hid inside a storage closet and listened to the security siren and the shouts of soldiers as they hurried by.

"Hey! Hold up!"

"General said he's already outside!"

"Yeah, but he wants us to secure the server room."

"What?"

"In case the son of a bitch doubles back."

The footsteps receded and Caitlyn opened the door a crack. She peeked out to see two soldiers disappear around the corner. She hurried after, staying far enough behind so they wouldn't detect her footfalls and caught snatches of their conversation as she followed.

"Who the heck would be dumb enough to break into this place?"

"FBI maybe?"

"Those deep state bastards have it in for us."

"And they have no clue who they're working for. No idea that Satan's the one pulling the strings."

"I almost feel sorry for 'em."

"I don't. Those devils deserve to burn."

Caitlyn poked her head around the corner to see the two guards standing at a steel door. The bigger of the pair peered at a keypad. "What's the code again?"

"Seven Sevens. For the seven seals!"

He punched in seven sevens. The indicator light turned from red to green and the door clicked open. They walked inside. Caitlyn waited until they closed it and shut it behind themselves. She hurried to the keypad and waited five more seconds before punching in the code. The door clicked open again, and she quietly stepped inside.

■　■　■

Flynn did his best to ignore the commotion as someone attacked the hangar's locked door with an axe or sledgehammer. The slathering dogs snarled, barked, and bayed. It was only a matter of time before the door came off its hinges and the dogs tore in after him along with the Army of God.

Flynn opened the Bradley M3 fighting vehicle and lowered himself inside. He pulled the hatch over himself, completely muffling the shouting, hammering and snarling. Flynn kept up with all the latest technological advances and often watched YouTube videos on the latest war planes, submarines, and fighting vehicles. From that research, he knew the supercharged six hundred horsepower, liquid-cooled engine powered the twenty-five-ton vehicle to a top speed of over forty miles an hour.

He settled into the snug driver's seat and looked over the control panel. The Bradley M3 required a three-man crew to properly operate it. A commander. A driver. And a gunner. As the driver, he wouldn't have access to the M240 machine gun, the M242 Bushmaster autocannon or the TOW anti-tank missiles. The only view outside was through a collection of four periscopes. It took some trial and error as Flynn flipped switches, pushed buttons, and turned knobs, but finally the engine started with a roar.

Flynn's teeth rattled as the power of those six hundred horses came to life. He put his left hand on the yoke and engaged a gear selector that looked absurdly complicated. He peered through the direct view bi-ocular periscope. Someone looked back at him. An angry face filled his entire field of view. The Army of God had obviously breached the hangar.

Someone pulled open the hatch. Flynn had neglected to lock it. *Shit!* He quickly shifted and flattened the gas. As the gears weren't identified, Flynn mistakenly engaged reverse instead of drive. The Bradley lurched backwards and the man who opened the hatch fell inside. Flynn kept his foot to the floor and the Bradley moved with expeditiousness, smashing backwards through the wall of the hangar.

The man who fell inside had a pistol. Flynn struggled to disarm him. The gun boomed and the earsplitting sound reverberated around the cockpit. The bullet ricocheted once and again before ending up in his attacker's very own arse.

Flynn twisted away the wounded man's gun and elbowed him in the face as they crashed into something that gave way immediately. The Bradley flattened fences and shrubbery and trees as it continued on its inexorable path to nowhere in particular. Bullets ricocheted off the armor. Flynn wondered why they were bothering to fire on him at all. His assailant tried to take him out with a choke hold. Flynn slammed the back of his head into his attacker's nose. He followed that up with an elbow to the throat. The man fell back, gasping, allowing Flynn to concentrate on his driving. He put his right eye up to one of the periscopes. At least a dozen men chased after him. Another periscope showed what lay ahead just down the hill.

General Jedidiah Anderson's massive cowboy castle.

. . .

As Caitlyn crept down the spiral staircase that led to the server room, the two guards continued to converse. Their voices echoed off the solid cement walls.

"So when the rapture happens, the Lord's leaving us here to fight the forces of the Antichrist?"

"No, we're raptured to heaven along with all the rest of the righteous."

"So who fights Hell's army?"

"We do. We become part of the Army of Heaven and return for the battle of Armageddon."

"So we're not here on Earth for the tribulation?"

"No, we are not."

"I find the timeline a little confusing."

"It's all part of God's plan and it's not for us to understand."

A thunderous clatter shook the server room. Dust fell from the ceiling and Caitlyn tumbled down the last few steps of the spiral staircase. She found herself in an expansive basement that looked far more high tech than the rest of the house. The air was cold and the floor was some sort of hard rubber. The servers stood in racks, and fluorescent lights and sprinkler heads dotted the acoustic tile ceiling.

The two guards stared in stunned wonderment at Caitlyn while the house trembled. Both fumbled for their weapons. Caitlyn sprang to her feet and swept their legs out from under them. As they fell, their heads bounced off the rubber floor. She disarmed them quickly and used a nearby spool of blue ethernet cable to bind their arms and legs.

She then pulled out the one terabyte flash drive she picked up at the Kmart in Provo and plugged it into a USB 3.0 port on the server terminal. The security protocols were rudimentary and, as an experienced hacker, Caitlyn easily found her way into the system. She did her best to ignore the ruckus above and worked fast. At one point the power went out, but the server, outfitted with the latest and largest battery backup system available, kept everything online. Still, if the house collapsed and the ceiling came down, she'd need more than an uninterruptible power supply to finish what she needed to do.

■   ■   ■

Flynn hadn't intended to drive the fighting vehicle into and through the General's lovely cowboy castle, but that was exactly what he did. The collision and subsequent crashing slowed the Bradley's acceleration to such an extent that two other soldiers climbed into the open hatch. While one pummeled Flynn's face, the other killed the engine, causing the giant fighting vehicle to discontinue its path of destruction. With the engine silent, Flynn could hear dozens of enemies screaming for his blood. They dragged him from the driver's seat and pulled him out of the Bradley's cockpit.

Flynn caught glimpses of the destruction the fighting vehicle had wrought. Wires sparked and flames roared as the exposed wooden beams burned. Flynn tried to cover up as dozens of fists and feet beat him into submission.

"Alive!" someone with a booming voice roared. "The General wants him alive!"

■　■　■

Once Caitlyn had what she needed, she untied the two soldiers and brandished one of the weapons she took from them. "RUN!" she shouted.

And they did.

She followed after them, up the spiral staircase, through the steel door, and into the smoke-filled corridor. Coughing and choking, Caitlyn dropped to the floor. She crawled forward under the heavy smoke, taking quick, shallow breaths as she searched for a way out. The heat was intense, even though the flames had yet to reach the corridor. Her eyes burned as she slithered forward, keeping low. Distant shouts spurred her to move as fast as she could, trying her best to keep her nose and mouth close to the ground. She grew increasingly faint, but worked to keep her panic down.

Caitlyn reached up to try every door as she crawled down the corridor. Finally, one opened. It led to the study she and Flynn first entered. She skittered across the floor and wriggled her way through the window. Dropping to the ground, she rolled away, hacking and choking.

Flames engulfed the building. She didn't see any of the Army of God as she struggled to her feet and ran. The cold Wyoming air pushed out the smoke and filled her lungs with life-giving oxygen. She headed for their pre-arranged rendezvous point. The spot where they left Alessandra's Maserati SUV. There wasn't much of a moon, and even though the stars were bright, they offered little ambient light.

Caitlyn wasn't sure what kind of distraction Flynn had created, but whatever he did knocked out the power and set Anderson's house ablaze. That was overkill as far as she was concerned, but then Flynn was nothing if not a drama queen. She tripped multiple times as she stumbled her way back to the Maserati Levante, hesitant to turn on her flashlight. Caitlyn didn't want to make herself a target. But once she was deep enough in the trees, she flicked it on and found her way back to the luxury SUV.

Flynn wasn't there. She waited and waited, but he didn't show. Flashlights flickered through the trees, followed by the rustling and crunching of leaves. The Army of God was almost upon her. *Did they catch Flynn? Did they kill him?* If she stayed here, they'd catch her and then this would all be for nothing. She couldn't risk it. She had to go. The voices were louder now. The flashlights closer.

She climbed into the driver's seat and started up the SUV. The men hunting her heard the engine. Shouts rose and flashlights danced as they ran in her direction. Caitlyn shifted into reverse and backed away from the tree before slamming it into drive. She looked back one more time, hoping against hope that she'd see Flynn. But all she saw was a bullet shatter the rear window glass.

Caitlyn hit the gas and roared off.

CHAPTER THIRTY-TWO

"I looked and beheld a pale horse and his name that sat on him was Death, and Hell followed with him. And power was given onto them over the fourth part of the earth, to kill with sword and with hunger and with famine and plague and the beasts of the earth.... And lo, there was a great earthquake and the sun became black and the moon became as blood... and the stars of heaven fell to earth... for the great day of his wrath has come and who shall stand against him?"
Revelation 6:8

General Jedidiah Anderson understood the stakes. They couldn't be higher. As God's right hand, his duty was to fulfill the prophecy and fight the final battle. The Archangel Michael might command heaven's army, but General Jedidiah Anderson, progeny of one of the Confederacy's greatest military leaders, commanded the Lord's mortal army on Earth.

The Army of God.

Every moment of his life had led him to this point. From his time at the U.S. Air Force Academy in Colorado Springs to the day he earned his pilot wings to his first command. He flew hundreds of sorties during Operation Desert Storm and earned multiple decorations for bravery and valor. He went on to command the 7th Bomb Wing at Dyess Air Force Base and later became the commanding general for the Air Expeditionary Forces in Kabul, Afghanistan. With each command, he saw how the prophecies were coming true. When President George W.

Bush handed him the reins of the Air Force Global Strike Command, he believed it to be God's will.

Anderson's swift ascension caught the attention of Satan, and the Prince of Darkness used his influence to precipitate the scandal that ended his career. Only those under the sway of Lucifer could believe that teaching the word of God was dishonorable. Those given the responsibility to launch the missiles needed to understand the Lord's plan. When those evil politicians asked for his resignation, he offered it gladly. The dark one had corrupted this country and its military. He knew he needed to work outside the system if he hoped to do the Lord's work. Raytheon recruited him to sell their weapons of war and he used those contacts to build and finance what would eventually become the Army of God.

The signs were clear. The catastrophic earthquakes and floods and wildfires. The devastating hurricanes and tornadoes and droughts. The wars. The famines. The plagues. The Four Horsemen of the Apocalypse were already here. War, Famine, Pestilence and Death stalked the planet in preparation for war. Soon Anderson would light the fuse and the battle would begin. Clearly, Satan wanted to stop him. Perhaps he wasn't prepared to fight. Perhaps he feared defeat. Whatever the reason, Anderson couldn't let the dark lord derail his destiny.

His evil minions tried to burn his house to the ground. They did serious damage, but a house constructed of stone and steel is mostly impregnable to fire. His state-of-the-art sprinkler system did much to slow the spread, but what really saved him was the rain. A downpour like he'd never seen sent by God himself to quench the flames.

Anderson captured one of Lucifer's minions, but the she-demon somehow slipped away. She was the real danger. The one who discovered his plan and brought it to the authorities. Luckily, he still had some influence. The military industrial complex made a lot of people a lot of money and those who benefited weren't about to let some young *Whore of Babylon* impede the cycle of endless war. Of course, most of them were motivated by greed and didn't see the larger picture or understand that all their earthly riches and pleasures were meaningless and transitory.

The she-demon failed in her mission. The servers escaped harm as did the armory and most of his men. A few sustained wounds, but there were no fatalities. Not even when that she-demon's accomplice crashed the Bradley Fighting Vehicle into his house. His castle held and would keep them safe until the good Lord called them home.

The she-demon's cohort feigned insanity, but Anderson knew he was crazy like a fox. His men took him to the pole barn where Anderson's own personal *Torquemada* would get Flynn to talk.

■ ■ ■

Flynn licked his fat lip and tasted the coppery tang of blood. It dripped down his chin and onto his lap. His wrists were securely strapped to the arms of some sort of antique metal chair. His legs were bound as well. The building was large and well-lit, with a cement floor, metal walls and a metal ceiling with two skylights. Flynn looked around at an impressive array of medieval torture devices, each labeled with printed plaques encased in plastic, as if this was some sort of museum. By leaning forward as far as he could and turning his head all the way to the right, he could read the writing on the plaque next to him.

The Hellfire Chair. Under the seat, a cast iron oven, filled with burning coal, raises the temperature of the metal and roasts those seated alive.

"Isn't history fun?"

Flynn turned to see a tall, smiling, bespectacled man wearing blue Dickies Coveralls. He had a tiny paunch, and a head shaved to disguise his pattern baldness. His outfit looked like something a mechanic would wear. His black steel-toe work boots glinted, polished to a high shine. The man took pride in his appearance and seemed somewhat gleeful and quite enthusiastic. He had a familiar voice. At first Flynn couldn't quite place it and then he realized he sounded a lot like Kermit the Frog.

"This particular torture chair dates back to 1487. I picked it up in Toledo, Spain. In the beautiful region of Castilla-La Mancha. Verdant plains dotted with vineyards, castles, and windmills. The Alcazar of Toledo sits impregnable above the city. I purchased this piece from The Museo de la Tortura. Some say it was used by Torquemada himself."

"And who might you be?"

"Oh, pardon me! I do get so excited by history. I'm Brian Snedeker, the Army of God's Grand Inquisitor."

"You're quite the antiquarian."

"I am indeed. I find great inspiration from our forebears."

"An impressive collection."

"One of the finest such collections in all the world."

"Is that an Iron Maiden?"

Brian's eyes lit up with pride. "It is indeed! Good eye! Of course, the use of Iron Maidens as an actual torture device is a fantasy created in the early 18th century when the literati of The Enlightenment created the myth of the Middle Ages as being uncivilized. Most Iron Maidens were built for display in museums of the time. The most famous being the Iron Maiden of Nuremberg. Some believe it was destroyed by an Allied bombing in 1944. But it wasn't. This is it. The actual Iron Maiden of Nuremberg."

"That's an amazing story."

"I know, right? I must say, it's refreshing to talk to someone who isn't screaming and crying and begging for his life. To what do you attribute your fearlessness?"

"Two things. Number one, my faith."

"In the Lord above?"

"In myself. Number two is that this isn't my first rodeo. I've been tortured before by expert sadists and have lived to tell the tale." Flynn looked around the room. In truth, he was stalling for time. "I do recognize a few of these devices, but not all of them."

"Many are quite old and quite rare." Brian walked about the room, pointing out various pieces and offering a quick summary of their history. "This rack dates back to the 1300s. I bought it from a museum in Prague. I acquired this pointy brass pyramid-like device from a torture museum in Amsterdam. The supplicant sits on the sharpened point and eventually it rips him in half."

"Ow."

Snedeker smiled and nodded with enthusiasm. "*Ow,* indeed." Brian strolled about the room, pointing out other devices. "That's a Spanish Cat's Claw. A Catalan Garrote. A Pear of Anguish. An ancient Greek Brazen Bull. That rat cage is from medieval Italy."

"I assume you have some rats for that."

"I do and they are hungry as heck, as I have yet to feed them today."

"And what information are you hoping to extract from me?"

"That's not my purview. General Anderson will ask you the questions. I'm simply here to encourage you to talk."

A door opened in the side of the barn and a man backed inside carrying some sort of metal bucket. Flynn saw he wore thick welding gloves. Smoking hot coals were piled high. One fell out as he crossed the room. So transfixed by the bucket of hot glowing coals, Flynn didn't glance at the man's face until he was almost upon him.

"Gabriel?"

"Flynn?" The man with the bucket stared at Flynn with surprise and delight.

Snedeker grinned. "You two know each other?"

"We used to be roommates," Flynn said with a smile.

Gabriel put down the heavy bucket. "What are you doing here? Are you in league with the devil?"

"Of course I'm not," Flynn replied.

"Then why'd you ditch me?"

"That was Caitlyn. That wasn't me."

"She's a she-demon, isn't she?"

"She does have a temper," Flynn agreed.

"So, why are you helping her?"

"Helping her? I'm not helping her. I'm trying to stop her."

"You are?"

"Yes. That's why I'm here. To join the cause."

Brian Snedeker looked at Flynn skeptically. "Really?"

"Gabriel can vouch for me," Flynn said.

"So you want to join the cause?" The skeptical question came from General Jedidiah Anderson himself as he entered Brian Snedeker's torture pavilion. Four burly militia men followed him inside.

"Why else would I be here?" Flynn queried.

"To sabotage the Army of God before the final battle can even begin. Someone wanting to join our cause wouldn't try to destroy my house with a Bradley Fighting Vehicle, would they?"

"It wasn't your house I was trying to destroy. It was the she-devil."

"The she-devil? You completely missed her!"

"So she's still out there?" Flynn tried to look concerned instead of relieved.

General Jedidiah Anderson stepped closer to Flynn. "The devil is a trickster, and so are his minions."

Flynn looked to Gabriel. "Gabriel, tell him who I am."

"You are a lost soul, seduced by the she-devil to fight for the Army of Hell."

"What? No! I only pretended to be on her side. I was working undercover."

"The Lord detests lying lips," Gabriel spat. "You left me behind, but I still got away. Made my way to San Jose. I located a library, found an open computer, and googled *Armageddon*. I was hoping for a sign from the almighty and he gave me one. General Anderson's Army of God. I made a pilgrimage here and unlike most mortals, when I told them I was an archangel in human form, they took me at my word."

Anderson nodded and looked at Flynn. "If Christ himself came back to Earth, the godless would lock him up in a psyche ward. For all we know, he's already here, pumped up with Thorazine, rotting in some dark padded cell. Now... tell me where to find Caitlyn Valentine."

Flynn shook his head. "I don't know. I wish I did. But I don't."

General Anderson settled his cold eyes on Brian Snedeker. "Show Mr. Flynn the horrors of Hell. If he doesn't die, if he manages to stay alive, and still claims not to know the whereabouts of that she-demon, then we will know he speaks the truth." He turned his gaze back to Flynn. "Either way, we will purify you with pain. The mortification of the flesh can be a path to forgiveness. I will return in two days. Survive this trial and perhaps you will feel closer to the Lord and even let him into your heart."

CHAPTER THIRTY-THREE

Anderson left with two of his militiamen. Flynn didn't hear the helicopter until the general opened the door. He glimpsed the bird sitting on its helipad a distance away, its position lights blinking in the darkness. The sun was down. Night had fallen. One of the two remaining militiamen shut the door, silencing the sound of the chopper.

"The room is well insulated," Flynn said.

"Sound proof," Snedeker replied. He nodded to Gabriel, who shoveled a few hot coals into the small cast-iron oven built into Flynn's Hellfire Chair. "So you can scream as loud as you want. No one will hear."

"I'm not much of a screamer," Flynn replied.

Snedeker grinned. "I guess we'll see, won't we?"

"Mr. Snedeker, would you mind if I asked you a question?"

"Not at all."

"How is it you came to become the General's Grand Inquisitor?"

"We met in Kandahar."

"Were you C.I.A. or Army Intelligence?"

"What does it matter?"

"I imagine you were an interrogator."

"You have an excellent imagination." He pushed up his glasses and nodded to Gabriel who shoveled a few more hot coals into the cast-iron oven.

Sweat ran down the side of Flynn's face as he watched Snedeker approach a large antique wooden table covered with a white tablecloth. Various instruments of torture lay in a carefully organized arrangement. There were scalpels and pliers, rubber mallets and bone saws, and some odd and unique handheld torture devices that Flynn hadn't seen before and hoped never to see again.

The iron chair heated up. The pain was bearable, but just barely. He caught Snedeker's eye. "You clearly enjoy your work."

"Is it that obvious?"

"What's the saying? Choose a job you love and you will never have to work a day in your life."

"Do you know Torquemada kept detailed records of what he did and how he did it? Accounts of the cries of torture victims and what elicited them. What loosened tongues and what loosened bowels. I applied his methods and learned from his mistakes and his successes. We used the same tricks and techniques in Kandahar. In 800 years human beings haven't really changed all that much. Not physically or psychologically. The anticipation of pain is almost worse than the actual agony itself. The trick is to make it so much worse than the victim ever imagined it could be."

Flynn winced and tried to hide it. "If I die here serving the Lord, then so be it."

"Hallelujah!" shouted Gabriel. "We will burn the corruption out of your heart and purify your soul so you can live for eternity in the Lord's everlasting paradise."

Flynn tried to lift his arms off the searing metal, but they were immovable. Snedeker sensed Flynn's agony and fed on it. He picked up a pair of pliers and used them to grip Flynn's nose. "The same nerves that give us such exquisite pleasure can also cause us the greatest pain. This cast-iron oven can reach temperatures of over eight hundred degrees. How's that scrotum feeling? Every square inch of that rather unattractive skin sack contains over one thousand nerve endings."

Snedeker grinned as he twisted the pliers. Flynn grunted and gritted his teeth. "I get the distinct sense you're trying to intimidate me."

"I bet your hacky sack is starting to smart," Snedeker said.

"What do you want! What do you want from me?"

"The truth."

"What truth? Who's truth?"

"Where is that she-devil?"

"I told you! I don't know!"

"Who do you work for?"

"His Majesty's Secret Service!"

"You don't work for Satan?"

"No!"

"You don't carry water for the Prince of Darkness?"

"No!"

"So Beelzebub isn't your primary employer?"

This time Flynn's "no" was a hoarse whisper. "No…"

Flynn saw Gabriel looking at him with some concern. "I think he's telling the truth."

"Only one way to find out." Brian Snedeker pointed at the last of the red-hot coals in Gabriel's bucket and then pointed at the oven under Flynn's Hellfire chair. "Mr. Flynn thinks he's in pain, but this will feel like a day at the spa compared to what Mr. Flynn will experience once I really get to work."

Gabriel looked reluctant as he scooped up the last of the hot coals.

The lights went out, plunging the barn into darkness.

Flynn could see the glowing coals in the bucket, but not much else.

"What the heck," Snedeker groused. "That stupid frickin' circuit breaker! I told Anderson we needed to increase the amperage. I wasn't even using the gosh darn electric chair for cripe's sake."

Someone undid the buckles holding Flynn in place on the Hellfire chair. First his ankles. Then his wrists. He stood and immediately collapsed. On the floor. In the darkness.

"What was that? Did you hear that? I think someone's here." Snedeker said.

"Yeah, I'm here," Caitlyn answered. "And I'm wearing night-vision goggles and holding a very large gun."

"Bullcrap," Brian Snedeker said. One second later the enormous gun boomed.

Snedeker yelled and fell. He hit the ground hard and made an *oof* sound.

That gunshot prompted the two militiamen to fire in the direction of the boom. Caitlyn's big gun boomed twice again. Two large bodies hit the cement.

A moment later, Caitlyn's hand rested on Flynn's shoulder. "Can you stand?"

"I'm a bit worse for the wear, but I do believe I'm mobile."

She helped him to his feet. "We better go before it blows."

"Before what blows?"

An immense explosion shook the barn. The violence of the blast created a kaboom so loud it even penetrated the barn's state-of-the-art soundproofing.

"What did you do?" Snedeker demanded. Apparently, he was still alive.

"I blew that armory to high heaven," Caitlyn replied.

Snedeker laughed an evil laugh. "You'll never escape! You'll never get out alive! You'll never—" The large gun boomed, shutting him up mid-sentence.

After an awkward pause, Gabriel's voice came up out of the darkness. "Hello, She-demon."

"Gabriel?" Caitlyn sounded surprised.

"Have you come for your revenge?"

"No, just Flynn."

"I knew you were one of Satan's hellspawn."

"I don't really have time for a long conversation, Gabriel. Are you okay?"

"Not really."

"Okay, well, we're going to leave now."

"Okay."

Caitlyn helped Flynn to the door and opened it. They stepped outside. In the light of the waxing moon, Flynn saw she was indeed wearing night-vision goggles.

"Did you get those from the armory?" he asked.

"I have a pair for you too and a large selection of weapons loaded into that tank over there."

Flynn spotted the M1 Abrams tank parked a short distance away. "You know how to drive a tank?"

"I do now," Caitlyn said.

Someone fired on them from the darkness. Others joined in. A bullet whizzed by Flynn's head and Caitlyn helped him inside the tank. He tried to sit, but his dangly bits wouldn't stand for it. So he kneeled instead. Bullets pinged and ricocheted off the armor as Caitlyn fired up the engine. She peered through the night-vision periscope and trundled them out of there. Flynn couldn't see where they were going or what was happening outside. He was just glad his gonads were no longer being grilled. It was then that Flynn realized he didn't have a stitch of clothing on.

"You're very quiet." Caitlyn said. "Are you okay?"

"I could use some pants."

"Yes, you could."

"And Bactine would be good."

"I grabbed a first aid kit from the armory. It's right by your feet."

Caitlyn fired the tank's machine gun. The sound was somewhat muffled inside the cockpit, but Flynn noticed that since she started shooting, fewer bullets pinged off the outer armor.

Flynn tapped Caitlyn on the shoulder. "May I ask where we're going?"

"Buffalo."

"New York?"

"Wyoming. It's about three hours east of here."

"You're driving this tank all the way to Buffalo?"

"Of course not. This beast only gets a half mile per gallon." She glanced at the fuel gauge. "And we're just about out of gas."

"So we'll be walking?"

"If that's your preference. Me, I'm taking the Maserati."

The tank stopped abruptly. Caitlyn threw open the hatch. She scrambled out and helped Flynn extricate himself. He moved slowly and winced painfully. The Maserati SUV sat just ahead. Caitlyn hopped in the driver's seat and Flynn rode shotgun. The cool, soft Nappa leather felt wonderful on his slightly burnt bum. The SUV started with a throaty rumble, punctuated by the crack of an AK bullet shattering one of the Maserati's back windows. More windows shattered, and more bullets punctured the side panels. Caitlyn jammed the car into drive and flattened the gas, kicking up gravel. The window next to Flynn's head exploded. A bullet buried itself in Caitlyn's headrest.

The Maserati took off like a rocket sled, leaving the Army of God in the dust. Flynn felt the back of his head and looked at the blood on his fingertips.

Caitlyn kept her eyes on the road. "You hit?"

"It's nothing. I'm fine."

"We need to get you some clothes."

"I don't disagree."

"I almost left you behind."

"But you didn't."

A pause as Caitlyn considered that. "No."

"Did you ever make it into the server room?"

"I did."

"And?"

She grinned. "I think I found the motherlode. Though I still need to sift through it to know exactly what we have."

CHAPTER THIRTY-FOUR

Built in 1880, the Occidental Hotel attracted both the famous and the infamous. Located near the foot of the Bighorn Mountains, the hotel quickly became the most renowned hostelry in Wyoming. Early guests included Buffalo Bill Cody, Teddy Roosevelt, and Calamity Jane, who drove freight wagons on the Bozeman Trail. Butch Cassidy and the Sundance Kid would occasionally stop by for a steak, a bottle of whiskey, and a night of high stakes poker. The saloon still sports its original 25-foot-long mahogany and brass bar. The heads of elk, moose, mule deer, and pronghorn antelope decorate the walls and look down on the ghosts of those who fought and died in the Johnson County War.

With the adrenaline dissipating, exhaustion permeated every cell in Caitlyn's body. She winced with every bruise and muscle pull, every scrape and laceration. She saw the pain as a blessing as it was the only thing keeping her awake. Blinking her bleary eyes, she navigated east on US Route 14. She passed a sign indicating they were on the Bighorn Scenic Byway and damn if it wasn't scenic as hell.

The sun had risen just an hour earlier and the views of the Bighorn Mountains were spectacular. Route 14 cut through mountain meadows and dense pine forests, rugged alpine peaks, and deep dramatic canyons with cascading waterfalls. Caitlyn kept looking at Flynn to get his reaction, but he was dead to the world. Snoring with his mouth open and totally naked. *What the hell am I doing dragging this nude lunatic halfway across the country?* Charming and attractive as he was, he was also certifiably nuts. But then again, he'd saved her bacon more than once. If not for him, she'd be dead or still locked in that loony bin. What did it say that he was the only one who didn't think she was crazy?

. . .

Flynn awakened with a start as Caitlyn sprayed ice cold Bactine all over his twig and berries.

"How's that feel?" she said.

Flynn gritted his teeth against the cold, but before long the relief spread. "Better."

"Good." She grinned and sang, "You broke my will, but what a thrill. Goodness gracious, great balls of fire."

She laughed and Flynn couldn't help but laugh as well. She dropped some clothes in his lap. "I found these in that box Sancho gave us."

"Thank you."

"Can you put those on while I check us in?"

"Check us in?" He looked through the windscreen and saw a block long, brick building with white western-style letters stretching across the top. *Occidental Hotel.* "I can do that."

"Good."

She handed Flynn the Bactine and slammed the passenger door. The burning sensation returned to his knackers and he dosed those dangly-bits with another burst. *Bloody hell.* That freak Snedeker certainly did a number on his nuts. The cotton boxers felt like barbed wire as he pulled them up. He cursed the fact that the black Hugo Boss trousers hugged him so tight. That was the look. Slim fit. And it took a while to slide them up over his flowers and frolics.

Caitlyn returned in twenty minutes. He assumed she used some of Alessandra's cash to pay for their room. She gently helped Flynn out of the car and up the steps into the ornate, antique-filled, western-style lobby. They climbed a long staircase. Every step was agony. Deer heads and cowboy art, ornate Victorian sconces and sepia-framed photographs of the Occidental in its heyday adorned the walls.

She'd booked them into the Cottonwood Suite because it had a king-sized bed and wasn't far from the ice machine. A plus for Flynn since he spent the next three hours icing his overcooked undercarriage. Caitlyn sat at the antique desk and plugged the flash drive into the Dell XPS laptop she also picked up at that Kmart in Provo. While Flynn soothed his goolies, Caitlyn searched through the files she found on the Army of God's server.

"Here we go," Caitlyn mumbled.

"Did you find something incriminating?"

Caitlyn nodded. "Sure did."

"Would you care to be more specific?"

"Are you hungry?"

"I am indeed."

"Me too. There's a place in the hotel that looks pretty good. Let's get some breakfast and I'll lay it all out for you. Of course, you'll have to put on some pants."

"I think I'm ready for that."

"All right then."

. . .

Caitlyn didn't realize how famished she was until she smelled the bacon and eggs, home fries, and fresh buttermilk biscuits arrayed in front of her. The Occidental Hotel's Busy Bee Café bustled. The coffee was hot and strong and so was their waitress: a strapping fifty-something redhead barely contained by her black Busy Bee t-shirt. She flirted with Flynn shamelessly and he didn't discourage her. He never discouraged anyone. Caitlyn found that both entertaining and a little irritating. Was that irritation jealousy? As much as she didn't want to admit it, Flynn had wormed his way into her heart. She knew it would never work. She knew they had no future. She wasn't even sure *she* had a future.

The waitress offered Flynn more coffee. "Can I warm that up for you, sugar?"

"Thank you, Shelly. I would love a little more."

She didn't offer Caitlyn more coffee and bustled off to warm up cups elsewhere. Gingham curtains, buffalo heads, and other charming western-style antiques, knickknacks, and gewgaws decorated the Busy Bee. A sign on the wall had a list of commandments.

Bee Humble. Bee Honest. Bee Kind. Bee Grateful. Bee Happy. Bee You.

Caitlyn caught Flynn gazing at her across the table.

He raised an eyebrow. "So, are you going to tell me what you found?"

She leaned in and lowered her voice. "The Church of the Prophecy and The Army of God bought a tactical nuclear device."

"Didn't we already know that?"

"We knew they *wanted* to."

"Do we know who sold it to them?"

"General Anderson works with both legitimate arms brokers and those who deal in illegal weapons and sales. Through those contacts on the dark web, he found someone who would sell him a suitcase nuke. I spoofed the general's IP address and contacted the sellers directly on the dark web. I told them I had another buyer interested in their merchandise and they responded almost immediately. Apparently, they have more than a few of them and are trying to unload them quickly."

Flynn nodded. "Are they in the former eastern bloc? I've read that Bulgaria has a thriving black market in plutonium and enriched uranium as well as actual nuclear warheads stolen from the former Soviet Union. They do all their business on the dark web."

"They're not in the former eastern bloc."

"So where are they?"

"Beloit, Wisconsin."

"Someone in Wisconsin is selling suitcase nukes?"

"So they claim," Caitlyn said.

"And you want to talk to them?"

"Yep."

"And find out exactly who they sold it to."

"I do."

"Did you set up a meeting?"

"I did. It's a fourteen-hour drive to Beloit from here. We can take turns driving and sleep on the way."

"There's no time to lose, then."

"Nope."

Shelly the waitress swung by with the coffeepot and pointed at Flynn's cup. He put his hand over it. "Thank you, Shelly, but I believe we're ready for the check."

CHAPTER THIRTY-FIVE

The dark web exists on what are called darknets: overlay networks that use the internet, but require specialized software, specific configurations, and authorization codes to access. On the dark web, private computer networks can communicate and conduct business without identifying a user's location or any other information. So terrorists and criminals can meet and conduct business on the dark web anonymously. Black markets on the dark web sell everything from child pornography and illegal drugs to stolen credit card numbers and illicit weapons and munitions. Proprietary data stolen from ransomware attacks is often dumped on the dark web and sold to the highest bidder. Most transactions are conducted using Bitcoin and other cryptocurrencies.

Powered by four cups of Busy Bee Coffee and the burning pain still nagging his naughty bits, Flynn took the wheel for the first leg of their journey. Though thrashed and battered with a shattered back window and a smashed front bumper, the Maserati Levante still ran like a top. Caitlyn slept in the backseat, curled up in the fetal position. Flynn figured the contact they were meeting operated under the aegis of the Russian Mafia. Who else would have access to suitcase nukes from the former Soviet Republic?

When billionaire Sergei Belenki hired him as a bodyguard, Flynn bumped up against the *Solntsevskaya Bratva*. They wanted Belenki dead and Flynn found himself caught in the crossfire. *Which Russian organized crime syndicate will I be dealing with this time? Who operates out of Chicago? Are they working with The Outfit?* He had history with that infamous criminal organization as well. A madman with a plan to irradiate the entire gold supply at Fort Knox used them and Detroit's Purple Gang to finance his ultimately unsuccessful score.

At the halfway point between Buffalo and Beloit, Flynn stopped for petrol and a visit to the loo. From there, Caitlyn took the wheel and Flynn stretched out the best he could in the backseat. He tried to get some sleep, but his anticipation for what they'd find in Wisconsin kept his mind racing.

He called to Caitlyn from the rear seat. "How can we be sure we're not driving into a trap?"

"We can't."

"So this man we're meeting. Do we know anything about him?"

"Nothing really. All I have is a code name and login credentials for a dark web marketplace called the Golden Crescent."

"So what's the going price for a suitcase nuke?"

"The seller is asking one hundred bitcoins."

"What's that in real money?"

"The current price for one bitcoin is almost twenty thousand."

"Twenty thousand times one hundred?"

"Two million dollars."

"A tidy sum," Flynn said with a smile.

"Chump change for a billionaire like Anderson."

"Indeed. So where are we meeting this seller?"

Caitlyn glanced at Flynn in the rearview mirror. "I'm supposed to message him when we arrive in town."

"We have the what and the why, but not the where or the when. For all we know, we could already be too late."

"If it already happened, I think we'd know."

"That just means it hasn't happened *yet.*" Flynn pointed out.

"Try to get some sleep while you can. You won't rest much once the shit hits the fan."

.   .   .

Flynn's fake mustache looked crooked. He tried to rearrange it, but the glue had already set. Steam filled the bathroom and he had to keep wiping the mist off the mirror. Caitlyn turned off the shower, pushed back the plastic curtain, and stepped from the tub, already wrapped in a towel. Flynn found her modesty endearing. "I like you as a redhead."

She pointed to the empty box on the counter. Clairol Nice'n Easy Perfect 10. "I couldn't decide between *Cool Summer Blonde* or *Caribbean Mahogany.*"

"Auburn suits your skin tone and complements your eyes. You must have some Irish in you."

"Scottish. On my father's side. My mom's side is German and Italian."

Flynn smiled and stepped closer. "Though you'd be quite striking as blonde as well."

"Are you flirting with me, Mr. Flynn?"

"Just stating the obvious."

It was Flynn who suggested they stop at the Walmart Supercenter across the highway from their motel to see what they could find to disguise themselves. Their escape from Hornitos was still a top story on cable news, and they couldn't afford to be recognized. The powers allied against them were clearly doing all they could to keep the story alive. Fox and CNN basically deputized every citizen in America to be aware, be afraid, and contact local law enforcement if the two were spotted. Besides the hair dye and Halloween costume supplies, they bought clothes to help them blend in even more. Caitlyn encouraged Flynn to dress like a small town midwestern dad. He bristled at first, but finally agreed. Flynn didn't enjoy wearing ugly or gaudy clothing. Unlike many spies, he wasn't a master of disguise.

He once posed as a Japanese fisherman, and that turned into a total debacle. He knew he wasn't fooling anyone and felt the same way now clad in oversized stone-washed high-waisted denim dad shorts, white tube socks, and clunky, chunky blindingly white sneakers. He wore black, semi-rimless, non-prescription nerd glasses, and a blue Chicago Cubs baseball cap. His baggy yellow t-shirt had the words "World's Best Farter… I mean father" emblazoned across the front. A bright blue fanny pack rounded out this unsightly ensemble. If the overall effect was to cause people to look away in horror, then so much the better.

Caitlyn assembled an equally hideous outfit. Baggy mom jeans stuffed with something that made her perfect bum larger and somewhat squishy. A shapeless purple polyester polka dot blouse, pink Crocs, and a multi-colored quilted shoulder bag completed her look.

Caitlyn's burner phone buzzed. The seller had texted her the meeting location. "Applebee's."

"Across the street?"

"It's the only one in town."

"You ready to do this?"

Caitlyn unwrapped a stick of gum and put it in her mouth. "Let's do it."

. . .

Applebee's was a six-minute walk from the Quality Inn. They passed Qdoba Mexican Eats and a Little Caesar's pizza before they reached the Applebee's parking lot. As they approached the front doors of the large casual dining establishment, Flynn imagined the burning glare of every eye in the parking lot. When he looked back, however, no one paid him any attention at all.

For the first time ever, Flynn fit right in with the general population. That thought chilled him to his core.

A bored and irritated young hostess looked up with a frown. Flynn wasn't used to that kind of reaction from the fairer sex. Most women perked up when they saw him. Young women. Old women. Didn't really matter. They'd straighten up and smile and look him in the eye. Often, they'd exhibit certain unconscious signs that signaled their amorous interest. They'd stroke their hair. Lick their lips. Coyly tilt their head and giggle for no good reason. But this young twenty-something couldn't be less interested. Flynn might have been invisible for all the attention she paid him. She barely looked up from her phone and her greeting was as bored and perfunctory as the look on her face. "Welcome to Applebee's."

"We're meeting someone here," Flynn said.

"Hmm?"

"We're meeting someone," Caitlyn repeated.

She nodded and briefly glanced up at Caitlyn. "Do you want to look around and see if they're here?"

Flynn noticed the name on her tag. "Thank you, Brittany."

She nodded, but didn't look at Flynn. He found Brittany's disinterest disheartening and deeply mortifying. The heat of humiliation rose up the back of his neck and he vaguely remembered experiencing that sort of embarrassment before. Flynn had to work to force it back down and into that secret part of himself that had no confidence or self-esteem. That weak and helpless part of his personality that he kept hidden and locked away.

Caitlyn charged off and Flynn pushed up his nerd glasses to follow. The seller said they'd be wearing a sweatshirt with an American flag on it. They searched the room for a huge, hulking Slavic-looking guy decked out in red, white, and blue, but the only diner in the room dressed in that sort of outfit was a white-haired grandmother-type with big plastic glasses. Her sweatshirt had red and white stripes decorated with sequins on one side and sparkly yellow stars on a navy-blue background on the other. Caitlyn approached and used their pre-arranged sign/countersign code. "Rainbow in the morning gives you fair warning."

"Ring around the moon? Rain real soon," croaked the elderly lady. She had no hint of a Russian accent, but sounded like someone from Minnesota.

Caitlyn scooted into the booth across from her, leaving room for Flynn to follow. The lady was round and rather large and barely fit in the booth. She had a cup of black coffee in front of her and the remnants of some sort of dessert. Melted ice cream and brownie crumbs. Smears of chocolate frosting decorated the corners of her mouth. "Were you followed?"

"No," Flynn said.

"Are you sure?"

"Yes." He stared at her.

"If you are law enforcement, you need to identify yourself as such."

"We're not," Caitlyn said.

She nodded, pushed away her plate, and dabbed her mouth with a cloth napkin. "We can't talk here."

"Where?" Caitlyn snapped her gum.

"Follow me."

CHAPTER THIRTY-SIX

It took the seller quite a while to extricate herself from the Applebee's booth, but once she did, she led Flynn and Caitlyn back into the parking lot, where they followed her to a brown, late-model Chevy Malibu. The seller frisked them both. Expertly and methodically. *Is she looking for guns? Wires?* She didn't say and Flynn didn't ask. He knew better than to come armed, but Flynn felt rather naked without his weapon.

"I apologize," the seller said. "But I can't be too careful."

Flynn nodded. "Understood."

The seller offered the shotgun seat to Flynn to better accommodate his long legs. Caitlyn sat in the back.

The older woman lit up an unfiltered cigarette before taking her handicapped parking permit off the rearview mirror and rolling down the driver's side window an inch or two to let the smoke out. She backed out of her handicapped spot and took a left on Milwaukee Road. The woman drove with confidence and puffed away. Squinting through the smoke, she caught Caitlyn's eye in the rearview mirror. "Name's Eunice. What's yours?"

"Judy," Caitlyn said. She pointed at Flynn. "That's Mike."

Betty nodded and merged on I-90 North.

"Where are we going?" Flynn asked.

"You'll see," Eunice said.

Twenty minutes later, they reached a two-lane country road and rumbled past vast fields of corn. Flynn wondered how a conservative-looking elderly white lady got her hands on tactical nuclear weapons. Was she the grandmother of an international

263

arms trafficker? He supposed it was possible. Even the worst of the worst had grandmothers. Flynn glanced at Caitlyn and raised an eyebrow. She smirked and shook her head.

A minute later, Eunice pulled the Chevy down a gravel road that led through a cornfield and finally to a farmhouse surrounded by a large lawn and a beautiful garden.

Eunice pushed open the driver's door and rocked back and forth twice before she dislodged herself from the driver's seat. "This way." She led them to the front doors of the sprawling two-story farmhouse.

Inside, the place was immaculate and decorated in Early American antiques. Braided area rugs covered the polished hardwood floor. The furniture looked handcrafted. A red floral Chippendale sofa sat across from two beautifully upholstered wingback chairs with carved American eagles. White doilies decorated the arms.

Eunice plopped down in one of the wingback chairs and directed them to the sofa. Once they sat, she searched Flynn and Caitlyn's eyes. "I assume you'd like to see the merchandise?"

Caitlyn nodded. "We would."

Eunice barked out the name "Walter" with such violence and volume both Caitlyn and Flynn couldn't help but jump. A moment later, a tall, older gentleman appeared from another room with a big smile on his face. He was rangy and raw-boned with huge hands and broad shoulders. Walter wore gray work pants, scuffed steel-toed boots, and a faded red and white checkered flannel shirt. He had a pleasant, welcoming smile and didn't seem nearly as taciturn as his partner in crime. Eunice introduced Walter as her husband.

Flynn offered Walter a charming grin. "I'm Mike. This is Judy." Caitlyn just nodded her head.

"Welcome to our home." Walt's voice was reedy and high-pitched.

"Thank you," Flynn said.

Eunice lit up another cigarette. "Before we show you the merchandise, we're going to need a good faith payment of ten bitcoin."

Caitlyn shook her head. "That's not what we agreed to. I need to know you have what we're looking for before we give you dime one."

Eunice narrowed her eyes. "It appears we are at a stalemate, then."

Walter wasn't about to let the sale slip through his fingers so easily. "Now, now, Eunice, I'm sure we can come to some kind of accommodation here."

"I agree," Flynn said. "But I'm sure you understand our skepticism. You seem like a very nice couple. How is it you came to acquire tactical nuclear weapons?"

"I don't think that's any of your business," Eunice barked.

Caitlyn rose up off the couch. "Look, *Eunice*, I'm not leaving here until you show me that suitcase nuke."

Eunice grunted and lifted herself off the eagle chair. "Are you threatening us, missy?"

"I don't want to hurt you, but I will if I have to."

Eunice laughed and looked at Walt. "She's threatening us!"

"That's funny to you?" Caitlyn said.

Eunice lumbered closer and stood nose-to-nose with Caitlyn. "I don't like threats."

Caitlyn put her hand on Eunice's chest to push her back. Eunice grabbed Caitlyn's wrist and twisted and turned and used her superior size to bring Caitlyn to her knees.

A shocked Flynn caught the surprise in Caitlyn's eyes as she tried to escape Eunice's grip. Eunice pulled her close and head-butted her viciously before using a sophisticated submission hold to force Caitlyn face down on the floor.

As Flynn stood to help, Walter pressed a stun gun into his neck. Thousands of volts surged through Flynn's nervous system and he lost control of his legs. Walt was fast and shockingly strong for such an elderly stick insect. He slammed Flynn's head into the edge of a colonial coffee table. Flynn saw stars and not just on Eunice's sweatshirt as she brought her shoe down on his face.

. . .

When Flynn came to, he couldn't move. His arms were zip-tied behind him and his legs were zip-tied together. He lay on his side on the floor next to an equally trussed and beat-to-shit Caitlyn. Both Eunice and Walter glared down at them.

Flynn suddenly understood what was happening and who Eunice and Walter were. He explained it with one word. "Systema."

"Excuse me?" Eunice said.

"I haven't seen it used in years, but you are clearly a master."

"I don't know what you're talking about."

"*The system.* Russia's indigenous martial art. Developed by the Cossacks a thousand years ago. Of course, it has morphed over the years. Refined and perfected by Spetsnaz and SMERSH. Dangerous. Deadly. Similar to Krav Maga in its simplicity, practicality, and single-minded brutality."

Eunice offered just the hint of a smile as she squinted at him through her omnipresent cigarette smoke. "You're smarter than you look. Especially for someone who would wear such a stupid t-shirt."

"You're Russian, but you have no accent. What are you? *Sleepers?*"

"I don't know what you're talking about."

"The Illegals Program. You're just the right age."

Caitlyn rolled over to glance at Flynn. "The Illegals Program?"

"That's what the Department of Justice called it. In the 1980s, the KGB inserted a network of undercover Soviet sleeper agents in every major city in America. They trained for years to lose their accents so they could pose as ordinary Americans. Many came as two-person teams and masqueraded as married couples."

Caitlyn stared at Walt and Eunice and then back at Flynn. "What? Like that TV show?"

"Exactly. Each agent is an expert in languages, electronic surveillance, munitions, martial arts, and weapons. Certain ones specialized in various sciences and technologies, including weapons of mass destruction. They inserted themselves in government, in law enforcement, in the military, and in major American corporations."

"You are out of your goddamn mind," Eunice said.

"What's your birth name? Svetlana? Natasha? Magda? You brought them with you, didn't you? You didn't buy them on the black market. They issued them to you."

Caitlyn struggled to roll over even more so she could look Flynn in the eye. "Issued what to who?"

"Miniaturized nuclear weapons. Suitcase nukes. Twenty years ago at a congressional hearing held in Los Angeles, a former Russian military officer claimed that Soviet KGB agents hid small atomic munitions in multiple locations all across the United States."

Eunice barked a harsh laugh. "Preposterous."

Flynn continued. "It's well documented. They hid conventional caches of weapons and explosives, which they planned to use to sabotage America's infrastructure. The suitcase nukes were developed at the Soviet Union's version of Los Alamos. Arzamas-16. The site of a former Russian Orthodox monastery. It was closed in 1923 when the monks were executed by the Bolsheviks. After the war, it became the Scientific Institute of Experimental Physics and the entire city was closed off from the rest of the world. The top scientists had handlers.

Bodyguards. They erased the identities of the residents from the national census. Officially Arzamas-16 didn't even exist."

Eunice lit up another cigarette and held it in her lips as she squinted at Flynn through the smoke. "You are well informed," she said with just the hint of a Russian accent.

"I'm a student of history," Flynn replied.

"So then you know what happened when the Soviet Union collapsed."

"You were abandoned."

"Yes. Left behind. Discarded. Forgotten. We kept to our mission even though those who sent us became businessmen. Politicians. Plutocrats. Oligarchs. Corruption, always a factor, became the organizing principle. The central philosophy. The Kremlin became a kleptocracy. Capitalism won. Communism lost. So we had no choice but to go with the flow. Become capitalists. Gangsters."

"Arms dealers."

Eunice picked a bit of tobacco off her tongue. "I spent the last thirty years working at Walmart. Walt here worked for the post office. Wisconsin isn't bad for most of the year. But from December to February, it's colder than a witch's tit in a brass bra. Much like Moscow. As we grew older, it became more difficult to live with that."

"The average high in January is twenty-nine degrees Fahrenheit," Walt said.

"The average low is fifteen fucking degrees," Eunice added. "With windchill, it's even lower. Often the temperature doesn't rise above zero for weeks at a time."

"We just want to move somewhere warm," Walt said.

"Hawaii," Eunice explained. "We have our eye on a beach house in Maui."

Caitlyn grinned. "Seriously? You're selling your suitcase nukes to terrorists so you can move to Maui?"

Eunice nodded and lit a cigarette with the one still smoldering in her mouth. "That's how Capitalism works. Supply and demand. We have an exceedingly small supply and there's an exceptionally large demand. In fact, we only have one suitcase nuke left. But apparently you and Mike are here under false pretenses. Who do you work for? Homeland Security? The FBI?"

"We're not here for you," Flynn said. "We're here to find out who you sold your second to last nuke to."

"So if we give you that information, you'll go on your merry way and leave us alone to sell our last nuke to whoever we want?"

"No, I'm sorry," Flynn said. "That would be irresponsible."

"Oh, I see. You want to take it and *not* pay us. Is that what you're saying?" Eunice smiled with tiny tea-stained teeth. "Do you know how much it costs to buy a beachfront house in Maui?"

"Millions, I imagine, but I'm afraid we have no choice. That nuke needs to come with us."

Eunice smirked. "Am I missing something here? Aren't you the ones tied up on the floor?" Eunice opened a drawer in a buffet cabinet and took out a pistol. She pointed it at Flynn.

"Wait! *Wait! What are you doing?*" Caitlyn asked.

"Shooting him and then you." She pulled back the hammer.

"CIA!" Caitlynn shouted. She pointed to Flynn with her nose. "And Mike's with British Intelligence. Do you really think we came here without backup?"

"Yes, because Walter shadowed you and watched to see if anyone was watching you and no one is. No one is watching you. You are all alone here."

"You're right," Flynn said. He rolled and rocked forward and then back and then forward until he sat in an upright position. "We are rogue operators, and Mike and Judy aren't our real names."

"No kidding," Eunice said.

"She is Caitlyn Valentine and I am James Flynn."

"Shut up, James," Caitlyn said.

"Caitlyn uncovered a deadly plot and, like you, was abandoned by her own government. To cover up their evil plan, those responsible had her declared insane and sent away to an institution. My people sent me to free her, and now we both are fugitives." Flynn shook off his glasses and looked Eunice hard in the eye. "Look at me, Eunice. Don't you know who I am?"

Eunice's mouth formed a perfect O and her eyes went wide as recognition dawned. "You're those two mental patients. The ones who escaped from that nut house in California."

"Oh, for fuck's sake," Caitlyn said.

"Here's your chance, Eunice. You once believed in something. You once hoped you'd make a difference. Well, I'm here to tell you that *this* is your chance. Join us. Help us. Together we can save the world."

Eunice picked a bit of tobacco off her tongue. "Yeah, I don't think so."

Flynn looked directly into the barrel of Eunice's gun. "Then do it. Shoot us. But know this. You won't just be killing us. You'll be killing yourselves. By selling that tactical nuke to those terrorists, you set in motion a plan to start World War Three."

Eunice looked unconvinced. "Why would anyone want to start World War Three?"

"Because they believe World War Three will be the final battle between heaven and hell."

"Now you just sound crazy."

"Because it is crazy, Eunice. But we're not the crazy ones. They are!"

"Maybe you're all crazy." She raised her pistol to shoot them, but Walt gently pushed the barrel back down.

"Hold on now, hon, I think there's a reward for these loony tunes."

"A reward?"

"100,000 dollars for each one. For information leading to their capture."

"Really?"

"If we turn 'em in, we can make some money. And if they tell anyone we're spies who tried to sell 'em a suitcase nuke, nobody's gonna believe 'em. Everybody already thinks they're crazy."

"Because they *are* crazy," Eunice said.

Walt and Eunice laughed and that laughter soon devolved into coughing and the hacking up of generous quantities of phlegm.

CHAPTER THIRTY-SEVEN

On January 24th, 2000, former KGB operative Stanislaw Lunev was the star witness at a Military Research and Development Subcommittee hearing chaired by Representative Curt Weldon (R-PA). Lunev testified that KGB agents planted hundreds of portable tactical nuclear devices disguised to look like small suitcases in various locations in Europe and the United States in the 1970s and '80s. Each one could be set to detonate within ten minutes and would produce a 10-kiloton blast.

The former Soviet spies left Flynn and Caitlyn zip-tied on the floor. Flynn's wrists were bound behind his back and he could get very little leverage to pull himself loose. Caitlyn had smaller wrists and hands and the plastic didn't cut as deep into her flesh. She strained to pull her hands through. The hard plastic scraped her skin raw.

The braided area rug in Eunice and Walt's living room smelled like wet dog. Or maybe that smell emanated from the dog itself, sitting ten feet away. The elderly cocker spaniel's eyes were glazed bluish-gray with cataracts.

Walt shouted into the phone in the kitchen. "No, I'm not kidding. It's the same two I saw on TV. Those two crazies from California."

Eunice joined in and shouted just as loud as Walt. "Tell 'em we got 'em tied up in the living room!"

"We got 'em tied up in the living room!"

A silent beat as whoever Walt spoke with obviously had a question or a comment.

"What's he saying?" Eunice wanted to know.

"He wants to know if I'm sure."

"Of course we're sure!" Eunice shouted.

"Of course we're sure!" Walt repeated.

As Walt described Caitlyn and Flynn in detail, Caitlyn used the blood that covered her hands as extra lubrication to finally pull her hands free. She pulled the gag out of her mouth and took a deep breath.

"Good girl," Flynn mumbled through his gag.

She tried to pull apart the flex ties that bound her ankles, but they were heavy duty and not about to budge. "I'm gonna need a knife or a saw to get my legs free," she whispered.

In the other room, Walt shouted into the phone. "Well, when can you get here?"

"What did they say?" Eunice prodded.

"They didn't and they don't seem to be in any damn hurry."

"Ask to speak to their supervisor."

"I wanna speak to your supervisor," Walt insisted. He listened to whatever whoever he was talking had to say and then said, "I don't care. I can wait. I want to talk to someone who can make a damn decision."

Caitlyn carefully rolled across the floor to make as little noise as possible. Luckily, both Walt and Eunice seemed hard of hearing. She pulled herself to her knees and a opened a door to reveal a hall closet heavy with coats and plastic boots.

Flynn motioned with his head towards another door on the other side of the room. Caitlyn nodded and rolled her way over. That door led to a stairwell.

"Basement," she whispered.

Flynn rolled closer and looked down the stairs. They were steep, but Caitlyn showed no hesitation. Using her hands, Caitlyn pulled herself down the steep staircase, being careful not to let her momentum get ahead of her. Flynn wanted to follow, but wasn't sure how.

"Where the hell do you think you're going?" Eunice shouted.

Flynn inched himself over the edge and proceeded to fall down the stairs. With his ankles tied together and his hands bound behind him, he fell with all the grace of a crash dummy. He collided with Caitlyn, who hadn't quite reached the bottom and they both tumbled the rest of the way down, landing in a heap on the hard cement floor.

Flynn, on his back and bleeding, looked up the stairs. Eunice stood at the top. She laughed. "Walt, you gotta see this!"

Walt appeared next to her. "Shit. Now we gotta carry them back up the damn stairs. Don't want the cops nosing around the basement."

"Are the police on the way?" Flynn mumbled through his gag.

"What did he say?" Eunice asked.

"Who the hell knows?" Walt answered.

Flynn glanced at Caitlyn. "Suitcase nuke," he said through his gag. Even though it sounded like *oo-cake-uke*, she still seemed to understand him.

She looked around the room and whispered, "Gotta be down here somewhere."

Eunice and Walt clomped down the stairs. Eunice carried a revolver. Walt cradled a shotgun. She holstered her weapon and zip-tied Caitlyn's hands again while Walt held his shotgun on her. Then he leaned his weapon against the wall and grabbed Flynn's arms. Eunice grabbed Flynn by the ankles. Grunting, they lifted him up off the floor.

Walt cried out and let Flynn fall, his head bouncing off the floor. "My goddamn back."

"I can't carry him up myself," Eunice hissed.

Walt angrily grabbed his shotgun. "Cut the ties on his legs. Let him walk his own ass up."

"What about her?"

"Her too."

Eunice cut the zip ties on their ankles, backed away, and pulled her weapon. "On your feet. NOW!"

Flynn struggled to stand. An aggravated Eunice gave him and then Caitlyn a hand before backing away again. She motioned to the stairs with her gun. "Let's go!"

"Up the stairs!" Walt shouted.

Caitlyn went first. Flynn followed. He knew they were lucky to be alive. Perhaps with the local constabulary, they'd have some chance to escape. After all, they were just a small-town police force. Not hardened KGB agents like Walt and Eunice. Flynn looked past Caitlyn to see the elderly cocker spaniel standing at the top of the stairs.

"Careful, Pumpkin! Stay right there," Eunice ordered. The old dog wagged its tail.

"Stay, Pumpkin! Stay!" Walt added.

"I can't believe you left the damn door open!" Eunice groused.

"Watch the stairs, Pumpkin!"

"Stay, Pumpkin! Stay!"

The old blind dog took a tentative step forward.

"No! No, Pumpkin!" Walt barked.

"*Stay*!" Eunice commanded.

Pumpkin didn't stay, but stepped off the top stair and took a header, somersaulting and tumbling and bumping into Caitlyn, who banged into Flynn, who smacked into Walt, who crashed into Eunice.

Walt's shotgun went off, blowing a hole in the ceiling. A startled Eunice tugged her own trigger and put a bullet in Walt's ass.

Walt dropped his gun as Eunice lost her balance. She tumbled straight back, smacking her head on the cement floor.

Caitlyn pulled her feet through her zip-tied arms and picked up Walt's shotgun. The old man tried to stand, but Caitlyn slammed the stock down on his head, knocking him just as cold as his pleasantly plump wife.

Pumpkin somehow made it to the bottom of the stairs, looking no worse for wear. She sniffed her unconscious mom and dad with curiosity. Flynn located a small handsaw in Walt's basement workshop and, within minutes, both he and Caitlyn were free. He then zip-tied Eunice and Walt while Caitlyn searched the basement for that last remaining suitcase nuke.

She found the suitcase on a metal shelving unit stacked with other old luggage. She set it on Walt's workbench and unlatched the latches. It was the size of a large briefcase and contained some kind of timing mechanism with a digital readout, and two large metallic cylinders which Flynn assumed contained the trigger explosives and the fissionable material. There was also a metal switch flanked by two red buttons. Clearly, this was mid-1980s tech. Flynn detected the musty smell of mildew.

"Be careful with that. It's very touchy," Eunice said. She lay on her side, trussed up with her own zip ties. She struggled against them before giving up with a frustrated grunt.

Walt slowly came to as well, blinking and disoriented as he looked around and slowly assessed their situation. He glared at the dog. "Fucking Pumpkin."

"It's not Pumpkin's fault you left the damn door open," Eunice said.

Flynn reached for something in the suitcase nuke and Caitlyn grabbed his wrist. "Careful. We don't know what we're dealing with here."

"Which is why I need to examine it," Flynn said. "Once we find the one they already sold, we'll need to know how to disarm it."

Caitlyn pointed at a keypad. "If there's a keypad, there has to be a fail-safe code." She looked at Eunice and Walt on the floor. "What is it?"

"What's what?" said Walt.

"The code."

"You want that code? You need to let us go."

"I don't think so," Flynn said.

"Then that bomb that we sold will be detonated and thousands will die," Eunice replied.

Flynn fingered various switches and buttons on the mechanism. "Where and who did you deliver it to, Eunice?"

"I'll let you know once you let us go."

"No, first you let us know, *then* I'll let you go."

"Listen, crazy man," Eunice said. "The police are on their way. What do you think they're gonna say when they find us being held prisoner in our own house?"

"They won't say anything, because by the time they get here, we'll be long gone. You'll have given us the name of the buyer and the code we need to disarm their device."

"And why would we do that?" Eunice spat.

Before Caitlyn could react, Flynn flicked the metallic switch and pushed the two red buttons. The digital clock immediately ticked backwards from thirty minutes.

"Oh, shit," Caitlyn said

"What did you do?" Eunice shouted.

"One-half hour from now, you, me, Caitlyn, Walt, Pumpkin, and everyone else within a ten-mile radius will be completely obliterated unless you tell me the secret security code."

"It's 22429," Eunice shouted. "22429!"

Caitlyn reached for the keypad, but Flynn pushed her hand away. "First, we need the name and location of the buyer."

"James, move!"

"I can't let you —"

She slammed her knee into his groin, shutting him up mid-sentence. As he bent at the waist and cupped his already injured balls, Caitlyn kneed him in the face, knocking him on his ass.

Caitlyn shouted to Eunice, "What's the code?"

"22429!"

Caitlyn punched in the numbers, but the countdown didn't stop. It sped up. "It's not working!"

"Maybe that's the code for the other one," Eunice murmured.

"They have different codes?"

"Of course they do."

"So what's the code for this one?"

Walt piped up. "I think it's 53617."

"Isn't it 56317?" Eunice asked.

"I think it's 5-3-6."

"You don't remember the code?" Caitlyn shouted.

"56317," Eunice said with certainty.

Walt nodded. "That sounds about right."

"*But you're not sure?*" Caitlyn shouted.

Walt nodded. "I think she's right. I think that's it. I'm pretty sure that's it."

Caitlyn punched in 56317.

The countdown didn't stop.

It sped up.

CHAPTER THIRTY-EIGHT

A ten-kiloton nuclear bomb detonated on the ground in New York City would explode with a flash brighter than the sun, briefly blinding people as far away as Long Island and New Jersey. A wave of searing heat would radiate outward from the explosion, followed by a massive fireball, the core of which would reach tens of millions of degrees. Few structures would remain standing. People would be vaporized. Buildings and trees within a one-mile radius would be severely burned or charred. Metal, fabric, and plastic would ignite, melt, or blister. The intense heat would set gas lines, fuel tanks, and power lines on fire, and an electromagnetic pulse created by the explosion would knock out most computers, cell phones, and communication towers within a several mile radius.

Caitlyn frantically punched in 53617. The countdown just sped up.

"Try 94681," Eunice suggested.

Caitlyn did and that didn't work either. The timer ticked down even faster.

"Fuck me!" Caitlyn shouted.

Flynn pulled himself to his feet, still clutching his injured knackers.

"Wasn't it a six number code?" asked Walt.

"Was it?" Eunice looked confused, and then she nodded. "Maybe... yeah... try 946810."

Caitlyn did. With less than five minutes left, the digital numbers flew by in a blur.

"We gotta get out of here!" Caitlyn shouted.

"No point." Flynn shook his head. "We'll never get far enough away."

"Shit!"

"Try that first number I gave you again," Eunice said.

Caitlyn couldn't believe how calm Eunice was. "What number?!"

"22429. Only this time, add a zero on the end."

Caitlyn punched it in and the countdown rate doubled. She backed away from it and looked at Flynn, her eyes wide with shock and defeat. "That's it then. We're done."

"It would seem so."

"Goddamn it!"

"I'm so sorry," Flynn said.

"You should be! You're the maniac who activated this motherfucker."

"I just want you to know I never entertained the possibility of a deep, intimate relationship with anyone. How could I? Who would understand the life I led? Who could take the chances I did? No one. And then I met you. And you understood me. You lived life as I did. And I knew, I *knew* in my heart, that you and I were meant to be."

"You really *are* crazy."

Flynn took Caitlyn's hand as she watched the clock tick down. She looked away and braced herself for total annihilation. The front of Walt's pants were damp with urine. Eunice just seemed perturbed.

Caitlyn looked back at the bomb and noticed a scrap of paper taped inside the top of the briefcase. It was yellow and curled up and when she unfurled it she saw five smudged numbers.

13524.

She punched all five digits into the keypad.

The countdown stopped.

Two seconds before detonation.

The bomb made a beeping sound and reset itself before going silent. No one moved. No one said a word.

Caitlyn finally stopped holding her breath. "Jesus."

Eunice glared at Walt. "Did you tape the code to the top of the case?"

"I guess I did," Walt mumbled. "In case we forgot it."

"And then you forgot you taped it there?"

"I guess I did," Walt admitted.

Eunice shook her head. "Mudak."

Flynn crouched down to talk to Eunice, still trussed up on the floor. "Look, if you and Walt want to keep the money the Army of God paid you for that nuke… that's fine with me. Take it and go to Hawaii. Buy that house in Maui. Live the rest of your lives working on your tans and swimming with the dolphins. Just tell us who you gave it to. Do that and the FBI never has to know who you are or what you did. The country that sent you here doesn't even exist anymore. That mission is over. Those days are done. Fate just handed you a second chance, Eunice. Don't let it pass you by."

Eunice glared at Flynn with her flinty gaze, but finally relented as the reality of the situation sank in. "Our buyer wanted to remain anonymous," Eunice said. "We arranged a rendezvous in Grant Park in Chicago. We gave them the device and they paid us in bitcoins, transferring the funds electronically."

Caitlyn let go with an exasperated sigh. "So you don't know who they are or how to find them?"

"No, I know who they are. I know exactly who they are. And I know exactly what they're doing. We planted a bug on the device. The KGB didn't train us to be fools."

CHAPTER THIRTY-NINE

Flynn and Caitlyn said goodbye to Pumpkin and loaded the deactivated suitcase nuke into the back of their beat-to-shit Maserati SUV. They left Eunice and Walter zip-tied on their floor. The police would soon be there to free them, but by then they'd be heading south on I-90.

The attack was to take place in Hollywood, California in approximately thirty-four hours. Flynn and Caitlyn knew they couldn't fly without risking capture. Driving cross-country was their only real option, but they were half a continent away. The fastest route west took them through Des Moines and Denver and south through Las Vegas. According to Google, they wouldn't reach Hollywood for thirty-one hours. Flynn didn't like cutting it that close and decided they had no choice but to call the FBI. He hoped to reach special agent Miranda Jacks. She had been a loyal ally in the past and he trusted her to get the job done.

Flynn put the burner phone on speaker and the FBI office answered after one ring. A cheerful recorded female voice said, "Thank you for calling the Los Angeles office of the Federal Bureau of Investigation. If you know your party's extension, you may dial it at any time."

"I do not."

"If you are a law enforcement officer reporting an emergency such as a bank robbery, please press zero. If you are calling to report a crime, please press 4."

Flynn hesitated and then pressed 4.

The call transferred and rang one time before a perky recorded voice answered. "You have reached the FBI's public access line. This call may be monitored or recorded for quality assurance, investigative or other purposes. For English press one."

Flynn did.

"Please choose from the following options."

"Jesus."

"If you wish to report online crime, email hoaxes, or scams press 1. If you wish to report suspicious activity, please press 2."

Flynn sighed and pressed two. An even perkier female voice answered the call. This one was live.

"Thank you for calling the FBI! May I have your first and last name, please?"

"Flynn. James Flynn."

Caitlyn shot him a look, and Flynn held up one hand.

"Your telephone number, Mr. Flynn."

"Is that really necessary?"

"It's standard procedure, Mr. Flynn."

"288-229-3558."

"And how can I help you today?"

"I'd like to talk to Special Agent Miranda Jacks."

"If you'd like to report suspicious activity, you can report it to me."

"I'd rather talk to Agent Jacks. She'll know who I am."

"Is she expecting your call?"

"No, she is not, but I'm an old colleague."

"Can I tell her what this is regarding?"

"Tell I have news of an imminent terrorist attack. I'm sure she'll want to take my call."

"Hold please."

Flynn glanced at Caitlyn to see her glaring at him. "Why'd you give them your real name?"

"So Miranda would take the call. She needs to know it's me."

Caitlyn sighed and shook her head. Ten long minutes went by before the call transferred. Someone picked up. A man.

"Special Agent Rodriguez."

"Hi, yes, I'm actually calling for Miranda Jacks."

"She is not available, sir, but I would be glad to take your information."

"I worked with Agent Jacks and I'd really prefer talking to her."

"Yes, but like I said, she isn't available."

"When will she be?"

"I can't really say, sir, but I'm with the FBI's Joint Terrorism Task Force and if this is an emergency, you want to talk to me. I understand you have information regarding an imminent terrorist attack?"

"I do, but—"

"Sir, Agent Jacks would just refer you to me anyway, as she doesn't handle counter-terrorism. That's my purview. Please, whatever you wanted to tell her, you can tell me."

"What's your name again?"

"Special Agent Rodriguez."

"All right then. Do you have a pen? You probably want to write this down."

"I'm going to type whatever you tell me directly into my computer, sir."

"Okay. Are you ready?"

"Yes, sir."

"Retired General Jedidiah Anderson commands the Army of God. They are allied with the Church of the Prophecy in Orange County, California. Together, they want to bring on Armageddon. The final battle between heaven and hell. To that end, they acquired a suitcase nuke from two Soviet sleeper agents who want to retire to Maui... Are you writing all this down?"

"Yes, sir."

"The Army of God's Special Assault Force is on its way to California. These aren't just suburban dads or weekend warriors. These are former special operators: Army Rangers, Navy Seals, Green Berets. They are masquerading as Hezbollah and intend to detonate that suitcase nuke in Hollywood two nights from now. The same night as the Academy Awards. For you see, they believe that the movie and TV stars who rule the culture are brainwashing the young and want to turn America into a socialist state ruled by black, brown, and gay people. They believe that those same Hollywood elites are the enemies of freedom and that by obliterating them, they will strike a blow for the real America. However, the Army of God has other ambitions. They believe this attack will infuriate the entire free world. Hezbollah will be held responsible. Iran will be implicated. And war will be declared. Their intention is to precipitate World War Three. Armageddon. The Final Days."

Flynn heard Agent Rodriguez typing for quite some time and when he finished he said, "Hold please."

Caitlyn gave Flynn a skeptical side eye. "Do you think he believed you?"

"Why wouldn't he?"

"They didn't believe me. They thought I was a crazy."

Ten more minutes went by before Agent Rodriguez returned. "Mr. Flynn?"

"Yes?"

"Are you the same James Flynn who works for His Majesty's Secret Service?"

"Yes!"

"We've been looking for you for quite some time, sir. Can you tell me where you are?"

"Interstate 90 in Illinois. On our way to California."

"Are you alone?

"No, I'm with CIA operative Caitlyn Valentine."

"Where are you on I-90?"

"We're approaching Rockford, Illinois, but what difference does that make? Time is of the essence here. They intend to launch their attack from the rooftop of the Hollywood Roosevelt Hotel. That way they can avoid the heightened security in and around the Dolby Theatre."

"Okay, Mr. Flynn, thank you for all you've done. Can you do me a favor now? Can you drive directly to the FBI resident agency office in Rockford? It's just a few miles away from where you are now. The address is 308 West State Street, suite 350. I'll have a supervisory special agent meet you there and take you to O'Hare airport. You and Ms. Valentine will fly directly to Los Angeles. I'll meet you both at LAX and together we will deal with this threat."

"You want to fly us to Los Angeles?"

"You said yourself, time is of the essence."

"Yes, good. I'm glad you're taking this seriously. Miss Valentine wasn't sure you'd believe me."

"What kind of car are you driving?"

"A Maserati Levante."

"A Maserati? Wow. Okay. Good. The agents are expecting you. I'll see you in a few hours."

"Thank you, Agent Rodriguez."

"Thank you!"

Flynn beamed at Caitlyn.

She didn't beam back.

■ ■ ■

Caitlyn had her doubts. She had experience dealing with Federal law enforcement and wasn't as trusting as Flynn. She parked the Maserati on the street. Two blocks away from the four-story brick office building where the small FBI office was located.

"Why are you parking here?" Flynn pointed back towards the office building. "There was parking right in front."

"I'm not sure I totally trust them."

"I understand why, but I believe Agent Rodriguez grasps the gravity of our situation."

"Maybe."

Flynn raised a curious eyebrow. "You don't agree?"

"I don't know. Why don't you walk over there and see?"

"You're being ridiculous," Flynn grumbled.

Caitlyn shrugged. "Maybe."

Flynn gave her an irritated look before climbing out of the SUV. Caitlyn climbed out as well and scanned the street. She didn't see an FBI SWAT team or any agents in blue FBI windbreakers. Maybe Flynn was right. Maybe she was just being paranoid.

As Flynn headed inside the brick building that housed the local FBI office, she stepped inside the storefront across the street. The Rockford Area Convention and Visitors Bureau. She pretended to look at brochures as she kept an eye on the building on the other side of the street. A bank took up the first floor. There were other businesses as well. She observed workers and customers entering and exiting and considered following Flynn inside, but hesitated.

She waited quite a while. Flynn did not re-emerge. What could he be doing in there?

A middle-aged lady in a blue pantsuit smiled and approached Caitlyn. "Is there something I can help you with?"

Caitlyn shook her head. "No, I'm just looking over your brochures."

"Are you here on business or pleasure?"

"Business."

"Oh, what business are you in?"

Caitlyn glanced back out the window to see the doors across the street open. A burly man in a dark suit appeared. Flynn, his hands cuffed behind him, followed after. Two other men in equally boring suits prodded Flynn forward and around the side of the building. Caitlyn pushed past the woman, hurried out the door and across the street, crouching behind a parked minivan as she eavesdropped on their acrimonious conversation.

"Where is she, Mr. Flynn?"

"Long gone from here! She told me not to trust you and dammit if she wasn't right."

"You need to tell us where she is."

"On her way to L.A. most likely! Doing what *you* should be doing! Preventing a terrorist attack that could very well destroy America's second largest city!"

Two of the agents exchanged amused glances.

Flynn was apoplectic. "You think this is funny? We're talking hundreds of thousands of innocent people!" He struggled to pull away. The agents fought to hold on to him.

"You need to calm down, Mr. Flynn."

Caitlyn crept closer as she followed, hiding behind one parked car after another.

"*Calm down*?" Flynn shouted. "They're trying to start World War III! Haven't you heard a single word I've said!"

The lead agent suppressed a laugh as they dragged Flynn into an outdoor parking lot and approached a blue van with an FBI logo on the side. "Please, Mr. Flynn. It's imperative we find Ms. Valentine. Just tell us where she is."

"Right behind you," Caitlyn said. "And I have a Glock 17 aimed at the back of your head. Turn and I promise I will put a bullet in each of you before you can clear leather."

CHAPTER FORTY

Flynn parked the Maserati SUV by the boat ramp on Pierce Lake in Rock Cut State Park, a large forest preserve not too many miles from the Rockford FBI office. There were dozens of parked cars with empty bunk trailers. The owners of those trailers sat on their boats, out on the lake, either fishing or sailing or floating aimlessly about, drinking beer and smoking pot.

Caitlyn found a pair of pliers and a screwdriver in the bed of an unlocked Ford Ranger. While Flynn detached the trailer, Caitlyn cracked the steering column and hot-wired the pickup. After Flynn transferred his cardboard box of clothing, the suitcase nuke, and their small arsenal of weapons, they hit the road west.

Two hours later, Flynn used his burner phone to call the FBI office in Los Angeles. He asked for Miranda Jacks and once again they put him through to Special Agent Rodriguez.

"Mr. Flynn?"

"Agent Rodriguez, you set me up."

"Where are Agents Metzger, Lindsay, and Timmons, Mr. Flynn?"

"They're alive. Unharmed. But if you don't start taking me seriously, *you* won't be."

"Threatening a federal agent is a felony."

"I'm not the threat, you bloody idiot. A nuclear device will be detonated in Los Angeles in less than twenty-four hours. Isn't that where you are? Los Angeles?"

"Mr. Flynn—"

"I told you where it's happening. I told you who's responsible."

"I'm sorry for the misunderstanding, but if you would just come in—"

"I want to talk to Miranda Jacks."

"Where are our agents, Mr. Flynn?"

"Tied up in the back of an FBI van parked at a Dick's Sporting Goods. Just a few miles from the FBI office there."

"Thank you. Now please, just let us help you."

"You want me to trust you?"

"Where are you now?"

"Heading for Los Angeles, obviously."

"We have an FBI office in Denver and we can fly you to Los Angeles from there."

"And why should I believe you this time?"

"I understand why you wouldn't, but I want a peaceful resolution to this."

"I'll see you in Los Angeles, Agent Rodriguez." Flynn hung up, opened the window, and tossed out his burner phone.

■ ■ ■

They hot-wired a Honda Civic at a Walmart Supercenter in Dixon and were halfway across Iowa before they heard a radio news report about three FBI agents being kidnapped and locked in the trunk of their own van by two escaped mental patients.

"The FBI knows where we're headed. They'll be watching the rest stops and the roads," Caitlyn said.

"I'm sure they will be. Which is why we're going to cut through Kansas and take the southern route. If we drive straight through and take turns, we can hit Hollywood in twenty-two hours. Just in time for the Academy Awards. "

"You know they'll be waiting for us at the Roosevelt."

"Let's hope so. If we're lucky, we'll lead them right to the terrorists. Can I borrow your burner?"

Caitlyn handed it over, and Flynn punched in a number. Sancho Perez answered after the third ring. "Hello?"

Flynn turned on the speakerphone. "Sancho?"

"Flynn?"

"Listen to me, my friend. You and your family are in grave danger."

"What are you talking about? Where are you?"

"I'm on my way to Los Angeles."

"The FBI called me about you."

"Never mind that. You need to take your family and you need to leave L.A. Get as far away as you can."

"Why? What's going on?"

"Approximately twenty-four hours from now, someone intends to detonate a nuclear bomb in the City of Angels."

"What? Why?"

"To start World War three."

"Jesus Christ!"

"I know it's a lot to take in, but you need to stay calm."

"What the fuck?"

"Pack up Alyssa and go. Get out of L.A."

"Alyssa's already gone, man. After what happened with Mendoza, she freaked."

"Where is she?"

"With her mom in San Diego."

"Good. You need to join her."

"Dude, you gotta call the FBI. Tell them what's happening."

"We did, but they think we're crazy. They even tried to arrest me."

"Are you kidding me?"

"I wish I was."

"Jesus Christ!" Sancho shouted.

"Sorry to be the bearer of bad news."

"I got some bad news too, bro."

"Worse news than my news?" Flynn asked.

"It's about Mendoza. He's still alive."

"What?"

"He escaped from the hospital. Ripped out his IV and overpowered the cop in the hallway."

"I shot that asshole right in the head," Caitlyn said.

"Yeah, I think you really pissed him off," Sancho replied.

Caitlyn banged her fist on the steering wheel. "Un-fucking-believable!"

"Apparently, that pendejo has a steel plate in his head. But maybe that nuke'll finally take his ass out," Sancho said.

"I wouldn't bet on it," Caitlyn mumbled.

"Well, let's *not* find out." Flynn said. "We need to go the Roosevelt, foil this plot, and take out those terrorists. *Then* we can worry about Mendoza."

"The Roosevelt Hotel?"

"That's where they plan to set off the bomb."

"What do you need me to do?" Sancho asked.

"I need you to go to San Diego. You're about to be a father. You have responsibilities."

"No way, man. My whole family's here in L.A. My mom. My abuela. All my cousins. All my friends."

"So tell them all to leave town."

"Are you fucking kidding me? They're all gonna think I'm crazy."

"I'm sorry, Sancho. I don't know what to tell you."

"Tell me what I can do to help."

CHAPTER FORTY-ONE

The first ever Academy Awards were held at The Hollywood Roosevelt Hotel in 1929. Built in 1927 and named for Theodore Roosevelt, the hostelry was financed by a consortium that included Douglas Fairbanks, Mary Pickford, and Sid Grauman. Over the years, the venue for the Academy Awards changed many times. From the Roosevelt to the Biltmore to Grauman's Chinese Theatre to the Shrine Auditorium to the Dorothy Chandler Pavilion, and finally in 2002, to the Dolby Theatre, right next door to Grauman's and across Hollywood Boulevard from the Roosevelt Hotel.

Traffic came to a standstill at Franklin and Bronson. The Academy Awards were scheduled to start in less than an hour. Caitlyn's anger and frustration grew as she searched for a side street that wasn't jammed. "Which way?"

Flynn, navigating from the passenger seat, pointed to a driveway leading to a Gelson's Market parking lot. "Pull in there."

"How far away are we?"

"Nearly two miles away, but we'll get there faster on foot."

Caitlyn cursed under her breath and pulled into the Gelson's lot, zipping around cars waiting for a spot. She double-parked their stolen Honda Civic, and both climbed out dressed to the teeth.

Besides the thousands in cash, the Maserati Levante, and her late husband's weapons, Alessandra gifted Caitlyn a garment bag full of her own clothes. The most elegant outfit was a low-cut black minidress designed by Versace and a pair of strappy Manolo Blahniks. Caitlyn had two inches on Alessandra and ten extra pounds of muscle, so the dress was a tight fit, but not unflattering based on the looks she received from the random male pedestrians on Bronson. Flynn looked elegant in his own vintage Armani tuxedo. They knew they needed to look the part if they hoped to fit in with the hoity-toity Academy Awards crowd.

Flynn led the way down Bronson. They crossed an overpass above the Hollywood Freeway. Cars and trucks whizzed by below as Flynn and Caitlyn made their way past a homeless encampment consisting of a collection of random tents that covered the sidewalk.

Caitlyn hated wearing heels and by the time they reached Hollywood Boulevard, her feet were killing her. An unwelcome breeze blew up her miniskirt as she tried to ignore the catcalls from all the rough-looking characters. Nothing glamorous about this part of the boulevard. Junkies, runaways, hookers, and petty criminals of all kinds stared at her as she wobbled by, barely staying upright in those stupid heels.

They traversed countless stars on the Hollywood Walk of Fame. Occasionally, Caitlyn would glance down at the names as she and Flynn pounded past them. Some she recognized. Most she didn't.

They cut south down El Centro, down an alley, and caught sight of four gangbangers blocking the way ahead, staring, grinning. Street predators in baggy jeans, hoodies, t-shirts, and flannels. They had neck tats and shaved heads and dead eyes. Caitlyn sighed.

The leader of the pack, the smallest of the four, raised both his hands to slow them down. "Whoa, whoa, whoa, what's the rush, pretty lady?"

"Step aside," Flynn said.

"You two going to the Oscars?"

Flynn didn't even break stride. "I'm not going to ask you again."

The guy lifted his hoodie to reveal a pistol jammed down the front of his pants. "And *I* asked *you* a motherfucking question."

"Yes, we're going to the Oscars," Caitlyn said.

"I knew it!" the leader said, his gold tooth gleaming. "Are you in the movies, mama?"

"No."

"Yeah, you are. Look at you. Your limo driver left you off way too soon, *chica*. But you're in my world now. This is Rebels territory." His three friends laughed. The gangbanger looked her up and down and licked his lips before stepping up close to Flynn. He was six inches shorter, but considerably wider. "You can go. The *chula* stays."

"I don't think so," Flynn said.

The leader laughed. "You a hero, *vato*?"

"She doesn't need me to protect her."

"No?"

"No. And if I were you, I'd move before you make a serious mistake."

"I'm making a mistake?" The gangbanger laughed. "*Cabrón*, you just made the worst mistake of your life. Every Five-O in L.A. is at the Oscars, man. Ain't no one coming to save you."

Caitlyn pulled the Glock 17 out of her handbag and pointed it at the asshole menacing Flynn. "Move aside," she said.

"*Órale! Mamacita* means business. You gonna shoot me, *hyna*?"

"If you don't fucking move."

The cholo laughed and reached for his gun and Caitlyn shot him in the hand, sending the pistol flying. Flynn drew his Desert Eagle and the other three took off running.

The *cholo* Caitlyn shot stared at the bloody hole in his hand. "*Qué carajos!?*"

"Run," she said as she pointed the gun at his head. "*Run!*"

He ran.

And so did Caitlyn and Flynn—out of the alley, down to Selma, and west to Highland. They didn't talk. They just hurried. Caitlyn struggled to keep up in her high heels. They didn't stop for lights, but ran right through intersections, causing cars to swerve and honk. Caitlyn ignored her screaming feet. Sweat ran down her face and burned in her eyes as she kept a steady pace behind Flynn.

A few pedestrians stopped to stare and watch as they ran by; past the Argyle Nightclub; past Hollywood and Vine; past the Dream Hollywood Hotel and Hollywood Urgent Care; past the Hollywood YMCA and Selma Avenue Elementary School. The sun hung low in the sky and reflected orange and red off the wispy clouds above. Flynn and Caitlyn headed for Hollywood Boulevard. The crush of fans and random pedestrians grew denser. Flynn took point, pushing his way forward, shoving through the crowd. Caitlyn followed in his wake.

The red carpet leading to the Dolby Theatre was walled off with a temporary barrier. There were cops and private security everywhere. Those gangbangers weren't wrong. Every cop in the city was there. Caitlyn spotted military-style trucks belonging to SWAT and the LAPD bomb squad. Canine units patrolled the streets, and on the rooftops she caught glints of sniper scopes. The Dolby Theatre and the surrounding block were virtually impenetrable.

The boulevard was closed between Highland and Orange Drive, and a chain-link fence blocked the way forward. A long line waited to pass through a private security checkpoint. Flynn ignored the line and stepped to the front. He waved the FBI badge he lifted off Timmons and Caitlyn used the one she took from Metzger. She prayed they wouldn't look too closely or want to see their accompanying ID. They didn't. Overwhelmed by the crowd, they just waved them through.

More security waited for them at the main entrance to the Hollywood Roosevelt, but they blended in with the rest of the fashionable crowd waiting to show their ID and invitations. Once again, the FBI badges magically granted them access. Soon they stood in the elegant lobby, packed with guests and party-goers, hotel staff, police, and security. It looked a bit like Caitlyn imagined it did in the 1920s, decorated in Spanish Colonial Revival with arched doorways, stone columns, and carved wood-paneled ceilings. A fire blazed in the grand fireplace, and giant cast-iron chandeliers hung from the high ceilings. In the center stood a large fountain decorated with hand-crafted Talavera tiles.

She figured the FBI were probably trying to blend in unobtrusively and wondered if someone there would recognize them. But with all the famous faces everywhere and everyone dressed in evening wear, they were basically invisible. Each celebrity had their own security contingent. Little did those celebs realize how useless their massive bodyguards would prove to be. All the muscles, menace, and bullets in the world wouldn't protect them from what was about to happen.

A large lobby sign showed the locations of the various Oscar parties being held on the premises. Every ballroom and venue had one, but the most prestigious party was The Women in Film reception being held on the historic rooftop. Wielding their stolen FBI badges like mystical amulets, Caitlyn and Flynn made their way onto the elevator and straight to the top.

The rooftop setting was breathtaking, an ironic counterpoint to the coming holocaust. The Hollywood Roosevelt sign towered above, all festooned with bright Italian lights. Alicia Keys sang jazz standards from an elegantly-appointed bandstand as the stars of Hollywood danced under the stars of heaven. Waitstaff in tuxes served flutes of champagne on silver trays. Celebs sat at tables draped with white tablecloths and dined on fancy canapés and sushi.

Caitlyn surveyed all the famous faces. It seemed so unreal. *If the Army of God have their way, every one of these famous faces will no longer be among the living.*

Flynn moved through the crowd effortlessly, totally comfortable in his own skin. She hurried to keep up and couldn't help but notice all the movie stars noticing him. She envied his innate self-confidence, his total obliviousness. Nothing seemed to faze him. There was something to be said for living in your own separate reality.

An older female voice called out her name. "Caitlyn?"

Caitlyn froze. Who the hell here would know her name? She turned and Alessandra Bianchi embraced her and then Flynn.

"What a surprise? What are you two doing here?"

Flynn grinned at Alessandra. "I can't speak for Caitlyn, but I'm enjoying the view."

It was then Caitlyn noticed the other famous sex symbols from the sixties standing in a little circle surrounding Alessandra.

"Ladies, this is James and Caitlyn." They all smiled as Flynn kissed each of their hands. Alessandra introduced them one at a time. "Jane, Ursula, Raquel, Shirley."

"I've admired you all from afar," Flynn said. "What a pleasure to finally meet you all in the flesh."

Jane studied Flynn's face. "Are you an actor?"

"You look very familiar," Raquel said.

"Have we met before?" Ursula asked.

"We may have in another life," Flynn replied.

"I agree," Shirley said. "I can tell you're an old soul."

"James!"

A beautiful young woman nearly shoved Caitlyn out of the way to reach Flynn. She gave him a huge hug, held him close and did not let go. A surprising pang of jealousy hit Caitlyn hard. The fresh-faced twenty-something beauty reminded her of that young actress from the Harry Potter movies.

Flynn held the girl at arm's length and looked at her with genuine affection. "Chloe! My goodness! How long has it been?"

"Oh, my God! I've been so worried! They moved you to that other hospital and I couldn't visit and then you escaped and—" Chloe looked at Caitlyn and recognition dawned. "Is this—"

"Caitlyn," Flynn said. "Meet Chloe. Chloe, Caitlyn."

Caitlyn recognized her now. She was the young actress Gary Goldhammer famously harassed. Chloe grabbed Flynn's hand. "What are you doing here?"

"Oh, you know. The usual. Fighting the enemies of freedom. Saving the world from megalomaniacs."

The ladies all laughed at that. All except for Chloe and Alessandra, who both understood that Flynn wasn't joking.

Caitlyn smiled at Flynn. "We better get to it."

Flynn nodded. "Indeed. It's been a pleasure, ladies. Chloe, when this is all over, let's catch up. It's been too long."

Flynn snatched a flute of champagne off a nearby silver tray and took off into the crowd. Caitlyn quickly followed.

CHAPTER FORTY-TWO

On the day of the Academy Awards, hundreds of LAPD officers, along with a commensurate number of private security guards, secure the block around the Dolby. A half-mile of Hollywood Boulevard is closed in either direction and bleachers are set up to accommodate the fans who want to watch the stars walk the red carpet. There's a lottery to win a coveted seat on those bleachers and the winners are thoroughly vetted. Many adjacent streets are also shut down. Armed men are stationed everywhere, eyeballing and inspecting, rousting and frisking and making sure no one unauthorized makes their way into the Dolby Theatre.

Flynn considered rushing back and telling the ladies to flee the city, but there wasn't time for them to get far enough away and it would just start a panic. So he headed away from the hubbub to where the caterers were set up. A ladder there led to a higher point on the roof, above the deck and all the party people. Before Flynn could put his foot on the first rung, someone called out to him. "Mr. Flynn?"

A tall, stocky Hispanic man in a dark business suit offered Flynn a smile. He was with a slightly younger, meaner-looking man who wasn't smiling. Neither dressed for the occasion and Flynn figured out who the bloke was before he even produced his FBI badge. "Agent Rodriguez?"

"Yes, sir, and this is my partner, Agent Paul."

"Have you seen any sign of the terrorists?"

"No, sir."

"Because you haven't been looking for them, have you?"

Rodriguez shrugged apologetically. "No, sir."

"Because you think we're both crazy."

"Not for me to say, sir."

"We were just about to search the upper part of the roof. Would you care to join us?"

"Actually, we'd like you both to come with us. We spotted you downstairs, but I didn't want to make a scene. I have backup if I need it, but I'd rather not raise a ruckus if I don't have to. I don't want to make a fuss and I don't want anyone to get hurt."

"We don't either, Agent Rodriguez," Caitlyn said. "So I apologize."

"For what?"

Caitlyn kicked Agent Rodriguez square in the nuts. Flynn did the same to a surprised Agent Paul. As they both bent over and grabbed their balls, Caitlyn clambered up the ladder leading to the higher part of the roof. Flynn followed, figuring that the FBI agents probably wouldn't start shooting willy-nilly. Not with so many celebrities milling about.

From the top of the roof, Flynn viewed the sun setting behind the hills to the west. As the sky grew darker, lights blinked on, illuminating the streets of Hollywood and the hills beyond. Much of the rooftop lay hidden in shadow as Flynn followed Caitlyn across the slanted surface of red ceramic tiles. He crouched to keep his center of balance low as he searched for the Army of God. What if they weren't here? What if they changed the plan? Changed the location? What if the FBI spooked them? What if Eunice and Walter lied?

Caitlyn climbed to a higher, flatter part of the hotel rooftop. Flynn followed and heard the muffled roar of industrial-sized HVAC systems with exhaust fans and vents. Electrical panels and electrical cables and steel conduit led to a spot even higher.

Flynn glanced back to see Rodriguez and Paul pulling themselves up over the edge of the roof. Caitlyn scrambled up the conduit like a spider monkey, quite the achievement in a little black minidress and three-inch heels. Flynn followed and briefly glanced down. One slip and he'd plummet hundreds of feet to the street below, slamming into the Walk of Fame, decorating the name and star of some dead Hollywood legend with his lifeless body. To stay focused, he kept his eyes on Caitlyn's behind as he climbed up the rest of the conduit. She disappeared over the edge. He scrambled to catch up. Her face appeared as he reached the top, startling him to such a degree he almost lost his grip. Her right index finger hovered over her lips as she pointed with her left index finger to the far side of the roof.

Flynn pulled himself up and over. Three huge guys dressed like caterers in white shirts and black bow ties, stood on the far edge of the roof. Caitlyn and Flynn, still in shadow, edged closer. These "caterers" wore tactical headlamps and black harnesses festooned with knives, guns, and grenades. One held the suitcase nuke with the lid flipped up to reveal the timing mechanism and the metallic cylinders with the trigger explosives and the fissionable material. From this distance, Flynn couldn't tell if the clock was ticking down. A fourth man appeared to be taking a video of the other three with his cell phone.

Flynn stayed low and slithered closer. Caitlyn crawled right beside him, furious at the fact that her miniskirt no longer covered her bottom. The man with the phone narrated as he shot the video of the other three. He used a phony Middle-Eastern accent.

"…for these infidels defile our youth with their blasphemous propaganda. They inflame the innocent with the sins of the flesh and turn them away from Allah. They desecrate their young souls with the promise of earthly pleasures and set them on a path of pure evil. The Jews created Hollywood to establish control over the rest of us. They elevate their so-called movie stars to the status of gods. They turn them into heroes and objects of desire to steal the hearts of our young, control their minds, and corrupt their fragile souls. Hollywood is the pantheon of these false idols, and tonight we shall destroy it along with all their counterfeit deities."

"FBI!" shouted Agent Rodriguez.

Agents Rodriguez and Paul slowly advanced, holding their guns in a two-handed stance. All four Army of God soldiers fumbled for their guns. Flynn and Caitlyn jumped to their feet and trained their weapons on the terrorists. Soon, the only one not holding a gun was the one holding the nuke.

Flynn called across the roof. "Did you set the countdown to give you enough time to get far enough away? I wouldn't imagine you gentlemen are suicide bombers. Not like *actual* Hezbollah."

"That's close enough," the man with the nuke said. The other three clearly had trouble deciding who to aim their weapons at.

"Weapons on the ground," Rodriguez shouted. "Do it now. You too, Flynn! Both of you! Guns on the ground!"

Flynn half turned and looked at Rodriguez. "Are you sure? If we put our guns down, it's four against two."

The Army of God Assault Squad quietly conferred and then did a surprising thing. They slowly holstered their guns. The one with the suitcase nuke closed and latched the case.

"I'm glad this didn't have to get ugly," Flynn said.

The Army of God squad backed to the edge of the roof and stood shoulder to shoulder. The one with the suitcase nuke offered Flynn a thin smile.

And fell straight back.

Right off the roof.

The other three followed.

"Shit!" Caitlyn shouted. She raced to the edge with Flynn right behind her. Climbing ropes were clipped to the sign. Looking over and down, she saw the four men rapidly rappelling down the side of the building. *"Shit!"* she shouted again.

"Don't you move," Rodriguez shouted. "Put your guns down and get on the ground."

"They're getting away!" Flynn shouted. "They're rappelling down the roof! You saw the suitcase nuke! You know this is real, right?"

Rodriguez, terrified and tongue-tied with indecision, had no answer. Flynn holstered his weapon and stepped to the edge of the roof. He glanced down to a valet parking area twelve stories below. Then he looked at Caitlyn.

"Do you know the South African method?"

"The what?"

"It's how mountaineers rappelled before the invention of harnesses and carabiners!"

"What are you talking about?" Caitlyn asked.

Paul left Rodriguez behind and stepped closer, his gun hovering between Flynn and Caitlyn. "On the ground! Now! Both of you!"

Flynn looped the ropes around his body and under his armpits and back through his groin. "You use the rope as a makeshift harness and use your body to create friction and slow your descent."

Caitlyn didn't look convinced. "Seriously?"

"Hold firmly with your right hand and brake with your left."

"Have you done this before?"

"No, but I watched a very informative video about it on YouTube."

"On the ground! I won't ask you again!" Paul shouted!

Flynn looked Paul in the eye and stepped off the edge, his feet against the building as he fell back. He rappelled straight down, much faster than he should have, his feet barely skimming the wall as the rope ground against his still tender testicles, tore through his tux and ripped the hair out of his armpits. He saw Caitlyn's face peering over the edge as he plummeted.

Flynn's crotch was on fire by the time his feet hit terra firma. Not metaphorically, but literally. There were no tendrils of smoke or rising flames, but the friction created quite a bit of heat. His balls were already screaming from the roasting and beating they took in Wyoming. Rappelling without a harness might not have been the best idea.

Flynn tried to ignore the pain as he scanned the area for his quarry. *There!* They disappeared around the edge of the building. He looked straight up, but didn't see Caitlyn or Agent Rodriguez rappelling down and couldn't wait for them to find the courage.

He followed the Army of God squad up Orange Drive to Hollywood Boulevard, where a large throng crowded the street. Many stood pressed up against the chain-link barrier separating the riffraff from the Hollywood royalty. Police and private security kept the crowd relatively orderly.

The crush consisted of movie fans and curious tourists and the usual array of costumed characters posing for pictures. Flynn pushed past a fat Spiderman, a skinny Superman, a large orange Elmo and a tiny Darth Vader. He did the back-and-forth tap dance to get around a beefy Wonder Woman and nearly collided with a chunky Chewbacca. His eyes never left his prey, even as they tried to hustle away.

"Flynn?" A hand settled on his arm. Turning, he found Sancho with a tall, slender Captain America. The Captain's real name was Tyler Jablonski. Flynn hadn't seen him in months. He and his sister, Chloe, and Alessandra Bianchi had helped him and Sancho defeat a super villain just last year. A man by the name of Goldhammer.

"They're getting away," Flynn shouted and pointed. "We have to stop them! They have the bomb!"

"Bomb?" asked a middle-aged lady next to Flynn.

"What bomb?" Her portly husband sounded panicked.

A twenty-something girl with purple hair yelled, "There's a bomb?"

Panic ripped through the crowd like an electrical current.

"Someone has a bomb!"

"A bomb!"

"Oh, my God!"

"A bomb!"

The crowd collectively screamed and ran in ten different directions. Flynn battled his way forward. The throng slammed and buffeted him about. Sancho and Tyler fought to stay with him as they followed the four terrorists. Police blew their whistles and tried to take control, but anarchy and chaos reigned. Flynn elbowed his way forward, flattening fans, tourists, and costumed characters alike. He even accidentally flattened a police officer.

■   ■   ■

Sancho's eyes widened when Flynn knocked the patrolman down. The angry officer scrambled to his feet, drew his taser, and fired at Flynn. Captain America banged into the cop just as he fired, and the darts hit Big Bird instead. The large, feathered fowl yelped and fell and flopped around on the ground.

Sancho jumped right over him and followed Flynn. Tyler Jablonski (aka Captain America) kept right with him. Wheezing with asthma and nearly out of breath, Tyler wasn't exactly a super soldier. The aspiring director worked at a comic book store and made extra money posing for pictures in front of Grauman's Chinese, dressed as his favorite superhero. Nevertheless, Sancho knew Tyler would do his best to keep up.

The crowd thinned as they reached Highland and now Sancho could see who Flynn was after. There were four of them. All dressed like waiters. One had a large briefcase.

Tyler could barely catch his breath. "Who are those guys?"

"Tell you later," Sancho wheezed. "Right now, we just gotta stop 'em."

One of the four stepped in front of a Ford Escape heading south on La Brea Avenue. The woman driving hit the brakes. Another of the four opened the driver's side door and dragged her out. She shrieked and screamed for the police as she fell. The cars behind the carjacked Escape slammed on their brakes, blocking all the traffic on La Brea.

Flynn stopped and rested his gun hand atop the roof of a car to steady his aim. But before he could pull the trigger on the terrorists, someone the size of a refrigerator tackled him. Sancho hurried closer. Flynn tried to break free. The monster of a man straddled and strangled him. Not until Sancho was almost upon them did he realize who the monster was.

Mendoza.

Hijo de puta!

Did that maniac follow him to Flynn?

Mendoza sat on Flynn's abdomen, crushing him with his weight while choking the life out of him. Sancho ran right at Mendoza and hit him with everything he had. And bounced right off. It was like trying to tackle a brick wall. The *pinche pendejo* didn't even flinch.

Sancho grabbed onto Mendoza's enormous arm and tried to dislodge him, but the monster's arm wouldn't budge. Flynn's face turned bright red. His eyes bugged out of his head.

"Let him go! Let him up!" Sancho shouted. "You kill him, you kill us all!"

"Fuck you," Mendoza growled.

Sancho poked Mendoza in his last remaining eye. The big man roared and let Flynn go to grab his injured peeper.

Tyler Jablonski jumped on the big man's back and yelled to his fellow costumed superheroes. "Need some help here!"

Fat Spiderman, the Not-So-Incredible Hulk, and a middle-aged Wonder Woman all piled on. Even chunky Chewbacca and large Elmo joined the fray. Mendoza bellowed and flailed and threw them off, scattering them as Flynn skittered away.

The Army of God squad took off in their highjacked Escape. A long black limo squealed to a stop right in front of Sancho. The driver's side window hummed down. Caitlyn sat behind the wheel. "Flynn!"

Flynn was already on his feet. He ran for the limo. Sancho and Tyler limped along after him.

They all jumped in. Mendoza tried to follow.

Flynn found a bottle of bubbly in an ice bucket and bashed it over Mendoza's head. Caitlyn hit the gas and Mendoza toppled backwards, but held onto the door frame as the limo roared away. The forward momentum slammed the door shut, smashing Mendoza's hand, but still he refused to let go.

Until Sancho poked him in his one good eye again.

The *sicario* let go to grab his injured eye and tumbled onto La Brea. Sancho looked out the back window to see the big man rolling down the street. He got to his feet as a car slammed into him, but barely staggered him. Mendoza wrenched open the door, ripped out the driver, and tossed him like a rag doll.

"Mendoza must have followed me," Sancho said.

Flynn sighed. "Obviously."

"He's like a Mexican Michael Myers, man. That *pendejo* just keeps on coming."

Flynn looked at the crinkled label from the champagne bottle he shattered on Mendoza's head. "This was a Krug '88. What a terrible waste." He pulled another bottle from the ice and began unscrewing the little wire cage on top. "Luckily, we still have a fine bottle of Veuve Clicquot. Let's hope it's chilled to the right temperature."

Tyler pulled off his Captain America mask. Sweat dripped down his face as he tried to catch his breath. Sancho looked out the window. The world shot by in a blur. The limo rocketed through an intersection as the light turned red. Cars skidded and squealed. A faint muffled boom echoed as two cars collided behind them. Sancho glanced through the Plexiglas partition — the speedometer hovered at 93mph.

Flynn popped the cork. "I believe they're driving a red Ford Escape."

Caitlyn nodded. "It's about a block ahead."

Sancho glanced out the rear window. A car sped after them. As it drew closer, Sancho could identify the driver. *Mendoza.* "Shit. We got company!"

"The more the merrier," Flynn said and handed Sancho a glass of champagne. Sancho gulped it down. Flynn poured two more. He handed one to Tyler and slid open the partition. Champagne sloshed as Caitlyn grabbed the glass and pounded it down. She handed Flynn the empty and floored it.

CHAPTER FORTY-THREE

After Flynn jumped off the top of the Roosevelt, Caitlyn pushed right past the two stunned FBI Agents. They yelled for her to stop and she yelled at them to *do their jobs*! After riding the elevator back to the lobby, she ran outside to search for Flynn and glimpsed him limping around the corner of the building. She hurried after and followed him into the crush of bodies on Hollywood Boulevard. Caitlyn climbed up on a planter to get a better view, and it didn't take her long to spot the Army of God squad. The crowd pushed one way, and they pushed the other way to get away from Flynn. *Who is that with him?* Was that Sancho?

Was that… Captain America?

Caitlyn hurried to a long line of limos parked north of the boulevard on Orange Drive. The drivers, smoking and shooting the shit, looked alarmed when Caitlyn put her pistol to the head of the first driver in line.

"Keys," was all she said.

He surrendered them without a word and she jumped behind the wheel and took off like a bat out of hell.

She picked up Flynn, Sancho, and Captain America and chased after the fleeing Escape. The extended, black Lincoln limo wasn't the easiest vehicle to maneuver. It had to be twenty-five feet long at least, and she lost count of how many cars she sideswiped as she tried to catch up to the Army of God squad.

The Escape weaved in and out of traffic and shot through red lights. Cars squealed and skidded and crashed into each other as

Caitlyn did her best to maneuver around them, south past Sunset, Santa Monica, Melrose, and Beverly. She struggled to close the distance and glanced at Flynn in the rearview mirror. He sat in the back, calmly sipping champagne. Flynn gave her a nod and pointed ahead. "I think they're turning."

The Escape cut a hard right on 6th Street. It skidded and slammed into a UPS truck before continuing on. Caitlyn wasn't sure the limo could make that corner, but she went for it, anyway. "Shit! Shit! Shit! Shit!"

The back of the limo slammed into that same UPS truck. Everyone's champagne sloshed, but at least the collision kept the Lincoln from spinning out. Caitlyn flattened the gas and the limo lurched forward. 6th Street was a lot less busy and had fewer stoplights, allowing the Escape to pull farther ahead. She glanced in the rearview. Mendoza was still on their tail, skidding around the corner and knocking over a mailbox.

Caitlyn floored it, but the limo had lousy acceleration compared to the Ford. The Escape made a left on Hauser. Caitlyn cut early to make the turn. She bumped over the curb and clipped a parked car. Still, she kept her eyes on the prize. The Escape didn't slow as it turned onto Wilshire Boulevard, directly into the path of a speeding pickup truck.

The collision spun the Escape around but didn't stop or disable it. Caitlyn cut a wide right on Wilshire and stayed with the Ford as it wobbled west.

"Run 'em off the road!" shouted skinny Captain America.

Caitlyn pulled up next to the Escape and slammed into it. She caught the surprised look of the driver as the cars collided. The Escape jumped the curb and knocked over a La Brea Tar Pits sign before flattening the green metal fence surrounding the property. It slammed into a towering palm on the edge of the largest tar pit.

Caitlyn pulled the limo to an abrupt stop. All her passengers lurched forward and banged their faces on the Plexiglas partition. She jumped out. Flynn, Sancho, and Captain America followed. The terrorists had already escaped from the Escape. Three had guns. One had that suitcase nuke. He held it high over his head and shouted, "I started the timer! It's too late! You can't stop it!" The ersatz Middle-Eastern accent was gone, replaced by a West Texas twang.

Flynn aimed his weapon at him. "Put the briefcase on the ground!"

Caitlyn pulled her own weapon. "Do what he says!"

She heard the roar of an approaching car and turned just as it collided with the back of the Limo. Mendoza jumped out and growled, his face red with fury.

The terrorist with the suitcase nuke took advantage of the momentary distraction to toss the briefcase as hard as he could into the middle of the tar pit. It landed with a wet plop.

Caitlyn ran to the edge of the shiny black pit and watched the briefcase slowly sink. "Oh, shit!"

The terrorists took off running. Flynn ignored them and raced for the tar pit. At the edge, he leaped like Superman and landed with a belly flop. The puddled water on top splashed.

"Flynn! What the hell?" Caitlyn shouted, but Flynn was on a mission and tried to swim through the thick, viscous gunk.

"If it sinks, we're sunk!" He dog-paddled and crawled and stretched as far as he could until the tips of his fingers touched the briefcase handle. He stretched even farther to wrap his fingers around it. But he couldn't turn. He couldn't move. He couldn't do anything but slowly sink.

■　■　■

Mendoza walked to the edge of the pit and watched Flynn. He lowered his gun. Puzzled, he looked at Sancho. "What is that *pinche pendejo* doing?"

"Trying to save the world," Sancho said.

"By drowning himself in a tar pit?"

"By grabbing that suitcase nuke before it sinks."

"Suitcase nuke?"

"Those guys we were chasing? Terrorists. They want to blow up L.A. and start World War Three and because of you, now they will."

Mendoza raised a skeptical eyebrow. "Are you shitting me?" Mendoza watched Flynn flail around in the tar. He had one hand on the briefcase as he struggled to stay above the muck. The more he flailed, the faster he sank.

"If Flynn dies, we all die," Caitlyn said.

She raced back to the wrecked limo and searched for something to throw to Flynn. She found jumper cables in the rear of the Escape and hustled back. The tar was now up to Flynn's chest. She tried to throw one end to him, but the cables weren't long enough. Flynn couldn't grab on. Caitlyn pulled them back and threw them again, but this time let go of the end. They landed with a wet plop next to Flynn. He managed to get a hand on one of the alligator clips. The twenty other feet of cable floated on top of the tar, too far away from the edge for anyone to grab.

Now up to his neck, Flynn continued to sink.

A flood of conflicting emotions buffeted Mendoza as he watched Flynn flounder in the tar. That *hijo de puta* made his life a living nightmare. But now that the *idiota* was about to die, Mendoza couldn't even enjoy it. Because thousands would die. Now *he* would die. Even in death, Flynn was flipping him the bird.

Mendoza heard running footsteps and watched with astonishment as that *al asno*, Sancho, raced to the edge of the pit and launched himself forward into the air. He landed with a loud belly flop. *Que chingados?* Did he want to die with that crazy man? Mendoza watched the little *pendejo* paddle forward far enough to get one hand on the end of the jumper cables.

"Someone grab my feet!" Sancho shouted.

Scrawny Captain America took a running jump and landed flat on top of the tar. He stretched to reach Sancho's ankles, keeping his head turned so he could still breathe.

Flynn was now up to his chin.

The fake superhero's shoes were maybe five feet away from the edge. So close, but not close enough. Big as he was, Mendoza knew he would sink like a boulder and drag them all down with him if he jumped in.

Mendoza looked at Caitlyn. Neither one said a word. She stared at the bubbling tar, steeled herself, and threw herself forward, reaching for Captain America's skinny legs. She grabbed his ankles, lifted her face away from the tar, and strained to look back at Mendoza.

He knew what she wanted him to do.

She wanted him to save Flynn.

Save them all.

Mendoza looked around. A small crowd now surrounded them. Two teenagers stepped forward, each one grabbing one of Caitlyn's legs. They pulled and strained and grunted, but that tar held tight. The briefcase couldn't be seen at all now and Flynn's nose hovered just above the black gunk.

All Mendoza had to do was nothing and Flynn would no longer be a problem.

Nothing would be a problem.

As far back as Mendoza could remember, life for him was suffering. Pain and suffering. Not until you died did the suffering end. Maybe it was time to end the torment. Maybe it was time to stop fighting the inevitable. Maybe it was time to accept the inescapable.

"*Puta Madre,*" mumbled Mendoza. He pushed the teens out of the way, grabbed Caitlyn Valentine's oily ankles, planted himself and pulled. He strained with every ounce of his being — all two hundred and ninety-two pounds of him. The tar did not give up its victims easily. It held tight to them, all of them.

Especially Flynn, now completely submerged. The harder Sancho pulled, the greater the suction effect created by Flynn's body. He was like a shoe stuck deep in the mud. Impossible to pull out.

Mendoza was a powerful man before he went to prison. But he pumped iron daily while incarcerated and could dead lift close to 550 pounds. He pulled with every muscle fiber he had and took a step back to dig in even deeper. Flynn and the others moved, but just barely. The teenagers grabbed his thigh-sized arms and aided his effort. Soon others in the crowd joined in, grabbing waists and legs and arms and pulling. All putting their collective strength and weight behind the rescue. But Mendoza was the engine. Teeth gritted, face red, muscles and veins on his neck bulging, his deep, guttural roar harmonized with all the other sounds of effort.

The top of Flynn's head emerged from the tar, totally covered in pitch. Mendoza focused on Flynn's oily black face. Slowly his neck and the top of his chest emerged. Mendoza dug in even deeper as he strained with each backward step until most of Flynn's body was on top of the tar, the jumper cables in one hand and that briefcase in the other. Soon he pulled Caitlyn completely out of the pit, spitting and gagging and blinking the tar from her eyes. Then came Captain America, also covered in black. Next was the *poquito gordito*, Sancho, sticky with pitch, on his knees, vomiting in the grass.

Last came Flynn, still clutching those jumper cables. He crawled up the muddy grass at the edge of the pit and wiped the tar out of his eyes. He staggered a few feet away and then sat heavily in the grass. Caitlyn crawled over and snapped open the briefcase. Mendoza could see some kind of mechanism. Metal cylinders and a digital clock all gummed up with tar.

The concerned citizens crowded closer, surrounding them in a circle as Caitlyn and Flynn scooped handfuls of black viscous goop from the case.

Flashing lights lit up the area as a patrol car pulled up. The officers hurried over and joined the crowd. One was a tall female, the other a shorter, burlier male. "What's going on here?" asked the female cop. "What is that?"

"A bomb," Sancho replied as he tried to wipe the tar off his tongue.

The cops and the concerned citizens all backed up. A few ran, but not everyone. Some watched from a distance away. Mendoza knew it wouldn't matter how far away they stood. Not if that briefcase really contained a nuke.

The female cop pointed at the bomb. "Better get away from that!"

"We need to call the bomb squad!" her partner yelled.

Curious, Mendoza stepped closer. The digital timer read 22:34 as the seconds ticked down. Maybe they *should* wait for the bomb squad? Did Flynn even have a clue? He was out of his fucking mind, but the woman wasn't. She was a boss-ass bitch. A force to be reckoned with. She actually shot him in the fucking head. But Mendoza didn't take it personally. He knew she was just defending herself. "Do either of you know what the hell you're doing?"

"We've disarmed one of these before," Flynn said.

Caitlyn wiped the black muck off what looked like a keypad.

The cops both had their guns out now. "You all need to step away from the bomb," shouted the lady cop.

"I'm calling the bomb squad!" yelled her shorter, burlier partner.

Caitlyn looked over at the two panicky police officers and talked to them in a calm, collected manner. "This is a suitcase nuke. So unless that bomb squad gets here in the next ten minutes, it's not going to matter."

The male patrolmen took a half a step back. His female partner stood her ground. "I won't ask you again! Move away from that bomb before someone gets hurt."

Caitlyn wiped tar away from the inside of the briefcase and revealed a curled up piece of paper taped to the top.

"What's that?" Mendoza asked.

"The deactivation code," Caitlyn replied.

Flynn scrutinized it. "One of the numbers is completely covered in tar."

Caitlyn tried to wipe it off, but all that did was smear the ink. "Shit."

"That's that then," Flynn said. "All we can do now is guess and hope we get it right."

Mendoza watched as the two cops edged closer. Mendoza pulled his gun and stepped between them and the bomb. "Back off."

"Put the gun down," ordered the female.

"Put it down!" shouted her partner.

"You pull that trigger and everybody dies," Mendoza replied.

Caitlyn punched in a code. "Shit."

"Bloody hell," Flynn replied.

Mendoza glanced at the digital readout. The countdown accelerated, the numbers flashing by twice as fast.

"Try again," Flynn said.

Caitlyn did. "Shit," she mumbled.

"Bloody hell."

Two more patrol cars came screaming up. Lights flashing. Siren shrieking. The cops climbed out with weapons in hand. Two of them had shotguns.

"Odds are better now," Flynn said. "Try again."

Caitlyn punched in the numbers.

"Shit."

"Bloody Hell."

With reinforcements now backing her up, the female cop shouted an order at Mendoza. "Drop your damn weapon! I won't ask you again!"

Mendoza shook his head. He could see the equivocation in the cop's eyes. He could also see the anger and outrage. Shit was about to go sideways. Then he heard the helicopter. It came roaring in from the west and blew dust everywhere as it touched down on Wilshire. The letters on the side read FBI.

Caitlyn tried another number.

"Shit."

"Bloody hell."

A half dozen FBI agents in blue windbreakers exited the helicopter and joined the Mexican standoff. The lead agent, a tall black woman in her early forties, immediately took charge. "Everybody stand down! Lower your weapons!" She glared at the cops. "You too LAPD." She then addressed Flynn directly. "Sorry, James, I came as soon as I got the message."

"Good to see you, Miranda!"

"The FBI bomb squad will be here soon."

"Not soon enough."

Mendoza watched the digital timer rapidly tick down. Caitlyn's right index finger hovered over the keypad.

"The odds are now 1 in 6," Flynn said.

"Not great odds," Caitlyn noted.

"Agreed. However, the only sure way to lose is to not make a bet."

All eyes focused on Caitlyn as she keyed in the code.

The countdown speed doubled.

Caitlyn froze.

Flynn quickly keyed in another code.

It doubled again, the red digital numbers now a blur.

Flynn frantically entered more digits with only three seconds left on the clock.

The timer stopped.

CHAPTER FORTY-FOUR

Miguel Alejandro Medina Perez was born at 2:00 p.m. on a Wednesday afternoon. Sancho and Alyssa named their new son after Sancho's late father. Little Miguel was two weeks late and weighed just over nine pounds. Alyssa's obstetrician had to induce labor.

Sancho held Alyssa's hand throughout the delivery. The harder she pushed, the harder she gripped Sancho's hand. He thought his fingers were going to break, but they didn't. Baby Miguel's head was huge. Sancho was sure it would never fit through Alyssa's *cuevita*, but it did, and soon Sancho could see his new son's impossibly fat face. His thick shock of black hair gave him the appearance of a giant troll doll. They say newborn babies can't see very well, but Miguel looked right into his father's eyes. Sancho felt the connection all the way to his soul.

At first Miguel didn't make a sound, but once he sucked in his first lungful of air, he let go with a shriek that made Sancho jump. Dr. Wiggins handed him to Alyssa. She cried and smiled at Miguel, and looked up at Sancho with happy tears. Sancho never felt so full of love and joy and wonder. He touched his son's tiny hand. Miguel grabbed his finger and held on tight. Like he'd never let go.

Two months later, Sancho held Miguel on his chest and sat on the couch in the tiny living room of their modest Pico Rivera townhouse. Alyssa decorated it inexpensively with art and area rugs and unique furniture from secondhand stores. The overall effect was warm, cozy, and colorful. Sancho's major contribution was the 60-inch flat-screen TV he bought soon after his promotion at City of Roses.

Miguel slept like a bag of cement. Once out, nothing could wake him up. His giant head rested on Sancho's shoulder, right next to a spreading pool of drool.

Sancho called to Alyssa. "It's starting!"

"I'm coming! I'm coming!" she replied from the kitchen. A second later, she appeared with a large bowl of popcorn and cold drinks for both of them. She set everything down on their Talavera tile coffee table and plopped next to Sancho on the couch. Through it all, Miguel remained silent and motionless.

Sancho turned up the TV. The words *Vice News Special Report* appeared on the screen along with some suspenseful-sounding news music. A moment later, the beautifully serious and familiar face of Bettina O'Toole-Applebaum filled the screen. "This is Bettina O'Toole-Applebaum with a Vice News Special Report."

They cut to another camera angle with Bettina's face on one side and video footage on the other. "Since I broke the story on Caitlyn Valentine and the vast network of corruption and domestic terrorism that she blew the whistle on, grand juries have been empaneled and indictments have been handed down. The FBI and ATF continue to investigate the ever-widening scandal.

"It's clear now that Caitlyn Valentine was framed by powerful forces. Her superiors dismissed her allegations as delusional. Arrested for the murder of a sitting U.S. Senator, they ruled her incompetent to stand trial and found her not guilty by reason of insanity. Of course, now we know that Caitlyn Valentine never should have been sent to Hornitos. Everything she claimed turned out to be true.

"A fringe, religious organization called the Church of the Prophesy framed her for Jeffers' murder. Aiding in this effort was the Army of God, a radical militia group. All of Ms. Valentine's charges have been expunged. Back working for the federal government, she is an integral part of their on-going investigation.

"Today, I have the rare privilege of interviewing Ms. Valentine here in studio. Because the investigation *is* ongoing, there are certain things she cannot reveal. However, there is still *much* she can talk about."

The camera angle changed again, and now Bettina sat across a table from Caitlyn.

Sancho grinned. "Look at her."

"Wow," Alyssa murmured.

"She cleans up pretty good, huh?"

"She's beautiful."

"Yet still somehow scary as hell."

Caitlyn wore a dark gray suit and an emerald green blouse that made her vibrant green eyes even more striking. Her dark hair looked a little longer and less spiky. Sancho could swear she was wearing makeup.

"Ms. Valentine, I want to thank you for coming into the studio today."

"Of course."

"I know there are certain aspects of the investigation you can't talk about, but I wonder if you can tell us a little about Mr. Flynn's involvement."

"Without Mr. Flynn, Los Angeles and many of its citizens would no longer be alive. He literally saved millions."

"I understand he helped you escape from Hornitos."

"Yes, he did." She smiled. "I kept trying to ditch him, but he is very persistent."

Bettina nodded and smiled back. "Yes, he is."

Sancho laughed. Alyssa grinned.

"Without Mr. Flynn's help, I never would have exposed those responsible."

"According to my sources at the Justice Department, retired four-star general and billionaire defense contractor Jedidiah

Anderson has been indicted along with Reverend Calvin J. Henderson, brother-in-law of the late Senator Alton Jeffers."

"I apologize, but I can only confirm what the media has already reported on."

"Can you tell us if they are being charged with the murder of the senator?"

"Sorry, but I can't reveal any details concerning an ongoing investigation."

"Do the authorities know who sold the Army of God those suitcase nukes?"

"Can't talk about that either. Sorry."

"Or how you and Mr. Flynn uncovered and then foiled this plot?"

Caitlyn shook her head. "Once the investigation is over and those responsible have been charged, tried, and convicted, I promise I'll sit down with you and tell you everything I can."

"I'm going to hold you to that."

"Please do. In fact, I believe this conspiracy and the story behind it would make a fascinating book and I can't think of anyone better to write it than you."

"Thank you."

Bettina looked down at her notes. "I understand Mr. Flynn is due to be released from Hornitos and will soon return to City of Roses."

"That's what I understand too."

Bettina offered Caitlyn a wry smile. "What about Mr. Mendoza?"

"He'll be returning to prison."

"Quite the unexpected hero."

"People can surprise us sometimes. Of course, to save himself, he had to save Flynn. So I'm not sure I'd say that he completely redeemed himself."

"I understand you saved Mr. Flynn's life more than once."

"And he saved mine more than once."

"Sounds like you two have developed quite a bond."

The camera moved close on Caitlyn. Her eyes grew shiny. "We did."

Sancho glanced at Alyssa to see her eyes were shiny as well.

A commercial came on and Alyssa immediately muted the sound. "You're driving up Thursday?"

Sancho nodded. "Caitlyn's coming with. She hasn't seen him for a few weeks."

"You staying overnight?"

"I booked us both rooms at the Best Western."

"Is she driving back with you two on Friday?"

"Yep."

"So they'll have a night alone together?"

Sancho smiled. "Yep."

"Good."

Alyssa wrinkled her nose and laughed. "Daddy has a diaper to change."

Miguel's face squinched up and turned bright red.

"Yeah, I don't think he's done yet," Sancho said.

CHAPTER FORTY-FIVE

Mendoza waited in line in the cafeteria and tried to decide on lunch. *Chicken tacos or fish sticks? With creamed spinach or macaroni and cheese?* As terrible as the food was at Hornitos, it would be even worse at Pelican Bay. His new lawyers, paid for by Goolardo, promised him he'd serve his time in a minimum-security prison like Lompoc or Victorville. But first, he needed to be legally declared sane and sent back to the state prison system. Based on his previous convictions, Pelican Bay fit the bill. Flynn, on the other hand, was being sent back to City of Roses.

Fucking Flynn.

The *idiota* sat at a table with Grace, Boyd, and Gabriel. Grace, a pleasant-looking middle-aged white lady, liked to grab guys by the balls. The former nurse was in here for strangling a bunch of old ladies on their deathbeds. Boyd shot up his high school before shooting himself in the head. Somehow, he survived and now rhymed every *stupido* thing he said. The FBI picked up Gabriel in Cody, Wyoming. The crazy *pendejo* flattened a Burger King while going through the drive-through in a *pinche* tank. *Loco hijo de puta.* But then every *hijo de puta* in this place was *loco.*

When he reached the lunch ladies, he pointed at the fish sticks. A short, bulky white lady in a hairnet plopped some food on a plate for him. He wasn't sure where they got the meat for the tacos and he didn't want to know. At least, whatever fish parts they used in the fish sticks were covered up by breading. Since he hated creamed spinach, he went for the macaroni and cheese, poured himself a black coffee, and crossed to Flynn's table.

Boyd grabbed his tray and jumped up like his pants were on fire. "Big fish. Red fish. Mean fish. Dead fish." Boyd fled. Grace followed and left her lunch behind. Gabriel, however, didn't go anywhere. He grabbed Grace's tray and started eating her leftover lunch.

Mendoza set his own tray down and took a seat across the table from his long-time nemesis.

Flynn offered Mendoza a warm smile. "Are you here to say goodbye?"

Mendoza didn't know how to answer that, so he didn't say anything. He just glowered.

"Well, I will miss your scintillating conversation and wry observations, but all good things must come to an end. I did want to thank you for saving my life. How does it feel to be a hero?"

"Hero?" Mendoza spat out the word with contempt. "I'm no hero."

"Well, some people think you are. The powers that be tell me you've been getting all kinds of fan mail. School children sending you hand-drawn pictures of their families. Beautiful women sending you… other sorts of pictures. Your Facebook fan page has over a million followers and someone even set up a GoFundMe campaign to take care of your legal expenses. Not that you need it with your old employer picking up the tab."

"I can't believe I saved your stupid ass."

"Maybe you're not the terrible person you thought you were. After all, this isn't the first heroic thing you've done. You helped me bring down Sergei Belenki."

"That was Goolardo. Not me." Mendoza jammed a fish stick into his mouth.

"There's good and bad in all of us, Mr. Mendoza. I'm no angel. To do what I do requires a certain amount of ruthlessness. But it's all in the service of the greater good."

"What about Gabriel?"

"What about him?"

"You okay with him being in here after what he tried to do?"

"Unlike you and I, Gabriel isn't in his right mind. He's mentally ill and for that we need to cut him some slack."

"So he's crazy and you're not?"

"You and I both were sent here under false pretenses, and now my time here is done. My mission has been completed and I need to return to headquarters. But I do believe we will see each other again."

"Count on it," Mendoza said.

■　■　■

Flynn was happy to leave Hornitos behind. He had sympathy for those who truly suffered from mental illness. To not be able to trust your own mind or sense of reality? Flynn couldn't think of anything more terrible. The patients here were a danger to themselves and others. Society needed to keep them here to protect everyone, but that didn't make it any less of a tragedy. The line between madness and sanity was slender indeed and even those who had lost all reason still had their lucid moments.

He brought nothing to Hornitos, so he had nothing to take with him. He said goodbye to Dr. Sahakian, Nurse Winston, and the few orderlies and guards he befriended. Quite a few new faces arrived since the last time he was here. Some looked familiar, but he couldn't remember their names.

He bid adieu to Grace, who tried to grab him by the balls one last time. Boyd offered him a cryptic rhyme. Gabriel, his old roommate, expressed some regrets as he bid Flynn goodbye.

"I'm sorry I assisted in your torture, buddy. I was deceived by the evil one to join the forces of darkness. I now believe that the Army of God was godless. It's not the first time men of faith were fooled by a false deity. Apparently, even an archangel can be bamboozled."

"Apology accepted." Flynn reached out.

Gabriel shook his hand. "You take care of yourself."

"You too."

"But keep your eyes open and trust no one. Evil walks among us and we must remain vigilant."

Flynn clapped him on the shoulder and headed out. A guard and an orderly escorted him through the locked ward and into the reception area where Sancho and Caitlyn waited to take him back to City of Roses.

Caitlyn looked beautiful, but somewhat sad. Flynn wondered what troubled her. Those responsible for framing her now faced prosecution. She was free. Exonerated. Vindicated. Now they could be together. What could be upsetting her? Perhaps she was just overwhelmed with emotion.

Flynn smiled at Sancho and embraced him. "Good to see you, old friend."

"Good to see you too, bro!"

Flynn glanced at Caitlyn. She wouldn't meet his eyes. "You okay?"

She nodded. "I'm good."

"Good."

Several guards in the reception area seemed very familiar to Flynn. Some of them now carried sidearms. Weren't lethal weapons prohibited? He recognized a few faces, but couldn't quite place them. Not until one guard in particular turned around to face him.

Retired General Jedidiah Anderson's icy glare was unmistakable. A tiny triumphant smile curled his lips as he drew his sidearm. *Bloody hell*! Every guard there belonged to The Army of God.

"Mr. Flynn, we meet again," Anderson aimed his Smith and Wesson 460 Magnum at Flynn's head. "Did you really think that God would let you get away with this?"

"God?"

"I am his right hand. His heavenly sword. And I am here to strike you down. For they shall know that I am the Lord when I lay my vengeance upon them!"

Flynn stood stock still. He knew a .452 magnum bullet could take his head clean off as Dirty Harry once famously said. And Flynn wasn't feeling lucky.

Caitlyn, however, swept the General's legs out from under him just as he pulled the trigger. He missed Flynn by inches and shot one of his own men. That man squeezed his own trigger in reaction and put a bullet through the foot of the man standing next to him.

Flynn tackled Sancho as bullets whizzed through the air. They crashed to the floor behind the reception desk. Flynn found two guards and two nurses bound and gagged and grunting for help. Flynn hit the black button behind the desk that unlocked the door to the locked wards.

Sancho crawled for the open door. Flynn and Caitlyn followed.

An angry General Anderson scrambled to his feet. "Smite those evil motherlovers!"

Gunshots boomed behind them as they raced down the corridor. Flynn glanced at Caitlyn. She had a gun. Likely taken off one of Anderson's soldiers. She fired back at them and caught one in the knee. He fell and took down two more when they tripped over him.

Flynn ducked into the TV and recreation room. Sancho and Caitlyn followed. Manu, the monstrous Samoan, Boyd, Grace, and Mendoza all stopped watching TV to watch them take defensive positions behind the couch, the chairs, and a big wooden table.

When the first two soldiers came through the door, Mendoza picked up the big screen TV and tossed it at them. Down they went. Others followed and piled inside. One pushed past Mendoza and aimed his pistol at Flynn. Grace grabbed him by the balls and took him to his knees. Boyd wrenched his gun away and hit him in the nose.

Anderson, the last one through the door, leveled his Smith and Wesson at Flynn's head. Caitlyn fired, but her gun was empty and clicked impotently. Flynn dodged sideways as Anderson put a bullet in his shoulder, spinning him around. He tripped over a coffee table and hit the ground hard.

One soldier smashed Caitlyn in the head with an expandable baton. She fell to her knees. Before he could hit her again, Manu nearly took his head off with a backhanded slap.

Sancho wrestled with a soldier on the floor, Boyd grappled with another, and Mendoza beat one of Anderson's true believers senseless with a folding chair.

Flynn struggled to get to his feet, but only made it to his knees. Jedidiah Anderson stood in the doorway, his furious eyes burning into Flynn. He pulled the pin on a hand grenade and rolled it across the floor before disappearing out the door. Flynn moved to throw himself on the grenade, but Mendoza landed on it first, smothering it with his impressive bulk. They locked eyes for just a moment. Flynn was sure Mendoza smiled. An instant before the grenade detonated, he gave Flynn the finger.

CHAPTER FORTY-SIX

Forest Lawn Memorial Park was founded in Glendale, California in 1906. One of the original owners, Dr. Hubert Eaton, firmly believed in a joyous life after death. He thought most cemeteries were "unsightly, depressing, stoneyards." He wanted Forest Lawn to be "a great park devoid of misshapen monuments and other signs of earthly death, but filled with towering trees, sweeping lawns, splashing fountains, and beautiful statuary." Its over three hundred acres are filled with full-sized reproductions of Renaissance sculptures like "Michelangelo's David" made from marble sourced from the original quarries in Carrara, Italy. Over a million tourists visit every year. Many of Hollywood's biggest, brightest, and dearly departed stars are buried there, including Clark Gable, Jimmy Stewart, Humphrey Bogart, Lauren Bacall, and Elizabeth Taylor.

Goolardo stood at the lectern in Forest Lawn Memorial Park's "Little Church of The Flowers." He looked out over those assembled to honor his late compadre. Flynn sat in the front row with his arm in a sling. A bandage decorated his forehead. To his right sat Sancho Perez. To his left perched a dark-haired beauty Goolardo recognized from the news. The CIA agent Flynn liberated from that mental hospital. Both displayed a similar number of bruises and abrasions. He spotted that old movie star, Alessandra Bianchi, and that journalist. *What's her name? Betty? Tina?* He didn't recognize many of the other faces. And there were quite a few. Goolardo was surprised at the size of the crowd, but then Mendoza had achieved much notoriety when he helped save Los Angeles from nuclear annihilation.

Goolardo hadn't ventured into the U.S. for quite some time. Not since he and Mendoza and Flynn foiled that crazy American billionaire's insane plan two years previously. He changed his appearance since then. Goolardo shaved his head, sported a gray goatee, and wore steel-framed glasses. His passport identified him as a professor from Lisbon, Portugal. He moved there from Costa Rica when he decided he missed the trappings of civilization.

Goolardo had continued to pay for Mendoza's legal expenses even when Mendoza defied him and tried to kill Flynn. Again. How ironic that in the end the big man died saving Flynn's life. Goolardo felt somewhat responsible for Mendoza's fate. That was why he paid for Mendoza to be buried at Forest Lawn. And why he stood at the lectern to say a few words.

"I'm very pleased to see so many people here to honor my friend, Mendoza. We haven't been as close lately, but we spent many good years together and at one time we were like this." Goolardo crossed the index and middle finger on his right hand and held them up next to his face. "He was a brave and loyal compadre. He did whatever I needed, no questions asked. But he was more than an employee to me. More than a friend. He was almost like a son. But I never gave him the respect or admiration he deserved. I withheld that from him. Left him wanting. I thought that might motivate him and it did, but not the way I imagined. You see, I didn't understand what he needed from me. I never told him how much I appreciated him. How much he meant to me. And now... I never will." A tear leaked from Goolardo's left eye and he wiped it away. He smiled. "Normally, this is the point where someone would tell a funny story about the recently deceased, but Mendoza was not a funny guy. Not fun. Not funny. We never spent much time talking about who we were or where we came from. In fact, I really didn't know a lot about him. I know he liked *cerveza*. I know he liked his steak rare. He *loved* rum raisin ice cream. And his favorite actor? Michael Clarke Duncan. He's buried right here at Forest Lawn.

"That's why I bought a plot here for Mendoza. Michael Clarke Duncan stood six-foot-five and weighed three hundred and fifteen pounds. Perhaps that's why Mendoza identified with him. Like Mendoza, he could be dangerous and intimidating and even terrifying, but deep down there was goodness inside of him. Now, don't get me wrong. Mendoza wasn't a gentle giant like Michael Clarke Duncan. He wasn't warm, kind, or cuddly. But he had a code. That's why in the end, he sacrificed his life to save the lives of the others. Mendoza died a hero and I guess that's why we're here. To honor that."

"Here! Here!" Flynn agreed and began to clap. Soon others joined in and before long, the Little Church of the Flowers echoed with applause.

■ ■ ■

After the memorial, Flynn tried to locate Goolardo, but the former head of the Goolardo Drug Cartel was nowhere to be found. Goolardo didn't go to the gravesite and Flynn couldn't find him among the mourners.

After the brief graveside ceremony, the crowd quickly scattered. Alessandra Bianchi walked up and embraced Flynn. He winced from his injuries and she whispered in his ear, "Are you okay?"

"I'm a little worse for the wear, but I'll survive."

"You always do," she said with a smile.

Chloe and Tyler were there as well. Flynn was glad to see them. He gave them both a hug. Tyler wore an actual suit rather than his Captain America outfit and Flynn clapped him on the shoulder. "I haven't had a chance to thank you, but I'd like to take that opportunity now. You didn't just help save me. You saved everyone. The entire City of Los Angeles."

"Of course he did," Chloe said as she put her arm around him. "He's Captain America."

Sancho and Alyssa joined the little conclave and everyone oohed and aahed over baby Miguel.

Alessandra seemed especially delighted to see the little one and took his tiny hand in hers. She smiled at Sancho. "He looks just like you."

"Fat and toothless with poop in his pants? Thanks."

Everyone laughed.

Then Flynn spotted Caitlyn. She looked stunning in her modest black dress. She gave everyone a hug and squeezed the blue bootie on Miguel's right foot before taking Flynn's hand. "Can we talk?"

"Of course."

She led Flynn into the Mystery of Life Garden a short distance away. She held Flynn's hand for a bit and then let go. Flynn tried to catch her eye, but she seemed reluctant to look at him. Instead, Caitlyn stared at the impressive statue that anchored the garden. Twenty-two life-size figures carved in Carrara marble all depicting life's many mysteries. A mother with a babe at her breast. Two young lovers sharing a first kiss. A little boy with an egg that just hatched in his hand. The words *The Mystery of Life* were engraved at the bottom.

Caitlyn strolled into a beautiful, flower bedecked, private garden with a handful of graves. Flynn followed and glimpsed headstones for Mary Pickford, Humphrey Bogart, and Joan Crawford.

"I'm moving to Europe," Caitlyn said. "I'll be joining the U.S. embassy in Berlin."

"The CIA is sending you to Germany?"

"I can't really say much more about it."

"When do you leave?"

"Friday."

"Friday?" Flynn stepped closer. "Has this been in the works for a while?"

Caitlyn nodded. "I need to put everything that happened here behind me. I need to move forward."

"I thought you were thinking about leaving the agency?"

"I changed my mind."

"Good. They need you. And maybe now they'll appreciate you."

She took Flynn's hand in hers. "I'm going to miss you."

"You don't need to."

"What do you mean?"

"I could go with you."

"Go with me?"

"I could ask for a transfer. Leave Pasadena."

"I don't think so."

"Then I'll resign. I'll leave the service."

"Leave the service?" Caitlyn had an odd smile on her face. Tears filled her eyes.

"I don't want to lose you."

"James —"

"All my life I've avoided long-term relationships. Living the life I led, I couldn't afford those kinds of close personal attachments. My life was too dangerous and I would only put those I love in peril. But you and I? We're cut from the same cloth. We live the same life and you... *you* are a force to be reckoned with. You understand the risks. You understand the stakes. We are made for each other, and I want us to be together."

"I care about you. You know I do. But I can't be with you. Not like that."

That was not what he expected to hear. "What do you mean, not like that?"

"We have to say goodbye."

"But I love you."

"I love you too, but we're not like everybody else. We can't have what normal people have. You have your path and I have mine, and it's time to say goodbye."

Flynn's tears blurred his vision. "I can't."

"You have to. But look at me. I'll always be your friend and I'll always be there for you if you need me."

"We can make this work. I know we can."

Caitlyn kissed Flynn on the cheek. "Goodbye, James."

She started backing away. Flynn followed, but she shook her head and held up her hand. Flynn stopped. He stayed where he was as she walked out of *The Mystery of Life Garden* and out of his life.

■ ■ ■

Sancho found Flynn standing in front of Errol Flynn's grave, staring at the weathered headstone. "Flynn, hey, I've been looking everywhere for you, man."

"I've just been walking."

"You okay?"

Flynn shrugged. "Why wouldn't I be?"

"Where's Caitlyn?"

"On her way to Berlin."

"Seriously?"

"I'm afraid so."

Sancho had seen Flynn happy, angry, amorous, amused, disgusted, joyful, and determined, but never had he seen him so sad. "I'm sorry, dude."

Flynn nodded.

"You want to join Alyssa and me for dinner tonight?"

"I'm sure you two are busy with the baby."

"Not too busy to eat dinner. Come on over, bro. I'll fire up the grill. Throw on some nice ribeyes I picked up at Costco."

"You're a good friend, Sancho."

"You can teach me how to make a martini and I'll teach you how to burp a baby."

"Tempting offer."

"Best one *you're* gonna get tonight."

Flynn nodded and curled his lips into a tiny smile. "The night is young."

And now, a sneak peek at Flynn's next escapade in...

CHAPTER ONE

Caitlyn Valentine hated wearing dresses and high heels. Especially tight, strapless, semi-see through dresses and four-inch-high stiletto heels. But Oleg picked this dress out for her personally. A Dolce & Gabbana. What he spent on the dress would probably feed a family of five for a year. But then Oleg Ivanov had more money than God. Even so, he wanted more. Billionaires always want more. Especially those who grew up poor. More wealth. More power. More prestige. More safety. Though safety was the one thing money couldn't guarantee. That tended to make them paranoid.

In business.

In life.

In love.

Oleg liked having Caitlyn on his arm, but he didn't completely trust her. He didn't completely trust anyone. Not even his wife, Anya. Since Caitlyn spoke fluent Russian, Oleg took certain calls on a secure line in his office. Caitlyn wasn't privy to those calls, but his London townhouse was built a hundred years previously and she discovered that sound often traveled from one room to another through the ancient air ducts. By climbing up on a priceless antique sideboard and putting her ear up to the ventilation grille in the library, she could hear the conversation in Oleg's office. One side of it anyway. That made it difficult to discern exactly what was being discussed. She did catch a few choice words, however.

Extortion.

Cyberwarfare.

Economic collapse.

Chaos.

Caitlyn heard footsteps in the corridor outside the office and hopped down off the sideboard, not easy in a skintight dress and high heels. The door opened moments after her heels hit hardwood. Oleg's wife, Anya, seemed startled to see her. The tall, striking, forty-something redhead spoke to Caitlyn in Russian-accented English. "My dear, what are you doing in here?"

"Waiting for Oleg to get off the phone."

She offered a devious smile. "It's always all business with him, isn't it?" Anya glanced at the grille high on the wall above the antique sideboard and then lowered her gaze to Caitlyn.

"But then it's all business with you too."

"I better get back to Oleg."

"Why?" She eyeballed the grille again. "Is his conversation over?"

CHAPTER TWO

Flynn maintained a discreet distance from his target. He kept her in view, but never looked directly at her. Prey can feel the eyes of a predator. Not that Flynn meant her harm. His mission was to protect her. She stopped in front of *Dancers in the Rotunda at the Paris Opera* by Edgar Degas.

Tall and slender with long jet-black hair and pale flawless skin, her blue-green eyes studied every detail of the painting, her expression inscrutable. She resembled the dancers on the canvas, her posture like that of a ballerina. Only the fine lines around her eyes and mouth hinted at her age. She moved with a confident athleticism through the various halls of the Norton Simon Museum, catching the attention of every male over the age of fifteen.

One man in particular eyed her as she ambled by. A rough character in the uniform of a security guard. Shorter than Flynn, but broad shouldered and solid. The guards at the Norton Simon carried no weapons. At least none visible to the naked eye.

The double-sided slit in the soft cashmere sweater dress showed off her shapely calves. That could account for all the attention. Or perhaps those watching her had more sinister motives. She slowed to scrutinize a bronze sculpture. Another Degas. *Little Dancer, Age Fourteen*. Eyes closed, head back, arms taut, the young dancer stood in a modified fourth position. Almost a *tendu croisè devant*. Flynn once dated a dancer in the Bolshoi, and she schooled him in the five basic positions. He then schooled her in a few more advanced ones.

His target moved on, unaware that anyone was watching her. She moved from room to room and gallery to gallery, slowing to pause and take in paintings like Botticelli's *Madonna and Child with Adoring Angel* and *Tulips in a Vase* by Paul Cezanne. Flynn stopped when she did and stared at whatever painting or sculpture stood before him. At one point, he felt her eyes on him, but didn't dare look for fear of giving himself away. When he finally turned and glanced in her direction, she was gone. He hurried to find her, but not too quickly, not wanting to reveal himself to those pursuing her.

He caught a glimpse of her outside in the sculpture garden, standing by the large, lush pond. At certain angles she reminded him of a love he had lost. Or at least misplaced. Caitlyn Valentine. Usually, Flynn was the one who did the dumping. He did it to protect himself as well as those he cared about. He couldn't afford to love too deeply. To do so would put those he cherished in great jeopardy. But Caitlyn Valentine understood the risk. She lived the same life he did. A life he promised to abandon if she agreed to do the same. Caitlyn, however, wasn't ready to settle down. Not yet. At least that's what Flynn told himself.

The Norton Simon's lush sculpture garden resembled Monet's Garden at Giverny. Flynn followed his beautiful target through the sunlight and shadow, keeping hidden behind various large bronze sculptures, cedar, and eucalyptus trees. He cut through some lavender and found her standing below a towering abstract statue by Henry Moore. As she turned, he frantically searched for somewhere to hide and found cover behind Aristide Maillol's *L'Aire*.

The statue was huge, and Flynn crouched next to the large nymph's naked buttocks. He peered over the curve of the recumbent nude's hip and caught his target looking right at him. Flynn ducked down and waited, wondering if she was looking at him or the sculpture. He crawled forward and peeked between the naked lady's hefty thighs and caught her eyes again. She grinned at him playfully and took off, disappearing into the trees.

Flynn hurried to catch up. He had no reason to be surreptitious as she'd clearly made him. He followed her back inside the museum and caught her rounding a corner. Others watched and followed as well. He had to find her before they did. He caught glimpses of her flashing him a naughty smile before disappearing around another corner. She played with him. Baited him. Was she leading him into a trap?

More people populated this part of the museum as it held a newer art installation. Flynn lost her in the crowd. He looked about frantically, desperate to find her in the throng. Then he caught sight of her mischievous face. She offered him a devilish smirk and disappeared through another doorway. Flynn followed, pushing through the crowd. He found himself in a long, empty corridor, lined with paintings from the Renaissance. There were two doors. Both locked. He raced to the far end and through an open archway into another smaller gallery with Italian paintings from the 14th century, all religious-themed, depicting Christ and the Madonna and the horrors of hell.

Flynn stood alone in the room, his target gone. *Did I lose her? Did they grab her? Have I failed her?* He turned to hurry back down the corridor. One of the previously locked doors abruptly opened. Someone grabbed him by the arm and jerked him inside. The door slammed shut, plunging him into darkness. The scent of Black Opium by Yves Saint Laurent filled his nostrils. An iPhone flashlight blinked on, illuminating her mesmerizing blue-green eyes. She stood inches away.

"You were watching me," she whispered.

"I'm not the only one."

"I was watching you too."

"Under whose orders?" Flynn demanded.

"My orders."

"Why would *you* be watching *me*?"

"Why wouldn't I be? Let's stop playing games, James. I see how you look at me. I know what you want."

"Miss Grossblatt, please…"

"Shelley. Call me Shelley."

"Shelley, listen—"

Shelley silenced Flynn with a kiss as she grabbed him by the arse. He tried to back away and bumped into the storage closet door. Her tongue forced its way past Flynn's lips. She pressed herself against him. Flynn desperately wanted to give in, but gently pushed her back until their tongues decoupled and he broke the suction created by their mouths.

"I'm not saying I don't find you attractive," Flynn whispered. "I find you very attractive. But I promised my superiors I'd refrain from dipping my pen in the company ink."

"James, look at me. Life is fleeting. We must take our pleasures where and when we can."

"I don't disagree."

"Then make love to me."

"I worry we might be in danger."

"Of course, we're in danger. Death stalks us all. But before I die, I want to live. I want to love. I'm not getting any younger. I don't want to wake up one day and discover that life has passed me by. If I don't take a chance, if I don't grab life by the balls—" Flynn flinched as she grabbed him by the balls. Not to the point of pain, but firmly and with great conviction. "Then why am I even here? Do you know what Henry David Thoreau said?"

"If a man does not keep pace with his companions, perhaps it is because he hears a different drummer."

"Yes, he did say that," she nodded. "But he also said I want to live deep and suck out all the marrow of life." She unbuttoned his button and unzipped his zipper and sank to her knees. "All good things are wild and free. There is no remedy for love but to love more." She put her iPhone face down on the floor, plunging the little closet into darkness.

.   .   .

Sancho Perez tried not to panic. Dr. Michaels assigned Sancho the task of monitoring Flynn and now Sancho had lost him. He'd looked away for just a moment, and Flynn disappeared. Flynn reminded him of his one-year-old son, Miguel. Once Miguel learned how to crawl, he would vanish in an instant, take off like a rocket, chasing the dog or the cat or whatever caught his interest. Flynn too often disappeared in the blink of an eye.

The higher-ups at City of Roses Psychiatric Hospital hadn't authorized an off-campus field trip for quite some time. Not since the fiasco at the paintball park last year. Dr. Michaels brought as many minders as patients this time, and Sancho was there specifically to keep an eye on Flynn. As a psychiatric nurse at City of Roses, he always anticipated the unexpected. But Flynn, who suffered from a severe delusional disorder, pushed the envelope when it came to unpredictability.

James Flynn believed that City of Roses served as a satellite headquarters for His Majesty's Secret Service, and that he operated as a secret agent with a license to kill. Sancho was an orderly when they first met. Flynn befriended him, encouraged him, and mentored him. Flynn helped him find his confidence and taught him to believe in himself and his abilities. The money he made on his adventures with Flynn paid for his college education and his house. They were like brothers, and that was why Dr. Michaels put Sancho in charge of keeping tabs on him. No one knew Flynn better than Sancho.

"*Mierda*," Sancho mumbled as he moved from gallery to gallery, nervous sweat beading on his forehead. He searched for a glimpse of Flynn's grey Brioni suit. No other patients dressed as fashionably as Flynn. Most wore sweats or jeans or shorts. He spotted a few of them staring at various paintings and sculptures or nothing at all.

Forty-something Mary Alice had freckles, graying red hair, and anger management issues. Three-hundred-pound, twenty-something Ty used a gangsta attitude to cover up his crippling anxiety. Eighty-two-year-old self-proclaimed genius inventor Quentin Smith suffered from delusions of grandeur. Rodney, a stout, sixty-something with a Santa Claus beard, struggled with substance abuse. Bob was bipolar. Zipper, a shy schizophrenic, dozed on a bench in front of a Goya.

Where the hell did Flynn get to? Flynn wasn't under lock and key at City of Roses. He was there voluntarily and could come and go as he pleased. Yet, the outside world wasn't a safe place for him. Not in his delusional condition. Whenever Flynn ventured outside the hospital walls, he regularly found himself in insanely dangerous situations. As a young dad, Sancho couldn't afford to take the same risks he once did. His days of saving Flynn from himself were over. He prayed his old friend hadn't wandered away from the Norton Simon.

Sancho spotted Nurse Durkin standing by an Alexander Calder. *Maelstrom with Blue.* The head nurse at City of Roses was Sancho's immediate superior. At six feet tall and two hundred pounds, she brooked no insolence and took no prisoners. Sancho considered asking her if she'd seen Flynn, but that would mean admitting he lost him. So instead, he continued on into the next gallery where he spotted the hospital's other chaperones: Nurse Alvarez, Nurse Benson, and Dr. Michaels.

Dr. Michaels, the head psychiatrist at City of Roses, was balding and slender. He sported a black goatee streaked with gray and Giorgio Armani eyewear. Michaels had an imperious attitude and hesitated to approve this outing. Somehow Shelley, the new art therapist, changed his mind. They had a certain contentious familiarity. Sancho wondered if they'd worked together before.

Shelley Grossblatt was a lot more attractive than her name. For a woman in her forties, she kept herself in good shape. Tall and slim with long black hair and blue-green eyes, she reminded him of the actress Kate Beckinsale. It's probably why every male patient of City of Roses signed up for art therapy. Flynn included. She was cold and stand-offish until Flynn started charming her. She loosened up. She smiled. She laughed. She...

Shit.

Sancho didn't see her anywhere in the museum. *Did she and Flynn disappear together?* He moved faster. Room to room. Gallery to gallery. No Flynn. No Grossblatt. And then he noticed Ty standing by a hallway door, his ear pressed up against it, a stupid grin filling his face. Sancho approached him and heard what Ty heard. Moaning and groaning and bumping and squeaking on the other side of the door.

Someone bumped into Sancho from behind. He turned to see Quentin, his hand cupped over his ear as he tried to hear what was happening behind the door. Rodney stood grinning next to him. Bob giggled behind a glowering Mary Alice. She did not look happy. Sancho knew she had a thing for Flynn, and she didn't react well to other women throwing themselves at him. Nurse Durkin headed in their direction, probably to see what all the fuss was about. That caught the attention of Nurse Alvarez and Benson and, finally, Dr. Michaels himself.

Everyone stood and stared at the entrance to the storage room, listening to the intimate sounds emanating from within. Durkin pushed her way forward, shoved Ty to one side, and pulled open the door, flooding the little storage room with light.

CHAPTER THREE

Norton Simon made his first fortune in sheet metal. He used that money to buy an insolvent orange juice bottling plant in Southern California. The company, renamed Val Vita Food Products, expanded its product line to include all kinds of fruit and vegetable products. He sold his company to Hunt's Foods in 1969. That same year he married Jennifer Jones, the widow of David O. Selznick, producer of Gone with the Wind. *Later, he bought Canada Dry, Avis Car Rental, and Max Factor. At one time, he was one of the wealthiest men in America with a net worth of over 10 billion dollars. He collected 8000 works of art over 30 years, and in 1975 opened the Norton Simon Museum in Pasadena, California.*

Flynn squinted into the light. A small crowd of people gathered outside the storage closet. Most were fellow agents or support personnel from His Majesty's Secret Service. Even M was there, though out in public everyone called him by his cover name, Dr. Michaels.

They stared at Flynn, and Flynn stared at them, and no one said a word.

Flynn's pants were down around his ankles. He wore no jacket, shirt, or tie. Shelley Grossblatt had even less on. Just a pair of black Manolo Blahniks. Flynn felt sheepish, but Shelley showed no embarrassment whatsoever. In fact, she appeared proud of her nakedness. Her impertinent breasts. Her brazen behind. Her long, flawless legs. She looked directly into M's eyes and offered a defiant smile. "Darling, would you please close the door?"

"How could you do this to me?" M sputtered.

"I'm not doing this to you, darling," Shelley said with a smile as she gestured towards Flynn. "I'm doing this to *him*."

Flynn raised his hand. "Sir, I'm sorry. This might seem somewhat…inappropriate, but I do have an explanation."

M's complexion changed from light pink to red. "An explanation?"

"Several enemy agents were eying Miss Grossblatt with ill intent and closing in. Miss Grossblatt thought it best we hide from view and pulled me into the closet with her. To throw off suspicion if any of them opened the door, I thought it best we appear to be…"

"Out!" M shouted.

"Sir?"

"Out of the closet, Flynn! Out! Now!"

Flynn stumbled out with his pants still around his ankles. He nearly tripped, but Ty caught him before he could fall.

M went to close the door, but Miss Grossblatt kicked it back open, banging M in the nose. "Look at me, Tony. For once, look at me!"

"I'm looking!" M shouted as he held his injured nose.

"But you don't see me. Not really."

"*Everyone sees you!*"

"Are you even attracted to me?"

"Of course, I am."

"Then why do you ignore me?"

"Shelley—"

"Do you even remember the last time we had sex?"

"Shelley, please! Don't do this to me!"

"I wouldn't have to if you would occasionally do something to *me*!"

"This isn't the time or the place."

"Of course, it is! You ignore me at home. You ignore me at work. You barely talk to me. We're barely roommates. How else was I going to get your attention?"

Recognition slowly dawned on Flynn as he pointed at Miss Grossblatt and then at M. "Are you two…"

"Yes, Mr. Flynn! We're married. Shelley is my wife!"

"But…um…you don't have the same last name."

"Because we wanted to keep our private lives separate from our works lives!" M shouted. "We wanted a firewall to keep things professional, and then my wife set that firewall on fire!"

"Sir, I'm sorry, I had no clue that you two… that you and her…that Shelley was your—"

"Nurse Durkin, please get the patients back on the bus! This outing is over."

M stepped into the closet and pulled the door shut behind him. Muffled shouting filtered through as the argument continued. Flynn hesitated and then opened the door. "Excuse me, but could you please throw me my—" His shirt hit him in the face, and M slammed the door.

．　．　．

Sancho sat next to Flynn in the transport van. Dr. Michaels sat up front next to Durkin. Shelley never boarded the bus. She left in an Uber, destination unknown. Sancho knew he'd take the fall for this. He wouldn't be surprised if Dr. Michaels fired him. The ride back to City of Roses was short and uncomfortable.

After dinner, Sancho found Flynn in his room, lying in bed, staring at the ceiling, his lips pursed with anger.

"Bro, are you all right?"

"I'm ashamed of myself."

"We talked about this."

"I know."

"You're out of control."

"I had no idea she was a married woman."

"None of us did," Sancho said.

"M seemed upset."

"No shit."

Flynn sat up and put his feet on the floor. "I was just trying to keep her safe."

"You did a little bit more than that."

"I didn't seduce her, Sancho. She seduced me."

"You've been getting seduced a lot lately."

"Not on purpose."

"Bullshit. You're putting out the wounded puppy dog vibe, and women can't resist that."

Flynn shook his head. "I don't know what you're talking about."

"You're heartbroken and they can sense it. They want to fix you. Comfort you."

"How is that my fault?"

"You're using sex to distract yourself from what you're feeling."

"Don't be ridiculous."

"Caitlyn broke your heart. The sooner you admit it, the sooner you can put it behind you."

"I admit I enjoyed my time with her, but a man who does what I do can't afford those kinds of feelings."

"You told her you'd give it all up for her and she turned you down. She hurt you. Rejected you."

Flynn looked down at his shoes. His face reddened with either anger or embarrassment.

Sancho sat next to him. "I'm not trying to make you feel bad."

"I'm worried about her."

"I'm sure she's fine."

"We talked every week. Even after she moved to London. But suddenly, she stopped taking my calls. And then her number was disconnected."

"When was the last time you heard from her?"

"Not in weeks. Frankly, I'm a little concerned."

"Maybe she just moved on. Met someone else."

Flynn shook his head. "No. Something isn't right."

"Is she back with the CIA?"

"I don't know. Even if she was, she couldn't say."

Sancho nodded. "I'll see what I can find out, but you got to stop with the Don Juan shit. Keep it up and Dr. Michaels might send you somewhere else."

"Well, if he would send me on a mission, I wouldn't need to distract myself with these frivolous escapades. I'm a double 0. I need a target. A mission. A purpose. I'm fit, I'm ready, I need to be out in the world, confronting our enemies."

A sharp rap on the door ended Flynn's diatribe. Nurse Durkin filled the doorway. "Let's go, Mr. Flynn. Dr. Michaels wants to see you."

Flynn nodded and stood. He glanced at Sancho. "This might be it. Wish me luck."

．　．　．

Flynn entered the anteroom to M's office. His loyal secretary, Miss Honeywell, typed at her computer. The voluptuous African American beauty wore her hair in exotic cornrows that hung halfway down her back. Flynn sat on the edge of her desk. She didn't look up.

"Miss Honeywell, you are a sight for sore eyes."

"Uh huh."

"Have you changed your hair, Miss Honeywell? It's quite fetching."

She looked up at Flynn with a smirk. "Mr. Flynn, are you flirting with me?"

"What if I was?"

"Then I would say your little head is getting your big head in all kinds of trouble."

"So, you heard?"

"Everybody's heard."

"I had no idea she was married."

"Or who she was married to."

"No, ma'am."

"You sure stepped in it this time."

"Apparently so."

Honeywell snickered and shook her head. "Go on in. He's waiting."

"Okay then. Until we meet again."

"Uh huh." Honeywell went back to typing.

M sat behind his desk, pointing at his couch. Flynn took the hint and sat. "Sir, if I may."

"You may not."

"I had no idea you were married to Miss Grossblatt. If I had the slightest inkling, I never would have—"

"Please stop talking."

"Of course."

"I'm not angry with you, Mr. Flynn. I'm angry with my wife. But that's a personal matter, and that's the last I'll speak of it. I don't take what you did personally. You're dealing with deep abandonment issues, and the end of your relationship with Miss Valentine only exacerbated that trauma. You're acting out. It's a cry for attention. I understand that."

"Sir, if I may—"

"I'll tell you when it's your turn to talk. Right now, it's my turn."

"Of course."

"I considered sending you elsewhere, but that would be admitting failure, and I haven't given up on you yet, Mr. Flynn."

"Thank you, sir."

"But I *am* restricting you to the premises. No more outings. No more visitors. No computer access. No phone privileges. You are on lockdown."

"You're not sending me on a mission?"

"Your mission is to make yourself whole. Get better. Integrate your personality. We're going to get aggressive with your treatment, and try things we haven't tried before. You've been here for over twenty years. My predecessors failed you. I won't. It's time we made a concerted effort to get you better.

"Yes, I agree I may suffer from a certain amount of PTSD, but that goes with the territory. No one does what I do and walks away completely unscathed. However, that's not what I'm worried about. I'm worried about Miss Valentine. Worried she might be in trouble. Since you're not sending me on a mission, I'd like to fly to London and make sure she's okay."

"What did I just say, Mr. Flynn? You're in no condition to go anywhere. For the foreseeable future, you are on lockdown."

CHAPTER FOUR

In 1934, a Hungarian doctor named Ladislas Meduna came up with the concept of using one disease to cure another. He injected a drug called Metrazol to induce epileptic seizures in a catatonic patient. After a number of treatments, the patient was able to walk, speak, and feed himself. But the technique often caused severe neurological damage. Italian neurologist Ugo Cerletti thought inducing seizures with electricity might be more humane. He first perfected this technique on dogs and then, in 1938, conducted the first human trial on a schizophrenic found wandering around a train station in Rome. With the application of 110 volts, they successfully induced a seizure. After ten more treatments, they reduced the schizophrenic's outward symptoms of psychosis and he returned to his wife and job and life in the community. This technique, known as electroconvulsive therapy or ECT, later became widespread, even though it produced certain side effects like loss of memory, confusion, headaches, nausea, and even heart rhythm irregularities.

Dr. Michaels told the staff he only wanted Flynn to find his true self. To that end, he was going to try every drug, technology, and technique known to modern psychological science. His stated goal? Break Flynn's delusion.

Instead, Sancho watched as he broke Flynn.

From his course work at Cal State, Sancho knew that delusional disorder was relatively rare. Because of his affection for Flynn, Sancho read a lot of the research literature, and learned of the various factors that might contribute to the condition.

Delusional disorder often ran in families, so there was likely a genetic component. But abnormalities in certain areas of the brain or a chemical imbalance might also contribute. Losing his mother and father at age ten had a major impact on Flynn. His years in foster care. The bullying. The isolation. The fact that he felt so helpless and all alone. It was no wonder he became the most powerful person he could imagine. Someone who had no fear. Someone who could handle any situation and survive anything.

Sancho snuck a peek at Flynn's file. Dr. Michaels put Flynn into intensive cognitive behavioral therapy. Michaels wanted Flynn to take a closer look at his notions and emotions. The goal was for Flynn to unlearn behaviors, reduce negative thoughts, and confront his delusional thinking directly. To help accelerate that, Michaels upped Flynn's meds.

First-generation anti-psychotics work by blocking dopamine receptors in the brain, but the side effects were no joke. Michaels started with chlorpromazine and thioridazine. They made Flynn incredibly drowsy and slow. He shuffled when he walked, and his face lost all emotion and expression. Flynn retained water, gained weight, and developed facial tics. His hands shook. He stopped exercising, stopped socializing, and slept away most of the day.

When Sancho tried to talk to Flynn, his old friend struggled to focus and form sentences. He seemed fearful, and confused.

Second-generation anti-psychotics like clozapine and ziprasidone blocked serotonin receptors and made Flynn restless and agitated. So, Michaels prescribed tranquilizers and anti-anxiety meds. Flynn grew slower, and sleepier, and more lethargic. He even started to drool.

Sancho tried to make an appointment with Michaels, but his secretary claimed he didn't have an opening for weeks. Finally, Sancho cornered him in the cafeteria one day as they both waited in line for lunch.

"Hey, Dr. Michaels, can I ask you a question?"

"Can we do this after lunch?"

"Flynn's not looking too good lately. Are you sure all these new drugs are necessary?"

"I wouldn't have prescribed them if I didn't think so."

"Are you sure you're not punishing him?"

"Excuse me?"

"For what happened with your wife?"

"What are you accusing me of?"

"I'm just saying—"

"I know what you're saying, Mr. Perez, and I do *not* appreciate it."

Michaels picked up his lunch, found an empty table, and took a seat. Sancho followed and sat across from him. "I'm not accusing you of anything. I'm just…I'm just saying…I don't like seeing him like this."

"No one does."

"Other doctors have gone down this route before. It just doesn't work."

"That's your expert opinion?"

"Look, I know I'm just a nurse, but I've known him a long time."

"Yes, you and Mr. Flynn are very close. Too close. So close you can't be objective about this."

"I don't think that's true."

"Mr. Flynn has been a resident of this institution for over twenty years. His treatment here has not been effective. If anything, he's fallen deeper into his delusion. We are not doing him any favors by ignoring his condition."

"I'm not saying we should ignore it."

"I know my predecessor, Dr. Nicholson, made a serious effort at one point to help Mr. Flynn. He tried antipsychotics. Anti-depressants. Even transcranial magnetic stimulation. And for a time, Mr. Flynn found his way back to reality."

"Yeah, but he wasn't happy. He wasn't himself."

"He was exactly himself and if Nicholson had stayed the course, Flynn would have finally been able to live a normal life. A life outside a psychiatric hospital."

"I don't know if that's true."

"Well, I intend to find out. Monday, I'm starting him on electroconvulsive therapy."

"Shock treatment?"

Dr. Michaels frowned at the disparaging nickname for the procedure. "ECT. It's non-invasive and it's performed under anesthesia. It'll help accelerate changes in Mr. Flynn's brain chemistry. The side effects are minimal. Mild headaches. Short-term memory loss."

"Short-term memory loss?"

"It's rarely permanent."

Sancho angrily slapped his hand on the table. Everything jumped. *"I don't like seeing him like this."*

"Lucky for you, you won't have to. I'm transferring you to another facility. I'm afraid you've become an impediment to Mr. Flynn's progress. You're enabling his behavior and reinforcing his delusion."

"Transferring me? Where?"

"To a facility in Long Beach."

"Seriously?"

"Unless you'd rather leave the employ of Health Management System Services entirely."

That took Sancho by surprise. "What?"

"Think about it." Dr. Michaels stood, leaving his tray and his dirty dishes on the table. "Talk to your wife. But let me know by tomorrow."

■ ■ ■

Transferred? Sancho couldn't believe it. He'd been there six years. He had never worked at another hospital. He felt at home at City of Roses and liked everyone he worked with. Well, mostly everyone. Not Nurse Durkin. And some of the orderlies were assholes. Especially O'Malley and Barker. But most of his fellow nurses were great. He even liked most of the patients. And Flynn…Flynn was the big brother he never had. If not for Flynn, he never would have married his wife, or finished college, or owned an Aston Martin DB 9 Volante. *Shit. Maybe Michaels is right. Maybe we are co-dependent.*

Sancho decided to give Michaels the benefit of the doubt. Long Beach wasn't that much longer of a commute. Maybe he needed to stretch his wings. Try something new. Part of him felt like he was letting Flynn down. But what if it was for the best? *What if I'm holding Flynn back?*

After lunch, Sancho went looking for Flynn. Before Michaels tried to fix him, Flynn spent most days reading, researching on the communal computer in the activity room, or working out either in the hospital's exercise area or in the outdoor courtyard on the little patch of grass between the picnic tables. He was better looking than Bradley Cooper and had a physique that would put Hugh Jackman to shame. Lean. Tall. Wide shoulders. A solid six-pack. The nurses would often lunch outside just so they could watch Flynn perform his shirtless karate katas. But Sancho didn't find Flynn in the courtyard or the exercise room or even his own room. He found him in the TV room.

Flynn never watched TV, but there he sat on the sofa, squished between Ty and Rodney. His puffy face the result of all the extra pounds he put on. Probably from the anti-psychotics. Still, between Rodney and Ty, he looked relatively petite. They watched a Magnum PI rerun. Well, Rodney and Ty did. Flynn slept like a drooling, bloated, pasty-faced baby.

Normally, Flynn dressed better than any patient in the place. He had a vast of collection of stylish clothes he bought from online vintage thrift shops. Designer suits from Versace and Armani and shoes from Gucci. Even his casual clothes were the best of the best. But today, someone had dressed him in gray sweatpants, plastic sandals, and a baggy yellow t-shirt decorated with the remnants of his breakfast.

A few other patients sat scattered around the room. Flynn's elderly roommate Quentin, who Flynn referred to as Q, played Uno with Doris Frawley and Mary Alice. Doris, a former 1940s pinup girl, claimed she dated L. Ron Hubbard and gave birth to the Antichrist back in 1952. Big-boned, freckle-faced Mary Alice beckoned Sancho over. She had a raspy three-pack-a-day voice and an East Texas accent. "What the hell are they doing to Flynn?"

Sancho shrugged. "They upped his meds."

"What the fuck for?"

"Dr. Michaels is trying something new."

"Are you shitting me?"

"No ma'am. Michaels wants to help him get better."

"He don't look better to me. He looks like crap."

"I don't disagree."

"He was such a beautiful man. Charming as all hell. Now look at him. It ain't fair. It ain't right. I know he had a thing for me. I saw how he looked at me. I intimidate most men. But not him. He was working up the nerve to finally make a move, and then Michaels pulls this shit? You know what anti-psychotics do to boners?"

"Nothing good, I'm guessing."

"No, sir. They are boner killers."

"He does look a little droopy."

"It's revenge, ain't it? Cause Flynn bumped uglies with his bride."

"I don't think so."

"Bullshit! He didn't even come on to her! That hussy came onto him! Took advantage of him. Because he's a man and men can't say no." Mary Alice looked up and immediately shut up.

Sancho followed her gaze. Shelley Grossman stood in the doorway. She wore a long, light blue linen dress that accentuated her modest curves. It was sexy without being provocative, and she likely wore it to impress the puffy couch potato who used to be James Flynn. By the look on her face, Sancho saw Flynn's condition shocked her. Eyes wide, full of tears, she glanced at Sancho. "Did my husband do this?"

Sancho played dumb. "Do what?"

She pointed. "*This* to Mr. Flynn."

Sancho tried to change the subject. "Are you teaching art today?"

"I asked you a question!"

"Of course, he did," Mary Alice replied. "And he did it because of *you*!"

Shelley Grossman flounced away angrily, headed in the direction of her husband's office.

Mary Alice grinned and got up. "Can we put this game on hold for a sec? I wanna stand outside Michaels' office and listen to the fireworks." As she headed off, she offered a raspy giggle. "This is gonna be good."

Sancho went to Flynn and grabbed him by the arm. "Brother, we need to talk."

He tried to pull Flynn to his feet, but Flynn was immovable, lodged as he was between Rodney and Ty. "How 'bout a hand here!"

Rodney and Ty struggled to stand up. Being as big as they were, moving from a seated position to a vertical one required some effort. They groaned and grunted and finally got upright. Between the three of them, they managed to get Flynn on his feet as well.

Sancho held his compadre by the arm and guided him down the hall. "I got something I need to say to you, and I just hope you can hear me."

Flynn grunted, then farted and wobbled as Sancho navigated him down the corridor. It took some time, but finally they reached Flynn's room. Sancho helped him onto the bed. Flynn lay flat on his back, his face slack, his mouth open, drool dripping.

"Flynn, can you hear me?" Flynn stared unseeing at the ceiling. Sancho shook him by the shoulder. "Flynn! *Flynn!*" Flynn's eyes slowly moved in Sancho's direction. "Nod your head if you can hear me!"

Flynn nodded his head.

Sancho sat on the edge of his bed. "Dr. Michaels is transferring me. He thinks I'm interfering with your treatment, and he might be right. I don't like seeing you doped up like this, but maybe it's for the best. I hope it's for the best."

"It's not," Flynn said with a strong, clear voice. He sat up.

"What the hell?"

Flynn shushed him, holding his finger to his lips, before leaning close and whispering in his ear. "I took the medication at first. I sincerely believed M wanted to help me with my PTSD. But when I started feeling the effects, it occurred to me that perhaps M had a hidden agenda."

"You're not taking the drugs?"

"I pretend to but spit them out later. I'm feigning the effects so as not to arouse suspicion."

"Are you kidding me?"

"No. Which is why I allowed Nurse Ramos to dress me in this appalling outfit."

"Well, you're doing a damn good job of faking it."

"I believe M is transferring you for the very same reason he's trying to drug me."

"What reason would that be?"

"He's working for the enemy."

"Enemy? What enemy?"

"Moscow most likely. Though it could be some international criminal cartel."

"What?"

"Someone got to him. Maybe they're blackmailing him with *kompromat*. Maybe they're threatening his family."

"You don't think it's about his wife?" Sancho asked.

"Maybe his wife was trying to warn me. Maybe that's why she tried to seduce me."

"*Tried?*"

"It was likely a cry for help."

"*Dude.*"

"It's not the first time His Majesty's Secret Service has been compromised."

"Look at me, man. You are spinning out here."

"Am I? Monday M intends to have me undergo ECT. Electroconvulsive Therapy."

Sancho nodded. "He thinks it might help you."

"Help me what?"

"See things more clearly."

"So, he's fooled you too?"

"What? No. I don't know."

"Well, I do. I'm going to continue to play along and see how far he takes this. I'm going to find out who's manipulating him. Find out if his handlers are the ones who took Caitlyn."

"You think someone took Caitlyn?"

Flynn stood, too upset to stay seated. "I told you, I've been trying to get a hold of her for weeks."

"Right, I know, but that doesn't mean someone took her."

"What other possible explanation could there be?"

"Maybe she's just…you know…busy."

"Too busy to let me know she's okay?"

"Maybe."

Flynn raised a finger in the air. "Or…maybe she's being held prisoner at some black site undergoing enhanced interrogation. They're probably trying to break her."

"Who?"

"Exactly! That's what we need to find out."

"*We?*"

"M doesn't want me communicating with anyone on the outside. No phone privileges. No computer access. He has me on lockdown."

"Look, if you don't like what Dr. Michaels is doing, you can go somewhere else. You're here voluntarily. You can leave anytime you want."

"How can I leave? M is my only lead. No, I need to play this out, but I'm going to need your help."

Sancho sighed. "What do you need?"

"A burner phone. Something untraceable."

"Why?"

"I need to contact Miranda Jacks."

"You want to call the FBI?"

"Perhaps she knows what happened to Caitlyn."

"I don't know if that's such a good idea."

"A burner phone, Sancho. It's the only way I can learn the truth. If turns out that Caitlyn is okay, then that's one less thing I'll have to worry about."

Sancho shook his head and rubbed his eyes. "A burner phone. Fine."

Footsteps approached. Flynn fell back on the bed. His eyes lost focus. His jaw went slack. Drool dribbled down his chin.

ABOUT THE AUTHOR

Haris Orkin is a playwright, screenwriter, game writer, and novelist. His play, *Dada* was produced at The American Stage and the La Jolla Playhouse. *Sex, Impotence, and International Terrorism* was chosen as a critic's choice by the L.A. Weekly and sold as a film script to MGM/UA. *Save the Dog* was produced as a Disney Sunday Night movie. His original screenplay, *A Saintly Switch*, was directed by Peter Bogdanovich and starred David Alan Grier and Vivica A. Fox.

He is a WGA Award and BAFTA Award nominated game writer and narrative designer known for *Command and Conquer: Red Alert 3*, *Call of Juarez: Gunslinger*, *Tom Clancy's The Division*, *Mafia 3*, *Dying Light*, *Evil West*, *Resident Evil: Shadows of Rose*.

www.harisorkin.com

NOTE FROM THE AUTHOR

I was a shy, skinny, bookish, bespectacled, and insecure twelve old living in the suburbs of Chicago when I first realized what I wanted to be when I grew up. I wanted to be Alexander Mundy in *It Takes a Thief*. I wanted to be Illya Kuryakin in *The Man from Uncle*. I wanted to be part of the Mission Impossible team. I wanted to be Jim West, Derek Flint, and Matt Helm.

I wanted to be James Bond.

Those men had no fear. They knew karate and could scuba dive and rock climb and skydive and ski and shoot the eye out of a flea at fifty yards. They were confident in any situation and were comfortable in their own skin. I think that was the biggest wish fulfillment fantasy of all for an awkward pre-teen struggling through puberty and that's what inspired James Flynn and his adventures.

At twelve I was terrified of girls. I was always picked last in gym class. I lived a life of perpetual embarrassment. In hindsight, that's probably how most twelve-year-olds feel, but at the time, I didn't know that. So I started lifting weights. I became a gymnast. I boxed. I studied karate. I became a rock climber and learned to ski and scuba dive. I even studied in London for a year and traveled the world.

But I never did become an international super spy. Instead, I became a screenwriter and game writer, creating wish fulfillment fantasies for other nerdy twelve-year-olds. Thank you for indulging in my fantasies. I hope you enjoyed the journey. I do believe Mr. Flynn is just getting started.

Please connect with me on Twitter and Facebook and feel free to ask me anything. This is a two-way conversation.

~Haris Orkin

NOTE FROM THE PUBLISHER

Word-of-mouth is crucial for any author to succeed. If you enjoyed *License to Die*, please leave a review online — anywhere you are able. Even if it's just a sentence or two. It would make all the difference and would be very much appreciated.

Thanks!
Haris Orkin

We hope you enjoyed reading this title from:

BLACK ROSE
writing™

Subscribe to our mailing list – *The Rosevine* – and receive **FREE** books, daily
deals, and stay current with news about upcoming
releases and our hottest authors.
Scan the QR code below to sign up.

Already a subscriber? Please accept a sincere thank you for being a fan of
Black Rose Writing authors.

View other Black Rose Writing titles at
www.blackrosewriting.com/books and use promo code
PRINT to receive a **20% discount** when purchasing.

www.ingramcontent.com/pod-product-compliance
Lightning Source LLC
Chambersburg PA
CBHW020547120726
47903CB00001B/158